# DEAD BY MIDNIGHT

**Center Point
Large Print**

Also by Beverly Barton
and available from Center Point Large Print:

*Cold Hearted*
*A Time to Die*

# DEAD BY MIDNIGHT

## BEVERLY BARTON

CENTER POINT PUBLISHING
THORNDIKE, MAINE

This Center Point Large Print edition
is published in the year 2010 by arrangement with
Kensington Publishing Corp.

The text of this Large Print edition is unabridged.
In other aspects, this book may vary
from the original edition.
Printed in the United States of America
on permanent paper.
Set in 16-point Times New Roman type.

ISBN: 978-1-60285-675-2

Library of Congress Cataloging-in-Publication Data

Barton, Beverly.
  Dead by midnight / Beverly Barton.
     p. cm. -- (Griffin Powell series ; 6)
  ISBN 978-1-60285-675-2 (library binding : alk. paper)
  1. Large type books. I. Title. II. Series.

PS3552.A76777D43 2010
813'.54--dc22

2009045403

# Prologue

*There it was again, that odd sound. It must be the wind. What else could it be? Possibly a wild animal, a raccoon or possum or even a stray dog. Bears are in hibernation this time of year.*

*Get hold of yourself. You're imagining things. Nobody's out there. Nobody is going to show up here in the middle of the woods in the dead of winter just to frighten you.*

Dean's bone-thin hands trembled as he pulled back the gingham curtain from the dirty window and peered out into the darkness. The quarter-moon winked mockingly at him through a thin veil of clouds, as if it knew something he didn't. The cold wind whispered menacingly. Was it issuing him a warning?

Releasing the curtain, he rubbed his hands together, as much to warm them as to control the quivering. He sure as hell could use a drink about now. Or something stronger, quicker. But he had learned to settle for strong coffee. A caffeine fix was better than no fix at all. He had been clean and sober for three years and he had no intention of allowing a few stupid letters to destroy his hard-won freedom from drugs and alcohol.

*Forget the damn letters. They're just somebody's idea of a sick joke.*

There were things he should be doing—stoking

the fire he'd built in the fireplace, checking supplies, preparing the coffeemaker for morning coffee, bringing in more firewood, putting fresh linens on the twin beds. Dean wanted everything to be in order before his brother got here. Jared, who was driving in from Knoxville where he taught biology at the University of Tennessee, would arrive sometime in the morning, and if all went as planned, they'd spend the weekend here. This was the first time they'd been together at their family's cabin in the Smoky Mountains since they were teenagers.

God, that had been a lifetime ago. Jared was forty-eight now, widowed, the father to two adult sons. His brother was successful in a way he would never be. Jared lived a normal life, always had and always would. Dean was a failure. Always had been and probably always would be. He'd been married and divorced four times. But he'd done one thing right—to his knowledge he had never fathered a child.

As he lifted the poker from where it was propped against the rock wall surrounding the fireplace, he glanced at the old mantel clock that had belonged to his grandparents. Eleven forty-seven. He should be sleepy, but he wasn't. He had flown in from LA earlier today and had rented a car at the airport.

Jared had sent him the airline ticket. His brother didn't trust him enough to send him the money. In the past, he would have used the money to buy drugs. He couldn't blame Jared. Dean had done nothing to earn anybody's trust. He might be clean and sober, but even he knew that it wouldn't take much to push him over the edge. If something happened, something he couldn't handle, he just might take the easy way out. He always had in the past.

Was receiving death threats something he couldn't handle?

Dean stoked the fire and replaced the poker, then headed toward the kitchen to prepare the coffeemaker. Halfway across the cabin's great room, he heard that pesky noise again. It sounded like footsteps crunching over dried leaves. He stopped dead still and listened.

Silence.

With his heart racing, his palms perspiration-damp and a shiver of uncertainty rippling along his nerve endings, he wondered if he should get his granddad's shotgun out of the closet. His dad had always kept a box of shells on the overhead shelf in the closet, well out of reach, when he and Jared had been kids. But what were the odds that he'd actually find an old box of shells?

He should have gone to the police after he received that first letter, but he'd waited, telling himself that each letter would be the last one. Over the past few months, he had received a total of four succinct typed notes. Each one had begun the same way. *Midnight is coming.*

What the hell did that mean? Midnight came every twenty-four hours, didn't it?

Dean went into the larger of the two bedrooms, the room his parents had shared on their visits here, turned on the overhead light, and opened the closet door. The closet was empty except for a few wire clothes hangers; and there in the very far left corner was his granddad's shotgun. He reached out and grabbed it. Just holding the weapon made him feel safe.

*Idiot. The thing's not loaded.*

To make sure, he snapped it open and checked. Empty. No shells. He raked his hand across the narrow shelf at the top of the closet and found nothing except dust. Had he really expected to find a box of shells?

Dean sighed. But he took the shotgun with him when he returned to the great room and laid it on the kitchen table. He rinsed out the coffeepot, filled it with fresh water, and emptied the water into the reservoir. After measuring the ground coffee into the filter, he set the timer for seven o'clock.

He still needed to bring in more firewood and put clean sheets on the beds. When he'd set his suitcase down on the floor in the second bedroom, the one he and Jared had always shared, he had noticed that the mattresses were bare. He had found the pillows and blankets in the hall linen closet, along with a stack of bed linens. He dreaded the thought of going outside, of getting chilled to the bone and facing his own fears. What if it wasn't an animal walking around out there?

*Wait until morning to bring in the firewood.*

But was there enough wood to keep the fire going all night?

"There are a couple of kerosene heaters in the shed out back," Jared had told him. "Just don't use them at night. It's safer to keep a fire going in the fireplace."

"Why haven't you put in some other kind of heat?" Dean had asked him.

"Because we hardly ever use the place in the winter. Besides, the boys and I enjoy roughing it, just like you and I did with Dad."

*Dad.* Dean didn't think about his father all that often. Remembering how completely he had disappointed his father wasn't a pleasant memory. His parents had loved him, had given him every advantage, and he had screwed up time and time again.

Dean put on his heavy winter coat—the one he had bought for a little of nothing at the Salvation Army thrift store. It was foolish of him to be afraid of the dark, scared to face a raccoon or a possum, or to think that whoever had written those crazy letters had actually followed him from California to Tennessee and was waiting outside the cabin to kill him.

Dean grunted.

*Don't be such a wuss.*

9

He flipped on the porch light and grasped the doorknob. The moment he opened the cabin door, the frigid wind hit him in the face and sent a shiver through his body. He closed the door behind him and headed toward the firewood stacked neatly on the north side of the front porch. Working quickly, he filled his arms to overflowing.

Dean turned and headed for the front door, then realized he'd have to shuffle his load in order to open the door. But before he could accomplish the task, he heard what sounded a lot like footsteps. The hairs on the back of his neck stood up. His heartbeat accelerated. He glanced over his shoulder and saw nothing out of the ordinary.

*Get a grip, man!*

Just as he managed to free one hand and grab hold of the doorknob, he heard the sound again. Closer. As if someone was walking in the leaves that covered the rock walkway from the gravel drive to the porch.

Dean took a deep breath, garnered his courage, and turned all the way around to confront the intruder. Suddenly, he burst into laughter. A possum scurried across the dead leaves not more than a foot from the porch steps.

"Son of a bitch," he said aloud as relief flooded his senses.

Still chuckling to himself, he turned back around, opened the front door, and carried the firewood into the cabin, leaving the front door open behind him. He dumped the firewood into the wood box on the hearth and stood up straight. Feeling the cold air sweeping into the house through the open door, he faced forward, intending to walk across the room and close the door. Instead, he froze to the spot. There, standing just inside the doorway, was someone—male or female, he couldn't tell—wearing a heavy winter coat, boots, gloves, and an oddly familiar mask.

"What the hell! Who are you?"

Dean tried to rationalize what he saw, but as fast as his mind was working, it didn't work fast enough to make sense of the bizarre sight. Before he could say or do anything else, the person in the mask pulled something from his—or her—coat pocket and aimed it at Dean.

A gun?

The person fired.

Once.

Twice.

Three times.

Dean reeled as the first bullet pierced his shoulder, and then dropped to his knees when the second bullet ripped into his leg. When the third bullet entered his chest, he heard two things simultaneously—the clock on the mantel striking the hour and the sound of his killer's voice.

"Dead by midnight," the masked murderer said.

Those were the last words Dean Wilson ever heard.

# Chapter 1

Lorie Hammonds slept until nearly eleven and woke with a mild hangover from having drunk too much champagne at Cathy and Jack's wedding. The moment her feet hit the wooden floor, she moaned. It was too damn cold for mid-March. As she reached down to the footboard of her bed to retrieve her robe, she danced her toes over the floor searching for her house shoes. Her big toe encountered one of the satin slippers. She slid her foot inside the soft warmth and glanced down to see if she could locate its mate. Only after getting out of bed and bending over to look under the bed did she find her other shoe. As she rounded the end of the bed, her hip accidentally made contact with the edge of the antique, gold metal storage bench.

Cursing softly under her breath, she realized this was probably not going to be a good day. After peeing, washing her hands, and splashing cool water on her face, she avoided glancing in the mirror and went straight down the hall to the kitchen. She checked the coffeemaker to see if she had remembered to prepare it last night. She hadn't. Great. That meant she'd have to wait for her morning pick-me-up. Working hurriedly, she ground the coffee beans, ran tap water through the faucet filter, and got everything ready.

While the coffee brewed, she tried to focus on

her usual Sunday-morning routine. Not being a churchgoer, she saved the first day of the week for leisure. Reading the morning newspaper from cover to cover, giving herself a manicure and a pedicure, spending the afternoon lounging in her easy chair with a good book, going to the movies, having dinner out with a friend.

But her best friend—her only true friend in Dunmore—was off on her honeymoon and would be gone two weeks. She didn't begrudge Cathy her happiness, her fourteen glorious days of uninterrupted lovemaking with her new husband. But Cathy's romantic dreams finally coming true only reminded Lorie of the impossibility of that ever happening for her.

Padding through the house to the front door of her 1920s clapboard bungalow located just outside the city limits of downtown Dunmore, Lorie sighed. Romantic dreams didn't come true for women like her. She'd had her one chance at happily ever after and she'd blown it big-time. Just because Cathy had gotten a second chance didn't mean she would.

She opened the front door, scanned the porch, sidewalk, and front yard, and located the Sunday paper hanging precariously between two small azalea bushes. Damn! It was raining like crazy, had probably set in for the day, and the cold March breeze felt more like a February wind. She shivered as she rushed down the steps, grasped the cellophane-wrapped paper, and ran back into the house.

She could smell the delicious coffee brewing. By the time she peeled off her wet housecoat and gown and put on something warm and dry, the coffee would be ready. After taking a couple of tentative steps down the hall, she stopped, said damn, and then turned and went back to the front door. She had forgotten to get Saturday's mail out of the box at the end of her driveway. She might as well do that now while she was already soaked.

After retrieving the mail and getting drenched to the skin, Lorie tossed the small stack of envelopes and the Sunday newspaper down on the half-moon table in her tiny foyer before she headed for the bedroom.

Ten minutes later, drinking her first cup of morning coffee, dressed in lightweight fleece lounge pants and a matching pullover, Lorie slipped the newspaper out of its protective cellophane sleeve and took the paper and her unopened mail into the living room. She relaxed in her plush easy chair, placed her feet on the matching ottoman, and scanned the morning headlines. The Life section of the paper was what interested her today. A color wedding photo of her best friend, Catherine Cantrell—no, she was Catherine Perdue now—stared up at her from the wedding announcements page. Cathy had never looked more beautiful.

Tears threatened, reaching Lorie's throat and lodging there. She swallowed hard. *Be happy, Cathy. Be happy. You so deserve it.*

And maybe that was the reason she would never be truly happy. Lorie Hammonds didn't deserve to be happy.

She folded back the page and laid the newspaper aside. She would cut out Cathy's picture and then look through the rest of the paper later. As a general rule, Saturday's mail was light, even at Treasures of the Past, the antique shop she co-owned with Cathy, but better to go through it now and toss out everything except the bills. She picked up one envelope after another, discarding half a dozen requests from various charities. If she regularly donated to each of these organizations, she would quickly give away her entire paycheck. She laid the one bill—her credit card statement—on the end table. She would write a check tomorrow and mail it off. Sooner or later, she would have to move into the twenty-first century and pay all her bills electronically.

One envelope remained in her lap. She picked it up and looked at it. Her breath caught in her throat.

*No, it can't be. Please, don't let it be another one.*

*Don't jump to conclusions. Just because it looks like the other one doesn't mean it's from the same person.*

She flipped over the envelope a couple of times, studying both sides carefully. Her name and address had been printed on a white mailing label. No return name or address.

*Just like the other letter.*

And just like the first one, it had been mailed from Tennessee, but this one was postmarked Memphis instead of Knoxville.

Lorie ripped open one end of the envelope and pulled out a single sheet of white paper. Her hands trembled as she unfolded the letter. For a half second, her vision blurred as she looked down at the message. Her heartbeat accelerated.

*Midnight is coming. Say your prayers. Ask for forgiveness. Get your affairs in order. You're on the list. Be prepared. You don't know when it will be your turn. Will you be the next to die?*

Lorie sat there staring at the letter until the words on the page began to run together into an unfocused blur. Her fingers tightened, crunching the edge of the letter. Closing her eyes, she tried to calm her erratic heartbeat.

This letter was identical to the first one she had received a month ago. The original letter had worried her, but she'd been in the midst of preparing for Cathy's bridal showers and upcoming wedding. She had decided it was nothing more than a crank letter from some nut who had nothing better to do with his time. After all, why would anyone want to kill her? It wasn't as if she was rich or famous. And as far as she knew she didn't have any enemies who would go so far as to threaten to kill her.

But here it was—a second letter. A second death threat. Could she simply ignore this one and toss it in the trash as she had the first one?

One really could have been a silly prank.

But two could mean that someone out there wanted, at the very least, to frighten her.

Or did they actually want to kill her?

Mike Birkett poured cereal into three bowls, added milk and blueberries, and set the bowls on the table. His nine-year-old daughter, Hannah, picked up her spoon and dug in while his eleven-year-old son, M.J., curled up his nose as he eyed the berries with disdain.

"Do I have to eat those?" M.J. asked, a slight whine in his voice.

"Yeah," Mike told him. "At least some of them. Okay? Blueberries are good for you."

"Who says?"

"I'll bet it was Ms. Sherman," Hannah said. "I've heard her talking about what she eats—stuff like protein shakes and tofu and soy milk and all kinds of yucky things like that."

"Figures," M.J. mumbled under his breath.

Mike knew that neither of his children especially liked Abby Sherman, the woman he'd been dating the past few months. And he really didn't under-

17

stand why. Abby had gone out of her way to try to make the kids like her, and she'd been very understanding when they had been rude to her on more than one occasion. What really puzzled him about their attitude was the fact that Abby actually reminded him of his late wife, Molly. It was one of the reasons he'd thought the kids would automatically accept her. Abby had the same cute look that Molly had, with her blue eyes and strawberry-blond hair. She was slender, athletic, and wholesome.

Abby was the sort of person he needed in his life, the type of woman who would make a good wife and mother.

Mike hurriedly wolfed down his cereal and forced himself to eat the blueberries he'd sprinkled on top. When he finished the last bite, he took a sip of his third cup of coffee and found it lukewarm.

"You two hurry up," he told his children. "Sunday school starts in less than an hour. If we're late again this Sunday, Grams will give us all a good scolding."

Since Molly's death nearly four years ago, his mother had stepped in and helped him. He didn't know what he would have done without her. His kids lived with him and he usually managed to get them off to school every morning. But his mother picked them up in the afternoons and looked after them until he came home from work. And whenever his duties as the county sheriff called him

18

away at odd hours, all he had to do was phone his mom. She'd been a lifesaver.

After being up late last night, dancing at his best friend's wedding, he would have liked nothing better than to have slept in this morning and let his mom pick the kids up for Sunday school. But as a single parent, he always tried to set a good example for his son and daughter, going so far as to eat blueberries.

Mike dumped the remainder of his cool coffee into the sink, rinsed out the cup, and left it in the sink along with his bowl and spoon. Glancing out the window, he groaned quietly. He wished the rain had held off for another day. Not only did they have Sunday school and church services this morning, but they were taking Abby out to lunch and then to an afternoon matinee in Decatur.

"I ate all the cereal and some of the blueberries," M.J. said as he dumped a few drops of leftover milk and three-fourths of the blueberries into the garbage.

Mike nodded and smiled. Whenever he looked at his son, he saw Molly. He had her red-blond hair, blue eyes, and freckles. Hannah, on the other hand, resembled him. Same wide mouth, square jaw, dark hair, and blue eyes. But Hannah had Molly's sweet, easygoing disposition and his son definitely showed the potential to be the hell-raiser Mike had been as a teenager.

When Hannah placed her empty bowl in the

sink, she looked at Mike and asked, "May I wear the dress I wore to Jack and Cathy's wedding to church this morning?"

"It's a little fancy for church, isn't it?" Mike knew little to nothing about young girls' clothes, but the floor-length green dress his mother had chosen for her to wear to the wedding wasn't something he thought appropriate for Sunday school.

"I like it a lot, Daddy. It's so pretty. It's the same color as Miss Lorie's maid of honor dress."

Mike groaned again. Lorie Hammonds was the last woman on earth he wanted his daughter to emulate.

"Wear that little blue dress with the white collar," Mike told Hannah.

"I wore that last Sunday."

"Then pick out something else. But you cannot wear the green dress you wore to the wedding."

"Oh, all right."

"Go on now. Brush your teeth and get dressed." Mike tapped the face of his wristwatch. "I want you two ready to go in twenty minutes. You can recite your Bible verses to me on the way there."

Mike left the kitchen as it was. He could load the dishwasher and wipe off the table and countertops later. He needed a quick shower and a shave.

As he walked through the house, heading for his bathroom, he tried his damnedest not to think about Lorie. He had spent more time with her this past week than he had in all the years since she returned to Dunmore. Usually, he avoided her like the plague. But they had been thrown together constantly the past few days because he had been Jack's best man and she had been Cathy's maid of honor. Now that the wedding was over, there was no reason for him to see her again, which suited him just fine.

Mike turned on the shower, stripped out of his pajama bottoms and T-shirt, and stepped under the warm water. Okay, so he had a hard-on just thinking about Lorie. So what? She was a beautiful, desirable woman and he was a normal guy whose body reacted in a normal way when he thought about someone he found attractive. Lorie was extremely desirable, but she was all wrong for him and his kids. Thoughts of Abby Sherman might not cause an instant arousal, but Abby was a lady, someone he could be proud of, someone suitable as a stepmother for his children.

Lorie Hammonds was a slut!

The weather fit her mood to perfection. Dark, dreary, and dismal. Maleah Perdue stood at the kitchen window and watched the morning rainfall, the heavy downpour veiling the backyard in a watery mist. She had spent her first night alone in her childhood home, the place that held many happy memories from the first seven years of her life. And a place that inspired nightmares if she allowed herself to think of the other eleven years she had lived here. Eleven years under the tyrannical rule of her cruel, abusive stepfather.

Shaking her head slightly to dislodge the unpleasant memories, she turned away from the window and picked up her coffee mug from the counter. She wasn't a breakfast eater. A piece of fruit or a glass of juice usually held her until midday, but she couldn't make it without at least half a pot of coffee. She was addicted to caffeine.

Carrying the half-full mug with her as she wandered leisurely from the kitchen to the small den at the back of the house, she wondered if the newlyweds had arrived in the Bahamas yet. Her older brother, Jack, and his bride, Cathy, had gotten married yesterday. She had been a bridesmaid.

Maleah groaned. God, she hated weddings. But she loved Jack and thought the world of Cathy, so she had agreed to be in the wedding party. The idea of a happy marriage was an alien concept to her. Jack remembered her parents being happy, back when the four of them had been your normal, average American family. But she'd been in the first grade when her father had died in a car accident and her memories of him were at best sketchy. What she remembered was her mother's marriage to Nolan Reaves.

By the time she was old enough to date, she had known that she would never get married. She would never be able to trust a man enough to pledge until death do us part.

When she sat down and curled up on the lush leather sofa, one hand holding her mug, she reached out for the TV remote. She surfed through the channels until she found a local station's early morning news program. Keeping the sound muted, she lifted the mug to her lips and sipped on the strong, sweet coffee. Black, heavy on the sugar, or rather the sugar substitute. A girl had to watch her figure, and in Maleah's case, being only five-four and curvy, keeping trim was a constant battle. Just as she settled back and relaxed, her phone rang. When she'd come downstairs half an hour ago, she had slipped her phone into the pocket of her cotton knit sweater. Four years as an agent for the Powell Private Security and Investigation Agency, based in Knoxville, had taught her to never be without her iPhone.

Checking caller ID, she smiled and placed her mug atop a coaster on the end table. "Morning," she said. "What's up?"

Nicole Powell, Maleah's boss and close friend, laughed. It was good to hear Nic laughing again. She'd had a rough year. For a while, Maleah had wondered if Nic and Griff's marriage could survive, but recently they seemed to have worked through their problems. And even though Maleah knew that Griff still kept secrets from Nic, it wasn't her place to interfere in her best friend's marriage.

"I wanted to let you know that Griff and I are

going away for a week, just the two of us. Sort of a second honeymoon. And I have no idea where we're going. Griff's keeping it top secret to surprise me."

*What is it suddenly with all these honeymoons?*

*Only two honeymoons,* she reminded herself. *Just because you're allergic to marriage and all the trimmings doesn't mean other people don't have the right to take a chance on happily ever after.*

"That's great. It sounds so romantic."

"If for any reason you need something while I'm gone, you'll have to go through Sanders," Nic said. "Naturally, Griff's leaving him in charge."

"I can't imagine why I'd need anything Powell Agency related. I'm on vacation. Well, sort of. House-sitting and keeping tabs on my nephew, even though Seth is actually staying with his grandparents, isn't exactly a vacation."

"How's that going—staying in your childhood home?"

"The old home place isn't the same. Jack and Cathy completely renovated and updated the whole house. Except for the bare bones, the interior is like an entirely different house. And they had the exterior painted in colors true to the time period, very similar to the way this old Victorian looked when it was built."

"So staying there isn't reviving bad memories?" Nic asked.

"A few, but nothing I can't handle."

"Good." Nic paused, then said, "Think positive thoughts for me—for us—will you? Griff and I love each other and our marriage is important to us, but we realize we have some fundamental problems. We're hoping we can work through a lot of things while we're away."

"Good luck. And I'll send tons of positive thoughts your way."

"Thanks. Talk to you when I get back. Bye."

"Bye."

Maleah slipped her iPhone into her sweater pocket.

She truly wished Nic and Griff the best. In the beginning of their marriage, they had seemed happy, seemed perfect for each other. Maleah would have laid odds that if any couple had a chance to make it work, Nic and Griff did.

Maleah had never been tempted to marry, even though she had received two proposals. As soon as a guy got serious, she broke it off and ran in the opposite direction. Both of her former serious relationships had been with wonderful men, either a real catch. She'd heard that Brad Douglas was now married and had twin daughters. She and Brad had enjoyed a two-year relationship and had even lived together for a while.

Back in college, she had lost her virginity to Noah Laborde. She had been in love for the first time. Noah had been handsome, intelligent, and every girl's dream come true. A week after graduation, he had popped the question. She had taken one look at the diamond solitaire he held in his hand and had broken out in a cold sweat. He'd been ready for marriage. She hadn't been, never would be. Less than a year later, a mutual friend had called to tell her that Noah was dead. Murdered. Even now, after ten years, it broke her heart to think that Noah never got the chance to live a full, complete life. It was so unfair. But then, she had learned at her mother's knee that life was seldom fair.

Lorie drove by Mike's house three times, trying to build up enough courage to stop, ring the doorbell, and tell the county sheriff that she had received her second death threat. He would ask to see both letters. She'd tell him she threw the first one in the trash. He'd look over the second letter, all the while wondering if she had written it to herself as an excuse to draw him into her life. Damn him! Did he honestly think she was that desperate?

And if he believed her, what would he do? Tell her to come down to the office in the morning and fill out a report? He certainly wouldn't take a personal interest. He'd hand her problem over to one of his deputies and that would be the end of it.

There had been a time when Mike Birkett would have gone to hell and back for her. But that had been when he had loved her, when he had thought she was going to be his wife and the mother of his children. That had been before she had gotten on a plane and flown to California to become a famous movie star. Seventeen years and a million heart-breaks ago.

Lorie slowed her Ford Edge SUV at the stop sign, glanced down at her wristwatch—2:46 P.M.—and wondered what the hell she was going to do. Who could she turn to for help?

Not Mike.

And not the Dunmore police. Even if they took the threat on her life seriously, what could they actually do?

What she needed was a private detective, someone who could find out the identity of the person who had sent her the threatening letters.

Lorie suddenly had a lightbulb moment and knew exactly who she could go to for help.

Fifteen minutes later, she pulled into the driveway at 121 West Fourth Street, parked her SUV, got out, and walked up and onto the front porch. She rang the doorbell and waited.

Maleah Perdue, Jack's younger, all-American, blond sister, opened the door and smiled. "Hi there. What brings you out on a day like this that's not fit for anybody or anything, except maybe ducks?"

"Are you busy?" Lorie asked. "Am I interrupting anything?"

"You're interrupting my game of solitaire on my laptop." Maleah laughed.

Lorie forced a tight smile. "I . . . uh . . . have a problem that I was hoping you could help me with."

"Well, come on in and tell me about it," Maleah said.

Lorie entered the large two-story foyer.

"Come on back in the den."

Lorie followed her best friend's sister-in-law. When they reached the small, cozy room, Maleah asked, "Want some hot tea or coffee?"

"No, thanks. Nothing for me."

"Have a seat."

Lorie nodded, but didn't sit down. "I want to hire you. I don't know how much you charge, but I need a professional."

Maleah stared at Lorie, then asked, "What's wrong?"

"I received a death threat in a letter about a month ago. I convinced myself that it was just a prank and threw the letter away and almost forgot about it. But I received a second letter identical to the first. It arrived in yesterday's mail, but I didn't open the mail until today."

"Did you bring the letter with you?"

Lorie dug in her purse, pulled out the envelope, and handed it to Maleah.

"Do you think you could get any fingerprints off the envelope or letter?" Lorie asked.

"Yeah, yours, the mail carrier's, and anybody else who might have touched it. But my guess is whoever wrote it made sure he or she didn't leave any prints."

Maleah removed the letter from the envelope and read it aloud. "Do you know anyone who might want to kill you?"

"No. No one."

"Does anything in the letter ring a bell? Any of the phrases sound familiar?"

"No."

"Do you have any idea what he—or maybe she—means by 'midnight is coming'?"

"No, not really," Lorie said. "Do you think this is for real, that someone is actually threatening to kill me?"

"I don't know, but you'd be a fool to ignore a second letter," Maleah told her. "I'm glad you've come to me. We'll get in touch with Mike Birkett and—"

"No!" When Maleah looked at her quizzically, Lorie explained. "I could have gone to Mike, but I didn't. He's not going to take this seriously. As you know, we . . . uh . . . we share some ancient history. I don't want to involve local law enforcement, especially not Mike. Not yet. Not until we know for sure that this is for real."

"Want my opinion?"

Lorie nodded.

"It's for real."

"Then you think somebody wants to kill me?"

"Possibly. At the very least, somebody wants to scare the shit out of you."

Had they all received the most recent letter? He could have mailed them from anywhere, but it seemed only appropriate for the letters to have a Memphis postmark, so he'd made a quick one-day trip back to Memphis. In the future, he'd mail the letters before leaving town. He liked to imagine each person's reaction when they opened the envelope, how they must have prayed that it wasn't another dire warning.

Smiling, he ran the tips of his fingers over his closed laptop where the letter was stored. There would be no need to write a new message each time after this, not when the original said it all so perfectly.

He could only surmise that each of them was puzzled by the letter, wondering who had sent it and why. Stupid fools!

Sooner or later, somebody, probably a smart FBI agent, would figure it out, but by then it would be too late. They would all be dead, the guilty punished, and a cruel, ugly part of the past erased. And the best part was that no one would ever suspect him.

He picked up the glass of chardonnay he had poured only moments ago and sat down in his favorite chair. As he sipped the wine, he lifted the remote control with his other hand and hit the Play button to start the DVD.

He owned dozens of copies of this particular movie, both on DVD and on video. If he could have purchased every copy ever made, he would have. And he would have destroyed all of them.

# Chapter 2

Derek Lawrence arrived late. He wouldn't have even considered attending if this wasn't his mother's sixty-fifth birthday bash. As a general rule, he deliberately avoided spending time with the woman who had given birth to him. But not being a total bastard, he had felt compelled to put in an appearance this Sunday afternoon at the party hosted by his sister, a party for family and a few close friends. He had known that to Diana a few close friends meant there would be no less than a hundred in attendance. His baby sister loved nothing better than to host a social event so that she could show off her fifteen-million-dollar estate on the outskirts of Nashville. Unlike their mother, who had come from a middle-class background, Diana had been born into money and had married money. He loved the girl, but the older she got, the more like their mother she became. God help her.

The house was buzzing with activity. In one glance, he counted thirty people milling about in the massive foyer and adjoining living room. A small band filled the place with music befitting the Queen Bee's birthday. Nothing common and vulgar. Classical and semi-classical only.

When a waiter carrying a tray of champagne flutes passed him, Derek grabbed a glass. He meandered through the crowd, nodding and smiling at those who glanced his way. Some he knew. Some he didn't. Others looked vaguely familiar. And then he spotted her—the most beautiful woman in the room. Alexa Daugherty. Too bad she was his first cousin. Derek chuckled to himself. Even if they weren't related, he would never take on Alexa. The lady was too high maintenance for his tastes. As a child, she had epitomized the saying "poor little rich girl." As a woman, she brought another catchphrase to mind—"rich bitch." His darling cousin had a reputation for chewing up men and spitting them out in little pieces.

The moment she saw him, she smiled and motioned for him to come to her. He made his way through the celebrators and when he reached Alexa, he leaned over and kissed her flawless cheek.

"I haven't seen you in ages," she said. "You're not still working for the FBI, are you? I believe Aunt Happy mentioned that you were an associate of Griffin Powell's. Is that right?"

Happy was Derek's mother. He had never heard anyone call her anything else. He wasn't sure where the nickname had come from or who had given it to her, but it certainly didn't suit the snooty, social-climbing woman he had known and hated for most of his life.

Before Derek could reply, a man he didn't know—midfifties, trim, well dressed—injected himself into the conversation. "We were just talking about this shocking murder case over in Memphis, and Alexa mentioned you used to be with the FBI, a profiler, I believe."

Derek nodded. His sister's crowd always found it fascinating that he had chosen to work in a field usually reserved for those not in their social circle—law enforcement.

Alexa slipped her arm through his, but she looked directly at the other man. "You simply must tell Derek all about it. The killer is still at large and the Memphis police have no idea who did it."

"Ward Dandridge." The man stuck out his hand. "It's a pleasure to meet you."

"Oh, silly me." Alexa giggled. Even her giggles sounded sexy. "I forgot that you two didn't know each other. Sorry about that."

Alexa was not an airheaded bimbo, despite appearances to the contrary. His guess was that she'd had one glass of champagne too many. Alexa was a brilliant woman with an IQ that bordered on genius. And he knew for a fact that she was a shrewd businesswoman who had recently taken over as CEO of her father's empire. The old man still maintained his position as chairman of the board, but he happily left the day-to-day running of Daugherty, Inc. to his only child.

"Do you know Tagg Chambless?" Dandridge asked.

"The former NFL halfback?"

"That's the one. Tagg and I are business associates. We both have an interest in one of the Tunica casinos." Dandridge downed the remainder of his champagne and motioned to one of the waiters, who quickly exchanged his empty glass for a full one.

"Didn't you date Chambless for a few months?" Derek winked at Alexa.

She gave him the evil eye, a look for which she had become notorious. Grown men had been brought to their knees in submission by that look alone.

When Ward Dandridge stared questioningly at Alexa, Derek laughed. "No, his name wasn't Chambless, was it? But the fellow was a football player, wasn't he? Not Chambless, though. If I recall, he was a big, burly brute with—what did you say at the time? Oh yes, that he had more muscles than brains."

"You're mistaken. That's not my type," Alexa said coolly. "But we're getting off subject. Ward did so want your thoughts on the murder case."

"And just what does Tagg Chambless have to do with the murder case?" Derek asked.

"Oh, the victim was Tagg's wife," Ward said. "Gorgeous woman, even if she was little more than a plastic doll. She'd had all sorts of cosmetic surgery. Everything from breast implants to rhinoplasty."

Derek wished he could think of a diplomatic way to escape. It had become apparent that Ward Dandridge loved gossip, and discussing other people's private lives bored Derek.

"I'd love to hear more," Derek lied. "Maybe later. I really should find Mother and wish her a happy birthday."

Alexa tightened her hold on Derek's arm, leaned close and whispered, "Stay. Please. Ward's a friend of Daddy's and I simply can't be rude to him."

"I'll make this quick," Dandridge said, apparently determined to drag an opinion out of Derek. "Mrs. Chambless, Tagg's wife, had quite a reputation. The lady used to be an actress of sorts. She starred in several"—he cleared his throat—"*adult* films and was a *Playboy* centerfold about ten or eleven years ago.

"The woman was shot numerous times, killed right there in her own home." Dandridge lowered his voice. "The police never released certain information, but Tagg shared a few things with me. Seems when the maid found her, she was naked and was wearing a mask of some sort. Odd, don't you think?"

"Yes, quite odd," Derek agreed.

"You would assume that she was raped, considering the fact she was naked, but Tagg said she wasn't. Raped, that is."

"Hmm . . ." Derek wasn't sure what Dandridge wanted him to say. Did the man honestly think he could come up with a profile of the killer with no more information than that?

"Oh God, who invited him?" Alexa asked with utter disdain in her voice.

"Who?" Dandridge inquired as he glanced right and left.

Derek followed his cousin's cold glare, which was aimed directly at a man Derek knew, liked, and respected.

"Camden Hendrix." Alexa spoke his name as if she were saying Attila the Hun. "The man is a barbarian."

Derek grinned when Cam looked his way and immediately came over to speak to him.

To break the sudden uneasy silence, Derek introduced the two men, who apparently knew each other by reputation. "And of course, you know Cam, don't you, Alexa."

"We've met." Icicles hung on her words.

"Looking as lovely as ever," Cam said, but did little more than glance briefly at Alexa before he turned back to Derek. "Good to see a friendly face. I thought maybe Nic and Griff would be here. I haven't seen them in a couple of months."

"I believe they're off on a second honeymoon,"

Derek said. "Something spur of the moment." As a Powell Agency employee, he had received the text message sent out that morning to inform everyone that Sanders was in charge while the agency's owners were away.

"Is that how you finagled an invitation to Aunt Happy's birthday party—because you're Griffin Powell's lawyer?" Alexa asked, knowing full well how rude her question was.

Cam chuckled. "Actually, your cousin Diana invited me. My firm is representing her husband's brother in his divorce case."

"I say, Hendrix, have you heard about Tagg Chambless's wife's murder over in Memphis?" Ward Dandridge asked, apparently interested in little else. "I had just cornered Derek to get his opinion about her unsolved murder."

Cam's mouth tilted in a smirking grin and it was obvious that he had barely managed not to laugh.

"We'll talk later," Derek said as he pulled away from the group. "I want to check with Mother and make sure she received her present yesterday." He glanced from Dandridge to Cam. "Why don't you tell Cam about the case? After all, he's famous for defending accused murderers." Derek kissed Alexa on the cheek and whispered, "Behave yourself, cousin."

Several minutes later, he found his mother surrounded by her country club girlfriends, women in her age group whose husbands' wealth afforded them a lifestyle only dreamed about by most.

Happy Lawrence Vickers Adams—married three times, widowed once and divorced twice—was still an attractive woman, thanks to great genes and a talented cosmetic surgeon. Tall, slender, elegant. No one would ever guess that Happy wasn't "to the manor born."

Their gazes met as he approached her and she quickly plastered a fake smile on her unwrinkled face. Derek couldn't remember the last time his mother had been genuinely glad to see him. When he reached her, she leaned close, offering him her cheek to kiss. He did as he was expected to do.

"Happy birthday, Mother."

"Thank you, dear. And thank you for the lovely jade bracelet. I'm sure I will enjoy wearing it occasionally."

With the necessary pleasantries out of the way, Happy turned her full attention back to her friends. Derek walked away, went through the kitchen and out the back door without searching for his sister to say hello or good-bye. He motioned for the valet to bring around his car, and within five minutes, he sped off down the long, winding drive and out onto the highway.

If he was lucky, he shouldn't have to make a command appearance again until Happy's seventieth birthday.

• • •

Lorie answered, as truthfully as she could, all of Maleah's questions about her past and present boyfriends and other relationships.

"I honestly can't think of anyone who would want to kill me," Lorie said, feeling more frustrated by the minute. "It just doesn't make any sense. I live as low-key a life as possible. I haven't had a date in months. I do my level best not to piss off anybody here in Dunmore. I just want to live my life without any major complications."

"A death threat is a major complication." Maleah shifted on the sofa, turning halfway to directly face Lorie. "You haven't noticed anyone following you or skulking around your house or your antique shop?"

"No. Not really. I mean, men sometimes look at me and I know they're mentally undressing me. Occasionally someone makes a crude comment. And at odd times, I feel like somebody's watching me, but I've never actually seen anyone, so I assumed it was just my imagination."

"Maybe. Maybe not," Maleah said. "Have you recently received any peculiar phone calls?"

"Are you talking about heavy breathing? Then no. And no one has called to talk dirty to me since the first year I moved back to Dunmore."

"What about online—any weird e-mails?"

"Nope. And I don't have a blog or anything like

that. Just a Web site for Treasures. And I don't Twitter."

Maleah shook her head, the action inadvertently bouncing her long, blond ponytail. Today, with no makeup on and wearing jeans and an oversized cotton sweater, she looked more like a fresh-faced teenager than an experienced bodyguard and investigator.

"I wish you had kept that first letter," Maleah said. "We have no proof you actually received the letter, only your word that you got it."

"Are you saying you don't believe me, that you think I'm lying?"

"No, of course not. I believe you, but when we go to the sheriff, he'll want proof."

"I told you that I prefer not to involve local law enforcement, not until we know for sure this isn't someone's idea of a sick joke."

"Look, I'm ninety percent sure that when I contact the Powell Agency for an okay to take your case, I'm going to be told that although we'll do an independent investigation, the sheriff needs to be notified."

Lorie groaned.

"Do I need to know more about you and Mike Birkett?" Maleah asked. "I was just a kid, twelve or thirteen, when you two dated and that's all I remember—that you two dated, were sort of pre-engaged and you broke it off and left town. But that was what—sixteen or seventeen years ago? Is there something going on with the two of you now?"

"God, no!" *Only in my dreams.* "You know the rest of my story, don't you? Everybody in town knows about how I disgraced my family, ruined my reputation, and made a complete and utter fool of myself after I left Dunmore. I jilted Mike and broke his heart. Now he can't stand the sight of me."

Maleah glanced away as if it bothered her to see the sadness that Lorie knew she couldn't hide. Her feelings were written plainly on her face.

"I'll have to talk to Mike," Maleah told her. "But I'll ask him to assign one of his deputies to your case. That's what he'd do anyway."

Lorie nodded, reluctantly agreeing. "So, what do I do now?"

"Do you have a security system at home?"

"Yes."

"Use it. Be aware of your surroundings at all times and take no chances with your personal safety. Do you carry a gun or Mace or—?"

"I have a small pistol that I keep in my nightstand," Lorie said. "And I carry Mace in my purse and I've taken a couple of self-defense classes."

"Put my number into your home phone speed dial and your cell phone so you can contact me instantly if you need me. At this point, I think providing twenty-four/seven private security would be premature."

"Yeah, I think it would be."

"If you get another letter, a phone call, sense someone following you or anything that raises a red flag in your mind, get in touch with me immediately," Maleah told her. "In the meantime, I'll ask for an okay from Powell's to work on your case and then I'll call Mike."

Lorie stood. "Thanks, Maleah. I appreciate your doing this for me. I guess I'm lucky that you decided to stay in Dunmore for a while."

Maleah got up and walked Lorie to the front door. She patted Lorie on the back. "Be careful, okay? But don't worry any more than you can help. At this point we have no idea what we're dealing with, whether the person who sent you the letters is some goofball who thinks this is funny or some nut job who gets his cookies off scaring women with threats or if we have the real thing on our hands."

Lorie opened the front door and then paused for a moment. "The real thing being someone who is going to kill me."

"Someone who plans to kill you," Maleah corrected. "We won't let that happen—you and me, the Powell Agency, and the sheriff's department."

After Sunday evening church services, Mike sent his kids to take their baths and get ready for bed. Tomorrow was a school day, the first day back following their spring break, which had come early

42

this year. He'd probably have a couple of hours of alone time after he tucked his kids in, time to kick back and watch a little TV or read a few chapters in the latest David Baldacci novel. For now, he needed to load the dishwasher and set it to start in the middle of the night. Later, he'd put out plates, bowls, cups, and silverware on the kitchen table for breakfast and afterward he'd gather the clothes he needed to drop off at the cleaners in the morning.

Just as he headed for the kitchen, the doorbell rang. *Who the hell?* It was nearly nine o'clock. When he opened the front door, he was surprised to find Jack's kid sister, Maleah, standing on his porch.

"Hi, Mike. Got a few minutes?" she asked.

"Sure, come on in." He escorted her to the living room. "Is there a problem? Something with Seth or—"

"Nothing personal. I'm fine. My nephew is fine," Maleah told him. "I'm here on business."

Frowning in confusion, Mike stared at her. "Explain."

"May I sit down?"

"Sure. Please sit. Believe me, my mama taught me good manners. I just forget them sometimes."

Maleah sat on the sofa. Mike eased down onto the wing-back chair directly across from her.

"You know Lorie Hammonds, I believe," Maleah said.

Mike nodded. His gut tightened.

"She has hired me, as a representative of the Powell Agency, to investigate two threats made on her life."

"You're kidding me."

"No, I'm quite serious."

"Don't tell me the Women for Christian Morality folks are after her again. Believe me, those ladies are harmless."

"I'm not familiar with that group, but I doubt they're involved in this situation. Lorie has received two letters, one a month ago and a second this weekend. Both letters were identical, both were death threats."

"Did you see the letters?"

Maleah nodded. "Yes, one of them, the most recent. Unfortunately, she threw the first one away thinking it was a crank letter."

"Hmm . . . I wouldn't take anything Ms. Hammonds says too seriously. She tends to be melodramatic sometimes. Actually, I wouldn't put it past her to have written the letter herself in order to get attention."

"To get whose attention—yours, Mike?"

His gut knotted painfully. "Yeah. Maybe."

"Do you think she's that desperate to have you pay attention to her that she'd fake death threats?"

Would she? Did he really believe she would go to that extreme just to draw him into her life? "I don't know. Probably not."

"Hey, I realize you two were an item when you

were teenagers and she broke your heart when she went off to Hollywood hoping to become a movie star. But that was a long time ago. Don't you think it's way past time to let bygones be bygones? I don't know Lorie all that well, but then neither do you. You knew the teenage Lorie. She's not the same person."

"You can say that again."

"I'm really not concerned about your personal issues with her. But I do need to know that, as the county sheriff, you will treat these death threats as seriously as you would if any other woman in your jurisdiction had received them."

"You have my word on it. Ask Ms. Hammonds to come to the office tomorrow and give a statement. I'll assign one of our deputies to question her."

"Thanks, Mike. I knew I could count on you." Maleah stood.

"Daddy," Hannah called out from down the hall. "I'm ready for my good-night kiss."

"Go on," Maleah told him. "I'll see myself out."


Lorie sat alone in her semidark bedroom, the only light coming from the adjustable floor lamp behind her lounge chair. Oddly enough, the silence was comforting, the familiar a safe haven. The security system was armed. Her handgun was nearby in the nightstand. She was safe, at least for now. And it was possible that she wasn't in any real danger, that whoever had written the two threatening letters would not follow through and actually try to kill her.

She had halfway expected to hear from Mike. Perhaps Maleah hadn't contacted him; perhaps she was waiting until morning. But Lorie knew that eventually, Mike would confront her. He wasn't likely to take the situation seriously. He'd think she concocted the whole thing in order to get his attention.

He couldn't be more wrong.

It had taken her nearly four years—ever since Molly Birkett had died and Lorie had hoped Mike would turn to her for comfort—to accept that Mike truly hated her and would never forgive her.

Lorie gently ran her fingertips over the open book in her lap—the Dunmore High yearbook from Mike's senior year. She had been a sophomore, only sixteen, and madly in love with Mike. Their first date had been for his senior prom.

She slammed the yearbook closed and dropped it to the floor beside the cream and gold damask chaise longue.

An odd idea came to mind. The corners of her mouth lifted into a sarcastic smile. The only person she could think of who might want to kill her was Mike. Of course, not literally kill her. But he would like nothing better than to make her disappear, to erase her and pretend she'd never existed.

As she considered possible suspects from her

life, past and present, she couldn't think of anyone who had ever truly hated her except Mike.

Her parents disapproved of her and were disappointed in her. Her father still wouldn't speak to her and although her mother would talk to her briefly over the phone, she refused to see her.

When she had lived in California and had been trying to break into show business, she had made a few friends and possibly a few enemies. But no one who would want to kill her, certainly not after all these years.

*What about Dean?*

She hadn't thought about Dean Wilson in ages. The last time she saw him was the day she'd caught a bus home to Alabama. He had followed her to the terminal and pleaded with her not to leave him. He'd been high as a kite. She supposed that, in a way, she had loved Dean. He'd been good-looking and exciting and charming. But in the end, he had been her undoing. And for that, she could thank him. After all, if he hadn't gotten her a small part in one of his movies, it might have taken her longer to realize how close she had come to hitting rock bottom. That final degradation had forced her to admit the truth to herself. She had failed miserably. She might have been pretty, had a small amount of talent and a great deal of ambition, but after nearly six years of trying to get a big break, she had gone from starry-eyed beauty pageant winner to a bit player in a porno movie.

Was it possible that Dean had sent the letters? The last thing he'd said to her had been a threat.

"Go ahead and leave me, bitch. But one of these days when you least expect it, I'll show up and make you sorry you were ever born."

At the time, she hadn't paid much attention to his drug-induced ravings. But . . . What if . . .

*Damn it, Lorie, why would Dean send you death threats now?*

# Chapter 3

Barbara Jean met the potential client at the front door, introduced herself as Sanders's assistant, and showed him down the hall to Griff's study. The door stood wide open and Sanders sat behind the antique desk, a somber expression on his face. She knew Sanders for the kind-hearted, caring man he was. She knew that he liked his tea without lemon, cream, or sugar, that he preferred to sleep on the right side of the bed, that he had a dour sense of humor and that he enjoyed classical music. His favorite color was yellow, his favorite snack was Cheetos, and his favorite season was summer. However, even now, after being this man's lover for nearly three years, she knew very little about the mysterious past he shared with his best friend and employer, Griffin Powell, and with the alluringly beautiful Dr. Yvette Meng. And that secretive past had made him the man he was today.

Although they were on intimate terms, friends as well as lovers, she thought of him as Sanders, his surname the one used by all who knew him, even Griff and Yvette. In their private moments, she occasionally called him Damar, but in reality, Damar was a man she didn't know, a man who belonged to a past that she could never share. A past that belonged to a dead wife and child.

Unlike Griff's wife, Nicole, her dear friend, she accepted the fact that Sanders had secrets he chose not to share with her. But where she managed to curb her curiosity about the man she loved, about the years he had spent with Griff and Yvette, the three of them captives of a madman, Nic probed relentlessly into the past. Nic needed to know; Barbara Jean did not. It was enough for her that Sanders loved her now, and that he was loyal to the commitment they had made to each other. Perhaps it was because she had known from the very beginning that she was not the great love of Sanders's life.

When she paused her wheelchair at the door, their guest waiting with her, Sanders rose from behind the desk. "Please come in, Mr. Chambless."

The tall, broad-shouldered biracial athlete resembled his photographs, a handsome man with a toned body. But where in every picture Barbara Jean had seen of him, he'd been smiling, today he looked as if he might never smile again. Grief hung on his shoulders like a heavy shroud. The man had lost his wife only a month ago.

When Tagg Chambless entered the study and strode across the room, Sanders came out from behind the desk and met him, his hand extended. Sanders was much shorter than the six-five former NFL star, but equally impressive in his own way. The first time she saw Sanders, she had thought he looked like Yul Brynner, the exotically handsome actor who had risen to stardom in the mid-twentieth century portraying the king of Siam in the Broadway production and later in the movie, *The King and I.* Same bald head. Same hot, dark eyes. Same regal, commanding manner.

"My lawyer, Robert Talbot, told me that the Powell Agency is the best money can buy," Tagg said as he shook hands with Sanders. "Seems Bobby and your agency's lawyer are old buddies."

"Yes, that is my understanding," Sanders said. "Camden Hendrix called me personally Saturday to set up this appointment today."

"Yeah. And you might as well know up front that I wanted to talk to Griffin Powell himself about this and was told he was unavailable."

"Mr. and Mrs. Powell are away on vacation."

Tagg nodded. "So I get the number-two man instead." He glanced back at Barbara Jean, who remained in the doorway. "What about Ms. Hughes?"

"Come on in, Barbara Jean." Sanders motioned to her and then focused his gaze on Tagg. "Just as I am Mr. Powell's associate and second in command when he and his wife are not available, Ms. Hughes is my associate and privy to everything that goes on at the Powell Agency." When Tagg made no comment, Sanders indicated a chair near the fireplace. "Please, sit down."

After Tagg took his seat, Sanders sat in the chair across from him. Barbara Jean entered the room and eased her wheelchair behind Sanders.

"I think Mr. Hendrix explained what I want," Tagg said.

"He gave me the basic details—that your wife was murdered approximately one month ago, the police have done all they can and have no suspects in the case, and you want to hire the Powell Agency to do an independent investigation."

Tagg leaned over, his shoulders slouching with weariness, and sank his large, clasped hands between his spread knees. With his gaze directed to the floor, he breathed in heavily and released a deep, tortured sigh.

"You have no idea what it's like to see your wife's dead body lying in her own blood . . . to know that she suffered." Tagg choked with emotion.

Barbara Jean's gaze locked with Sanders's and without saying a word she conveyed her concern. He closed his eyes for just for a second and she understood exactly what he was reliving in that dark moment and how the other man's words had touched a sharp, painful chord in Sanders's very private memories.

51

Sanders cleared his throat. "I'll oversee the case personally, but I'll put one of our top agents in charge of the investigation. His name is Holt Keinan. I called him in from Knoxville last night and he's ready to return to Memphis with you today to handle things in the field. He will need your full cooperation. Do you understand?"

"He'll have it," Tagg assured Sanders.

"Whatever you share with us will go no further, even if you've been involved with anything illegal. But in order for us to do our job, we have to know about anything that might have the slightest bearing on your wife's murder."

"No one I'm associated with killed her. I'm sure of that. Nobody was out to get me through Hilary."

"Nevertheless, we will be digging into your and your wife's personal lives, past and present."

Tagg clenched his teeth and nodded.

"The more you can tell us, the more time we can save investigating and having to find out things you could have told us." Sanders paused, giving Tagg a chance to inject information into their conversation. He didn't. Sanders continued. "You seem to think there's no one in your life who posed a threat to you or your wife—what about someone in your wife's life? Somebody from her past? Or someone—?"

"It's no secret that for a while, when she was in her early twenties, Hilary went from being a Las

Vegas showgirl to a star in several low-budget adult movies."

"By adult you mean pornographic movies?"

"Yeah. Hilary was a beautiful woman. She had a great body. And she loved showing it off. She loved life . . . loved sex. When we met, she gave up the movie business and her agent was none too happy. This guy wore two hats, one as an agent and another as a producer of porno flicks. He told Hilary that she'd regret leaving him to marry me, that she'd miss the business and come back to him the first time she caught me in bed with another woman."

"Did she?" Sanders asked.

When Tagg looked him in the eye, his gaze questioning, Sanders clarified. "Did she ever catch you with another woman?"

"From the day we married, there was never anyone else for either of us. It's been that way for the past seven years."

"Who was this guy, the agent-cum-producer?"

"Travis Dillard."

"Did your wife have any contact with him over the past seven years or perhaps only recently?"

"No, none, not over the years or recently."

"We will check into it, find out if there is any reason to think he might be involved." Sanders glanced at Barbara Jean. "See if Holt is free to join us and then have coffee prepared and served in approximately twenty minutes."

"Certainly." Barbara Jean wheeled out of the room and headed straight for the kitchen. Holt would be there having a late breakfast. She had spoken to him less than fifteen minutes before Tagg Chambless's arrival.

The moment Cam Hendrix had contacted Sanders to tell him about Hilary Chambless's murder, she had known Sanders would agree to take the case. He identified with any man who had lost his wife in such a brutal way. And each time he became involved in a case such as this, he relived his own wife's death at the hands of a monster.

Charles Wong placed the letter back in the envelope, tore the envelope into several pieces, and dumped the pieces into the kitchen wastebasket.

"We're off," his wife Lily called to him from the living room. "Don't forget that you're picking the girls up from school today."

"I won't forget," he told her. "I'll be there on time. Three o'clock sharp."

"Oh, and Charlie, call me after the interview, okay? Good luck, babe."

"Yeah, sure. Thanks."

When he heard the front door slam, he released a loud huff as he poured himself another cup of coffee and opened the caramel crunch breakfast bar he had laid out on the counter after he had cleared the kids' cereal bowls from the table. Right now, Lily was supporting the four of them—herself, him, and her twin daughters, Jenny and Jessy. Since he'd been laid off shortly before Christmas, more than three months ago, he had signed up for unemployment and become a househusband. He had gone on numerous job interviews; today's interview was number twelve. Unfortunately, he wasn't qualified for much. His last job had been at a local plant where he'd been a janitor. Today's interview was for a job as a bagger at the grocery store two blocks from their duplex apartment.

When he'd met Lily three years ago, he had been on the verge of giving up, of taking an overdose or jumping off the nearest bridge. They had met at an AA meeting. He had never known anyone like her. For him, it had been love at first sight. She had survived a teenage pregnancy, a boyfriend who abused her, parents who abandoned her, and a drinking problem that had almost cost her custody of her girls. But she had turned her life around and had helped him do the same.

They had been married for a year, had a decent apartment, managed to survive on one paycheck, and were doing their best to be good parents. He adored Jenny and Jessy. Who wouldn't? They were seven-year-old replicas of their mom. And they were calling him Daddy now. Their own father never had been a part of their lives.

Charlie sat down at the small kitchen table, ripped open the breakfast bar, took a bite, and then washed it down with coffee. When he had lost his job in December, he had believed that was the worst thing that could happen to him, but he'd been wrong. In early January, he had received the first letter. He had dismissed it as nothing more than a stupid prank and threw the letter away. Then the second letter, identical to the first, had arrived in February, right before Valentine's Day. Even though that one had unnerved him, he had torn it up and tossed it in the garbage. As far as he knew, he didn't have any enemies who hated him enough to want to see him dead.

Then Saturday, the third letter had arrived, another word-for-word replica of letter number two. He knew the message by heart.

*Midnight is coming. Say your prayers. Ask for forgiveness. Get your affairs in order. You're on the list. Be prepared. You don't know when it will be your turn. Will you be the next to die?*

For the past couple of days, he'd been thinking about what he should do. Lily had enough on her mind with her job as a waitress, the two girls, and their barely having enough money to make ends meet. The last thing she needed was to find out that someone was sending her husband death threats. If he went to the police, what could they do? Not a damn thing. And what could he do? He had no idea who had sent the letters. Even when he had ended up in the gutter—literally—a few years back, he hadn't encountered anyone who'd want to kill him. All he could do was watch his back, be careful, and not take any chances. And as far as he knew, Lily and the girls were safe. The letters had not mentioned his wife and kids, so he hoped that meant that only he was in danger. But from whom? And why?

Maleah would have preferred dealing directly with Nic, but that wasn't an option right now and she needed permission to take Lorie Hammonds's case and use the Powell Agency's resources to investigate. That meant contacting Sanders in order to get his approval. When she had called Griffin's Rest earlier today, she had spoken to Barbara Jean.

"He's in a meeting with a potential client. I'll have him call you as soon as possible."

That had been two and a half hours ago. If Nic had been there, she wouldn't have kept Maleah waiting. But she and Sanders were not close friends, simply coworkers at the agency. It wasn't that she disliked Sanders. Quite the contrary was true. She liked and respected Griff's right-hand man, but she found his formal manners and his military bearing if not exactly intimidating then at the very least forbidding. From the first time she had taken her turn as head of security at Griffin's Rest, a position that routinely rotated among agents, she had thought it odd and at the same time rather endearing that the solemn, austere Sanders and the sweet, gregarious Barbara Jean were a couple. It was obvious to everyone that she adored him and that he, in his own way, cared deeply for her.

It wasn't until she and Nic had become close friends that Nic told her Sanders had, years ago, lost his wife and child. If Nic had known the particulars of the tragedy, she had not seen fit to share the information with Maleah. Sanders himself was as secretive about his past, if not more so, than Griff was; but Barbara Jean was an open book. Everyone who knew her knew she had been paralyzed in a devastating car accident and after many surgeries and years of physical therapy, she had been left a paraplegic. She considered herself lucky to have survived and found joy in her life every day. The topic she chose not to discuss, but that everyone at Powell's was aware of, was the fact that her younger sister had been one of the many victims of the Beauty Queen Killer, who had also murdered the first wife of one of Griff's best friends, Judd Walker.

Maleah was deep in thought—remembering the last time she had seen the Walkers, Judd and his new wife and their two young daughters—when the phone rang. She recognized the number immediately. Griffin's Rest.

"Hello."

"I received your message," Sanders said.

"Then you know that I called to get your okay to take on a new client."

"Lorie Hammonds is a friend of your brother's wife. Is that correct?"

"Yes, Lorie and Cathy are best friends."

"And Ms. Hammonds has received two letters threatening her life?"

"Yes."

"Have you notified the local authorities?"

"I have. I personally spoke to Sheriff Mike Birkett last night."

"And you believe that the situation warrants the Powell Agency becoming involved."

"Yes. Pro bono. Ms. Hammonds is not a rich woman."

"I see."

Maleah could tell by the tone of Sanders's voice that he was actually considering denying her request. "Look, I'm on vacation, but if you'll give me an okay to take Lorie on as a client, I'll work without pay for the duration of my time off from the agency."

Silence.

*Damn it, say something.* But when he remained silent, she knew he was thinking about her proposition.

"Agreed," Sanders told her. "You took time off to stay in Dunmore for two weeks, on a paid vacation. Use that time to begin the investigation, and if when your vacation comes to an end you have found evidence that Ms. Hammonds's life is in danger, then Powell's will pick up the tab for continuing the investigation."

She breathed a quiet sigh of relief. "Thank you. I assume this means that the agency's resources are at my disposal?"

"Certainly. However, unless you can show me the necessity of additional agents becoming involved—"

"I don't think Lorie needs a personal bodyguard at this point, but if she does, I'll handle it."

"Then feel free to proceed. And if while Griffin and Nicole are away, you require anything else, simply let me know."

"Yes, thanks. I will."

"Good day, Maleah," Sanders said, ever the courteous if somewhat stern gentleman.

Lorie had changed clothes four times that morning. The routine of bathing, doing her hair, applying makeup, and dressing usually took about an hour, less if she hurried. But today it had taken her two hours. When she had put on the first outfit and checked herself in the mirror, all she had seen was how large her breasts looked in the clingy yellow cashmere sweater, a Christmas present from Cathy and Jack this past year. She certainly didn't want Mike to accuse her of using her sexuality to gain attention or, God forbid, to entice any of his deputies. The second outfit had gone too far in the opposite direction, the long-sleeved, mid-calf-hemmed dress making her look as if she were trying to downplay her attractiveness. Her third attempt had been jeans, the legs tucked into black boots, and a hooded black rhinestone sweatshirt. Too youthful. Mike would think she was trying to look like a teenager. Finally, she had chosen a pair of charcoal dress slacks, a silvery gray silk blouse, and a simple black sweater.

When she walked into the sheriff's department, all eyes turned toward her. What was wrong with these people? But she knew that, to a person, all of Mike's employees either knew firsthand or had heard through local gossip about Mike and her, about their past relationship and the fact that Mike now despised her.

Her heart raced and moisture coated the palms of her hands. She was so nervous that you'd think she was a criminal who had been caught red-handed. Instead, she was the victim or at the very least, the potential victim.

A middle-aged female deputy, her brown hair cut short and styled in choppy disarray, approached Lorie, a noncommittal expression on her face, neither smiling nor frowning.

"Good morning, Ms. Hammonds. I'm Deputy Ladner. The sheriff has assigned me to take your statement."

Lorie nodded and offered the woman a hesitant smile, which was not reciprocated. Instead the deputy said, "Come with me, please."

As instructed, Lorie followed the woman to what she assumed was the deputy's workstation. She pulled out a chair for Lorie and motioned for her to sit. Deputy Ladner sat behind her metal desk, picked up a pen and paper, and interrogated Lorie. Or at least that was how Lorie felt, as if she were being given the third degree. Five minutes later, apparently finished, the deputy handed the pen and file form to Lorie.

"If you'll sign"—she tapped her finger on the dotted line—"right here, please."

Lorie hurriedly read over the form, then signed it and laid it and the pen on the desk. She looked directly at the deputy. "Thank you."

When she rose to her feet, the deputy did the same. "You'll let us know if you receive another letter or a phone call or—"

"Yes, of course," Lorie said. *For all the good it will do me. This woman doesn't believe a word I've said. She thinks I made the whole thing up. No doubt Mike told her to do her duty, but warned her not to take me seriously.*

"Is Sheriff Birkett in his office?" Lorie asked.

"Uh . . . yes, I believe he is," Deputy Ladner replied, "but . . . er . . . I'm sure he's busy. Is there anything else I can do for you, Ms. Hammonds?"

Without replying, Lorie turned and walked away hurriedly, every step taking her closer to Mike's closed office door. Just as she reached the half-glass door and could plainly see Mike sitting behind his desk, a cup of coffee in his hand, Deputy Ladner grasped Lorie's arm.

She turned and glared at the other woman, who loosened her hold and then dropped her hand away.

"You can't see the sheriff right now," the deputy said.

Lorie glanced around the room and noted that to a person, everyone in the sheriff's department was staring at the two of them. She smiled. "Why not? It's obvious he isn't busy."

Before Deputy Ladner could do little more than clear her throat, Lorie watched while Mike put down his cup, stood up, and walked to the door.

When he opened the door, the deputy jumped back. "Sir, I told Ms. Hammonds that you were unavailable."

"It's all right, Lana. Ms. Hammonds doesn't like to follow the rules. You may go now. I'll handle this."

Lana Ladner? The name certainly didn't suit the plump, plain female deputy. The name was far too fancy for such an ordinary-looking woman.

When Lana walked away, Lorie flashed Mike with a lavish smile. Totally fake, of course.

"I take it that I'm what you intend to handle," Lorie said.

Mike grabbed her arm and dragged her into his office, then closed the door behind him. "You wanted to see me. Here I am."

"You're really pissed about this, aren't you?" When he cocked an eyebrow as if saying I-don't-know-what-you-mean, she elaborated. "You don't like my invading your territory, even with a valid complaint."

Mike snorted.

"I know you don't believe that I'm in any danger. You think I concocted those two death threats, don't you?"

"One letter," Mike corrected. "Maleah explained that you threw the first one away . . . if there was a first one."

"You egotistical son of a bitch. You actually think that I'm so determined to get back into your life that I'd fake death threats." She punched her index fingertip into his chest. "Get this straight." She repeated the punching motion again and again as she said, "I got the message loud and clear. You don't want me. You wish I had never come back to Dunmore. You think I'm poison. Fine. Now, listen up—I'm over you. Finally. I wouldn't have you if you were served to me on a silver platter with a gold apple in your mouth."

He stood there and stared at her, his blue-black eyes wide with surprise.

She lifted her finger from his chest and balled her hand into a tight fist. "Someone has sent me two letters telling me that I'm going to die. It may be somebody's idea of a sick joke or it could be that out there somewhere there's a crazy person who intends to kill me. So, do your job, Sheriff. I'm a tax-paying citizen of your county."

Lorie turned and left his office, ignored the wide-eyed department personnel, and marched straight out the front door.

# Chapter 4

He exited the small commuter airplane, hoisted his vinyl carryall over his shoulder, and went directly to the car rental kiosk. If anyone remembered seeing him, they would describe him as a gray-haired man with a mustache and goatee. They might add that he wore sunglasses and dressed in wrinkled khakis and a plaid shirt. And if the airline passenger list were ever checked, his real name wouldn't appear, only the name on his phony ID.

He was a smart man. He had covered all his bases.

Within twenty minutes, he was behind the wheel of a low-mileage Ford Taurus and halfway across town. Charles Wong, aka Charlie Hung, lived in a duplex on Rider Avenue. The adjoining apartment had been recently vacated and was For Rent. Charlie now had a wife and a couple of stepkids, and was presently unemployed. It was amazing how much you could find out about a person by simply using the Internet.

He turned off the main street that went straight through Blythe, Arizona, population ten thousand, a quiet little border town southeast of Yuma. From what he could tell, the town was overrun with Mexicans and he figured half of them were illegals.

He slowed down as he drove past Charlie's apartment, but he didn't see anybody, not even a stray dog. His first stop would be at the Blythe City Diner, where Charlie's wife was employed. He had called earlier and found out she was working the evening shift. If he was lucky, she'd be the talkative type. All he needed to know was what night he could kill Charlie, a night when neither she nor her daughters would be at home. If necessary, he could wait for just the right moment, and in the meantime, he'd simply choose the next person on his list and come back for Charlie later.

Tagg Chambless stared at the two envelopes he held in his hand, both neatly sliced open, probably with Hilary's pearl-handled letter opener. He held them up, showing them to the Powell agent who had accompanied him home to Memphis a few days ago.

"I found these this morning," Tagg said. "In one of her lingerie drawers. They were hidden beneath the scented lining. I guess when the police searched our bedroom, they somehow overlooked these."

Holt Keinan glanced from Tagg's haggard face to the nondescript white envelopes he clutched tightly in his closed fist. "What are they?" He sure

66

as hell hoped they weren't love letters some other guy had written to the man's now deceased wife.

"Death threats," Tagg replied, a catch in his deep voice.

Holt focused on the envelopes. "Mind if I take a look?"

Tagg handed the letters over to Holt, who laid one down on a nearby end table in the den and then slipped the single page from the other envelope, unfolded it, and read aloud. " 'Midnight is coming. Say your prayers. Ask for forgiveness. Get your affairs in order. You're on the list. Be prepared. You don't know when it will be your turn. Will you be the next to die?' "

"Why didn't she show me these letters?" Tagg asked. "Why did she hide them from me?"

Holt inspected the envelopes. Typewritten. No return address. One was postmarked Knoxville, Tennessee, and the postmark on the other was smudged, making it illegible. The messages were identical.

"Any idea who might have sent these to your wife?"

Tagg shook his head. "I'm certain she didn't know anybody from Knoxville."

"Where the letters were mailed may or may not be important. But the message is important. You're right—these are definitely death threats."

"You think the person who murdered Hilary is the one who sent her these letters?"

"I think it's a good possibility."

"Is there any way to find out who—?"

"Probably not," Holt said. "But I'll overnight these to our lab."

"Shouldn't I show them to the police?"

"Let me handle that. Our lab will get to the letters immediately. With the police, it could take weeks . . . or longer."

Tagg sucked in a deep breath. "Yeah, you're right. The police have gotten nowhere. I'm pretty sure they think that I'm involved with some unscrupulous business partners and one of them had my wife killed. They're wrong. I've tried to tell them that, but they won't believe me. I'm putting my trust in the Powell Agency. I expect you to uncover the truth and find out who killed Hilary."

"The only promise we can make is that we will use every resource available to us to find your wife's killer and we won't stop looking until we either find the person responsible or you tell us to stop."

"Understood."


Sanders sipped on the cup of hot tea that Barbara Jean had, only moments ago, brought to him there in Griffin's study. During the past few years, he had come to rely on her as a friend, a lover, and an assistant. She meant more to him than she would ever know. His love for her was deep and sincere. He would willingly lay down his life and die for

68

her. Barbara Jean possessed a sweet, gentle nature and a warm, friendly personality, where on the other hand, he was quiet, stern, and very much an introvert. He preferred his own company to the company of others.

After his wife's death so long ago, he had believed that he would never be able to love another woman. And there had been no one of importance in his life until Griffin brought Barbara Jean to Griffin's Rest three years ago. She had been the only witness who could possibly identify her sister's killer, and thus her life had been in danger. They had kept her under twenty-four-hour-a-day protection until the killer was finally caught. By that time, she had become a member of the household and had accepted a position with the Powell Agency. And little by little, as time had passed, he had grown to love her.

As Sanders drank the tea, he thought about Holt Keinan's recent phone call concerning the Hilary Chambless murder case. He had sent Holt to Memphis with Tagg Chambless on Monday to begin the private investigation, and this morning new evidence had shown up. Tagg had discovered two threatening letters that had been sent to his wife before her death. The question was—why had she hidden the letters instead of showing them to him?

"I'm overnighting the letters to our lab," Holt had said. "I doubt anything will show up that will help us, but it needs to be done and we can get to it a lot quicker than the police."

Sanders wished that Griffin was here. Griffin was much better at dealing with the authorities than he was. And someone would have to explain to the Memphis PD why those letters hadn't been turned over to them immediately. Maybe the explanations could wait until Griffin returned from the island retreat where he'd taken Nicole for a second honeymoon.

His years as a career soldier made it more difficult for Sanders to rebel against authority, to ignore rules and regulations. Even when he had lived under Malcolm York's domination, little more than a slave, he had been a good soldier, obeying commands, always doing what he was told. Griffin was a different type, a rebel, a risk taker, a nonconformist. Griffin made his own rules. And Sanders would follow Griffin anywhere, even through the gates of hell.

And why not? They had already been there and back together. And they had survived.

Even if his wife and child had not.

A soft rap on the outer door of Griffin's private study alerted Sanders that Barbara Jean had returned, probably bringing him a second cup of tea and a snack. She had no doubt noticed how little he had eaten at lunch. The responsibility of being in charge of the Powell Agency weighed heavily on his shoulders.

"Come in," Sanders said.

Barbara Jean eased open the door, but didn't enter the study. "Mr. Wilson just arrived. He's waiting in the living room."

"I am ready to see him."

"All right." She looked directly at Sanders. "Promise me that after your meeting with Mr. Wilson, you will come to the kitchen for an afternoon snack."

The corners of his lips lifted ever so slightly. He almost smiled. Sweet Barbara Jean. A mother hen if ever there was one. She was the type of woman who should have had half a dozen children to smother with love and attention. But she would never have a child. Nor would he.

"I promise," he replied. "Now, send in Mr. Wilson."

She nodded, then turned and wheeled down the hallway.

Within minutes, a tall, slender man wearing a dark blue suit and a burgundy and blue striped tie stood in the open doorway. As Sanders came out from behind the desk, he inspected his visitor from the top of his gray streaked dark hair to his leather shoes. He appeared to be in his late forties or early fifties and from his demeanor, Sanders would have surmised that he was a confident, successful man. Of course, the background check on Mr. Wilson had given him that information. Jared Wilson was a professor at the University of Tennessee in

Knoxville. He and Griffin were both alumni of the school and had known each other for years, so when he had contacted the Powell Agency, he had immediately been given an appointment with Sanders.

"I am sorry that Griffin is unavailable," Sanders said as he held out his hand to his visitor. "He and Nicole are on a second honeymoon. But I can assure you that I and the Powell Agency will assist you in any way possible."

"Thank you, Mr. Sanders." Jared exchanged a firm handshake with Sanders. "Griffin knows about my brother's murder. He was kind enough to send flowers and he and Nicole attended the funeral."

"Is your brother's murder the reason you're here?" Sanders indicated with a sweep of his hand for the other man to sit. When Jared took one of the two chairs flanking the fireplace, Sanders took the other one.

"Yes." Jared rubbed his hands together. "The Sevier County sheriff's department has no suspects, and although they say the case is still open, I think they've marked it off as unsolvable."

"I see."

Jared's gaze met Sanders's calm, cool stare. "I want to hire the Powell Agency to do a private investigation. I want to know who killed my brother and why."

"I am sure that Griffin is familiar with the particulars of your brother's death, but I am not. I wish I did not have to ask you to go over the details for me, but—"

"I'll do whatever I need to do. Don't be concerned about upsetting me."

"All I need today are the basic details," Sanders told him. "Just enough to give me an idea of where to start. All of the agency's resources will be utilized and I will put two of our best agents on the case immediately. You will be dealing directly with them, but you may contact me at any time with questions or complaints."

"That sounds reasonable," Jared said.

"Ben Corbett and Michelle Allen are two of our best investigators. They will start tomorrow morning."

"Do I work out the arrangement for payments with you or a secretary or—"

"When Griffin returns, the two of you can discuss that." Sanders sat ramrod straight and looked squarely at Jared. "How was your brother killed? When and where? And who discovered the body?"

Jared took a deep breath. "He was killed in January at our family's cabin in the mountains outside of Gatlinburg. He and I were planning to spend a few days together. It was to be a reunion of sorts. We hadn't been close, not since we were teenagers. We took different paths in life."

Sanders could hear the regret in the man's voice and noted the sheen of moisture in his eyes. He would like to give comfort, but he simply did not know how. It was not in his nature. "Then you are the one who discovered his body?"

Jared swallowed hard. "Yes. I found him." He paused for a few seconds. "He was naked and lying on the floor in the middle of the living room. He had been shot several times. I'm told the fatal bullet hit his heart." He swallowed again. "It was the damnedest thing."

"What was?" Sanders asked.

"Whoever killed him had not only stripped him naked, but they had put a mask on his face."

"A mask? What sort of mask?"

"An elaborate mask, the kind you'd see at Mardi Gras or some fancy masquerade ball."

"I see." Was it simply an odd coincidence that both Jared Wilson's brother and Tagg Chambless's wife had been shot several times, stripped naked, and adorned with a fancy mask? "Do you know if your brother had received any death threats? Had someone sent him any letters warning him that he was in danger?"

"Not that I know of, but Dean lived in Los Angeles and we hadn't seen each other in years. He wouldn't have confided in me, especially not over the phone. Why do you ask?"

Sanders shook his head. "I was curious if perhaps your brother had been threatened in any way before he was killed."

"I really have no idea. Is there anything else you need from me today, Mr. Sanders?"

Sanders stood. "No, thank you, Mr. Wilson. I think I have all I need for the time being. Our agents will contact you in the morning."

After he saw Powell's newest client to the door, Sanders considered the possibilities. Two similar murders did not mean they were connected. But what were the odds that the MO of two separate murderers now being investigated by Powell's would be identical?

He entered the diner, searched and found Lily Wong serving behind the counter, and quickly took a seat on one of the padded stools. While waiting for her to notice she had a new customer, he pulled the plastic-coated menu from the rack that also held a variety of condiments. She came over, set a glass of water in front of him, and asked if he had decided what he wanted.

"Today's special sounds good," he replied and casually glanced at her.

She smiled at him. Lily was a pretty young woman with a mass of rich dark hair neatly confined in a ponytail, large silvery blue eyes, and full, pink lips. He stared at her name tag. "And a cup of coffee, please, Lily."

"Yes, sir. I'll place your order and then bring your coffee."

He nodded and returned her pleasant smile, a smile he believed was genuine.

*I'm sorry that I have to kill your husband, Lily.*

*But he must die, just as the others must die. I know you won't ever understand the reason his death is necessary and I'm sorry for that, too.*

She set the filled coffee mug in front of him. "Cream or sugar?"

"Just sugar," he replied.

She pointed to the small bowl that held individual packets of sugar and artificial sweeteners. A customer at the end of the counter called her name and requested more coffee.

He watched her as she made the rounds up and down the counter, making sure every customer was well taken care of with fresh coffee, tea, cola, and water. And when she brought his plate, she laid down extra napkins beside it.

"You seem to be very adept at your job," he said.

"Thank you. I try my best."

Before he could advance their conversation, she glanced down at her apron pocket. "Excuse me. I need to take this call."

Undoubtedly she kept her phone set on vibrate instead of ring while she was at work.

She moved away from him to the end of the counter where no one was sitting, pulled her phone from her apron pocket, and said, "Hi, honey."

He pretended to be engrossed in the chicken fried steak, mashed potatoes smothered in gravy, and the green beans on his plate. While eating, he listened carefully to every word Lily Wong said.

"Oh, Charlie, that's wonderful. When do you start?" she asked. "Monday?"

Apparently Charles Wong had found a new job.

"We should celebrate this weekend, maybe Saturday night," Lily said. "We can't tomorrow night. Remember I'm doing that mother-daughter campout thing with Jenny and Jessica's Brownie troop." She lowered her voice to a soft whisper. He strained to hear what she said. "We'll be home by ten Saturday morning and I promise that I'll get a babysitter for the girls so that you and I can have our own private celebration."

As soon as she returned her phone to her pocket, she walked over to him and asked, "Is everything all right? Do you need more rolls or coffee?"

"No, thanks, I'm fine." He offered her a big, friendly smile.

If Lily and her daughters wouldn't be at home tomorrow night and Charlie would be, then tomorrow evening at midnight would be the perfect time to kill him.

The minute Maleah hung up the phone after her conversation with Sanders, she brought up Mike Birkett's number from her list of contacts. When she had agreed to take Lorie Hammonds's case, she had thought it a good idea to include both the sheriff's private number as well as the department's number.

During the four days she had been on the job, she

77

had spent most of that time digging into Lorie's past and present acquaintances. When she had lived in the LA area, Lorie had encountered a few unsavory characters and had even lived with one, a guy named Dean Wilson, who, under the stage name of Woody Wilson, had starred in a string of low-budget porno movies.

And as fate would have it, just that morning, she had received information via Powell's investigative research department that Dean Wilson was dead. He had been murdered in January and his killer was still at large. His brother had discovered Dean's body at the family mountain cabin outside Gatlinburg, a short drive from Knoxville.

She remembered that Lorie had mentioned the first threatening letter she received had been postmarked Knoxville. Before talking to Sanders, Maleah had thought perhaps it was nothing more than an odd coincidence that Lorie's old lover had been murdered only a couple of months ago.

"These two murders—Dean Wilson and Hilary Finch Chambless—cannot be a mere coincidence," Sanders had said. "Both were shot several times, both were stripped naked, both were wearing fancy masks. Add to that the fact they were both porno stars and had worked together in numerous films and you pretty much erase the possibility of coincidence."

"What about threatening letters?" Maleah had

78

asked. "Did Dean Wilson and Hilary Chambless receive letters?"

"Jared Wilson did not know anything about his brother receiving threatening letters. But Hilary Chambless received two letters, the wording identical on both and the same as the ones Lorie Hammonds received."

"We have to take these threats seriously. Lorie told me that she made one porno movie, just a bit part, but the stars of that movie were Hilary Finch—better known then as Dewey Flowers—and Dean 'Woody' Wilson."

"Notify the local authorities, as well as Ms. Hammonds," Sanders had instructed her. "And I will call Derek Lawrence. He should arrive in Dunmore tomorrow. You will work together on this case and the two of you will share all information with Holt Keinan and with Ben Corbett and Michelle Allen. Holt is in charge of the Chambless case. Ben and Michelle start work on the Wilson case tomorrow. Since it is obvious the three cases overlap, this will be a joint effort, as of now."

Maleah groaned silently. The last person on earth she wanted to work with was Derek Lawrence. The man was a cocky, egotistical know-it-all. He'd been an FBI profiler and now worked as a consultant for the Powell Agency. In the course of various cases, their paths had often crossed, but whenever possible, she avoided the man as if he was the bubonic plague.

Maleah tapped Mike Birkett's private number when it appeared on the iPhone screen and waited for him to answer. Whether the man liked it or not, he was going to have to take Lorie's death threats seriously. Unless she missed her guess, there was a serial killer out there somewhere.

Lorie took the one-serving freezer packet out of the refrigerator, opened it, and slid it onto a microwavable plate. She had prepared the lasagna two weeks ago and divided it into six servings, eaten one, and frozen the rest for future meals. Today had been a long and tiring day at Treasures. Not only did they sell antiques, their store had a home décor and gift section. With Easter just around the corner, quite a few customers were taking advantage of the pre-Easter sale that would run from today until the Saturday before Easter. With Cathy away on her honeymoon, Lorie was in charge of the shop. Unfortunately, their two part-time clerks had been unavailable today. One, a student at UAH (the University of Alabama in Huntsville), had Thursday classes and the other, a stay-at-home mom, had a sick child she couldn't leave.

While the lasagna plate rotated inside the microwave, Lorie kicked off her heels—she wore heels almost all the time in order to add a few inches to her petite five-one height—and reached into an upper cupboard for a glass. Just as she picked up the wine bottle from the counter, she heard the doorbell ring. Checking the microwave clock, she noted it was six thirty-nine.

She padded through the house and to the front door in her bare feet. She hated panty hose and seldom if ever wore any. She looked through one of three small panes of glass in her front door and saw Mike Birkett and Maleah Perdue standing on her porch. With jittery fingers, she unlocked the door, opened it, and unlatched the storm door.

"What's wrong?" Lorie asked. "Why are y'all here?"

"May we come in?" Maleah asked.

Lorie nodded and stepped back to give them room to enter. Once they were inside, she closed and locked the door.

"Come on in." Lorie indicated the living room to the left of the small foyer.

With all three of them standing, Lorie glanced from Maleah to Mike, who lowered his gaze and refused to look directly at her.

"The news isn't good," Maleah told her.

Lorie's heartbeat went wild. "The letters . . . the death threats . . . they aren't a hoax, are they?"

"I'm afraid not," Maleah replied. "It seems that, more than likely, whoever sent you those letters has already killed two other people."

# Chapter 5

"I want to assure you that the sheriff's department will cooperate fully with the Powell Agency and do everything we possibly can to keep you safe," Mike Birkett said, his voice calm and even, showing absolutely no emotion.

"We have every reason to believe that you're in danger," Maleah said. "It's imperative, now more than ever, for you to be extremely careful. I'm suggesting that you stay with me at Jack and Cathy's, at least until they return from their honeymoon."

"You think I need a bodyguard?"

"I believe it's better to be safe than sorry."

"What led you to the conclusion that the person who is threatening me has already killed twice?"

"It seems that the brother of one victim and the husband of another have hired the Powell Agency to investigate their loved ones' deaths. When Sanders—who is Griffin Powell's assistant—discovered the similarity in the two murders, it was not a giant leap to connect them. And only today, the husband discovered two letters that his wife had kept hidden. The wording in those letters is identical to the wording in your letter," Maleah explained. "And it really wasn't a surprise to find out that the victims knew each other and they had worked together years ago."

Lorie's mind whirled with thoughts of how she

might be connected to the other victims. Focusing her attention on Maleah, she ignored Mike completely. He was here only because he had to be, because he was the sheriff. She didn't kid herself, didn't for one minute think he gave a damn if she lived or died.

"Who were these people?" Lorie asked.

"The woman was Tagg Chambless's wife," Maleah said. "Hilary Chambless. She was the second victim."

The name didn't sound familiar to Lorie. "I don't know a Hilary Chambless."

Maleah nodded. "The first victim, at least as far as we know, was a guy named Dean Wilson."

Lorie gasped. Her stomach flip-flopped. "Dean Wilson? In his late forties? Lived in LA? Was originally from Tennessee? That Dean Wilson?"

"Yeah, that seems to fit the info his brother gave Sanders. You knew him, didn't you?"

"Yes." Her gaze zipped toward Mike. "I knew Dean Wilson. We were . . . uh . . . friends when I lived in LA. How . . . ? Why . . . ?"

"He was shot several times," Maleah said.

"Poor Dean." Years ago, she had loved him.

Mike looked at her, studied her face, and for a split second, she saw genuine concern in his eyes. But he glanced away hurriedly, as if he couldn't bear to look at her. Why did he have to act this way? Even if they could never be friends again, did he have to go on hating her forever?

"But you say you didn't know Hilary Chambless. Is that right?" Maleah asked.

"No, I didn't—Oh my God! Was her maiden name Finch?"

"That's right. And she had a stage name, too. Dewey Flowers."

Lorie wished that Mike wasn't here, that he was not involved in this, that she didn't have to talk about her sordid past in front of him. But what did it matter really? It wasn't as if her past was a secret. He knew what she had done, who she had been, how she had lived those last few years in California.

"I knew Dean and Hilary," Lorie admitted. "Hilary was just an acquaintance. Dean and I were . . ." She cleared her throat. "We lived together for a while."

"Then you know they made several porno movies together," Maleah said.

"Yes, of course I know. I told you that I had a bit part in one of those movies." Lorie glared at Mike, who lifted his gaze from the floor and glared at her.

"When was the last time you saw either of them?" Mike asked.

"Not since I left LA and came home to Dunmore."

"Heard from either of them since then?"

"No."

"You've had no communication of any kind with either of them?" Maleah asked.

"None."

"Do you know of anyone from the time y'all worked together who might have wanted to kill them?"

"No. I have absolutely no idea why anyone would want to kill either of them or kill me. And my only connection to either of them is in the past, nearly ten years ago."

"I figured you'd have no idea who the killer might be," Maleah said. "It could be something as crazy as an unbalanced fan who for some reason has decided to kill the actors from his favorite films."

"Great. I had a bit a part in one adult movie ten years ago and now I'm targeted by some nut job who happened to like that stupid movie."

"Karma's a bitch," Mike said, his voice a low grumble.

Lorie and Maleah snapped around and stared at him.

"That was a damn cruel thing to say," Maleah told him.

A red tinge crept up Mike's neck and quickly darkened his face. "You're right." He looked at Lorie. "I shouldn't have said what I did."

"No, you shouldn't have," she said.

He snorted and then looked at Maleah. "I'll have a patrol car drive by Jack and Cathy's every hour once Lorie's staying with you and by Treasures when Lorie's at work. If I had the manpower, I'd assign someone to her, but she's got you so she really won't need police protection on a twenty-four/seven basis."

"Thanks." Maleah grabbed Mike's arm. "Let me walk you out, Sheriff." She shot Lorie a quick glance. "I'll be right back. Why don't you go pack a bag?"

Lorie hated the thought of being forced to leave her home. But what if the person who had killed Dean and Hilary really did intend to kill her? Her best chance of survival could well be having Maleah Perdue as her bodyguard.

Maleah gave Mike a well-deserved tongue-lashing, reminding him that his actions toward Lorie Hammonds were completely unprofessional and most decidedly uncalled for.

"I don't believe you're naturally a cruel or vindictive man," she said. "But you've treated Lorie as if she doesn't deserve even common courtesy. If I didn't know better, I'd think you enjoyed hurting her and that you don't give a rat's ass if somebody does kill her."

"That's not true. At least the part about my not caring if somebody kills her. I don't wish Lorie dead."

"Are you saying that you enjoy hurting her?"

"Yes. No." He shook his head. "Damn, I don't know."

"What's the matter with you? That woman in

86

there"—she pointed to the front door—"is in danger. Some unknown person out there somewhere has targeted her as one of his victims. And what do you do? You act like a vindictive ex-lover. You know what that tells me?" When he didn't respond, she elaborated. "It tells me that you still have some very strong feelings for Lorie, that whether you want to or not, you still care about her."

"That's a damn lie! I hate her." Crap! He hadn't meant to blurt it out like that. But Maleah had pushed the wrong buttons. Or maybe she had pushed all the right buttons to force him to admit his true feelings.

"I don't have to deal directly with you from here on out," Maleah told him. "When Jack gets back from his honeymoon, assign him to this case. Or go ahead and put one of your other detectives in charge. It'll be better for everyone involved that way."

"Good idea. You and Jack should work well together. But as the sheriff, I need to stay involved if one of our citizens is being threatened by a serial killer."

"Fine by me as long as you can keep your personal feelings under control. I'll report to you until Jack comes home."

"Okay." Mike stepped off the porch, but paused and glanced back at her. "By the way, how often does a serial killer forewarn his victims?"

"I have no idea," she admitted. "But the Powell Agency is sending in a profiler first thing tomorrow, and I'm sure he'll have all the answers."

"Derek Lawrence?"

"That would be *the* man."

"Good. I got to know Derek last year when he helped us out on the Fire and Brimstone case. He and Jack got pretty buddy-buddy."

"Yes, I believe they did." She barely got the words out through her partially clenched teeth. "God knows why my brother took a liking to such an egotistical SOB."

"Watch out, Ms. Perdue, now your unprofessional attitude is showing."

Grinning, Mike walked off and didn't look back. He got in his car and drove away, doing his best not to examine too closely his feelings for Lorie Hammonds.

Derek Lawrence had worked with Holt Keinan a couple of times in the past few years. He liked and respected the Powell agent who was a former sharpshooter for the Birmingham SWAT unit. Although they had little in common, their backgrounds as different as night and day, they had hit it off the first time they met.

When he saw Holt halfway across the bar at Logan's Roadhouse, he held up his hand to acknowledge he'd seen Holt motioning to him. At seven-thirty on a Thursday evening, the bar wasn't terribly crowded. He figured most of the customers were waiting to be seated in the restaurant.

He shook hands with Holt, then took the bar stool beside him.

"What'll you have?"

Derek eyed the other man's bottle of Guinness. "Same as you."

Holt placed the order with the bartender, then turned back to Derek. "Our table should be ready in about ten minutes or less."

"Sounds good." The bartender handed Derek his drink. He turned up the bottle and swigged down several large gulps before setting the bottle on the bar. "I interviewed Jared Wilson, the other victim's brother, this afternoon and the Sevier County sheriff's office sent me copies of Dean Wilson's case file. I thought we could go over whatever you've got on the Hilary Chambless case after dinner tonight and then compare the two cases. In the morning, I'll head out for Dunmore, Alabama, where Perdue is working on a case that involves a potential victim."

Holt grinned. "Perdue? You two still locking horns?"

Derek chuckled. "No doubt she's told everyone that I actually do have horns and a tail and carry a pitchfork as well as breathe fire and eat live rattlesnakes."

Holt almost choked on his beer. Instead he

spewed it into his hand, then wiped his hand off on a cocktail napkin. "Damn it, man, warn a guy next time, will you? Whatever you did to her, it must have really pissed her off. As long as I've known Maleah, I've never seen her react to anybody the way she does you."

"Maybe I remind her of somebody," Derek said. "To my knowledge, I've never done anything to the lady. Perdue stays as far away from me as she possibly can."

"Hmm . . . Who knows? She's a woman and there's no use trying to figure out how a woman's mind works. But you know, you might ease the tension between you two a little if you'd start calling her Maleah instead of Perdue."

"Nope. She's Perdue to me. And I'm that cocky, know-it-all SOB as far as she's concerned."

"Whoa there. Did she actually call you that—to your face?"

Derek took another swig from his bottle. "Not to my face. I happened to overhear her a few months back when she was talking to Nic Powell about me."

The buzzer Holt had laid on the bar went off, red lights blinking and the black disk vibrating. "That's us. Our table's ready."

An hour later, with steaks, baked potatoes, and half a dozen yeast rolls consumed, Derek and Griff compared notes over after-dinner coffee. The loud shit-kicking music and the din of customers provided audio camouflage for their conversation, but they were both careful about mentioning any names in such a public place.

"The murders are too similar to be a mere coincidence," Derek said. "If we knew for sure the mountain cabin victim had received threatening letters, it would erase any doubts I might have. But the truth of the matter is the bodies being nude and their having been shot several times wouldn't link them, but the fancy masks being placed on their faces tells a different story."

"The nudity and the masks are part of the killer's MO, right?"

Derek grinned. "Went through the training course at Quantico, huh?"

"Yep. When I was with the Birmingham PD."

"Then you know two murders don't make a serial killer," Derek said. "But the fact that the UNSUB has threatened a third person—one connected to the other two victims by past association, if nothing else—indicates this guy has the potential and if he isn't stopped, he'll go on killing."

"Seems he definitely has a hard-on for former porno stars. No pun intended." Holt grinned.

"Yeah, seems so. But my gut tells me that there's more to it than that."

"Like what?"

"Not sure yet."

"This Hammonds woman in Dunmore—seems she's Maleah's new sister-in-law's best friend, so the case is going to get personal, at least for Maleah."

Derek nodded. "If I were Sanders, I'd take Maleah off the case and assign an impartial agent. But I'm an easygoing kind of guy and not prone to rocking the boat by questioning the captain's orders."

"I know Sanders," Holt said. "If Maleah can't do her job, he'll replace her."

"Any chance you could persuade him to do that before I arrive in Dunmore tomorrow? It would save me a hell of a lot of trouble if I didn't have to deal with her."

Holt chuckled. "Something tells me that if there's a man alive who can handle Maleah Perdue, it just might be you."

Mike kissed Hannah's forehead, said good night, and closed her bedroom door. He moved to the next room, peeked in, and grinned when he saw that M.J. was already asleep, his long-legged little body sprawled across the rumpled covers. He tiptoed across the floor, lifted M.J. just enough to grab the covers with one hand, and pulled them up and over his son.

As he headed toward his small home office, an eight-by-eight space that had once been a walk-in pantry, he thought about what a lucky man he was to have two great kids, a loving and helpful mother, and a job he truly liked. If Molly were still alive, his life would be damn near perfect.

Even after four years, he still missed her as if she'd left them only a few months ago. His sweet Molly. She had been everything a man could ask for in a wife. They'd had a good life. They'd been happy.

He knew that when Lorie Hammonds had come back to town, Molly had worried about how he would react, but she had never brought up the subject. At least not to him. He might never have known about her insecurities where Lorie was concerned if his mother hadn't come to him.

"You need to make it perfectly clear to your wife that Lorie Hammonds is your past and that she and the kids are your present and future," his mother had told him.

He'd been dumbfounded that Molly had felt Lorie could pose a threat to their marriage.

"I'll tell her that she has nothing to worry about," Mike had assured his mother. "The only feelings I have for Lorie now are loathing and disgust."

"I'd keep that to myself. Those are powerfully strong feelings. It's best if Molly doesn't see how much Lorie still affects you."

"She doesn't—"

"You forget who you're talking to, boy. I was around when Lorie left you high and dry. You loved that girl with everything in you. Those kinds of feelings don't die. You just bury them deep and hope and pray you can keep them buried."

He had denied that beneath his seething animosity for Lorie the love he had once felt for her still existed. And he'd kept on denying it all these years.

*I don't love her. She means nothing to me. Less than nothing.*

*Then stop thinking about her, you dope.*

He walked into the office, flipped on a light, and pulled out his swivel chair. After plopping down in the Office Depot special—on sale for $99.99—he glanced at the shelves above his computer desk. A row of photos spread across one shelf, school pictures of Hannah and M.J., various photos of him and his kids. And one photo of his family, taken two years before Molly died.

*I loved you, Molly. You were the best thing that ever happened to me.*

His gaze traveled over the books and magazines stored on the shelves and settled on his old yearbooks. He hadn't looked through them in years. In fact, right after Lorie dumped him, he had tossed all four yearbooks in the trash. His mother had retrieved them and kept them for him.

Half standing, he reached up and yanked his senior yearbook off the shelf. As he settled back into his chair, he opened the book and flipped through it. Dust particles flicked off the pages and danced in the air, their images appearing in the iridescent light from the overhead fixture. He smelled a hint of mustiness.

And then he stopped flipping through the pages

and opened the book at the sophomore photographs. A sixteen-year-old Lorie Hammonds smiled up at him, her dark eyes sultry even then. His body tightened with desire. It had been that way since the first time he'd noticed her. That much between them hadn't changed. As desperately as he wanted to deny it, he had to admit that he still wanted Lorie.

They had been in lust long before they fell in love. From the get-go, sex between them had been explosive. She'd been a virgin. He hadn't. Being a good-looking jock, he'd had his pick of easy lays from the time he was fifteen. But Lorie had been different. She had been his, only his, the girl he wanted to marry and make the mother of his children.

Mike slammed the yearbook closed and tossed it on the floor.

"Damn you, Lorie! Damn you to hell."

# Chapter 6

Derek parked his Vette in the driveway, got out, locked it, and stretched his long arms over his head. He had driven in from Memphis this morning, a good three-and-a-half-hour drive, and hadn't made any stops as he'd crossed the entire state of Mississippi. The farther east he had traveled, the hillier the landscape, going from flatland through the Magnolia State to the tentacles of the

Appalachian Mountains that spread into the northern and eastern sections of Alabama. After retrieving his suitcase from the trunk, he glanced around, taking in the beauty of the renovated Victorian house and the peaceful street lined with large, mature trees beginning to come to life in the early days of spring. Dunmore was an old town, seeped in Southern traditions that grounded it in the past. And yet when he had spent quite a bit of time here last year, he had seen glimpses of change, of people looking to the future.

When the Powell Agency had sent him there last summer, he had gotten to know Perdue's older brother, Jack, a local deputy, rather well. He had liked Jack as instantly as he had disliked Jack's sister. Odd thing about the vibes you picked up from people. He figured Jack for a combination of hardened soldier and good old boy, a man's man as well as a ladies' man. But Jack's days of carousing were over. Less than a week ago, Derek had attended Jack and Cathy's wedding. The following morning, he'd left his motel room and driven straight to the Nashville area, to his mother's birthday celebration.

Now here he was back in Dunmore and doomed to work with Perdue on a new and rather intriguing case. He figured the best way to handle their precarious partnership was not to take the woman seriously. She was big-time uptight, at least around him. He had told her more than once that what she needed was to lighten up, and a good start would be to go out and get herself laid. She hadn't taken his suggestion in the spirit in which it had been given, which was only with the best intentions, of course.

Chuckling to himself, Derek headed up the walk that led to the front porch. Bet Perdue couldn't wait to see him.

When he rang the doorbell, he didn't expect to see a tall, lanky teenage boy open the door and invite him in.

"Aunt Maleah's on the phone," Seth Cantrell told him. "She's talking to somebody at the Powell Agency, getting some information about the case y'all are working on. She'll be with you in a minute."

Seth was Jack and Cathy's son, although Jack and Seth had met for the first time last year. Jack, a former Army Ranger, had been MIA during the Gulf War back in the early nineties. A pregnant Cathy had married another man who had raised Seth as his own. When Jack had come home to Dunmore last year, he had not only discovered that his long-lost love was a widow, but that he was her sixteen-year-old son's biological father.

As Seth led Derek out of the foyer and down the hall, he asked, "Have you had breakfast?"

"Nope, sure haven't," Derek replied.

"We've got leftovers," Seth told him. "A stack of pancakes, some sausage links, and I just put on a fresh pot of coffee."

"Sounds good. I'll take it all, starting with the coffee."

By the time Maleah joined them, a good ten minutes later, Derek had finished off the pancakes and sausage and was downing his second cup of coffee. Seth had explained that even though he was staying with his grandparents while his parents were off on their honeymoon, he had stopped by for breakfast with his aunt since he had only a half day at school today.

"I see you've made yourself at home." Perdue glanced from his empty plate to his suitcase resting against the table leg at his side. "You aren't planning on staying here, are you?"

"As a matter of fact—"

"There are two perfectly good motels here in Dunmore. Take your pick."

"Now, Perdue, don't be that way. You've got more than enough room here in this big old house to put me up."

"He's got you there," Seth said.

Perdue gave her nephew an eat-dirt-and-die glare.

Derek laughed. "Think of it as an adventure. The two of us working side by side, living under the same roof, getting to know each other."

She huffed loudly, not even trying to hide her aggravation.

He hated to even think it, hated to resort to an old cliché, but damn if Perdue wasn't downright pretty when she was pissed. *You're beautiful when you're angry.* He could think it, but God help him if he said it.

For all her faults and shortcomings, being unattractive wasn't one of them. Maleah Perdue was what had once been referred to as an all-American beauty. Five-four, a trim hourglass figure, blue eyes and golden blond hair. She looked like the kind of girl men used to dream about taking home to meet their mamas.

Seth broke the uneasy silence in the room when he cleared his throat and then said, "I hate to eat and run, but I'm supposed to meet some of the guys at ten."

"Are we still on for lunch and a movie Sunday?" Perdue asked.

"Sure are." He glanced at Derek. "Good to see you again, Mr. Lawrence."

"Same here, kid."

The minute Seth exited the back door, Perdue sat down at the kitchen table, taking the chair directly across from Derek.

"You're not staying here," she told him.

"I'll bet if Jack were here—"

"He's not."

"What are you afraid of, Perdue? Afraid you'll succumb to my many charms?"

She groaned, and then burst into laughter.

He didn't know whether to be insulted or just laugh along with her. He chose the latter.

Chuckling, he looked her right in the eye. "I'm glad to see you have a sense of humor."

Her laughter died away, but the smile remained.

"We're both grown-ups, both professionals," he said. "We're going to be working together for as long as it takes to find our killer and put him behind bars. That could be weeks or even months. You're going to have to find a way to put aside your personal feelings for me and—"

"I have no personal feelings for you. None."

"Prove it."

She huffed again as she narrowed her gaze and glowered at him. "Dare I ask how?"

"Let me stay here." When she didn't respond, he added, "Separate bedrooms, of course."

Her big blue eyes widened for a split second and then she grinned. "Were you always like this, even as a kid? God, if you were, I don't know how your mother put up with you."

"I was. And she didn't. I'll have you know that I'm a trust-fund baby. I was reared by a series of highly trained nannies and first-class private schools."

"Of course you were. Pardon my ignorance."

"And you grew up in this house, didn't you, you and Jack?"

Her smile vanished and a storm-cloud frown darkened her expression. Instead of replying to his question, she shoved back her chair and stood. "Come on. I'll show you to one of the guest bed-

100

rooms. You can unpack and then we can discuss the new information that just came in at the agency."

"What sort of information?"

"Several things, but the most interesting is the title of the only movie that my client, Lorie Hammonds, ever made. The stars of that film were Dean Wilson and Hilary Chambless, aka Woody Wilson and Dewey Flowers."

"Some stage names, huh? So, what was the title of the movie the three of them made together?"

"*Midnight Masquerade*," Perdue said.

"Well, I'll be damned."

Lorie and Cathy usually closed up shop at six on Friday and Saturday nights, but with Easter fast approaching, Lorie had extended the closing until seven for both nights. Three lingering, undecided customers, who wound up buying nothing, had pushed closing time to seven fifteen. Just as she waved good-bye to the last to leave—Paul Babcock, one of their regulars—and was in the process of closing and locking the front door, she saw Mike Birkett park his truck directly in front of Treasures.

What the hell was he doing here?

She stood in the open doorway and waited for him to emerge from his Ford F-150 pickup. He got out and walked toward her. Her heart skipped a beat. Why did he have to be so damn good-looking? And why, dear God, why did she still want him more than she'd ever wanted any other man?

"Closing up?" he asked as he approached.

She nodded. "Uh-huh."

"Got a few minutes?"

"Sure. Come on in."

After he entered Treasures, she locked the door and placed the CLOSED sign in the window. When she turned around, she almost bumped into him. He stood so close to her that only a few inches separated her body from his. She sucked in a startled breath and eased backward, intentionally putting some space between them.

"I won't keep you long," he said.

"That's all right. I'm in no hurry."

"I just thought that maybe you . . . Well, it is Friday night, and—"

"I don't have a date."

"Good." His cheeks blotched with embarrassment. He coughed and then cleared his throat. "I didn't mean it's good that you don't have a date. I meant it's good that I'm not keeping you from anything important."

"I knew what you meant."

He nodded. "You didn't move in with Maleah last night." He worded it as a statement of fact, not a question.

"No, she actually spent the night at my house and left early this morning. She was expecting Seth over for breakfast. And Derek Lawrence was supposed to arrive sometime this morning to assist her with my case."

"Is she staying with you again tonight?"

"No, I'm going home this evening, packing a few things, and moving in with Maleah until further notice." Lorie wished Mike would stop looking right at her. His intense scrutiny unnerved her. "What is it? Do I have dirt on my face? A black hair growing out of my chin?"

"Huh?"

"You're staring at me as if I've suddenly grown an extra head or something."

"Sorry. I . . . uh . . . Why don't I follow you home and then escort you over to Maleah's after you pack a bag."

Had she heard him correctly? Was Sheriff Birkett, the man who thought she was only one step above pond scum, actually worried about her?

"Why?" she asked.

"Why what?"

"Why the pretense of being concerned about my welfare?"

"I'm the sheriff. You're a citizen of my county whose life has been threatened. I'm just doing my civic duty."

"Bull. You could have sent a deputy to check on me."

"You've been monitored all day today," he told her. "Between my men and Chief Ballard's police force, somebody's been by here every hour since you arrived at Treasures this morning."

"So to what do I owe the honor of your visit this evening? Why put yourself out for little old me?"

"Damn it, Lorie, that smart mouth of yours—" Grimacing, he clenched his teeth together and snorted. "I came by here to apologize."

"What?"

Their gazes met and locked. For a split second, she thought she saw something achingly familiar in the way he looked at her. But the expression vanished so quickly that she realized she had probably imagined it.

"I let my personal feelings get in the way of doing my job," he admitted. "I had no right to assume you were lying about being threatened and to dismiss your concerns as if they were nothing. I'm sorry."

To say she was stunned was a gross understatement. She never thought she would live to see the day that Mike would ever again apologize to her for anything.

"I'm sorry, too," she told him. "I'm sorry that I gave you reasons to believe I'd do anything to get back into your good graces. I should have accepted the fact, years ago, that you didn't want to have anything to do with me . . . and with good reason."

He shuffled uncomfortably. "Yeah, sure. Apology accepted. So, what about you?"

She forced a fragile smile. "Apology accepted."

"Good. Why don't I help you close up shop and then I'll follow you home."

"There's nothing to do except turn out the lights, get my purse, and lock the back door on my way out."

"I'll walk you to your car," he said. "You're parked in back, right?"

"Right."

She glanced at him briefly. He smiled. Her nerves tingled with awareness. This was the first time since her return to Dunmore that Mike had smiled at her.

*Don't make too much of it. He's just doing his best to be civil, to do his job, to prove to you and Maleah—and probably to Jack and Cathy—that he won't allow his personal feelings to interfere with doing his duty.*

Mike loaded Lorie's suitcase into her Edge SUV and closed the hatch. "All set?"

"Yes, but it's really not necessary for you to escort me to Maleah's. I'm sure you'd rather be home having dinner with your children."

"Hannah and M.J. are visiting Molly's parents over in Muscle Shoals this weekend. Carl and Gail picked them up right after school today. They stay with them on average one weekend a month and they go over for a couple of weeks every summer."

"I know your wife's parents appreciate your being so generous with the kids."

"It's what Molly would have wanted."

Lorie smiled and nodded before moving away from him and grasping the driver's side door handle. "I'm ready to go."

"I'll be right behind you."

As soon as she pulled out of her driveway, he started the truck's engine and fell in behind her. He really wasn't sure why he was doing this.

Paying penance, maybe.

His feelings for Lorie hadn't changed. He still hated her, still wished she would leave Dunmore and never come back, still wanted to drag her off to the nearest bed and fuck her like crazy.

But he owed her the common courtesy of showing her that the sheriff's department intended to do everything possible to keep her safe. He might despise Lorie, but he couldn't bear the thought of someone killing her. She might deserve some of the bad things that had happened to her, but she didn't deserve to die.

*You're an idiot, Birkett. A damn idiot.*

Lorie didn't deserve any of the bad things that had happened to her. Just because she'd left him high and dry, had broken his heart and nearly destroyed him didn't mean she should be punished forever for wanting a life he couldn't be a part of. She had begged him to go to LA with her.

"Oh, Mike, it'll be so much fun," she had said. "We can both get jobs. You can go to school at night until you get your degree and I can sign with

106

an agent and get small parts in TV at first. And later on, when you're a big-time LA detective and I'm a movie star, we'll be the envy of every other couple in Hollywood. Just think how romantic that is—the detective and the actress."

Those had been her dreams, not his. She had wanted a glamorous life surrounded by the rich and famous. All he'd ever wanted was to finish college, work for local law enforcement, get married, and raise a family. He was a simple man with simple wants and needs. Lorie had been—and probably still was—a complicated woman with the kind of wants and needs he could never fulfill.

It had been his choice to stay in Dunmore and not follow her to LA. At first, she had called him every day, then every week and then every month. He would never forget the last time she'd called and the things they had said to each other.

"Honey, forget all that fame and fortune bullshit and come home where you belong."

"Oh, Mike, why can't you understand? I just got a speaking part on a *Law and Order* episode. I want you to be happy for me. I want you to fly out here and—"

"I can't."

"You mean you won't."

"Yeah, okay. I won't. I don't belong out there and neither do you."

"That's where you're wrong. I'm not going to live and die in Dunmore, Alabama, and waste the talent the Good Lord gave me. I've got a good singing voice and I'm taking acting lessons and my teacher says I'm a natural. And I'm told I have the kind of looks that will help me go far in the business."

"You do what you have to do," he'd said. "And I'll do what I have to do."

"What you have to do doesn't include me anymore, does it? You've stopped loving me . . . if you ever really did."

"How can you say that? I love you so damn much it hurts," he had told her. "And I miss you something awful. It's you who doesn't love me. If you did, you'd come home and we'd get married the way we planned. In a few years, we could save up enough for a house and our first baby."

"I don't want a baby! Not now. Not for years and years."

In the end, Mike had been forced to accept the fact that Lorie would never come back to him, that he had lost her forever.

It had taken him years to get over her, to move on with his life, and he could thank Molly for that. She had been his salvation. All the dreams he'd once had that included Lorie, all the plans the two of them had made together, he had fulfilled with another woman, with Molly. Thinking about his children, he knew that was the way things were meant to be.

He wasn't the kind of man who wasted his time

looking back and wondering what if? or wished for things that he couldn't have.

Yeah, sure, he could have Lorie, could have had her when she first came back to Dunmore, could have had her before and after Molly died. He could probably still have her. But the Lorie he had known and loved no longer existed. His Lorie was as dead to him as Molly was. The Lorie who had come to him a sixteen-year-old virgin, the girl who had been his and only his. The teenager who had planned her future around him and the family they would one day have.

The Lorie Hammonds who had returned to Dunmore nine years ago was a bruised and battered, used and discarded whore. God only knew how many men she'd had sex with, not just in that sleazy porno movie she'd made, but during the years she had been trying to get her big break. Just about every man in Dunmore had seen her in that film. He had seen the movie once, and the sight of her and what she'd been doing had made him sick.

Why she had ever thought when she returned to Dunmore, her reputation in tatters and her life worthless, that he would forgive her, that they could be friends again, he'd never know.

Mike had been so lost in his thoughts that he almost missed Jack and Cathy's driveway and had to slam on his brakes and back up a few yards. Lorie parked her SUV, got out, and opened the back hatch. He pulled his truck up behind her vehicle, killed the motor, and got out.

He rushed over to her, grabbed her suitcase, and said, "Here, let me get that for you."

She released the suitcase without protest and started walking toward the porch. He kept in step alongside her. When they reached the front door, she rang the doorbell and they waited together.

"I appreciate the escort, Sheriff," she said in a soft, sexy voice that caressed every nerve in his body.

"You're welcome, Ms. Hammonds. Just doing my job."

When the door opened, Derek Lawrence stood in the doorway. "Hello, Lorie." He reached out, grasped her hand, and pulled her over the threshold. He glanced around her and spotted Mike. "Hello, Sheriff. Nice of you to see Lorie here all safe and sound." He held out his hand. "Here, let me take her suitcase."

Reluctantly, Mike handed over the suitcase. "Where's Maleah?"

"On the phone at the moment," he said. "Seems the newlyweds called to check on Seth and on the old homestead."

"She isn't going to tell them about me, is she? I don't want them worrying while they're on their honeymoon," Lorie said.

Derek put his arm around Lorie's shoulders and ushered her inside the foyer. "I'm sure she won't

110

say a word. And there's no reason for anyone to worry about your safety. You have two Powell Agency employees acting as your bodyguards. And may I say what a pleasure this job is for me."

Mike cleared his throat. Derek glanced over his shoulder. "Oh, are you staying for dinner? Perdue didn't say. I set the table for three, but I can add another—"

"No thanks." Mike had the sudden urge to punch Derek Lawrence. "I've got other plans." When Lorie looked at him, he said, "If you need me, I'm just a phone call away."

"I'm sure she won't need you," Derek told him.

With that said, Mike nodded, turned and tromped off the porch. Cursing under his breath, he got in his truck, backed out of the driveway, and couldn't get away fast enough from the image of Derek Lawrence's arm draped around Lorie's shoulders.

# Chapter 7

After locking the door and securing it so that no one with a key could enter, he took the laptop from his suitcase and carried it with him to the desk in his motel room. He retrieved the DVD from the pouch on the laptop case, flipped open the plastic case, and carefully removed the disk. With steady fingers, he inserted the disk into the side slot on the computer and waited for the movie to load. He reached over to the far side of the desk, upended a glass, and quickly added ice from the ice bucket that he had filled earlier. As the film credits played, he poured a cola into the glass. He didn't need to read the credits. He knew them by heart.

*Midnight Masquerade.* Written by Casey Lloyd and Laura Lou Roberts. Directed by Grant Leroy. Produced by Travis Dillard.

He kicked back in the chair and turned sideways to prop his feet up on the edge of the bed.

Dewey Flowers and Woody Wilson were the stars, the main players in this piece of filth.

Dewey and Woody would never make another sinful movie such as this. They had been punished for their wickedness, for polluting the minds and hearts of everyone who saw this movie; punished for their parts in destroying the lives of the innocent who were adversely affected by the pornography industry, this sickeningly vulgar movie in particular. There was an ironic form of justice in the fact that he was the one who was righting the wrongs they had committed. He supposed that he had known for years that it was his fate to someday seek retribution.

And not only for himself alone.

His gaze settled on the screen. Watching the depraved acts that had been captured on film no longer nauseated him the way it once had. Over the years, he had become immune to the disgusting obscenity, the bestial perversions.

Well-endowed men and big-breasted women

frolicked about at a costume ball, but their only costumes were beautiful masks covering their faces. They kissed and licked and sucked one another, their bodies entwining in an orgy of carnal acts. Two men, one wearing a devil mask and the other an intricate court jester/joker mask, laid a voluptuous black woman on the floor and while one penetrated her, the other one toyed with her silicone-enhanced tits.

The two men were Charlie Hung, a strikingly handsome man of Asian descent, and a big, rugged blond—Sonny Shag. The dark-skinned beauty, whose red sequined mask had fallen off and lay on the floor beside her, was Ebony O.

In the background the two stars danced, their bodies rubbing seductively against each other. Woody placed his hands on Dewey's waist and lifted her high into the air, then let her slide down the front of his body until she was on her knees, his erect penis directly in front of her face.

In the background three young women—a blonde, a brunette, and a redhead—held hands and danced in a circle, the long, colorful ribbons on their masks floating around their shoulders and caressing their naked breasts.

Puff Raven, the tall, elegant brunette.

Cherry Sweets, the exotically beautiful redhead.

And Candy Ruff, the sex-kitten blonde.

Their stage names were ridiculous, of course, but the suggestive pseudonyms were simply part of the fantasy. Other movies produced by the one and only Travis Dillard had starred some of these same actors, and in each film the credits had read like a who's who of stupid suggestive names.

He had lost count of how many times he had watched *Midnight Masquerade*. Hundreds of times. Maybe thousands of times.

He knew the dialogue—what little there was—by heart. And he could mimic every grunt, groan, moan, and scream of delight.

He saw the women's faces—and God help him, their naked bodies, too—in his dreams. One particular face in particular. The woman he loved. The woman he hated. The woman who had ruined his life. The woman who had made him the man he was today.

As much as Lorie appreciated being guarded by Maleah and Derek, she resented the fact that some lunatic's actions had run her out of her own home. Whoever this guy was, she hoped the police caught him before he killed again.

For the life of her, she couldn't think of anyone she'd ever known who might want to kill her.

She placed her suitcase at the foot of the ebonized Federal-style double bed that dominated this guest room on the second floor of Jack and Cathy's home. Crisp, black-edged, white Schweitzer linens lent a modern elegance to a room filled with antiques. The Bijou linens were handmade in Italy from pure Egyptian cotton. Lorie and Cathy used this type of luxury linens when decorating the homes of clients who didn't mind paying a little more for the very best. On occasion, she had personally splurged on less expensive items, things like Chanel perfume and a thirty-fifth birthday present for herself—a little white Brahman shoulder bag she had eyed at Belk department store for weeks. These were the only types of luxuries she could afford on her income. And oddly enough, the girl who had once thought fame and fortune would make her happy was perfectly content being an antique shop owner in a small town and living on a modest budget.

"Hey, there," Maleah said as she walked up to the open door and stopped. "Sorry I had to send Derek to meet you and show you to your room. I was on the phone with Powell headquarters." Maleah's gaze surveyed the exquisitely decorated bedroom. "I hope this room is okay. You can take a look at the other two guest bedrooms and use either of them, if you prefer."

"This room is fine. As a matter of fact, this is the bedroom that I helped Cathy design and decorate."

"Is it really?" Maleah laughed. "I suppose I should confess that I told Derek to show you upstairs to one of the rooms. I didn't specify which one. He chose this room for you."

"Mr. Lawrence is a former FBI profiler, isn't he?

That probably means he has a certain sixth sense when it comes to people."

Maleah snorted. "Don't tell him that. His ego is oversized as it is. The last thing he needs is flattery from a pretty woman."

Lorie saw Derek Lawrence approaching about the same time Maleah apparently heard him. Groaning, Maleah made a snarling face, letting Lorie know how she felt about Derek.

"Perdue, did you say something about a certain part of me being oversized?" Derek winked at Lorie.

Smiling, Lorie winked back at him just as Maleah turned around and said, "I was referring to your ego." When he opened his mouth, no doubt with a stinging retort on the tip of his tongue, Maleah warned him, "Do not say another word. I'm in no mood for it. Do you hear me?"

Clicking his heels together in military fashion, he saluted her. "Yes, sir. Uh, I mean ma'am."

Turning back to Lorie after effectively silencing Derek, at least temporarily, Maleah said, "I had requested a list of everyone associated with the movie you made, *Midnight Masquerade*, the actors, writers, director, producer, et cetera. The office e-mailed me the list of the credits and I just got off the phone with my boss's former associate, FBI Special Agent Josh Freidman. I wanted to fill him in on what we think we're dealing with to see if he thinks the situation warrants FBI involvement. It's quite possible that you're not the only other person associated with that movie who has received threatening letters."

"If I know Freidman and his superiors, they aren't going to jump in with both feet until they're sure there's a serial killer on the loose." Derek slipped around Maleah's left side and entered the bedroom so that he stood between Lorie and her.

Maleah shot him a disapproving glare, but other than that, pretty much ignored him. "I thought that after dinner this evening, we might go over the list and see if you recall anything that sends up a red flag. A disgruntled coworker. Any affairs gone wrong. Disputes, arguments, fights. Someone who for any reason might still hold a grudge."

"All right," Lorie said. "I can't think of anything right offhand, but once we start talking more about the film, I might remember something. To be honest, I've spent the past ten years doing my level best to forget I ever did something so monumentally stupid."

"We all make mistakes," Derek said. "Especially when we're very young and eager to make our mark on the world."

Lorie heaved a deep, regretful sigh. "Some mark on the world, huh? Parading around buck naked and having sex on film."

Silence. No one said another word for at least a full minute.

"Sandwiches for supper in about fifteen minutes," Maleah said. "Why don't you settle in and come to the kitchen when you're ready."

"All right." Lorie plastered a phony half smile on her face. "If you'd like, I can help you with dinner, and not just tonight. I'm actually a fairly decent cook."

"Thank goodness." Derek chuckled. "I was afraid that during my stay here, I'd wind up eating cereal and sandwiches seven days a week."

"Oh, cry me a river." Maleah rolled her eyes. "What's wrong with your doing the cooking or your picking up takeout? It's bad enough that I have to put up with your staying here. I certainly don't intend to go out of my way to pamper your spoiled ass."

"I'll have you know that my ass is not spoiled."

Maleah grabbed his arm by the shirtsleeve and dragged him out of Lorie's room. As they walked down the hall toward the staircase, Lorie could hear them continuing their verbal sparring match. She couldn't help wondering what the problem was between those two.

Putting everything else from her mind, including her curiosity about Maleah and Derek, as well as her past misdemeanors and her present predicament, Lorie opened her suitcase. She had brought only two changes of clothes and underwear and the bare necessities, including a condensed version of her usual toiletry items. When she needed more clothes, she'd simply go home and pick them up.

The best-case scenario would be the police catching the killer before he struck again; then she'd be able to go home before Cathy and Jack returned from their honeymoon. The worst-case scenario—the killer would come after her before he was apprehended.

Thank God she had gone to Maleah with the second letter instead of tossing it in the trash as she had the first one. And thank God Maleah had taken her seriously and had believed her immediately.

*Mike believes you now.*

She placed her underwear in an empty top drawer of the mahogany highboy, positioned as if it were a three-sided piece, in the corner near the adjoining bathroom.

Mike had been civil to her this evening. Actually, he'd been more than civil. He had been almost kind to her. She had seen a fleeting glimpse of the old Mike, the man who had once loved her.

She removed two outfits encased in clear plastic garment bags from her suitcase and hung them in the Habersham armoire. Her fingertips caressed the armoire's distressed wood, a part of the item's fine craftsmanship, and lingered over the delicate artwork that decorated the surface.

Mike was simply doing his job. She shouldn't read more into him apologizing to her for not believing her life was in danger than what it was— a simple apology. Nothing more. Nothing less.

She couldn't allow herself to continue hoping for

the impossible. She doubted that Mike would ever be willing to be friends again, let alone lovers.

The full-face joker mask—constructed of papier-mâché, glue, floated whitening and acrylic colors—lay on the motel room bed staring up at him, mocking him, reminding him of her degradation. Charlie Hung had worn this mask in every scene in which he had ravaged the female actors. It was only fitting that it would be his death mask.

He carefully slipped the mask into the black plastic bag and then turned his attention to the Beretta, an Italian import, 9mm with a ten-shot magazine. When he had purchased the pistol, he had made sure it could never be traced back to him. For the right price, a guy could buy just about anything and remain anonymous.

Money talked.

Hell, money screamed.

He placed the gun in the bottom of the small tote, then wrapped the mask in tissue paper and laid it over the pistol before zipping up the 14" x 16" black vinyl bag. After checking the time on the digital bedside clock—6:08 P.M.—he carried the tote to the closet and set it on the floor.

He went back to the bed, pulled two pillows from beneath the comforter, and stacked one on top of the other. Then he lay down, stretched out, and closed his eyes. Step by step, he went over his plan. Parking the rental car a couple of blocks away and walking to Charles Wong's home. Ringing the doorbell. Introducing himself. The disguise he'd be wearing would prevent anyone who might see him entering or leaving the Wong house from giving the police an accurate ID. Tonight, he would wear a black wig and mustache, a gold earring and a wash-off neck tattoo, along with fake leather pants and jacket. A costume that could be easily disposed of in the motel's Dumpster.

In less than six hours, he would kill Charlie Hung and leave Mrs. Charles Wong a grieving widow.

Payback could be deadly!

Lorie carried her glass of wine from the kitchen into the adjoining family room, which boasted a wall of floor-to-ceiling windows and two sets of French doors that led outside onto the old-fashioned screened porch. She loved everything that Cathy had done when she decorated this house, although she would have preferred dark wood in the kitchen. Cathy preferred white cabinets and appliances, and had accented the clean, bright white with touches of a dark-stained wood in the flooring, the island top, and an overlay on the massive range hood. Both the kitchen and family room combined elements of the old with the new, retaining the integrity of the Victorian with the convenience of the modern.

While Lorie chose one of the two gold chenille armchairs separated by a walnut Sheraton table, Derek sat across from her on the moss green, camelback sofa. He smiled at her before taking another sip of his wine. During dinner, she had found herself liking Derek Lawrence more and more and was puzzled as to why Maleah seemed to dislike him so intensely. He had been charming and funny, and had put her at ease. Although she didn't really know him, she sensed that he was the type of man who didn't judge others harshly or by standards few people could live up to. Not the way Mike did.

Damn it, she had to stop comparing every man she met to Michael Birkett.

"So, how long have your worked for Powell's?" Lorie asked.

"Hmm . . . almost five years. I was sort of at loose ends when I left the Bureau, and as luck would have it, Griff called and offered me a consulting job and put me on a retainer I could hardly refuse."

Maleah snorted as she joined them. They glanced up at her. She shrugged. "Nothing. Don't mind me."

"Something tells me that Perdue doesn't approve of independently wealthy men actually working for a living," Derek said.

"Oh, are you independently wealthy, Mr. Lawrence?" Maleah asked mockingly. "Then the rumors about the men in your family having squandered most of their fortunes on wine, women, and song must have been vastly exaggerated."

A quick flash of annoyance passed over Derek's handsome face before he grinned and then laughed. "That was hitting below the belt. Keep that up and Lorie will think you don't like me."

"I don't like you," Maleah told him and returned his insincere smile.

Lorie cleared her throat. "I thought that after dinner, we were going to discuss the cast members of *Midnight Masquerade*."

"We were," Maleah said. "We are. I've got the file folder with the computer printouts on the kitchen counter." She set her glass on a decorative coaster on the table between the armchairs and hurried back into the kitchen.

"Let me clear up the matter of my economic status, not that it's anyone's business," Derek said, his voice loud enough for Maleah to hear him in the adjoining room. "Although there's a great deal of truth to the rumors about the men in my family, they didn't actually squander the entire fortune. And my very wise and very frugal paternal grandmother set up sizable trust funds for each of her three grandchildren."

Before Lorie could think of a proper response, Maleah sailed back into the room, the file folder in her hand. She completely ignored both Derek and his confirmation of being a trust-fund baby.

"Here we are." Maleah plopped down on the huge mushroom-shaped ottoman draped in a green and gold silk material. She opened the folder and handed several printouts to Lorie. "This is a list of actors who starred in the movie, along with the names of the producer, writers, director, and so on."

Lorie clutched the papers in her hand and focused on the top sheet, reading over the names slowly, doing her best to remember each person and anything of importance she could recall about them.

"Just take your time," Maleah said. "If it'll help, I'll go over each name with you."

In her peripheral vision, Lorie noticed that Derek had relaxed as he sipped on the wine and had closed his eyes. Was he napping? Or just thinking?

"Let's start with Hilary Finch and Dean Wilson," Maleah suggested. "What do you remember about them?"

"Not much about Hilary. I didn't really know her. She wasn't overly friendly with her female costars. Not hateful to us or condescending. She mostly ignored us. What I do remember is that she looked like a Barbie doll, all plastic perfection. And at the time, rumor had it that she and Travis Dillard were having a hot affair."

"And Travis Dillard was the producer, right?"

"Uh-huh. The producer of *Midnight Masquerade* and quite a few other porno movies. And he was also an agent for numerous wannabe stars, most of whom wound up in his movies. Me included."

"Dillard was your agent?"

"That's right."

"How well did you know him?"

"Well enough not to like him or trust him," Lorie said. "But I learned that lesson the hard way."

"I hate to ask this, but did you ever have a sexual relationship with Dillard?"

"No, but not for his lack of trying. He had a reputation for having laid every single one of his female clients. I figure that sooner or later, he would've cut me loose if I hadn't put out, but at the time, I was living with his major star—Dean Wilson—and he didn't want to do anything to antagonize Dean."

"You and Dean Wilson lived together?"

"Yes. For nearly a year. I thought I loved him and I believed he loved me. It was one of the most miserable years of my life. I finally realized that my big dreams of fame and fortune would never come true. I was living in a seedy apartment with a guy who was addicted to drugs and alcohol and who had introduced me to a life I hated. Dean's the one who talked me into doing a bit part in *Midnight Masquerade*."

"When was the last time you saw Dean Wilson?" Derek's question momentarily startled her.

Lorie's gaze connected with Derek's and she saw only kindness and compassion in his dark brown eyes. "Nine years ago when I left LA to come back home to Dunmore. He followed me to the bus station and tried to stop me from leaving. He actually threatened me."

"But he didn't follow through with his threats, did he?" Derek asked.

"No, he didn't."

"And you never saw him again?" Maleah asked. "Or heard from him? No phone calls? Letters? E-mails?"

"No. We had no communication whatsoever. Not since the day I left him and that god-awful life behind me."

"Have you seen or heard from anyone connected to the movie since your return to Dunmore?" Derek set his empty glass on the sharp-edged 1940s-era coffee table, the top shining with a high-gloss black lacquer finish.

"No," Lorie replied. "But other than Dean, I really didn't know anyone else. We were just acquaintances, not friends."

"Did you have a problem with anyone, other than Travis Dillard?" Derek inquired.

"By problem, do you mean did any of the other men hit on me?"

"That, or did you know if any of the women didn't especially like you or didn't like one another?"

"Grant Leroy, the director, propositioned me, but didn't seem offended when I turned him down. I think he and Terri Owens, aka Candy Ruff, wound up having a short-lived affair. And several of the other guys made passes at me, but that's as far as it went.

"Like I said, Hilary Finch pretty much ignored all her female costars. The rest of us got along okay. Outside of work, I seldom saw any of them."

"Why don't you keep the list," Maleah said. "Think about what went on during the filming of that particular movie and if anything, even something you think is insignificant, comes to mind, let me know."

"Let us know," Derek added.

Maleah shot him an are-you-still-here? glare and then turned back to Lorie. "You look beat. Why don't you go on up to bed?"

"I don't want to leave you with the dirty dishes and pots and pans."

"Go on," Derek told her. "I'll help Perdue clean up the kitchen."

Maleah groaned, making her displeasure known to anyone within earshot.

Charles Wong roused slowly, at first uncertain what had awakened him. And then the doorbell rang again and again, loud enough to be heard over the racket coming from the television. Someone was at his front door. But who the hell could it be? He glanced around the room and realized that he had fallen asleep in the living room, on the sofa, while watching the late-night newscast. With Lily and the girls gone on the overnight Brownies camping trip, he had snacked for supper, then fixed himself a bowl of popcorn and settled in to watch TV. He missed his wife and stepdaughters. Being with them reminded him of how lucky he was and that working at being a better human every day had its rewards.

The doorbell kept ringing.

"All right, I'm coming," he called loudly. "Be right there."

Barefoot and wearing a pair of loose-fitting sweatpants and a T-shirt, he got up, glanced at the time on the DVD player—11:52—and padded across the room. When he reached the front door, he paused before opening it.

"Yeah, who's there?" he asked.

"Hey, man, it's me. Let me in. I got a six-pack and some of the good stuff."

Charlie didn't recognize the man's voice. He probably had the wrong house. Charlie unlocked the door and, leaving the chain latch on, eased the door open a couple of inches.

"Come on, man, let me in. I need to pee real bad."

The guy didn't look familiar. Black hair, black mustache, dressed in cheap leather and sporting a sizable tattoo on his neck, he looked like some of the guys Charlie had known in his past.

"Look, buddy, I think you've got the wrong house."

"You're Charles Wong, right? You're married to my cousin Lily, right? Didn't she tell you I was in town and she offered to put me up a couple of nights?"

Lily's cousin? "No, she didn't mention you."

"Hey, sorry about that. I guess she forgot. Probably too busy with plans for that overnight camping trip with the girls' Brownie troop."

Charlie breathed a bit easier. Apparently his midnight visitor really was Lily's cousin. Otherwise, how would he know about the Brownie troop's camping trip?

Charlie removed the safety latch and opened the front door. "Come on in. I'm afraid you'll have to bunk on the sofa. We don't have a guest bedroom."

"No problem. I'm grateful you'll put me up a couple of nights while I'm in town." He entered the living room and closed the door behind him.

Charlie noticed the small tote bag in his hand. "You're traveling light, aren't you?"

"Just a change of underwear and my shaving kit." He set the bag on the floor.

Charlie turned around and walked back toward the sofa. When he heard an odd noise behind him, he glanced over his shoulder. His eyes widened in shock when he saw the weird mask the man now wore. Charlie's mind whirled with questions, but suddenly he recognized the mask at the same time he noticed the gun in his night visitor's hand.

"What the hell?" Charlie got out before the guy aimed and fired.

The bullet hit Charlie's left leg, just below the knee.

He stared at his shooter with total disbelief as he went down to the floor, his hands gripping his bleeding leg.

"Who are you? What's going on?"

The man fired the pistol a second time, the bullet piercing Charlie's shoulder. This man was going to kill him. He had opened the door and let some crazy person into his home. Thank God Lily and the girls weren't here.

"Don't do this," Charlie said when the man hovered over him.

He aimed the gun directly at Charlie's head and said, "Dead by midnight."

Then he fired the fatal shot.

# Chapter 8

Maleah and Derek had agreed to split the day guarding Lorie, even though Derek wasn't officially a Powell agent. At this point, neither of them believed Lorie was in imminent danger since both of the other known victims had been killed at night, probably sometime around midnight. Derek had driven to Treasures with Lorie that morning and promised to stay in the background as much as possible so as not to arouse her customers' curiosity.

"Gossip is one of the favorite pastimes in small towns," Lorie had told them. "And since the first day I returned to Dunmore, I've headed the list of favorite gossip topics. I don't want to give the busybodies, especially the WCM ladies, anything to speculate about. And tongues are bound to wag when they see you hanging around the shop all morning."

Even though it wasn't quite one o'clock and she wasn't due to relieve Derek until two, Maleah scooped up her shoulder holster, wallet, Powell ID badge, and car keys from the top of the dresser in her bedroom. Plans had changed.

After racing down the back staircase, she set the alarm, exited through the back door, and locked it behind her. Once settled into her GMC Yukon Denali and headed downtown to Main Street, she slipped on the Bluetooth earpiece and hit Mike Birkett's number. He answered on the fourth ring.

"Maleah?"

"Yeah, it's me."

"What's up? Is Lorie all right?"

"Lorie's fine and I want to keep her that way."

"Something's happened."

"Oh, yeah, you could say that." She kept her gaze glued to the view through the windshield. Too many wrecks occurred when people were distracted by talking on their cell phones. She didn't want to become another statistic. "I just got off the phone with Sanders, Griff Powell's number-two

131

man. The agency has been keeping close tabs on any reports of foul play involving the list of people involved with making the one and only adult film Lorie was in. It seems that another cast member has been murdered."

"Does Lorie know?"

"I'm on my way to Treasures as we speak to give her the bad news. Sanders received the information about fifteen minutes ago and contacted me immediately. A guy by the name of Charles Wong was found shot several times, the fatal bullet right to the head. Sanders personally called the police chief in Blythe, Arizona, the little border town where Wong lived, and managed to get some info that wasn't released to the press. It seems that Wong had been stripped naked and was wearing a mask."

"Son of a bitch. It has to be the same perp. It's the same MO."

"I agree. That makes three victims that we know of, three actors who appeared in *Midnight Masquerade*, one killed each month since the first of the year. Sanders is going to contact Nicole Powell's old friend, Special Agent Josh Freidman, at the Bureau and share what info we have. We seem to definitely have a serial killer on our hands and we're going to need all the help we can get to find and stop him before he kills again."

"Before he gets to Lorie," Mike said.

"Yeah, before he gets to Lorie."

"Is Derek with you?" Mike asked.

"He's at Treasures with Lorie."

"I'll meet y'all there. See you in about ten minutes."

Shontee Thomas twirled around and around on the podium, the full skirt of the satin bridal gown she wore swishing against the tulle netting beneath. She had never been this happy in her entire thirty years on earth. At long last, everything was coming together in the best way possible. In exactly two months, she would marry the most wonderful man in the whole world, Anthony Trice Johnson. They had met a year ago, introduced by mutual friends at the Atlanta nightclub Tony owned. Their relationship had started off on the fast track from the first date, which had ended at Tony's apartment, in his bedroom, in his bed. At the time, she had been working as a waitress six days a week at a local restaurant and taking night classes to become a masseuse. A real ladies' and gentlemen's spa masseuse, not a hooker using the term "masseuse" as a cover for her real occupation.

In the beginning, Shontee had hoped Tony would never have to know about her past as a porn star. She had made half a dozen films in her late teens and early twenties before quitting the business and undergoing antibiotic treatment for an unpleasant venereal disease. When she, along with three more of Travis Dillard's clients, had tested positive for gonorrhea, her agent and producer had been forced to close down production on his latest movie. But after she and Tony had been dating for about three months, he had come right out and asked her if she'd made some porno movies using the name Ebony O.

She had wanted to deny it, to lie to him, to tell him he'd gotten her mixed up with some other woman. But instead, she had told him the truth, the whole truth, about her life before and after she'd made those movies for Travis Dillard's Starlight Productions. She'd thought for sure Tony would turn tail and run. But he hadn't.

"I'm not especially proud of a lot of things I've done to get where I am today," he'd told her. "I'm no saint myself. Why should I expect my woman to be? I love you. What you did when you were just a kid doesn't matter to me. The only thing that matters is that you love me and treat me right."

"Oh, Tony, I do love you and I swear I'll always treat you right."

She was one damn lucky sister and she knew it. She was going to be Mrs. Anthony Trice Johnson and live in a big fancy house with hot and cold running servants. She was already driving a cute little Mercedes convertible and wearing a three-carat diamond. Life didn't get any better than this.

"You look like a dream," Tony said from where he stood in the doorway watching her. "A wet dream." He winked at the gasping saleslady.

"Behave yourself," Shontee scolded him.

"Aren't you going to wear a veil?" he asked.

"I don't want a veil," she said. "I want to wear a tiara. Diamonds and pearls. Something glittery and classy at the same time."

"Diamonds and pearls! Woman, do you think I'm made of money?" he teased.

"We have some lovely rhinestone and freshwater pearl tiaras," the saleslady informed them.

Tony chuckled as he walked across the room and held open his arms. Shontee didn't hesitate to sail off the podium and straight into his arms. He caught her around the waist, his big hands clasping her securely, and then set her on her feet. After he kissed her soundly, he glanced at the saleslady, a wide, toothy smile spreading from ear to ear.

"If my fiancée wants diamonds and pearls, that's what she'll get. The genuine articles. No fake stuff for her."

"Yes, sir. Of course, Mr. Johnson."

Everybody knew who Anthony Trice Johnson was and showed him the proper respect, always calling him Mr. Johnson. Tony was a fucking mul-timillionaire, that's who he was. A guy who had grown up in the projects and made something of himself. He owned a string of nightclubs in six major cities: Atlanta, Nashville, Memphis, Louisville, Birmingham, and Tallahassee. And little Shontee Rachelle Thomas from Greenville, South Carolina, a bastard child born to a fourteen-year-old girl who had been raped by her own cousin, was going to be Mrs. Somebody Important.

*It doesn't matter where you came from or who your mama was or how you got born. All that matters is who you are now. Tony Johnson's fiancée, soon to be his wife and the mother of his children.*

Shontee's hand instinctively went to her belly at the thought of one day giving Tony a son. Thank God, those two abortions she'd had more than ten years ago and that bout with gonorrhea hadn't screwed up anything inside her. She'd talked to her doctor right after Tony proposed, just to make sure her body was functioning like it should, that there was no reason why she couldn't get pregnant.

*Thank you, Sweet Jesus, thank you. I might not deserve so much happiness, but I sure do thank you for it.*

Lorie knew the moment Maleah walked into Treasures that something was wrong. She wasn't due to relieve Derek for another hour.

Doing her best to concentrate on ringing up Mrs. Hightower's order, Lorie tried to dismiss the thought that there might have been another murder. "Will there be anything else? You know we've marked all our Easter items twenty percent off this weekend."

"Nothing else today. But I'll be back next weekend when you mark the Easter stuff down a little more."

Lorie forced a smile. Eloise Hightower was one of her best customers, a lady who loved to decorate and to collect. Lowering her voice to a whisper, Lorie leaned toward Mrs. Hightower and said, "Next weekend, we'll mark down to twenty-five percent off, but that's as low as it will go until after Easter, then we'll have a fifty-percent-off sale."

Eloise grinned as if she'd just been awarded a prize. She whispered, "I won't tell a soul."

Lorie hurriedly wrapped the breakable items and placed them carefully in three separate small plastic sacks before putting all of Eloise's purchases in a large heavyweight paper bag with handles.

Glancing across the room, she watched while Maleah approached Derek, who had been sitting at an antique writing desk working crossword puzzles in a puzzle book he'd brought with him. Lorie's heartbeat accelerated.

*It's bad news. I know it is.*

After handing the bag to Eloise and thanking her for her business, Lorie slipped from behind the counter. The chime over the front door jangled as Eloise left, and less than a minute later, it jangled again, alerting her that a new customer had just entered the store. Pausing for a second, she glanced toward the entrance. Mike Birkett, wearing jeans, sneakers, and a seen-better-days Roll Tide sweatshirt, looked right at her.

Butterflies danced in her stomach.

Would the day ever come when she could look at him and not want him?

Mike had always been good-looking. Tall at six-two, and muscular, with wide shoulders and a broad chest. His hair was that deep black that glistened with navy blue highlights, and he wore it long enough so that it curled just above his collar. But it was his eyes that were so remarkable. At a distance, they appeared black, but on closer inspection, they glistened a dark indigo blue.

Mike moved his gaze away from her and scanned the shop until he saw Maleah and Derek. As he headed toward them, Lorie rushed to catch up with him, but was waylaid by another customer.

"Do you have any more of those pastel lights, the kind I can use to decorate my Easter egg tree?" Carol Greene asked. "I can't find the ones I bought last year and I've looked high and low."

"I've sold out of them," Lorie told her. "But I'm expecting more in a new shipment that should arrive by Wednesday."

"Oh, good. Would you put back a couple of strands for me?"

"I'll be more than happy to. Is there anything else I can help you with today?"

"That was it. The kids would be so disappointed if I didn't decorate that little weeping willow we've got in the front yard."

As soon as Carol walked off, Lorie made her way straight to where Maleah, Derek, and Mike were involved in a hushed conversation. She glanced around the shop and noticed that there were two customers still rummaging around. One customer, Paul Babcock, was shuffling through the assortment of antique postcards, the display arranged on top of one of the various glass cases in the store. Paul could spend hours searching for just the right card to add to his collection. She didn't recognize the other customer, a young woman who seemed to be simply browsing.

As she approached them, Maleah, Derek, and Mike stopped talking and turned to face her. She ran her gaze from Maleah to Derek and then to Mike. Their somber expressions concerned her.

"What's going on?" she asked.

"Is there any way we can talk in private?" Maleah asked. "Don't you have somebody who comes in to help on weekends?"

"One of my part-time workers has a stomach virus. The other, who wasn't supposed to work today, went out of town for the weekend."

"Could you close the shop for, say, thirty minutes?" Derek asked.

"I could, but I still have two—" The doorbell chime jangled. Lorie looked over her shoulder. The lone remaining female customer—the one she didn't recognize—walked out onto the sidewalk as the shop door closed behind her.

"Paul Babcock is deaf in one ear, but he refuses

139

to wear a hearing aid," Mike said. "He was in a hunting accident a few years back. I think we can feel certain he won't overhear anything from where he's standing over there."

Maleah looked right at Lorie. "There's no easy way to say this, so here goes. A man named Charles Wong was murdered last night in his home in Blythe, Arizona. His wife and young stepdaughters found his body this morning when they returned from an overnight camping trip."

Lorie remembered Charlie. He'd had a wicked sense of humor and was always playing practical jokes. She had really liked him. How awful that he had become the killer's most recent victim.

"Do you think that the same person who killed Dean and Hilary killed Charlie?" she asked.

Maleah nodded. "Same MO, I'm afraid. Shot several times, one final fatal shot to the head. He was naked and the killer had placed a fancy mask on his face."

A flash of memory jolted Lorie. Charlie Hung dancing around the *Midnight Masquerade* set between takes wearing a pair of gym shorts and that strangely beautiful joker mask. All the masks for the movie had been purchased secondhand, but were good quality party masks. The joker mask was stark white, each side marked with a different color stripe, one red and one black, and a glittery gold star accented the left eye-slit.

"The mask—was it a joker mask?" Lorie asked.

"I don't know," Maleah replied. "I didn't ask about specific details."

"Why do you ask?" Derek questioned.

"Because . . ." She swallowed and deliberately avoided looking at Mike. "Charlie wore a joker mask in the movie."

"We need to find out if each of the victims was wearing the same type of mask they wore in the film," Maleah said.

"If the killer somehow got hold of the original masks from the film and is using them to decorate his victims, Powell's might be able to find out what happened to those masks after the movie was completed," Derek added.

"I'll contact the office and have our investigative staff see what they can find out. It's possible we could even come up with a name, especially if someone purchased all the masks at one time."

"Possible, but not likely," Derek told her. "The movie was made ten years ago and those masks were part of the costumes, which were probably used over and over again and then disposed of by either tossing them in the trash or selling them. Tracking down the buyer or buyers would be an iffy proposition."

"What about Charlie?" Lorie asked. When the other three stared at her, she elaborated. "He was a nice guy, a goofy, funny guy who liked to play practical jokes. I remember him laughing all the time, as if . . . Before this happened . . . before he was killed, was he doing okay? You mentioned a wife and stepchildren. I guess he was able to turn his life around once he left LA, just the way I did."

She looked at Mike then and found him staring at her, his expression surprisingly sympathetic. Odd how, over the past nine years, she had become accustomed to his hostile glares and cold, disapproving expressions.

"Do you mind staying on for a while to keep an eye on Lorie?" Maleah asked Derek. "I really need to—"

"Why don't you both go?" Mike suggested. "Do whatever you need to do to move things along. I don't work on weekends, unless there's an emergency. My kids are with their grandparents. And all I had planned for this afternoon was doing a little housecleaning and laundry, which I can do tonight. I'll stay here at Treasures with Lorie."

"Are you sure?" Maleah asked.

"Yeah, I'm sure."

Derek grabbed Maleah's elbow. "Let's go, woman."

She jerked free of his hold and flashed him an eat-dirt-and-die look, then turned to Lorie. "From here on out, I don't want you to be alone, not here at Treasures or at the house or even to and from work. Even though, so far, this guy has killed only at night, we can't be certain he won't strike in broad daylight."

"I understand. Better safe than sorry," Lorie said.

When Maleah and Derek walked away, Lorie looked at Mike. "Have you had lunch?"

"Just some cheese and crackers around eleven this morning. Why? Want me to order lunch for us?"

"Uh . . . no, I . . . You'd do that, share lunch with me?"

"Why not? I've got to eat. You've got to eat. No reason we shouldn't share a meal." He glanced around the store, still empty except for Paul Babcock, who was deeply engrossed in the antique postcards. "What do you do when you're here alone?"

"I close the shop for half an hour," she replied. "I lock the door and place the CLOSED sign in the window."

"Okay. So, tell Paul you're closing for lunch while I order us something. What do you want?"

"I'm not picky. You choose."

"The Ice Palace has some great sandwiches and they deliver downtown." When she nodded and smiled, he asked, "Do you still like roast beef on wheat with horseradish?"

"Yes, I do." *Be still my heart. Mike remembered my favorite sandwich.*

"Me, too. Barbeque chips and dill pickles?"

"Absolutely."

"Mind if I get dessert?"

"I don't mind," she told him. "As a matter of fact, I'd love a piece of their lemon icebox pie."

Mike grinned. "Two pieces of lemon icebox pie."

Life was strange. She'd been back in Dunmore for nearly nine years and during all that time, Mike had been barely civil to her and had never smiled at her. And suddenly today, when it had become obvious that her name was on a madman's hit list, Mike had smiled at her for the second time. Did that mean he actually cared about her safety, that although he might not want her to be a part of his life, he didn't want anything bad to happen to her?

If only she didn't have to worry about the possibility of being killed, she could appreciate Mike's new attitude a lot more.

Did she dare hope that she and Mike could at least be friendly acquaintances from now on? If so, that was all the more reason to do everything she could to stay alive.

# Chapter 9

Lorie walked Paul Babcock to the door. "I'm glad you found several new postcards to add to your collection. I'm expecting a shipment in sometime next week from the antique dealer in Memphis. I'll call you when it arrives."

"Sure do appreciate it, Lorie," Paul said, his wide smile deepening the dimples in his round, rosy cheeks.

When she followed him out onto the sidewalk,

Mike came up beside her and slid his hand beneath her elbow. Startled by his touch, her stomach turning flip-flops, she barely managed to wave good-bye to Paul as he headed for his car.

Once Paul was out of earshot, Mike said, "You shouldn't be out here in the open like this. You're an easy target. Come back inside."

Before she had a chance to respond, a teenage boy carrying a large brown sack jaywalked across the street and came straight toward them. As he drew closer, she recognized him as one of Seth's buddies from school, but she couldn't recall his name.

"Y'all ordered lunch from the Ice Palace?" the kid asked.

"We did," Mike told him. "Bring it on in and I'll pay you."

Once back inside Treasures, Lorie went behind the counter, reached down, and lifted her purse from the bottom shelf. She pulled out her wallet. "Lunch is my treat." She looked at the delivery boy and asked, "How much?"

"Twenty-one fifty," he told her as he set the sack on the counter.

Lorie pulled out a twenty, a five, and a couple of ones, making sure to add a decent tip, and handed the bills to him.

"Thanks. Hope y'all enjoy your lunch," the boy said as Mike escorted him to the door.

"I'm sure we will," Mike replied and then added,

"In the future, don't jaywalk. It's illegal, you know, even in Dunmore."

The kid's face turned bright red. "Yes, sir, Sheriff Birkett. I won't do it again."

Mike closed and locked the door. Lorie came out from behind the counter and turned the OPEN sign in the window so that it read CLOSED.

"I think you scared him half to death," Lorie said.

"I wouldn't have said anything to him since most of the people in Dunmore jaywalk all the time, but because I'm the sheriff, I felt I had to at least act like I uphold that particular law."

"I'm sure it'll be a good while before he jay-walks again."

Mike picked up the sack off the counter. "You've got a room in the back with a table and chairs, don't you?"

"I do. Table, chairs, microwave, and refriger-ator," she said.

He followed her to the back of the shop and when she opened the door and flipped on the over-head light, he glanced around the small kitch-enette. She and Cathy had painted the one-window room a bright, cheerful daffodil yellow and sur-rounded the old free-standing sink with a base draped in navy blue gingham. Navy gingham place mats at the yellow table for two added to the overall color scheme. The old unmatched wooden chairs had been painted white and Lorie had hand-painted yellow daffodils on the backs of each and added navy gingham cushions.

"Hannah would love this room," Mike said. "Her bedroom is yellow. It's her favorite color."

"Yes, I know," Lorie admitted as she placed the lunch sack on the wooden counter between the sink and the refrigerator. "As you know, I see your children at the Interfaith Youth Council meetings that Patsy Floyd oversees. And before you chew me out, I know that once you learned I'd been talking to them, you ordered me to stay away from them. I promise you that I don't seek them out. But when Hannah and M.J. speak to me, I talk to them. Hannah told me all about how your mother helped her redo her room as a ninth birthday present."

"I shouldn't have reacted that way, telling you not to speak to my kids." Mike opened the refrigerator and removed the jug of iced tea. "It's not as if you're a threat to my children. Warning you to stay away from them was a knee-jerk reaction."

"Is that another apology?" she asked as she reached up and opened the single white cupboard over the counter and retrieved two tall glasses.

"Yeah, I guess it is."

"Hmm . . . apology accepted." She smiled at him and he smiled back at her. "There's ice in the freezer. You pour the tea and I'll set the table."

"Okay."

They worked together seamlessly, as if they'd been doing it for years. When everything was ready, sandwiches, chips, and pickles on bright yellow dinner plates, dessert on small navy blue plates, and forks for their pie placed atop white napkins, Mike pulled out a chair for Lorie. She had almost forgotten what a gentleman he had always been.

After they were seated, he looked across the table. "Why the sly smile and quiet little chuckle?"

"Oh, I was just remembering how you were always such a gentleman with the ladies despite having a reputation as a hellion."

Mike grunted. "My mama expected me to be a hellion when I was young, just like my daddy before me. But if I'd ever been anything less than a gentleman to a lady, she'd have beat the living daylights out of me."

"Miss Nell is certainly a real lady. I always thought the world of your mama."

"And she did of you." Mike looked down at his plate. "These sandwiches sure look good."

"I appreciate your treating me like a lady even if you don't think of me that way now."

"Let's not go there," he said as he picked up one half of the sliced roast beef sandwich. "It's best to leave that subject alone."

"You're right." She lifted her napkin, unfolded it, and laid it across her lap.

"You sure do set a fancy table. Everything's real pretty."

*Oh, Mike. You're trying to be nice to me, trying*

*so hard. Thank you. For whatever reason and for however long it lasts, I appreciate your kindness.*

They ate in relative silence for a while, but when the quiet became blatantly obvious, Lorie racked her brain trying to think of something to say. There were so many subjects they needed to avoid.

"I don't guess you've heard anything from the newlyweds?" she asked. "Maleah talked to them briefly. They called to check on Seth."

"I haven't heard a word. Not that I expect to. If any two people deserve an uninterrupted, blissful honeymoon, Jack and Cathy do."

"I agree. Their getting back together after all these years was a minor miracle."

Mike grunted.

"Not many people get a second chance," Lorie said.

Mike nodded. "Nope, they don't."

Silence returned. Suddenly her delicious sandwich tasted like cardboard.

Mike picked up his dessert plate and set it in the middle of his empty dinner plate. "Look, Lorie, we need to get a few things straight."

Her heartbeat thundered in her ears. "All right."

"I've been a real ass to you since you came back to Dunmore. I'm sorry about that. And I hate that you're in danger now, that some crazy guy might show up at any time and try to kill you. As the sheriff, I and my staff will do whatever we can to protect you and to help the Powell Agency. But that's as far as it goes. Understand?" When she stared at him, confusion no doubt written plainly on her face, he said, "You and I can be acquaintances who are civil to one another, but we can't be friends. You have to know that. And there's no way in hell we can ever be anything more to each other."

*Don't cry. Oh, God, don't cry.*

She swallowed hard and took a deep breath before replying. "Yes, of course. I understand."

Griff and Nic were returning to Griffin's Rest tomorrow evening, and by Monday morning, they would be in charge of the agency again. But until then, Sanders was handling everything, including notifying the FBI about the three almost identical murder cases that Powell's had been hired to investigate.

Derek checked the time on his wristwatch—3:48 P.M.

"I sure could use a cup of coffee," he said. "And something to eat since we both missed lunch."

"If you think I'm going to play servant to your lord of the manor, think again," Maleah said, her hackles raised and her fangs bared.

What was it with this woman? Why did she take almost everything he said the wrong way?

"What the hell are you talking about?" he asked.

"I'm talking about your expecting me to prepare coffee and fix you something to eat. I'm not your servant. And just because I'm female and you're male does not make me any more capable of preparing food than you are."

Derek chuckled as he skimmed his gaze over her slightly flushed face, her bright, blue eyes glaring at him and her full lips moist and slightly parted. He didn't know what amused him more, her ridiculous reaction to a simple comment or the fact that he actually found her attractive, especially when she was pissed at him. Every time she got upset with him, he thought the same damn thing.

*Wonder how she'd react if I actually told her that she was beautiful when she was angry?*

*She'd serve your head to you on a silver platter, that's what she'd do.*

"As a matter of fact, I was about to suggest that I prepare coffee and a couple of sandwiches for us," Derek said, "while you download and print out the info that Sanders is e-mailing us."

"Oh." For half a second she looked as if she was on the verge of apologizing, but that moment passed and instead she said, "Okay. That works for me. I don't want any mayo on my sandwich, only mustard, and I take my coffee—"

"With sugar," he finished her sentence. "Or rather a pack of Splenda now that you've cut back on your sugar intake."

She stared at him, a dumbfounded expression on her face.

"I notice little things," he explained. "I'm a highly skilled profiler, remember?"

"I know, but stop profiling me. I don't like your noticing anything about me."

"Yes, ma'am. As of right now, no more profiling, no more noticing things about you, like how you prefer your coffee."

She huffed. "I'll be in the den. When the coffee and sandwiches are ready, let me know."

Smiling, he nodded. She clamped her mouth tightly shut, turned and walked down the hall. Whistling softly, Derek headed for the kitchen.

Fifteen minutes later, carrying a large serving tray, he breezed through the open den door. "Our afternoon snack is ready."

She glanced up from where she sat on the sofa, her lap covered with pages of info that Sanders had sent them concerning the most recent murder and how it connected to the two previous ones.

Derek placed the tray on the coffee table and sat down beside Maleah. She gathered up the papers, scooted over as far as she could away from him, and laid the neatly stacked sheets on the side table to her left.

He poured and prepared the coffee to her liking and handed her the cup.

"Thanks."

"You're welcome." He glanced past her at the stack of papers. "Any new information we need to discuss about the case?"

"I don't know. I've only had a chance to quickly scan the info Sanders sent, and so far nothing jumps out at me."

"How do you feel about Sanders sending the two of us out into the field together?" Derek asked, knowing full well that she hated the very idea of spending so much time with him.

Their working closely together on this case should prove to be an interesting experience for both of them.

"I'd rather he sent someone else with you and left me here in Dunmore to act as Lorie's bodyguard. But considering my personal connection to Lorie, I understand why he thinks it's best to send in Shelley Gilbert."

"You should have told him that you could remain objective, that you could separate your personal feelings about Lorie from doing your job as her bodyguard."

"And if I had told him that, I'd have been lying." Sipping on the coffee, she glanced at him over the rim of the china cup. "But you knew that, didn't you?"

"Lorie's your sister-in-law's best friend. When Jack and Cathy return from their honeymoon, they're going to become deeply involved, thus making it practically impossible for this case not to be very personal for you."

"Tracking down everyone associated with *Midnight Masquerade* and finding out how many of them have received threatening letters is going to be a time-consuming bitch."

"It's not just a matter of Powell's warning these people and finding out if they've received letters," Derek reminded her. "It's about evaluating each one of them to see if I—we—get even the slightest hint that one of them is our killer."

"That could wind up being a total waste since it's possible that the killer wasn't connected to the film's production." Maleah eyed the thick sandwiches on the tray atop the coffee table.

"Thin-sliced turkey," Derek told her, and when she gave him a questioning look, he explained. "The sandwiches are turkey. I added lettuce and tomato, but left off the onion. No mayo for you. Mustard only."

She picked up a halved piece of the sandwich and took a bite. "Delicious."

"We aim to please." He bit off a large chunk of his sandwich, chewed, swallowed, and reached for the iced tea glass.

"Sanders is having the office compile a list of porno film crazies, guys who have stalked porn stars or made threats against them."

"That could be a very long list. There's no way Powell's can check out all of them unless we're going to spend the next year tracking them down."

"We'll have to do some process-of-elimination work," she said. "See if any of them were obsessed with this one particular film or the stars."

"So, Powell's is starting with warning the actors while you and I branch out and interview everyone else associated with *Midnight Masquerade*, right?"

"Right. On Monday, we're going to interview the movie's producer, who was also the agent for a number of the actors, including Lorie. Travis Dillard's bio reads like a trashy erotica novel. The guy sounds like a real sleaze."

"I thought you just skimmed the info Sanders sent."

"I did, but the info on Dillard . . . well, let's just say a few words here and there caught my attention."

"Any of those words imply potential killer?"

"No, not really. But they more than imply scum of the earth." After finishing off half her sandwich, Maleah nibbled on the potato chips Derek had put on their plates.

"I'd never peg Lorie Hammonds for the kind of woman who would have gotten involved in the porno business." Derek munched on his dill pickle.

"She was young," Maleah said. "She made a huge mistake and she's been paying for it ever since. Nobody in this town has ever let her forget she bared it all in *Playboy* and then did even worse by getting a bit part in that one movie."

"Why did she come back here? She had to know she would have to deal with the town's scorn. She could have started over someplace else where no one knew her."

155

"I don't know. You'd have to ask her, but my guess is that, at the time, Mike Birkett had something to do with why she came back to Dunmore."

"Birkett, huh? The old boyfriend? I picked up on some strong vibes between them the first time I saw them together."

"I was about thirteen when Mike and Lorie were engaged. She walked out on him before the wedding and went to California," Maleah said. "I haven't lived in Dunmore since I left for college, so I haven't exactly kept up on local gossip. All I know is what my brother told me. It took Mike quite a while to get over Lorie, but he finally married someone else, had a couple of kids, got elected sheriff, and—"

"Lived happily ever after."

"Not hardly. His wife had cancer. She died four years ago."

"Tough break," Derek said.

"Yeah, it was. Mike's a good guy."

"And Lorie?"

"What about Lorie?"

"I sense that she's a good woman despite her notorious past."

"On that, Mr. Lawrence, we can agree. I think fate handed Lorie a raw deal. She's already more than paid for her sins. And now she's on a killer's hit list and unless we can keep her safe . . ."

"We will," Derek said. "Powell's will keep her guarded twenty-four/seven and local law enforcement will do their job as backup. But what you and I accomplish by interviewing everyone associated with *Midnight Masquerade* could well result in our finding the killer and stopping him before he can get to Lorie."

"Dear God, I hope so."

# Chapter 10

The Powell jet landed shortly before noon, Eastern Standard Time. Sanders picked up Nic and Griff at the private airport and drove them home. On the ride to Griffin's Rest, they talked business. Sanders brought them up to date on the three new Powell Agency clients and how the cases had turned out to be related.

"Hell of a coincidence," Griff said.

"Three separate murder investigations that no doubt have the same killer," Nic said. "Yeah, I'd say that was one hell of a coincidence."

As much as she loved being a part of Griff's agency—correction—their agency, Nic couldn't help thinking about their very recent second honeymoon. It had been wonderful to spend an entire week without giving other people's problems a thought. Selfishly, a part of her wished that she and Griff could live a different life, a simple, uncomplicated life with both of them working simple, nine-to-five jobs that never involved a life-or-death scenario.

But when she had become an FBI agent, she had chosen a profession in law enforcement, hadn't she? That job had sometimes entailed danger and at the very least occasional excitement. And when she had married Griff, she had known that he would spend the rest of his life trying to right wrongs, trying to help those who couldn't help themselves. Fate had placed the two of them in the unique position of being able to work outside the system to seek justice. Coming from a background at the Bureau where she'd tried to be a by-the-book agent, she had not adapted instantly to the way Griff ran his agency. But she had come to understand that too often the guilty got off scot-free and the innocent suffered without ever receiving justice or even closure. The Powell Agency tried to tip the scales in the victim's favor.

As soon as Sanders stopped the limo in front of the house, Griff helped Nic out, kissed her cheek, and said, "I need to go over a few things with Sanders. I'll catch up with you later."

"All right." She smiled at him and then went inside, not turning around to watch while he and Sanders took the car to the garage behind the house.

They were home. Back into the maelstrom of Powell Agency business. Nic supposed she should drop into the kitchen to say hello to Barbara Jean, but what she wanted to do was contact Maleah ASAP. She knew Barbara Jean would be overseeing a late Sunday lunch for the four of them, so she would talk to her shortly. But having just learned from Sanders that Maleah had been paired with Derek Lawrence on these latest combined cases, Nic thought she should check with Maleah to see how their twosome was working out.

As soon as she closed the door to her bedroom suite, she flopped down on the chaise longue, dumped her purse to the floor, and grappled inside to find her phone. She hit Maleah's prepro-grammed number and waited.

"Nic? Are you at home or—?"

"We just got in," Nic said.

"So, how was the second honeymoon—every-thing you wanted it to be, I hope?"

"Everything and more," Nic admitted, flashes of memorable moments in Griff's arms flickering through her mind.

"That's wonderful. I'm so glad for you. For both of you."

"I understand you're involved in a new and very interesting case that is connected to two other new cases and that you're paired with Derek Lawrence." Nic waited for the explosion of exple-tives, but when Maleah remained silent, Nic asked, "Want me to take you off the case entirely and assign someone else?"

"No," Maleah told her emphatically. "I want to be involved with this case. After all, one of the potential victims is my sister-in-law's best friend."

"I could reassign you, put you with one of the other agents working on the case and send someone else to California with Derek tomorrow. All you have to do is say the word."

"I'm tempted, believe me. But that would be asking for special treatment, taking advantage of our personal friendship. I won't do that, no matter how I dread the thought of spending days on end with that man."

"I really do understand," Nic said. "There was a time, years ago, when I felt the same way about Griff. Back when I was with the Bureau, just the sight of Griffin Powell made we want to scream, usually scream at him." Nic laughed.

"My God, don't you dare compare Derek and me to you and Griff. I am not attracted to Derek Lawrence in any way, shape, form, or fashion. And he certainly isn't attracted to me. There is no deep-buried sexual tension waiting to explode between the two of us."

"Did I say there was?" Nic knew what it was like to deny your feelings, to pretend that you despised a man when on a subconscious level, you really had the hots for the guy. The first time Griff and she had made love, they had set the sheets on fire.

"It's not complicated. I just don't like his type. Never have. Never will. He's arrogant, domineering, and expects to always get his way."

"He's also handsome, brilliant, charming, and rich."

160

"None of which necessarily combine to make a good man."

"I think Derek is a good man beneath all those other sterling qualities. You have to know that he deliberately says and does things to bait you. He enjoys setting you off."

"Maybe he does, but for the life of me, I can't imagine why."

"Want me to tell you what he said about you?"

"No." Maleah snorted. "I'm not sure."

"I happened to hear him tell Griff that he finds you amusing. And Griff warned him to be careful, that one day he may push you too far and you'll shoot him."

Maleah laughed. "That gives me a great idea."

"Which is?"

"The next time I go to the Powell shooting range, I'll have a photo of Derek blown up to poster size and use it for target practice."

"You're wicked."

"So I've been told." Maleah paused for a second and then said, "Don't worry about me. I can handle Derek. I won't like it, but I can do it. You just concentrate on yourself and your marriage."

"That's what I've been doing. I told you that everything is fine. Why is it that you seem concerned? Is there something you know that I don't know?"

"No, of course not. It's just that I'm aware of what a rough year you and Griff have had and I want to see you stay as happy as you are now."

"Thanks. You're a real friend."

"Takes one to know one."

The moment she said good-bye to her best friend, Maleah started feeling guilty. She knew that Griff was still keeping secrets from Nic. Months ago, she had accidentally overheard a conversation between Griff and Dr. Yvette Meng, heard just enough to know that there was something important going on in Griff's life that he hadn't shared with his wife. But he had shared it with both Yvette and Sanders. The only thing she didn't know was whether this "something" was a secret from his past or his present.

Less than five minutes after she ended her conversation with Nic, Maleah's phone rang. Pushing aside her thoughts about Nic and Griff, she answered on the fourth ring.

"Perdue here."

"It's Griff," he said.

"Welcome home."

"Thanks. I assume Nic will be calling you today, if she hasn't already called."

"We just spoke."

Without commenting on her response, Griff said, "Sanders has briefed me on our three new cases. I understand that he assigned you and Derek to interview people associated with *Midnight Masquerade*, starting first thing tomorrow. Do you have a problem working with Derek?"

162

"No, sir."

"Are you sure?"

"I'm sure."

"Good. Then Shelley Gilbert will drive down from Knoxville and be in Dunmore by tonight. She'll take over from you so you'll be free to fly to California with Derek in the morning."

"Yes, sir."

"Are your brother and his wife aware of what's happening with Ms. Hammonds?"

"No, they are not. They're still away. None of us wanted them to cut their honeymoon short."

"I realize this case is personal for you," Griff said. "In a way, it's personal for me, too. I don't know if Sanders mentioned it, but the first victim's brother, Jared Wilson, and I go way back. We're both UT alumni and Jared is a professor there now."

"Sanders didn't go into detail, but I assumed that you and Mr. Wilson had at the very least a passing acquaintance."

"I've told Sanders that I want to expand the investigation. You and Derek will be in charge, but I plan to send out other agents to do some of the legwork. These agents, as well as Holt Keinan, Michelle Allen, and Ben Corbett, will report to you and Derek and to me. Y'all will follow up on their reports and dig deeper whenever you or Derek think it could lead somewhere."

"Do you want me to explain this to Derek or—?"

"I'll do it. I want to talk to him myself."

"Of course."

"That's it for now," Griff said and ended their conversation with those succinct words.

Maleah slipped her phone into her pocket. On her way upstairs to pack, she bumped into Derek on the landing. Before she could do more than glare at him, his phone rang and he quickly nodded to her and headed downstairs. Griff certainly hadn't wasted any time phoning Derek. She wondered if he'd ask her new partner if he had a problem working with her. Probably. Everyone at the agency knew about the animosity between them. And yes, she admitted that, for the most part, it was her fault. She wasn't very adept at keeping her mouth shut. She talked too much. Her mother had been a quiet, almost shy woman. Her brother Jack wasn't much of a talker, either. But one of the things she remembered about her father—other than his wide smile and loud laugh—was that he was an extrovert, a friendly man who never met a stranger.

What would Derek reply when Griff asked if he could work with her? He'd probably laugh and then say something to the effect of "I never met a woman I couldn't handle." She could almost hear him spouting off those exact words.

Arrogant son of a bitch!

Maleah hadn't realized she was mumbling to herself until she heard someone ask, "Who's an arrogant son of a bitch?"

She whirled around and saw Lorie standing in the doorway of the guest bedroom.

"Sorry. I was thinking out loud. Don't pay any attention to me."

"Do you know what time Ms. Gilbert will get here? I've started packing and I have to admit that I'm eager to go home."

"You do know that Jack and Cathy would be more than happy for you to stay here until—"

"I'm sure they would, but I really want to go home. And I don't want them in the line of fire, when . . ." Lorie took a deep breath. "If the killer comes after me, the last thing I want is to put Jack or Cathy or Seth in danger."

"I understand."

"I thought you would. I . . . uh . . . I'd like to ask a favor."

"Sure, what is it?"

"Would you keep me informed about what's happening, how the case is going? After all, it's my life that's in danger. I have a right to know—"

"You don't have to convince me. I agree. You have every right to be kept in the loop and I promise that I'll call you with regular updates. How's that?"

Lorie managed a fragile smile. "Thank you."

Both of them heard the doorbell.

"I'd better get that," Maleah said. "You stay here until I see who it is."

"I've got it," Derek called from below.

Maleah raced down the stairs and arrived in the foyer just as Derek opened the door to Mike Birkett and a broad-shouldered, auburn-haired man wearing tan dress slacks and a blue blazer. Although he wasn't traditionally handsome, masculinity oozed from his pores and sparkled mischievously in his hazel brown eyes. Maleah liked him on sight. There was a gentle calmness to the man, and his warm smile expressed an easygoing manner.

Mike made the introductions quickly. Derek Lawrence, former FBI profiler, now a Powell Agency employee. Special Agent Hicks Wainwright, from the Birmingham field office.

"And this is Maleah Perdue," Mike said. "She's the Powell agent that Lorie Hammonds hired as soon as she received the second of two threatening letters."

Maleah shook hands with the federal agent. When he smiled at her, she returned his smile. Her gut instincts told her that Hicks Wainwright was her kind of guy.

"Special Agent Wainwright has been assigned to investigate the three murders we believe are linked and make a judgment call on whether or not the Bureau should form a task force," Mike explained.

The usually charming Derek said rather gruffly, "It won't take much investigating to figure out that we're dealing with a serial killer."

Mike and Maleah stared at Derek, both surprised

by his tone of voice. But Wainwright seemed not to notice and replied, "I'm sure I'll discover that you're right. And if I do, I've been instructed by SAS Josh Freidman, from headquarters in DC, to ask for the Powell Agency's cooperation. We don't want to work at cross-purposes, do we? And I'm sure your team does not want to interfere once this becomes a federal case."

"Of course we don't," Maleah said. "The Powell Agency always does everything possible to work with law enforcement, local, state, and federal."

Derek grunted. Mike cleared his throat.

"I'd like to talk to Ms. Hammonds," Wainwright said. "I understand she'll be going back to her home tonight and will have the protection of both Sheriff Birkett's deputies as well as a private body-guard."

"That's right," Mike said. "A patrol car will be assigned to park at Ms. Hammonds's home every night from ten until one. We're assuming the killer won't deviate from his MO, which includes killing his victims sometime around midnight."

"Sounds like y'all have all your bases covered." Special Agent Wainwright focused on Maleah. "Will you be personally guarding Ms. Hammonds?"

"Actually—" Maleah began, but was cut off by Derek's response.

"Ms. Perdue will be working with me. We're flying into LA tomorrow to begin interviewing people who were involved in making the movie that

167

connects the three victims with Ms. Hammonds."

Maleah bit her tongue to keep from telling Derek that she was perfectly capable of speaking for herself. Instead, she swallowed her aggravation, ignored Derek, and smiled pleasantly at Hicks Wainwright. "As I was saying, actually, another Powell agent, Shelley Gilbert, will be taking over as Lorie's personal bodyguard. She's driving in from Knoxville. We expect her to arrive later this evening."

Wainwright nodded. "Good. Good. Now that we have that settled, may I speak to Ms. Hammonds?"

"I'll get her," Maleah said, and then turned toward the stairs.

She had barely reached the landing when Lorie came out of her room and met her. "I kept my door open and overheard what y'all were saying. So, the FBI is involved now, huh?"

"It seems so, which is probably a good thing. A very good thing. You'll have not only the Powell Agency and all its resources working to find the killer, you'll also have the power and resources of the Federal Bureau of Investigation at work on your behalf."

"And the local sheriff," Lorie reminded her.

"You're right. We should never underestimate the importance of local law enforcement."

He adored Lorie Hammonds. She was beautiful and kind and sweet and sexy as hell. He had worshipped her from afar for a couple of years, but she didn't really see him as anything other than an acquaintance, a nice hometown guy who had always treated her like a lady. Everybody here in Dunmore knew she was still hung up on Mike Birkett and the damn fool wouldn't give her the time of day. At least not until recently. Now the sheriff was sniffing around Lorie, acting all protective and concerned. Too little too late as far as he was concerned. It wasn't fair that Mike got to step into the role of Lorie's knight in shining armor. Given half a chance, he would take on the role himself. He dreamed of the moment Lorie would look at him and see that he was the man she'd always needed, the man who would do anything for her.

One of these days, he would work up the courage to ask her for a date. He'd walk into Treasures and go right up to her and say, "How'd you like to go out Friday night for dinner and a movie?"

And she'd say, "Whatever took you so long to ask me out? I'd love to go."

That would be the first of many dates, evenings that would end up back at her house, in her bed, the two of them screwing like crazy all night long.

Just the thought of touching Lorie gave him a hard-on.

Hidden in the shadows outside Jack and Cathy Perdue's home, he wondered what all the activity going on inside the house was about and how soon he could find out any details. Whatever concerned Lorie, concerned him, because whether she knew it or not she belonged to him.

Later that evening, Mike pulled his truck into the parking lot adjacent to the sheriff's office where Special Agent Wainwright had left his car. As soon as he killed the engine, Mike reached to open the driver's side door, but Wainwright's comment stopped him cold.

"Ms. Hammonds is even more beautiful now than when she made *Midnight Masquerade*."

Mike swallowed hard. "You've seen the film?"

"Yeah, strictly in the line of duty, of course." Wainwright chuckled.

*Do not lose your cool. This man doesn't know you were once engaged to Lorie. As far as he's concerned, this is just guy talk, nothing more and nothing less.*

"Yeah, sure." For the life of him, Mike could not fake a smile.

"It's a good thing the Powell Agency has assigned a woman to guard Ms. Hammonds. I can see where a guy could easily get personally involved when the client is a woman like Lorie."

"You're assuming a great deal about her simply because she made one porno movie."

Wainwright narrowed his gaze and studied Mike. "The lady's past had nothing to do with my comment. The fact that she's gorgeous and vulnerable and a guy could drown in her big brown eyes is what I was talking about. Just interviewing her for half an hour gave me a pretty good idea what kind of person she is."

"Care to elaborate?"

"You wouldn't have a personal interest in the lady, would you?"

Did he? Hell yes!

"My only interest in Lorie Hammonds is in my capacity as the sheriff of this county. She's one of the citizens that I'm sworn to protect."

Wainwright smiled. "Then the fact that you two were once engaged doesn't factor into your feelings about her?"

Wham! A two-by-four right between the eyes. That's how Wainwright's question affected Mike. Rendered momentarily speechless, he stared at the FBI agent.

"When I'm assigned to a case, I do my research, Sheriff Birkett."

"Then you know that there has been nothing between Lorie and me since she came back to Dunmore more than nine years ago."

"Nothing? No feelings whatsoever, huh? I find that hard to believe."

"Believe it."

"It must have been difficult for you when she came back to Dunmore, knowing every man in town had not only seen her naked in *Playboy*, but had watched her screw a couple of guys on film."

It took every ounce of Mike's self-control not to punch Wainwright in the mouth. With his jaw clenched and his hands balled into tight fists, he glared at the man.

Wainwright looked Mike right in the eye. Neither of them blinked. Neither flinched. Finally, Wainwright asked, "Did you hate her? Do you still hate her?"

A low, guttural growl rose from Mike's chest and crawled up his throat. Only his clenched teeth diluted the sound from a roar to a rumble. "What are you really asking?"

"Do you hate Lorie Hammonds enough to want to see her dead?"

"You son of a bitch! Are you implying that I'd—?"

"It's a legitimate question," Wainwright told him. "And to answer your question—no, I do not think that you're in any way involved with the murders. But someone could easily use the murders as a smokescreen to hide behind if they wanted Lorie out of the way."

"You're talking about a copycat murder? Why would you think I or anyone else in Dunmore could hate Lorie enough to want to see her dead?"

"I like to get the lay of the land where all the players are concerned, and you were the only one on my possible suspects list who had reason to truly hate Lorie Hammonds. Let's just say that I can mark that particular scenario off my list. It's

172

obvious that whether you know it or not, you still have some strong feelings for the lady."

"You're wrong."

"Am I? Then why did you turn ten shades of green when I mentioned how it must have felt knowing so many other men had seen your former fiancée in all her naked glory?"

# Chapter 11

He was dying. His doctor had delivered his death sentence shortly after Thanksgiving this past year. Merry Christmas and Happy New Year. He'd had four long months to learn to accept the reality of his situation. Pancreatic cancer. Stage four. Original prognosis: a few months, a year at most. He knew he was already living on borrowed time.

Travis Dillard smoothed his fingertips over the cold, glossy surface of his mahogany desk, a twenty-five-thousand-dollar antique that his decorator had chosen for his home office ten years ago. He had surrounded himself with only the best money could buy because he could afford it. He had lived in a house worth thirty million, owned a dozen high-dollar automobiles, smoked Cuban cigars, drank Krug Grande Cuvée champagne, and wore Moreschi shoes and Astor & Black hand-tailored suits.

But that had been then. This was now. Divorce in California was expensive and although he had managed to hide some of his assets with wives three and four, wife number five had outsmarted him by stashing away millions neither he nor his lawyer had ever been able to find.

He turned and gazed out the vast expanse of windows that showcased a splendid view of the Pacific Ocean. Beauty unparalleled in nature—except for the exquisite human form, both male and female in their prime.

Travis sighed heavily. Ah, for the good old days. *Be grateful for what you have, you old son of a bitch.*

It wasn't as if he lived in poverty. He still owned the beach house he had inherited from his second wife, Valerie. Dear Valerie, to whom he owed so much. She had been the one who had taught him how to enjoy the finer things in life. Although he had never loved her—had he truly loved any of his wives?—he would forever be grateful to her for leaving him her millions.

And he still owned the rights to forty of his films, adult movies that had been rereleased recently on DVD. The income off those movies didn't afford him the luxury lifestyle to which he had been accustomed, but it did pay the bills and allowed him and his latest wife to maintain the façade of wealth. Dawn—his sixth wife—was young and gorgeous and sported the best body cosmetic surgery could give her. She wasn't overly bright, but after his fifth wife—the one who had taken him to the cleaners—Travis was perfectly content being married to a gorgeous, airheaded bimbo.

By his standards, he had lived a good life. Hell, he'd lived a great life. How many men could say they had screwed hundreds of lovely ladies? From his first fuck at the age of fourteen, he'd had his pick of sweet pussy. Not that he was all that handsome himself, just an average-looking Joe. But he had a big cock and a big ego and women seemed to love both of his best assets.

If he had his life to live over again, would he do anything different? Hell, no! He had lived every moment of his life to the fullest and had no regrets.

Well, maybe one regret. The doctors claimed that his two-packs-a-day smoking habit had probably caused the cancer that was now killing him.

But why him? Damned if he knew. Bible-thumpers would say he was getting his just punishment. Screw 'em all, every last sanctimonious hypocrite out there. There wasn't a heterosexual man alive who didn't enjoy the pleasures of looking at, touching, and using a woman's body. The films he'd made catered to the normal human desires that existed in everyone.

"Mr. Dillard?" Louie Tong cleared his throat. "Your guests are due to arrive shortly. Do you wish for me to—?"

"Is it that late already?" Travis turned and faced his housekeeper of twenty years, a man he called friend, possibly the only real friend he had.

"Did you compile all the information I asked for?"

"All the information is in the red binder there on your desk," Louie said. "I placed it there earlier today."

Yes, of course, he had. Travis remembered now. Odd how easily he forgot things these days. "Thank you. It had slipped my mind."

"Will there be anything else?"

"No, I . . . uh . . . I'm just wondering about these murders. Someone has killed Hilary and Dean and Charlie. Hilary and Dean were some of the best in the business. I loved them both, you know." He chuckled, remembering how often he had "loved" Hilary. God, she'd been a wild woman in bed. "And Charlie was a real card. The guy had a wonderful sense of humor. I loved him, too."

"Yes, sir, it's a shame what happened to them."

"Damn shame. They were all far too young to die." Travis slammed his fist down on the antique desk. "Damn it, I'm too young to die! People live to be a hundred these days. I should have had at least another twenty years."

Louie stared at him, a look of concern and sympathy in his black eyes.

Travis waved his hand in the air and grunted. "When those Powell agents arrive, show them into the living room. I'll be in there drinking some of my Macallan scotch and smoking one of my Havanas. I'm going to enjoy every day I've got left, drinking and smoking and screwing to the end."

• • •

Travis Dillard had agreed to meet with them at four-thirty at his beach house on the Pacific Coast Highway. The Powell Agency office in Knoxville had quickly pulled together more info on Dillard, including the particulars of the property he owned. It seemed that he had been forced to sell his Bel Air mansion, which he had acquired through marriage to an heiress a good twenty years ago. The woman had been much older than Dillard and had died of an apparent heart attack after two years of marriage to the up-and-coming porno filmmaker.

"Wife number two financed Dillard's first ten movies," Derek read from his laptop screen. "But after her death, wives three through five pretty much bankrupted the guy, especially wife number five. All he owns now is the place in Malibu, a couple of antique cars, and the rights to more than forty of his films."

Maleah turned their rental car off onto the drive leading from the highway to Dillard's house. "How old is he?"

"Hmm . . ." Derek scanned the file that the agency had sent this morning. "Sixty-six. Why?"

"And his present wife is how old?"

"Twenty-two."

"Figures. Is she a porno star?"

"She was, but once she married the boss, she became a silent partner in his business and gave up acting."

177

Maleah parked the rental in front of a modern architectural creation of white stucco—two levels, walls of floor-to-ceiling windows, and a breathtaking view of the Pacific. She let out a long, low whistle. "What's this place worth?"

"The estimated worth is $11,950,000, which makes it one of the less pricey pieces of real estate along this stretch of Malibu."

"That means he's far from broke, at least not until the new wife divorces him and gets her half."

"Won't happen. She signed a prenup. Unless she stays married to Dillard until he dies, she gets one million in cash and that's it. Guess the guy finally wised up."

Maleah grunted. As far as she was concerned Travis Dillard was a scumbag, the lowest of the low, who catered to the baser elements of human nature and preyed on stupid young girls with stars in their eyes.

She opened the car door and got out, meeting Derek under the vine-covered overhang that protected the front entrance.

"Pull in your claws and play nice," Derek told her. "If Dillard senses your hostility, he'll clam up immediately and refuse to cooperate. We want him friendly and talkative. Whatever you do, do not accuse him of anything. Got it?"

"Don't talk to me as if I'm some green recruit who doesn't know—"

The front door swung open, and standing just

over the threshold, a small Asian man of indeterminate age stared at them.

"We're here to see Travis Dillard," Maleah said.

"We have an appointment," Derek added. "We're with the Powell Agency. I'm Derek Lawrence and the lady is Maleah Perdue."

"Come this way, please. Mr. Dillard is expecting you." Without a backward glance, the man walked off, leaving Maleah and Derek to follow him.

A rectangular tiger-print rug covered the foyer's ceramic porcelain tile floor and an elaborately decorated Chinese cabinet, painted black and red, stood against the left wall. They entered the huge living room, at least 30' x 30', two of the four walls filled with windows that overlooked the Pacific. Maleah barely stifled a startled gasp when she saw the expansive view of beach and ocean. But she managed to focus on the bone-thin, bald man who rose from one of the two white sofas flanking the stucco fireplace.

This old, haggard, bald man was Travis Dillard? He looked much older than sixty-six, more like eighty-six. And although he still resembled the photo they had of him, she would have pegged him for Dillard's father instead of the man himself. But then cancer could do that to a person, ravage their body and render them gaunt and pale.

"Ms. Perdue and Mr. Lawrence to see you, sir," the man who had met them at the front door announced.

"Thank you, Louie." Travis smiled, flicked the ashes from his cigar, and placed it, still smoking, in an ashtray on the glass and steel coffee table. "Please, you two come in. Come in and take a seat."

Maleah noticed the half-empty glass of liquor—her guess would be whiskey—on a tile coaster beside the ashtray. When a guy was dying, she supposed it didn't matter how much he drank and smoked.

She and Derek sat on the white sofa across from the identical one on which Dillard sat.

"You're from some private detective agency, right?" Dillard asked.

"The Powell Private Security and Investigation Agency," Maleah replied.

"Hmm . . . that's the one headed up by that famous guy—what's-his-name Powell, the billionaire."

"That's correct. Griffin Powell," Derek said. "And the agency has been hired by the families of Hilary Finch Chambless and Dean Wilson to do a private investigation into Mrs. Chambless's and Mr. Wilson's deaths."

"Damn shame about Hilary and Dean. And Charlie, too. I was just saying that to Louie"—he tossed up his hand and pointed at his servant still standing at attention halfway across the room—"earlier today. Good people, all three of them."

Maleah supposed that in Travis Dillard's world

the three victims had been good people. But not in the real world, the one inhabited by the vast majority.

"Oh, yeah, either of you care for something to drink? Louie can make tea or coffee or mix up a cocktail or—"

"Nothing, thank you," Maleah said, her voice a bit sterner than she had intended.

Dillard dismissed his servant with a quick glance before he focused on Maleah, studying her for a couple of seconds. "You got the looks, honey. How old are you? Twenty-eight? Thirty? They prefer 'em younger and younger these days, but there's a market for older chicks like you."

"I beg your pardon?" Maleah glared at the old man. Had he actually told her that she had what it took to be a porno star? When she heard an odd sound coming from Derek's direction, she snapped her head around and glared at him. Noting that he was on the verge of laughing out loud, she gritted her teeth to keep from losing her temper.

"Don't take offense, honey," Dillard said. "I just paid you a compliment." He glanced at Derek. "What is it with smart, professional women that they can't take a compliment from a man when they hear one?"

*I can take a compliment when I actually hear one.* The comment was on the tip of Maleah's tongue, but she managed, with great difficulty, to refrain from saying it aloud.

181

Derek shrugged. Damn the man! He winked at her, then grinned at Dillard before asking, "Do you have any idea who killed three of your former stars?"

"Don't have the foggiest." He shook his head.

"How long has it been since you last saw each of them?" Maleah asked.

"Years."

"So you've had no communication with any of them recently."

"Nope."

"Do you keep in touch with any of the people—actors and others—who were associated with *Midnight Masquerade*?" Derek asked.

Dillard reached out and picked up a red binder from the sofa cushion beside him. After flipping through several pages, he paused, pulled a pair of reading glasses from his shirt pocket, and put them on. He skimmed the information and then glanced from Derek to Maleah.

"I got Louie to compile some info for me on all the people involved in the making of that particular movie. It was a good ten years ago. I've made quite a few movies since then, a few well-received independent artsy productions, with real actors." He tapped the folder with his skeletal index finger. "I read over the names of everybody who had anything to do with *Midnight Masquerade* and I have to admit that there are a few I don't even remember. Not my stars, mind you, but some of the others." He grimaced as if hating the fact that his memory failed him. "To answer your question, yes, sure, I've kept in touch with a few of the people. Not many. Some are actually still in the business."

"Really," Maleah said. "Who's still in the business? And who are you still in touch with?"

"Well, Laura Lou Roberts, one of the two writers who worked on *Masquerade*, is still writing for a few other producers even though she's battling emphysema. She's an A-number-one bitch, but she writes the kind of stuff I want. And she's getting a little long in the tooth at nearly sixty, but it's not like she's showing her tits and ass on film."

Dillard laughed, the sound grating on Maleah's nerves. *This guy really is a sleaze.*

"Anyone else?" Maleah tried not to show her disgust.

"One of the cameramen, Jeff Misner, is a director now. He directed my last film, *Down and Dirty*, a few years back. He's married to the former Puff Raven, aka Jean Goins. She was in *Midnight*, too. She's doing some hot videos for the Internet and getting filthy rich. And I used to hear from Sonny Shag Deguzman, up until last year. He was over in Europe somewhere and I suppose he's still there. As far as I know, the other cameraman on that movie, Kyle Richey, is in Mexico. The first few years he was down there, he sent me some eager young things dying to be in the movies." Dillard lowered his voice to a whisper. "Young girls, if you know what I mean."

Yes, Maleah knew exactly what he meant. Underage girls, some as young as eleven or twelve, who were sexually exploited and those depraved acts were filmed by ruthless, criminal scumbags like Dillard.

Just as she opened her mouth to speak, Derek jumped in quickly and said, "Can you think of anything that happened during the filming of *Masquerade* that could have created some really bad feelings? You know, jealousy, professional or personal? Any fights? Any problems that resulted in violence, even if only minor altercations?"

Maleah took a deep breath, her heart gradually slowing to a normal rate as the anger boiling inside her subsided. For once, she was thankful to Derek for butting in and stopping her from shooting off her mouth. If she'd said anything whatsoever, the loathing and revulsion she felt for Travis Dillard would have been more than obvious. And antagonizing the depraved old bastard would do nothing to help them solve this case.

"Hell, there was always catfights among the women. That was a given," Dillard said, a smirking grin on his wrinkled face. "Nothing like a couple of naked broads rolling around on the floor, scratching and pulling hair."

"Any fights out of the ordinary?" Derek asked.

"I know where this is going. And the answer is no, I don't recall any incident that would make me suspect someone connected to *Masquerade* has gone on a killing spree ten years after the fact." Dillard reached out and picked up his whiskey glass, took a swallow, and shuddered. "Sure neither of you want a drink? This is eighteen-year-old Macallan scotch, costs me a hundred and sixty dollars a bottle, but it's worth every penny."

"I'm tempted," Derek said amiably. "But no thanks."

"Who handled the fan mail for your actors?" Maleah kept her voice calm and even.

"My secretary handled everything that came in for the actors I represented. The others—I have no idea."

"Were there any threatening letters after the release of *Masquerade*? Or any particular zealous fan who—?"

"There was that one guy." Dillard grunted. "Damn. Can't remember his name. Henry? Hewitt? Nah, doesn't sound right." He snapped his fingers. "Hines. His name was Hines."

"What about this guy named Hines?" Derek asked.

"He's a porno movie aficionado and a huge fan. He tried to get on the set a couple of times. Had to have him escorted off. He wrote to just about every actor in the movie more than once. I thought at the time the guy seemed obsessed with that one movie in particular."

"Does Mr. Hines have a first name?" Maleah looked Dillard in the eye.

"Yeah, sure, I just can't put my finger on it, but I can get Louie to call Etta and see if she remembers."

"Etta?" Derek and Maleah asked simultaneously.

"My old secretary. She'd probably remember the guy's name. Hell, she might even still have some of the letters he wrote. My actors never answered their own fan mail, you know. That was part of Etta's job."

"How can we get in touch with Etta?" Maleah asked.

"I'll get Louie to call her. We keep in touch. She and her latest girlfriend even come over for dinner occasionally. They live here in Malibu. She rents an apartment on Las Flores Canyon Road. If she's home, I'll ask her to come over and you can talk to her this evening."

"Thank you," Derek said.

For the life of her, Maleah couldn't thank this slimy old bastard, not even when he had given them their first real lead in their case.

"I want to know why you've got Tyrell following me everywhere I go," Shontee screamed at Tony. She was angry and hurt because she thought he didn't trust her. What had she ever done to make him think that she would betray him in any way? "Damn it, tell me why! I have a right to know why you believe you can't trust me."

"Stop your bitching, woman." Tony tried to grab her by the shoulders, but she jerked away from him and planted her hands on her hips. "Don't act like this."

Shontee's bottom lip trembled. Tears pooled in her eyes.

"Baby, I can't stand seeing you so upset." He held open his arms. "I trust you. I swear I do. I've had Tyrell following you to protect you."

Shontee swallowed and then swiped the teardrops from her eyelashes. "Protect me from what? From who? Has somebody you do business with threatened you?"

Tony shook his head. "Nobody would dare threaten me."

"Please, tell me—"

"Just wait here," he said as he walked across the room to his wall safe hidden behind a sleek platinum-framed mirror.

She waited, nervous and uncertain, as Tony opened the safe, reached inside, and pulled out several plain white envelopes. He closed the safe and turned to her. What was in those envelopes? Photos of her from the past?

When she stared at the envelopes, he held them out to her. "They're pretty much identical, all four of them. You know my assistant opens all our mail and—"

"I know, I know." She grabbed the envelopes out of his hand.

"You've received a letter each month, starting in late December. The fourth one arrived this past Saturday."

Her hand trembled. "Why did you keep these from me? Why hide them away in your safe?"

"Read one of them," Tony told her.

She dropped three of the envelopes down on the armchair near where she stood, then inspected the one she held in her hand. Her name stood out against the stark white background. There was no return address, only a Knoxville, Tennessee, postmark. Slowly, cautiously, she eased the single typed page from the envelope, unfolded it and read the brief note.

*Midnight is coming. Say your prayers. Ask for forgiveness. Get your affairs in order. You're on the list. Be prepared. You don't know when it will be your turn. Will you be the next to die?*

"Oh my God!" She released her hold on the letter and let it float down onto the floor. "Tony?"

When he held open his arms this time, she raced into the comforting embrace he offered.

"Now you understand why I've had Tyrell keeping a close watch over you whenever I'm not around. Somebody is threatening you, baby, and I haven't been able to find out who the motherfucker is."

• • •

Etta Muro handed Travis Dillard a large manila envelope, then turned and shook hands with Maleah and Derek. The woman was at least six feet tall, rawboned, darkly tanned, and sported a short, spiked haircut. She wore billowy beige gauze pants and a matching blouse. A large gold and turquoise pendant hung from a leather chain around her neck. Maleah guessed that she was close to sixty and one of the few women in the LA area who hadn't had cosmetic surgery, although she kept her hair dyed a bright reddish orange.

"We appreciate your meeting with us," Derek said, offering the woman his charm-the-birds-from-the-trees smile. The only problem was that this particular bird preferred her own sex, so his machismo was totally lost on her.

"Travis told me that this involves a murder investigation, that somebody killed Woody and Hilary and our sweet Charlie." Etta shook her head. "Now, who'd do something like that?"

"What's in here?" Travis held up the large over-stuffed envelope.

"Fan letters that we received about *Midnight Masquerade*," she told him. "I've got the folder labeled. Put on your glasses so you can read." She turned her attention back to Derek. "Most of that mail was for Hilary, a few for the other women, and even some for the guys."

"Mr. Dillard said there was one fan in particular

189

who was obsessed with this movie," Derek said. "He believes the guy's last name is Hines."

"Duane Hines," Etta stated emphatically. "He wrote a letter to everyone in the movie. He'd written to Hilary before then, and wrote to several of the stars later about other movies they were in. The guy's a real nut. We had to have him arrested once when he attacked one of our guards who had escorted him off the set."

"When is the last time Duane Hines contacted anyone involved in *Midnight Masquerade*?" Maleah asked.

"He's a persistent cuss, I'll give him that." Etta grunted. "He sent Hilary another letter sometime last fall. And come to think of it, he sent one to another of the actors from *Masquerade* at the same time. The bosomy redhead." Etta rubbed her chin. "Nice girl. Not cut out for our business. She used the name Cherry Sweets." Etta chuckled as she glanced at Travis. "She was one you never did nail, wasn't she?"

Travis snorted. "It was only a matter of time. If she'd stayed around long enough, she would have spread her legs for me."

"Lorie Hammonds," Etta said. "That was her real name. I wonder what ever happened to her."

# Chapter 12

The sun heated their naked skin as they played together in the river, the water refreshingly cool in contrast to the hot summer sunshine. Laughing, Lorie lifted a handful of water and threw it into Mike's face.

"You'll pay for that," he warned her.

When he reached for her, she didn't put up even a token resistance. He yanked her up against him, her breasts, covered only by two strips of cloth and a string tie, pressed into his hard, naked chest. As he cupped her butt with both hands, he lowered his head and claimed her mouth in a hungry kiss. She opened for him, took his tongue inside and closed her lips around him. He groaned deep and low, the sound rumbling from his throat.

Every cell in her body came alive, tingling, igniting with an internal fire that nothing except making love with Mike could extinguish. But only for a little while, only until he touched her again. It had been that way for both of them from the very first time he had kissed her.

With his arm around her waist, he walked her out of the shallow backwaters of the river, their bodies dripping wet as they stepped onto the shore. He slipped his hand inside her bikini bottoms and caressed her buttocks. Her femininity tightened and released. Aroused by his touch, her body instantly prepared for mating. Her nipples hardened. Moisture gathered between her thighs. Her feminine core swelled with anticipation.

Mike led her off into a secluded area in the nearby woods where earlier they had spread a blanket and eaten their picnic lunch. With sunlight dappling through the thicket of decades-old trees, he laid her down on the ratty old quilt he kept in the trunk of his prized Mustang. How many times had they made love on that quilt?

Sighing dreamily as she looked into the face of the man she adored, Lorie reached up for him and drew him down to her. He kissed her mouth, her cheeks, her neck, and the upper swell of each breast. Then he pushed aside her clinging arms and lifted her just enough to untie the bikini top and whip it off her. Totally exposed from the belly button up, she wriggled with pleasure as his hands explored every inch of her hips and butt while his mouth moved over her breasts and stomach. When he nuzzled the edge of her bikini bottoms, she lifted her hips enough for him to drag them down and off. The minute she was completely naked, he buried his face in the triangle of auburn curls between her thighs. His tongue snaked out, seeking and finding her clitoris.

He licked. She whimpered.

He stroked. She shivered.

He sucked. She cried out his name.

Alternating his moves, he used his mouth and

tongue to bring her to the brink while his fingers rose to her breasts to give them equal attention.

Lorie speared her fingers into his thick black hair, encouraging him to give her what she so desperately needed.

He increased the tempo of his strokes until she came, her orgasm rocketing through her, exploding inside her, shaking her from head to toe. Crying out with pleasure, she clung to him while he lifted himself up and shucked out of his wet swim trunks. Fully erect, his penis jutted forward from a bed of black curls. She reached up and touched him. He groaned.

"I love you, Lorie. God in heaven, I love you!"

He thrust into her fully, her slick, wet body more than ready for him. He lifted her hips to bring her closer. She wrapped her legs around his waist and moved sensuously against him.

"I love you," she whispered as he delved and withdrew, delved and withdrew. "Love you . . . love you . . ."

Seconds later he came, grunting and trembling. His release triggered a second climax for her and the moment she came apart beneath him, Mike eased down on top of her, wet with sweat and panting softly.

She kissed him again and again.

He slipped off her and stretched out at her side. They lay there together, sated and happy, young and in love.

"Do you think it will always be like this?" she asked.

"Yeah, I think it will," he replied. "Even after we've been married twenty years and have half a dozen kids."

She rolled over onto her side and kissed his damp, darkly tanned shoulder. "Giving birth six times will probably ruin my figure. In twenty years, I'll be fat and flabby and—"

"And still sexy." He ran his fingertips across her chest, from collarbone to collarbone. "Don't you know that I'll always love you and want you, no matter what? Nothing can ever change the way I feel about you."

She sighed contentedly. "I'll love you forever, Michael Birkett."

Forever . . . forever . . . forever . . .

Lorie woke suddenly, the word *forever* on her lips.

She sat straight up in bed, her skin moist with perspiration, her body remembering the orgasm she'd had in her dream. A dream that had seemed so real.

It was real, or at least it had been. Years ago when she and Mike had been together, a couple of kids who'd had no idea what the future held for them.

A soft rap on her bedroom door brought Lorie completely back to the present. She glanced at her bedside clock. 5:45 A.M. Nearly an hour before her alarm would go off.

"Yes?" Lorie called.

"Are you all right?" Shelley Gilbert, the Powell agent who had replaced Maleah, asked her through the closed door.

"Yes, I'm fine."

"I thought I heard you crying out and I wanted to make sure everything is okay."

"Come on in," Lorie said. "See for yourself. I was dreaming and must have been talking in my sleep."

Shelley eased opened the door and peered into the semi-dark bedroom. She scanned the entire area and then smiled at Lorie. "If you're getting up, I'll go put on a pot of coffee."

"The coffeemaker is preset for six-thirty, but yes, please reset it to start immediately. I'll join you in a couple of minutes."

"Sure thing."

Shelley had arrived Sunday night and Lorie had liked her immediately. Medium height and solidly built, the thirty-something woman looked the way Lorie thought a female bodyguard should—intelligent, nondescript in appearance, and with a tough glint in her keen blue eyes. Her short, wash-and-go brown hair, a minimum of makeup, sensible, low-heeled black shoes, and all-business attire consisting of tan slacks, white shirt, and a black blazer only added to her overall aura of competence.

Although their conversations hadn't gotten personal, not beyond the basic facts, Lorie felt comfortable around Shelley. And she felt safe. Shelley seemed more than capable of defending not only herself, but Lorie, too.

Doing her best not to think about the erotic dream that had given her an orgasm, Lorie hurried into the bathroom.

After flushing the commode, she washed her hands, dampened a cloth, and washed her face. Staring at herself in the mirror, she ran her fingers through her disheveled hair.

"It was just a dream," she told herself.

No, it was more than a dream. It was a memory of a long-ago summer day when Mike had loved her and everything had been good and clean and right in her world.

Duane Hines lived in a little town called Carey, Missouri, seventy-five miles south of St. Louis. He had been easy to locate. The last two letters he had written and sent in care of Dillard's Starlight Production Company—one letter to the late Hilary Finch Chambless and the other to Lorie Hammonds—had included his return address. If the man was a killer, he was a damn stupid one.

At present, Derek and Maleah Perdue were assigned to locate and speak to potential suspects. The main office in Knoxville had the job of locating all the *Midnight Masquerade* actors. Each actor was being notified about the deaths of their three costars and asked if they had received any threatening letters during the past few months. Only if Nic and Griff believed that there might be a crossover in the potential victims and possible suspects categories would Derek and Perdue personally interview that actor. And the decision would be based on facts unearthed by Powell's investigation.

Derek preferred to drive, but he hadn't made an issue of it with Perdue, knowing full well that she was a lady who needed to be in charge. He would bet his last dime on one fact—somewhere in Perdue's past there was a man who had subjected her to complete and humiliating submission. All the signs were there, even if she wasn't aware of it.

The more time he spent with Maleah Perdue, the more fascinated he became with her. Despite her bristly attitude toward him, he found himself liking her. He liked that she was smart and spunky and worked diligently at keeping her emotions under control. He figured it really bothered her that he got under her skin.

Was there something about him that reminded her of the man in her past?

What other reason could there be for her to dislike him so intensely? It wasn't that he expected everybody to love him. Hell, even his own mother didn't love him. But for the most part, people in general liked him. After all, he was a nice guy, wasn't he?

"Look for number ten," Perdue told Derek as she

turned off the main road and drove into the Poplar Creek Trailer Park.

A couple of minutes later, Derek pointed to a small, rusty trailer anchored beneath a couple of towering poplar trees. "There it is."

"Lovely place." She turned up her nose.

"Now, now, don't be judgmental."

"Oh, shut up."

Perdue pulled their rental car up beside an older model Harley-Davidson motorcycle. She got out and marched up the rickety wooden steps in front of the single door. Derek waited a few feet behind her while she knocked several times.

No response.

"He should be home," she said. "Our report stated that he was laid off from his last job a month ago and is drawing unemployment."

Perdue knocked again.

The door eased open and a dark-haired man in jeans and a wifebeater undershirt that exposed his hairy chest and arms looked at her and smiled. "Well, hello there."

"Duane Hines?" she asked.

"Sure am, sweet thing. And just who are you?" His grin widened, revealing uneven, discolored teeth.

Derek wondered in what universe did this skinny, yellow-toothed degenerate think that a woman such as Maleah Perdue would actually give him the time of day.

"I'm Ms. Perdue, with the Powell Private

Security and Investigation Agency," she told him. "I'm here to ask you a few questions about your obsession with the movie *Midnight Masquerade*."

He stared at her as if she were speaking a foreign language, then burst into laughter. "You're kidding, right?" His bloodshot, watery brown eyes narrowed as he ran his gaze over Perdue's body, pausing at her breasts.

"She's not kidding." Derek stepped forward, coming up beside her.

Hines's smile vanished when he saw Derek. "You a private dick, too?" He inclined his head toward Perdue. "You with her?"

"Yeah, I'm with Ms. Perdue. And we'd like to ask you a few questions."

"Maybe I don't want to talk to you," Hines said. "Maybe I just want to talk to her." He grinned lasciviously at Perdue.

"I'm sure that can be arranged, a private talk between the two of you," Derek said. "But you should know that the lady carries a ten-shot Ruger P93. And I've seen her at target practice. She's good. Damn good. Besides that, I've heard that she can disarm an opponent twice her size without breaking a sweat."

Perdue glanced over her shoulder at Derek and barely restrained the smile twitching the corners of her mouth.

"You're not cops, just PIs." Hines frowned. "I don't have to talk to you."

"No, you don't have to talk to us," Perdue said. "But one call and I can have the Carey PD out here in ten minutes flat. If you'd rather talk to them—"

"Who hired you?" Hines looked from Perdue to Derek. "One of them bitches from that movie? Writing fan letters isn't against no law. I haven't done nothing illegal."

"Would you prefer to have this conversation out here for all your neighbors to see and speculate about, or would you rather invite us in?" Derek asked.

Hines glanced around and saw that several of the trailer park's occupants were milling around outside their trailers and doing their best not to be conspicuous about their curiosity.

"Come on in." Hines stepped back inside his trailer and left the door open.

The interior, though shabby and cluttered, looked and smelled fairly clean, which surprised Derek. Hines swiped a stack of magazines off the sofa and copies of *Playboy*, *Penthouse*, and *Hustler* scattered over the floor.

"Take a load off." Hines pointed to the seen-better-days plaid sofa.

Derek waited for Perdue to sit and then he sat beside her, leaving a couple of feet between them, making sure he didn't invade her personal space.

"Before I answer your questions, I want you to answer mine—who hired you?"

"Our agency represents the families of two of the

*Midnight Masquerade* actors," Perdue said. "You probably know the actors as Dewey Flowers and Woody Wilson."

"Dewey Flowers," Hines sighed. "Now there is one sweet piece of . . ." He caught himself before finishing the vulgar expression and looked right at Maleah. "I've had more than one wet dream *starring* Miss Flowers, believe you me." His puzzled expression scrunched his face. "Did her family hire you to track me down and warn me to stop writing her? 'Cause that's all I've done—just write her some letters telling her how much I like her."

"When was the last time you wrote to Ms. Flowers?" Derek asked.

"Hmm . . ." Hines rubbed his thumb over the beard stubble darkening his chin. "Sometime last year. Never heard back from that one."

"You didn't happen to send any letters to her home address this year, did you? Letters telling her that she was going to die?" Perdue focused directly on Hines.

"Hell, no! Is that what's going on here? Somebody's written Miss Flowers and threatened her? It wasn't me. Swear to God, it wasn't. I wouldn't harm a hair on that pretty little head of hers. Besides, where would I get her home address?"

Derek's gut told him Duane Hines was probably telling the truth. No doubt he was a sexual deviant and an altogether reprehensible human being, but those undesirable qualities did not make him a murderer.

Derek and Perdue exchanged brief looks that he interpreted to mean they were in agreement about Hines. And ten minutes later, they left the trailer park and headed back to the airport where they would eat supper and catch a night flight to Laredo.

Once on the road a few miles from the trailer park, Derek broke the silence between them. "My educated guess is that whoever our killer is, he has the means to buy airline tickets from wherever he lives to Knoxville, Memphis, and Arizona."

"Yeah, I agree. And Hines looks like he doesn't have two nickels to rub together."

"Our killer isn't necessarily wealthy, but not only does he have to have enough money for airline tickets and enough to afford the fancy masks he left on each victim, but possibly fake ID, disguises, and hotel rooms. And he has to be able to take time away from his job."

"Travis Dillard could afford to pay for airline tickets to just about anywhere and it's possible he still owned the masks used in the movie."

"You aren't allowing your prejudice against Dillard to form your opinion of him, are you?" Derek asked.

"Maybe," Perdue admitted. "But I say we cross Hines off our suspects list or at the very least move him to the bottom. And for now at least, we put Dillard at the top of that list."

"I agree," Derek said. "For now. But I figure Dillard's physical condition would make it difficult for him to carry out the murders."

"Difficult, but not impossible. Besides, he has enough money to hire a professional."

"We agree again." Derek grinned. "Amazing, isn't it, how much we're beginning to think alike. We may wind up being best buddies after this case ends."

Keeping her eyes glued to the road ahead, she replied, "No way in hell."

Lorie lifted her gaze from the article in *Tea Time*, a magazine for tea party enthusiasts, and glanced across the room to where Shelley Gilbert sat immersed in a paperback novel. She had taken off her jacket before dinner, but she still wore her shoulder holster.

Lorie folded a page in the magazine—an advertisement for a teapot vendor—and laid the magazine aside. At the beginning of the year, Lorie and Cathy had decided to branch out at Treasures and include tea party items and perhaps even in the future rent the empty store next door to their antique shop, renovate it, and use it as a tearoom.

She missed Cathy and would be glad when she returned from her honeymoon. Four more days. But she dreaded having to tell her best friend what was happening in her life. In less than two weeks, her whole world had been turned upside down.

Because her life had been threatened, she now had a 24/7 bodyguard.

As if sensing Lorie was looking at her, Shelley glanced her way and smiled. Lorie returned her smile and said, "I'm thinking about fixing myself a root beer float before bedtime. Want one?"

"Make that a Seven-Up float for me, if you have Seven-Up. I'm not a big root beer fan."

"One Seven-Up float and one root beer float it is."

Shelley got up, laid her book in the chair, and followed Lorie into the kitchen. Lorie entered first, stopped dead still and gasped. She hadn't yet turned on the overhead light and the only illumination came from the dim hallway sconces and the three-quarter moon shining through the kitchen window.

"What is it?" Shelley asked quietly as she paused behind Lorie.

"I could've sworn I saw someone outside peeking in the kitchen window."

"Are you sure?"

"No, I'm not sure. It could have been my imagination. I've been pretty jumpy lately, but—"

"You stay here," Shelley told her. "I'm going out the back door and I want you to lock it behind me."

"Be careful," Lorie said.

Shelley pulled the 9mm from her shoulder holster, eased open the door, and walked onto the back porch. Doing as she'd been instructed, Lorie locked the door. But she pulled up the Roman shade covering the glass top half of the door and peered out into the darkness. Shelley left the porch and entered the yard. Lorie held her breath.

"Stop or I'll shoot," Shelley called loud and clear.

Oh God! What if Shelley had caught the killer? She checked her watch. Nine fifty-eight. Nowhere close to midnight. But maybe he'd been casing her house, checking out her comings and goings, and ascertaining the danger in trying to get past her bodyguard.

Suddenly, from out of nowhere, Shelley reappeared, a man about five-ten walking slowly in front of her, his hands held high above his head in an I-surrender-don't-shoot gesture.

"Call nine-one-one," Shelley shouted. "I've caught our intruder."

After she sent a patrol car to Lorie's house, the dispatcher had called Mike. He had contacted his mother, asked her to come over and spend the night to look after Hannah and M.J., and then he had broken the speed limit from his house to Lorie's. When he arrived, Deputy Buddy Pounders opened the door for him.

"What have we got here?" Mike asked.

"Ms. Gilbert caught the guy red-handed," Buddy said. "He was snooping around outside the house."

"Was he armed?"

"No, sir, not unless you consider a camera a weapon."

"A camera?"

"I'm a reporter," a voice called out loudly.

"The guy's a reporter for the *Huntsville Times*. He showed me his credentials. He's legit."

Mike stomped into the living room, where he found Shelley Gilbert standing over a cowering young man sitting on the sofa, a look of sheer terror on the guy's face. Then Mike scanned the room and found Lorie standing in the arched double doorway that led into the dining room.

"Are you all right?" he asked.

She nodded. "Just a little shaken up."

Mike turned around and glared at the reporter. "What's your name?"

"Ryan Bonner, sir."

"What the hell did you think you were doing sneaking around outside Ms. Hammonds's home? Do you realize that at the very least, she can charge you with trespassing?"

"Yes, sir. I—I was just trying to snap a few pictures of Ms. Hammonds without her knowing it. And I thought maybe I might overhear the ladies' conversation. I really need an exclusive in order for the paper to hire me as a full-time reporter."

"What sort of an exclusive did you think you'd find here?" Mike asked, hoping his gut instincts were wrong about why this guy wanted a story on Lorie.

"Hey, it's no secret that something's going on, that Ms. Hammonds has a bodyguard. And don't ask me how I know. I don't have to reveal my sources."

"You're right, you don't. But you do have the right to call a lawyer."

"Are you going to arrest me?"

"That depends."

"I won't be bullied into not writing my story," Ryan said. "I've done my research about Ms. Hammonds, you know, or should I call her Cherry Sweets? That was some *sweet* centerfold she posed for, but nothing to compare to that movie she made."

Mike saw red. Literally. The rage inside him boiled over and it took every ounce of his self-control not to punch Ryan Bonner in the mouth.

# Chapter 13

"Buddy!" Mike bellowed the deputy's name.

"Yes, sir?"

"Escort Mr. Bonner down to headquarters."

"You can't arrest me!" Bonner shouted.

"Take him in for questioning." Mike grinned. "And by all means, let him call his boss at the *Times* or his lawyer or anybody else he wants to call. But under no circumstances is Mr. Bonner to be released tonight. Understand?"

"Yes, sir."

"This is police harassment," Bonner whined.

Mike turned his back on Bonner while Deputy Pounders led him to the patrol car. He knew there wasn't anything he could do to stop the gung-ho reporter from writing an exposé about Lorie's past. It wasn't as if her years in LA were a big secret. But after being back in Dunmore for nine years and slowly making a life for herself here, Lorie had earned a second chance, at least with the townspeople. But if Bonner retold Lorie's old story—from hometown beauty queen and talent contest winner to *Playboy* centerfold and porno star—tongues would start wagging and the ladies from the WCM would get riled up all over again. Lorie would become the center of attention for all the wrong reasons.

He paused outside the front door, his thoughts a mixed jumble that he needed to straighten out before seeing Lorie again.

Did he really believe she deserved a second chance? Yes, of course she did.

Just not a second chance with him.

*Damn it, man, you want her. You know you do. Every time you see her, all you can think about is how it used to be between the two of you. You want to touch her. Hold her. Kiss her. Make love to her.*

What he wanted and what was good for him were two different things. Lorie was all wrong for Sheriff Michael Birkett and his two children.

He had to keep things on a professional level;

otherwise, he'd wind up in a sticky situation that could damage his career and wreak havoc on his personal life. And he could wind up hurting Lorie more than he'd already hurt her.

Taking a deep breath, Mike reached for the door handle, opened the door, and walked into the house. He found Lorie pacing the floor in the living room and Shelley Gilbert standing guard. Both women turned to face him.

"Buddy is taking Mr. Bonner to headquarters," Mike said. "If you want to press charges for trespassing or—"

"Does he know about the death threats?" Lorie asked.

"I'm not sure, but I don't think he knows anything specific other than the fact you have a bodyguard."

"How could he have found out?"

"Any number of ways," Mike said. "Maybe one of your neighbors snooped around and found out what's going on or even somebody working for me might have inadvertently let something slip and it got passed on. It's hard to keep secrets in a small town."

Lorie sucked in a deep breath and released it slowly.

"I can hold Bonner overnight for questioning, but that's it unless you press charges. And I'm not sure you want to do that."

"Why wouldn't I?"

"He knows about your alter ego, Cherry Sweets," Mike told her.

God, how he hated the pain he saw in her eyes. "Bonner wants to do an exposé on you—then and now—in the hopes it will get him a promotion to full-time status at the *Huntsville Times*."

"He can't do that! He has no right," Lorie said. "I'll hire Elliott Floyd and threaten to sue him and the newspaper if they print one word about my past."

"You can do that and you probably should, but you have to know that if what they print is the truth—"

"Their version of the truth." Lorie wrapped her arms together around her waist in a hugging gesture and closed her eyes.

Shelley cleared her throat. "If you can stick around for a while, Sheriff, I need to contact the agency about this," Shelley said. "We'll want all the info on Ryan Bonner we can get. And we'll want it now." She glanced at Lorie, who stood in the middle of her living room, a dazed expression on her face. "I won't be long, okay?"

Lorie nodded. "Okay."

When they were alone together, Lorie sad and on the verge of tears, Mike's male instincts urged him to comfort her.

*Talk to her. Reassure her. But don't touch her.*

"Just when I thought things couldn't get any worse, this had to happen." Lorie looked at him.

"Not only do I have a serial killer who intends to make me one of his victims, but I have a zealous reporter who plans to exploit my life story in order to get a promotion." She laughed, the tone despondently mocking. "What's that old saying about if not for bad luck I'd have no luck at all?"

"I'm sorry. I wish I could do more to help you."

"You really mean that, don't you?"

"Yeah." Mike took a tentative step toward her and then halted when she was within arm's reach. It would be so easy to pull her into his arms, to hold her against his body, to brush his lips over her temple, to tell her he'd die before he would let anyone harm her. "You've got twenty-four/seven protection with Ms. Gilbert, and between her and the patrol car I've assigned to keep watch shortly before and after midnight every night, you're relatively safe. As for that damn reporter—everybody in Dunmore already knows about the *Playboy* spread and the porno movie."

Lorie swallowed. "My illicit past has come back and bitten me in the ass big-time. No matter what I do, how hard I try to be a good person, how much penance I pay, I can't obtain a pardon."

"Don't." He reached out to her, his hand hovering over her shoulder. "Don't do this to yourself."

"What's the matter, Sheriff, don't have the stomach for watching my self-flagellation?"

His hand fell away, down to his side, as he kept

211

his gaze focused on the agony he saw in her eyes. "I don't know what to say. Tell me how I can help you."

"Don't you dare feel sorry for me! I don't want your pity."

"Damn it, Lorie, don't be so stubborn."

She threw up her hands in an I-give-up gesture. "Why did I ever think this town would allow me to live down my past when the man who once professed he would love me forever, no matter what, can't forgive me?"

"Lorie, please . . ."

"Please what? Understand why you feel the way you do? Do you have any idea what it's like to look into the eyes of the man you've loved since you were sixteen and see nothing but disgust and pity?"

He stared at her, momentarily unable to speak or move, while her words soaked into his brain. Her words—*the man you've loved since you were sixteen*—played over and over in his head. Surely she didn't mean that she still loved him. How could she love him after the way he had treated her all these years?

"Please leave," Lorie told him. "I appreciate everything the sheriff's department is doing to help me, but from now on I don't see any reason for you to stay personally involved."

"I . . . uh . . . I'll let Ms. Gilbert know that I'm leaving," Mike said, unable to think of anything else to say.

Lorie rushed past him and down the hall toward her bedroom. Mike clenched his jaw tightly. He had handled that all wrong. But then him doing that with Lorie wasn't something new. He had been handling his feelings for her in the wrong way ever since she returned to Dunmore.

Why hadn't he listened to his mother and to Molly years ago when they had both encouraged him to forgive Lorie?

"She ruined her life and practically destroyed herself in the process," Molly had told him. "And she lost you." His wife had caressed his cheek. "How horrible for her. I can't imagine what it would be like to lose you."

"You'll never lose me, sweetheart."

She had smiled at him, that beautiful smile that he still saw every day whenever he looked at his son.

"You should be kind to her," Molly had said. "Go to her, tell her that you forgive her, that you'll be her friend."

His Molly had been kind and generous. Despite the fact that in the beginning, she had felt threatened by Lorie's return, she had overcome her fears and found it in her big, loving heart to plead with him to forgive Lorie.

He would have done anything for Molly, especially during the final year of her life, but that one thing—forgive Lorie. Molly had to have known what it had taken him years to figure out, that his inability to forgive Lorie had as much to do with him still loving her as it did with him hating her.

*Molly, Molly. I'm sorry, sweetheart, if I ever gave you any reason to doubt how much you meant to me. I loved you. I miss you every day.*

"You're still here?" Shelley Gilbert asked as she walked into the living room. "Lorie said you were leaving."

"I was just going," he replied.

Shelley nodded.

"Is she all right?" He glanced down the hallway.

"Not really. She was crying, but doing her best not to."

"Take care of her."

"That's my job."

"There will be someone outside for the rest of the night," Mike said.

"Thanks. I think we'll be okay."

Mike let himself out, went to his truck, and got in. He sat there behind the wheel for several minutes, then finally started the engine and backed out of the driveway.

Lorie came awake abruptly, her body trembling, her thoughts in utter chaos. The nightmare had seemed so real. A masked figure in a black cape had chased her through downtown Dunmore in broad daylight. She had been completely naked. Exposed. Ridiculed by the outraged citizens, led by the ladies from the WCM. And Mike had stood on the corner, his arms crossed over his chest, a condemning glare in his dark eyes, and done absolutely nothing to help her. She screamed, pleading with him to save her. The masked stalker had grown larger and larger until his form blocked out the sun, leaving her hovering in a shadowed corner, weeping, frightened, and waiting for death.

Allowing herself a few minutes to shift from the horror of her nightmare to the safety of reality, Lorie sat up, tossed back the covers, and slid to the edge of the bed. She sat there, her bare feet on the floor, and considered the meaning of her dream. It made a weird kind of sense. The masked stalker was the unknown killer who posed a danger to her life. Mike's disregard for her was no mystery. And the utter fear that she had felt was perfectly normal, considering she was marked for death.

After getting out of bed and slipping into her house shoes, she found her robe at the foot of the bed and put it on. The bedside clock read 3:50 A.M. The last time she had noted the time, it had been shortly after midnight.

She had cried herself to sleep.

If she were alone in the house, she'd go to the kitchen and make coffee. But she didn't want to wake Shelley.

Moonlight streamed in through the windows, casting a soft, creamy glow across the floor. She followed the moonlit path to the windows and looked outside at the front yard. Her heart caught in her throat when she saw the familiar truck parked in her driveway. Mike's Ford pickup. What was he doing there? Had he been there all night?

She didn't want him there, didn't want him standing guard over her house, over her. Damn him, why couldn't he just go away and leave her alone? She didn't need him. Didn't want him.

*Liar!*

Securing the tie belt of her robe around her waist, Lorie opened her bedroom door and tiptoed down the hall. Before she reached the living room, Shelley called to her.

"Lorie? Are you all right?"

"I'm fine. Just restless. Go back to sleep."

"If you're up, I'm up."

"I'm sorry. I didn't want to disturb you."

Wearing a pair of gray sweatpants and an over-sized Georgia Bulldogs T-shirt, Shelley walked toward Lorie.

"Mike's outside," Lorie said.

"He's been there all night."

"I'm going out there to tell him to go home."

"I can do that for you."

"No. I want to talk to him."

Shelley nodded. "I'll disarm the alarm system and watch you until you reach his truck."

"Thanks."

For a few seconds, Mike thought he was hallucinating. He had been thinking about Lorie, remembering how it had once been between them, worrying about the danger she was now in, wishing he could erase every bad thing that had ever happened to her. And now here she was walking down the sidewalk, coming straight toward his truck. As she approached, he debated whether to open the door and step outside to meet her or just wait for her.

He waited.

She pecked on the window. He rolled down the window and looked at her.

"What are you doing here?" she asked, her tone none too friendly.

"It's not even four o'clock yet." He answered her with a question. "What are you doing up at this time of the morning?"

"We need to talk."

"Do we?"

"Unlock the passenger-side door," she told him.

"Okay."

She rounded the truck's hood, opened the door, and climbed into the cab. Turning sideways, she faced him. He laid his arm across the back of the seat, his hand almost touching her shoulder.

"Shelley told me that you've been parked out here all night."

"She's right. I have."

"Why?"

"Why what?" he asked.

"I have a private bodyguard. I don't need you hovering over me."

"I'm not hovering. You were inside. I was outside. Plenty of distance between us. You're the one who knocked on my door and invaded my space."

"Don't do this," she told him. "Don't blow hot and cold. It's not fair to me. It took me a long, long time to accept the fact that we could never be anything to each other ever again, not even friends. Your concern for me now is sending me mixed signals. I can't handle that."

"I'm sorry. It was never my intention to—"

"To feel sorry for me, to show me a little human kindness."

"To confuse you," he corrected.

"Well, I am confused. Not just about you, but about me, and about this whole damn mess that my life has become."

Unable to stop himself, he moved his hand a couple of inches until he touched her shoulder. Apparently taken off guard, she jumped and then went rigid. Their gazes met there in the semidark interior of the truck cab, which was illuminated only by the moonlight.

"I don't want anything bad to happen to you," he said. "I keep hurting you even though I don't mean to . . . not anymore. I—I guess if I'm completely honest, I have to admit that I'm confused, too. I've hated you for such a long time. Now . . ."

"Now?"

"Now I don't know for sure, except I know I want to keep you safe. I want to protect you from the person who's threatened to kill you, from guys like Ryan Bonner, from the censor of every narrow-minded prude in Dunmore."

She sat there staring at him, her eyes wide with wonder, her mouth slightly parted. "You have a hero complex, you know that, don't you?"

He chuckled. "Yeah, I guess I do. I used to be your hero, didn't I?"

When he squeezed her shoulder, she scooted closer and reached up to lay her hand over his.

"Once upon a time . . ." Her voice trailed off to a whisper. "You were everything to me, my hero, my lover . . . my life."

"My mother told me that the reason I hated you so much was because a part of me still loved you," Mike admitted.

Lorie remained completely silent.

"I think Molly agreed with Mom."

"Oh, Mike."

"Molly knew I loved her, that I'd never betray her. We had a good life together. She gave me two fantastic kids. If she were still alive . . . I wish you could have known her. You two would have liked each other. It's my fault that you never got the chance to . . ." He swallowed hard. "I'm sorry, Lorie, sorry for so much."

She brought his hand to her lips, turned it palm side up, and kissed the center of his open hand. Her kiss burned like fire. He closed his eyes for a second and prayed for strength.

Easing his hand from her gentle grasp, he said, "No more mixed signals, no more confusion."

She looked at him with hope in her eyes. His next words erased that hope.

"A part of me does still care," he admitted. "And I'd be lying if I said that as a normal, red-blooded man, I didn't want you. But . . . we can't . . . I can't . . . I have to think about Hannah and M.J. and what's best for them. They have to come first."

"I understand."

"Do you?"

"My sordid past makes me unsuitable step-mother material."

"God, Lorie, I'm sorry."

"So am I."

She pulled away from him, opened the door, and jumped out of the truck. He sat there and watched her hurry up the sidewalk and back into her house.

"Damn, damn!" He beat his clenched fists against the steering wheel.

# Chapter 14

After the unsettling night before, Lorie had decided not to open the shop until eleven, so she was still at home when the phone rang at ten fifteen that morning. She looked down at the portable phone on the kitchen counter and checked the caller ID. She didn't recognize the caller's name. Anthony Johnson.

Shelley glanced at her and then at the phone.

"Let the answering machine get it," Lorie said.

After the fourth ring, the answering machine clicked on, with Lorie's voice reciting her number and asking the caller to leave a message.

"Lorie, if you're there, please pick up," a female voice said. "It's Shontee, Shontee Thomas."

Lorie grabbed the phone off the base. "Shontee?"

"Thank the Good Lord you're there. I can't tell you how much I need to talk to you. I'm about half out of my mind and know you must be, too. Somebody from the Powell Agency called me this morning, asking me if I'd gotten any threatening letters, telling me that somebody sent Dean, Hilary, and Charlie letters and then killed them."

Lorie remembered Shontee as a bubbly, fun-loving girl with huge brown eyes and an infectious laugh. They hadn't known each other very long— they met during the filming of the one movie they'd made together.

"Then you've received the letters, too?" Lorie asked.

"Yeah, four of them," Shontee replied. "My fiancé hid them and didn't show them to me until yesterday. Good thing he did or when the Powell Agency called this morning, I wouldn't have known what they were talking about. They said that they're contacting everyone who was involved with *Midnight Masquerade*."

"Did whoever you spoke to tell you that I've

hired the Powell Agency and so have Dean's brother and Hilary's husband? We've hired them to do an independent investigation to find out who sent the letters and killed Dean, Hilary, and Charlie."

"That's one of the reasons I'm calling—Tony, my fiancé, wants us to be part of this deal. He says we need to be in the loop on all the info."

"I agree with your Tony. The more we all know, the better off we are. It's too late to save Dean and Hilary and Charlie, but the rest of us can band together and help one another. The Powell Agency should be working for all of us."

"Do you have a bodyguard?" Shontee asked.

"Yes, I have someone from the agency with me twenty-four/seven. I'm sure they can provide a bodyguard for you."

"Tony's already taken care of that. He keeps several bodyguards on his payroll. He's a nightclub owner, and rich men like him need protection. Oh, Lorie, I wish you could meet my Tony. He's a great guy and I'm crazy about him."

"It sounds like you've really turned your life around. I'm happy that you found someone special. You deserve to be happy."

"So do you. Whatever happened with that old boyfriend? Did you two get back together? I figured you were married by now and had a couple of kids."

"It didn't happen," Lorie said. "I'm still single."

"What about the guy?"

"He married someone else."

"Ah, that's too bad."

"Shontee, be careful, will you? The letter writer has killed three people already. The FBI will probably become involved. They're looking at this guy as a serial killer."

"I will, and you take care, too, you hear me? And when this is all over and they've put him behind bars, you'll get an invite to my wedding. We're based in Atlanta, so we're not that far from you there in Alabama, a five-hour drive at most."

"I'll be there," Lorie said. "Nothing will keep me away."

After her conversation with Shontee ended, she turned to Shelley. "Have you heard anything from Maleah and Derek? Maleah promised to keep me updated, but I haven't heard from her yet."

"I haven't heard from her personally. But then they wouldn't call me directly with any information they uncover. They would contact the agency and probably speak to Mr. or Mrs. Powell."

"Did you know that the agency is getting in touch with everyone connected to *Midnight Masquerade*? That was Shontee Thomas. She got a call this morning."

"Forewarned is forearmed," Shelley said. "Yes, I knew Powell's intended to try to contact everyone involved with the movie. I believe they're starting with the actors, since so far the ones killed were actors."

"So they think all the actors may have received letters and are in danger?"

"That's what we need to know."

"Why would the killer warn us? It doesn't make sense."

"The killer warning his victims in advance shows a great deal of either stupidity or monumental ego or possibly both."

Suddenly a thought occurred to Lorie, a reason why the killer might forewarn them. "He wants to frighten us, doesn't he?"

"Most definitely. He probably derives a great deal of satisfaction from knowing everyone will now take his threats seriously."

"He's killed one person each month this year, in January, February, and March. It's April now, so that means he'll kill again, doesn't it?"

"Unless he's found and stopped, yes, he'll kill again."

Maleah and Derek crossed the border into Mexico a little after noon that Wednesday. They had flown into Laredo, grabbed a quick bite of lunch, and rented a Jeep. An hour later, they entered the town of San Pedro, little more than a large village rich in colonial character. The town square consisted of a fountain and a statue of what appeared to be a Catholic priest wearing a hooded robe. A block off the main street that ran through town east to west, they saw men hawking hats and trinkets and boys offering to shine shoes.

"In a town this size, finding the hotel where Kyle Richey works shouldn't be a problem," Maleah said as she maneuvered their rental onto a back street.

"You're right. That's it up ahead. The yellow building on the right."

A large, faded sign hanging over the entrance read HOTEL GARCIA. The colonial era structure, painted a cheerful sunshine yellow, possessed a welcoming façade. A couple of young boys, probably no older than twelve, rushed toward the Jeep the moment Maleah parked in front of the hotel. Both began jabbering quickly, too quickly for Maleah to understand much of what they said. Her Spanish was so-so at best, and local dialects left her baffled.

Derek got out of the Jeep, pulled two five-dollar bills from his pocket, and handed one to each of the boys. Maleah understood that he had paid them to keep an eye on the Jeep and figured that had been his way of getting the pesky kids to leave them alone.

The interior of Hotel Garcia surprised her. The lobby floors were a colorful terra-cotta tile and the wooden staircase boasted an elaborately carved balustrade. The very pregnant clerk behind the check-in desk rose from the chair where she was sitting and flipping through a magazine. She looked up and offered them a wide, welcoming smile.

225

"Welcome to Hotel Garcia," the woman said in heavily accented English.

"We're looking for a man who works here," Maleah said. "Kyle Richey."

"Is he here now?" Derek asked.

"*Sí, sí.* Kyle is here." She turned and looked at the closed door directly behind her. "In his office."

Maleah and Derek exchanged glances. "Please tell Mr. Richey that we would like to speak to him."

She nodded. *"Sí."* She knocked on the door, called out "Kyle," and opened the door.

A tall, slender man with shoulder-length brown hair secured in a ponytail rose from behind an old wooden desk and spoke to the woman in Spanish. They conversed briefly and the man, whom Maleah recognized from old photos, came out into the lobby.

"I'm Kyle Richey," he said. "I'm the manager here at Hotel Garcia. How may I help you?"

"Mr. Richey, I'm Maleah Perdue and this"—she nodded to Derek—"is my associate, Derek Lawrence. We work for the Powell Private Security and Investigation Agency based in Knoxville, Tennessee."

Richey grunted. "Did one of my ex-wives hire you to track me down?"

"No, sir," Maleah replied. "We're here concerning the recent murders of three actors you worked with when you were a cameraman for Starlight Productions."

Richey frowned. "Who was murdered? Dare I hope it was that bastard Sonny Deguzman?"

"Mr. Deguzman was not one of the victims," Derek said, "but considering your past history, I can see why you might want the man dead."

"Yeah, I wouldn't shed a tear if someone had bumped him off."

"The victims were Dean Wilson, Hilary Finch, and Charles Wong." Maleah studied him closely, examining his response.

"Damn! Wilson was okay, I guess, even if he was every bit as much a prima donna as Hilary. Those two were a match made in hell." He chuckled. "And everybody liked Charlie. What the hell happened to them?"

"I believe I told you that they were murdered," Maleah said.

"Who killed them?"

"We don't know. We were hoping you might be able to help us with our investigation."

"Hey now, you don't suspect me, do you? The only body I had anything against was Sonny. And he isn't dead, is he?"

"What about your ex-wife, Charlene Strickland? Considering the fact that you nearly killed her when you discovered she was having an affair with Sonny and wound up spending several years in prison for assault, I would imagine you still harbor some ill will toward her."

Richey's face flushed. He glanced at the hotel

clerk. She came to him and slipped her arm around his waist.

"Luisa knows about my past." Richey placed his hand over the woman's protruding belly. "I've made a new life for myself since my release from prison four years ago. Luisa and I got married and we're expecting our first child in about three weeks. I've put the past in the past. I have no reason to want to harm anybody connected to my days as a cameraman with Starlight Productions."

"I'd like to believe you," Maleah said. "Can you account for your whereabouts since the first of the year? Have you made any trips across the border, say to Tennessee or Arizona?"

Luisa began speaking rapidly in Spanish. Richey hugged her to him and whispered softly. She stopped talking immediately and smiled at him.

"I haven't left Mexico in well over a year. Hell, I haven't left San Pedro since before Christmas when I took Luisa to Mexico City to visit her folks."

"Let's say that we believe you." Derek looked directly at Richey. "We can eliminate you as a suspect, but not necessarily as a potential victim. Have you received any threatening letters recently?"

"Threatening letters?" Richey looked genuinely puzzled by the question.

"Some of our victims all received letters telling them that they were going to die," Maleah said. "As have other actors who were in *Midnight Masquerade*."

"Well, I'll be damned. No, I haven't gotten any threatening letters. Maybe whoever is doing the killing is just after the actors."

"Possibly," Derek said. "Any chance you'd know someone from your past who would have a reason to want to kill the actors from that particular movie?"

Richey shook his head. "Not really. Unless, of course, Travis Dillard actually followed through with some threats that I heard he made."

"Explain," Maleah said.

Richey shrugged. "It was years ago. But word was that when Hilary quit the business, Dillard threatened her. She was his biggest star and everybody knew he was hung up on her. He would have married her in a heartbeat, if she'd have had him. Could be he finally made good with his threat and he killed the other two to make it look like Hilary was just one of several victims."

"Interesting theory," Derek said. "You know Dillard's dying, don't you? Stage four pancreatic cancer."

"Wish I could say I was sorry, but what goes around comes around. Dillard treated me okay, I guess, but the man was a real SOB."

Maleah couldn't agree with Richey more. Dillard was a real SOB. But he had no history of violence, where on the other hand, Kyle Richey did. He had almost killed his ex-wife, Charlene

229

Strickland, another *Midnight Masquerade* alumna. Was it possible that his theory of killing several people to cover up the motive for a single murder was his idea and that Charlene was his real target?

Mike could have sent one of his deputies to inform Lorie that Hicks Wainwright had recommended to his superiors that an FBI task force be formed ASAP. And it was possible that the Powell Agency already knew and had informed Shelley Gilbert.

As he stood on the sidewalk outside of Treasures of the Past, he tried to rationalize his reasons for being here. He was just doing his duty as the county sheriff. Jack and Cathy would appreciate him taking a personal interest in Lorie's case.

*Yeah, sure, whatever you have to tell yourself.*

Just as he reached to open the door, a customer came out of the shop, someone he recognized, but he couldn't recall her name. The woman paused, smiled at him, and said, "Afternoon, Sheriff."

"Afternoon," he replied, still unable to remember exactly who the middle-aged woman was.

Glancing inside, he noticed Shelley busily running a feather duster over a section of china and glassware that occupied several antique cabinets arranged in the left back corner on a raised platform. From that vantage point, she could see just about every square foot of the shop, including the checkout counter. He suspected that whoever had leaked the info about Lorie being under twenty-four/seven protection hadn't realized the trouble they had caused. He figured that at least half of the small crowd milling around inside the shop were curiosity seekers and not customers. Gossip traveled fast in these parts. It was only a matter of time before the entire town knew. And if—make that when—Ryan Bonner convinced his boss at the *Huntsville Times* to run the exposé on Lorie that he had planned, everyone in north Alabama would follow the story of the former *Playboy* centerfold whose life was being threatened by someone from her sordid past.

Mike walked over to the checkout counter where Lorie was busy wrapping a silver tea service in bubble wrap.

"Busy afternoon," he said.

"You should have been here earlier," she told him. "When Shelley and I arrived at eleven, we had a block-long line waiting to get in."

"Selling much?"

"More than I thought I would. Mostly small stuff, knickknacks and such. Of course, my feeling like a bug under a microscope has been an added bonus. Apparently a lot of the folks I know and some that I don't are curious to see what a real bodyguard looks like. I think Shelley has been a disappointment to most of them. They were probably expecting some big, broad-shouldered guy wearing sunglasses and an earpiece and brandishing a semiautomatic."

Mike grinned. "Glad to see you haven't lost your sense of humor."

Returning his smile, she gently placed the wrapped tea set items into a heavy cardboard box and set the box under the counter. "I have a customer who wants this shipped to her daughter in Birmingham as a birthday present."

Mike nodded. "I've got some good news and some bad news."

"Good news first, please."

Mike leaned across the counter and lowered his voice. "Special Agent Wainwright is contacting his superiors and requesting a task force be formed. Now we'll have not only the Powell Agency hunting down the killer, but the FBI, too."

"The more manpower, the better. Right?"

"Right."

"Do I want to hear the bad news?" she asked.

"This morning, Ryan Bonner's boss at the *Huntsville Times* sent one of the newspaper's legal eagles to represent our overeager reporter. We had to release Bonner."

"Then he's free to write his exposé."

"I'm afraid so, if his boss gives him the green light."

"As if knowing someone plans to kill me isn't bad enough, now I'm faced with the possibility that my daily life will become a living hell again," Lorie whispered as she glanced around to make sure no one overheard her.

Mike knew she was as aware as he was that all of her customers were watching the two of them. To a person, everyone in the store pretended to be shopping while they strained to overhear their conversation.

Suddenly Lorie clapped her hands together, the action momentarily startling Mike and gaining everyone's attention. "Ladies"—glancing around, she spotted four men scattered about in the shop—"and gentlemen, I have an announcement. As most of you know, I'm Lorie Hammonds, one of the owners of Treasures of the Past. I'm sure all of you know our sheriff, Mike Birkett."

Mike threw up his hand as he looked around the shop at all the inquisitive faces. He had no idea exactly what Lorie was up to, but whatever it was, apparently he was right smack-dab in the middle of it.

"But there's someone here y'all don't know," Lorie told them. "Shelley, wave at the folks, will you?" Taken by surprise, a what-the-hell-are-you-doing? expression on her face, Shelley waved the feather duster. "Shelley is my bodyguard. You'll be seeing her here at the shop every day. She'll be with me wherever I go. She carries a big gun and knows how to use it. She's been hired to protect me. It seems that my wicked past has finally caught up with me and somebody wants to see me dead."

The crowd buzzed with excitement, everyone

talking at once, the din growing louder by the second.

"Why the hell did you do that?" Mike demanded.

"I honestly don't know," Lorie admitted. "It just felt right."

As Shelley made her way through the crowd of at least twenty-five customers, everyone she passed took several steps back, as if they weren't a hundred percent sure she wouldn't use her big gun on them.

Mike cleared his throat. "Show's over for today, folks. If you're buying something, line up and check out. If you're not buying anything, please exit through the front door. Ms. Hammonds is closing up shop"—he glanced at his wristwatch—"in ten minutes."

"Shutting me down, Sheriff?" she asked, a deceptively perky smile curving her lips. "Afraid I'll cause a riot?"

He ignored her and turned to Shelley as she approached. "I think you should take Lorie home and let her calm down. She's not thinking straight at the moment. Otherwise she wouldn't have made a public spectacle of herself."

"I'm thinking perfectly straight, thank you very much," she told him. "And if you think that little confession was making a public spectacle of myself, then just stick around until I do show-and-tell."

"Sheriff Birkett is right," Shelley said. "I don't

know what set you off, but you are acting irrationally."

Lorie huffed. "Two against one. It's not fair." She giggled.

"Damn," Mike cursed under his breath. "Escort her out the back way and take her home," he told Shelley. "I'll get rid of all these people and close up the shop."

"Isn't he forceful and commanding," Lorie said to Shelley. "My big, strong hero."

"Get your purse, Lorie," Shelley said. "We're doing as the sheriff suggests and going home now."

Lorie retrieved her purse from beneath the counter, pulled a key chain from inside, and tossed it to Mike. "Lock up for me, honey." Then she turned around and went through the shop and out the back way, with Shelley at her side.

"Sorry, folks, I'll have to ask everyone to leave the shop now. Please do so quickly and orderly," Mike said.

When the customers began leaving, following his instructions, Mike heaved a deep sigh of relief. He hadn't seen Lorie act this way since they were teenagers and she'd gotten royally ticked off. The young Lorie had been a firecracker, her actions emotional and often illogical. She reacted first and thought things through later. That specific personality flaw had been what had prompted her to go to LA seventeen years ago, believing that fame and fortune awaited her. Not until it was too late had she realized that she'd chosen to walk a tightrope without a safety net under her.

The woman needed a keeper. Always had and always would.

There had been a time when he would have gladly taken that job, taken it for a lifetime. But that was then and this was now.

# Chapter 15

On Saturday morning, Special Agent Hicks Wainwright held a press conference in Birmingham announcing the formation of a task force that would investigate three recent murders believed to be the work of a serial killer. He kept the facts to a minimum, stating that the two of three murders occurred in Tennessee and the third in Arizona. When asked, he gave the names of the three victims, but did not elaborate on anything about them or their deaths.

Mike Birkett sat in his den, his television tuned in to Birmingham's ABC 34/40 station, and watched the interview as he drank his fourth cup of coffee. Wainwright had phoned him late last night to tell him about the scheduled interview.

At 7:00 A.M., Hannah and M.J. were both still in bed. Saturday was the one day of the week during the school year they could sleep late. In his effort to be a good parent, Mike censored what his kids watched on TV, but with him being the sheriff, he had found it impossible to shield them from the local news reports. If they didn't see it on TV and he didn't explain what was going on, one of their classmates was bound to fill them in. And more often than not, they were misinformed and he'd have to go into more detail than he liked in order to correct the erroneous facts.

"Is there a specific reason you were chosen to head the task force?" a female reporter asked Wainwright. "You work out of the field office here in Birmingham and none of these murders occurred in Alabama."

"I can't be specific concerning the reasons I was chosen," Wainwright told her. "But I want to reassure the citizens of our state that we believe the general population is in no danger from this killer. We have reason to believe he—or she—has targeted someone in Alabama, as well as several other states. And before anyone asks, no, we will not release the identities of the potential victims to the media."

"Even if you can't give us their names, can you tell us anything else about these potential victims?" a bespectacled, white-haired reporter asked.

"No, I'm afraid not."

"Then what can you tell us about why the FBI believes the killer is targeting these particular people?" a familiar voice called out from the crowd of TV, newspaper, and magazine reporters.

The camera panned across the media swarm and stopped on the speaker.

"Son of a bitch!" Mike cursed under his breath.

There stood Ryan Bonner, all five feet ten inches of brash and inquisitive trouble. Big trouble.

"In order to protect those involved, I'm afraid that information must remain classified." Wainwright pointed to another reporter, who had held up his hand and waved frantically.

Before his colleague got out a single word, Ryan Bonner called in a loud, demanding tone, "Isn't it a fact that the three victims were former adult film stars and that the potential victim in Alabama is also a former porno actor?"

"No comment," Wainwright said and pointed again to the other eager reporter.

"Any comment on the fact that the one film the three victims and our Alabama connection have in common is titled *Midnight Masquerade*?" Bonner shouted.

"Again, no comment." Wainwright visibly tensed as the camera zeroed in on two agents who approached Ryan Bonner and escorted him out of the press conference.

Mike cursed again, mumbling the obscenities to himself. Everybody in town knew the title of Lorie's one and only movie. And now it was simply a matter of time before that damn eager beaver reporter, Bonner, put the information in the newspaper for everyone to read about, think about, snicker about. Lorie would have to relive the shame of her past all over again, just as she had when she had first returned to Dunmore.

Freedom of the press could be a double-edged sword, cutting down the guilty and the innocent alike. And in Lorie's case, the guilty who had already paid for her past sins.

Maleah and Derek had flown out of Laredo late yesterday and arrived in Fayetteville, Arkansas, last night. On their assignment to question all the possible suspects on their short list, they were zigzagging across the United States and had detoured into Mexico yesterday. Today, they would question Casey Lloyd, who had coauthored the script for *Midnight Masquerade*. The Powell report on the guy read like a soap opera. Boy genius pens first novel at eighteen, hits the *New York Times* bestseller list, and is hired to coauthor the script when his novel is optioned for the big screen. Lloyd became the toast of New York and LA. By the age of twenty-four, unable to repeat the phenomenal success of his first novel, he was a has-been wonder boy with an expensive cocaine habit. After a series of dismal failures—a novel and several movie scripts—Lloyd gladly accepted Travis Dillard's offer to work with the semifamous pornography writer Laura Lou Roberts, who had starred in numerous "stag" films in the seventies.

A knock on her hotel room door snapped Maleah from her thoughts.

"Perdue, let me in," Derek said. "I've got coffee and Danish."

Overcoming the urge to check her appearance in the mirror, Maleah tromped barefooted across the room, unlocked and unlatched the door, and looked from Derek's smiling face to the sack he held in his hand.

How the hell could he look so fresh and chipper this early in the morning? It was barely eight o'clock. Obviously, he had already showered, shaved, ironed his slacks and shirt, and gone downstairs to pick up their breakfast.

As he entered the room, he glanced at her casually. She cringed, knowing full well what she must look like in her baggy pajamas and with her hair uncombed. So, why should she care how she looked? It wasn't as if she wanted to impress the man. God forbid.

He set the sack down on the corner desk, opened it and pulled out two Styrofoam cups. "This one is yours." She accepted the cup from him. "I've got bear claws and apple and cherry Danish."

She snapped open the spout on the coffee cup's plastic lid, took a sip of the hot brew, and sighed. "I'll take the cherry Danish."

After placing his cup on the desk, he pulled a stack of napkins from the sack and laid them on the

240

desk; then he tore open the sack and spread out the selection of goodies.

"Griff called." Derek pulled out the desk chair and sat.

"When?" Maleah picked up a napkin and the cherry Danish and took the armchair to the left of the desk.

"On my way downstairs to get breakfast for us."

"And?"

"And the FBI is now officially involved. Special Agent Hicks Wainwright is heading the task force. He made an announcement to the press this morning outside the Birmingham field office."

"What does this mean for our private investigation? Did Griff change our orders?"

Derek shook his head. "Nope. Griff said to stick to the plan, send in a daily report, and if anything comes up he thinks we should share with the Bureau, he'll notify them."

"So we're still going to talk to Casey Lloyd today?"

"If he shows up for his weekly SAA meeting," Derek said. "Otherwise, we'll have to track him down since we haven't been able to find a home address for him."

Maleah took a big bite out of her Danish, savored the sweet taste, and then hurriedly washed it down with several sips of the sweet coffee. It really irked her that Derek remembered how she liked her coffee.

"How does a guy go from being a teenage literary genius to a thirty-five-year-old recovering drug and sex addict?" Maleah wondered aloud.

"Bad luck. Poor choices. Fate. Who knows?" Derek picked up a bear claw and immediately chomped into it.

"What did you tell Griff when he called?" she asked.

Derek stared at her questioningly.

"About your professional assessment of the three possible suspects that we've interviewed," she explained.

Derek took a swig from the coffee cup, set it down on the desk, and wiped his mouth with a napkin. "I told him what I told you—that I think Travis Dillard is capable of cold, calculated murder. And he's smart enough to pull off killing three people without leaving any evidence to link him to the crimes. Duane Hines is a couple of bricks shy of a load, but I doubt he's a killer. Besides, he doesn't have the money for plane fare and elaborate masks."

"I don't think Kyle Richey would risk destroying the life he's built with his new wife," Maleah said. "Just my opinion, of course. I don't have your credentials as a profiler."

"I agree. Besides, Richey's the type who would kill in the heat of passion. He's not the cold, calculating type who would plan and execute a series of murders."

"That means for the time being, Travis Dillard is our chief suspect."

"The agency is checking on his whereabouts when each of the murders took place. If he has a concrete alibi for just one, he's not our guy. Unless he hired a hitman."

"After we talk to Casey Lloyd today, that leaves only one more person on our interview list. Grant Leroy, the director."

"Actually, Griff added another name to the list."

Maleah widened her eyes and glared at Derek. "You'd think Griff would inform me of what's going on. After all, I am the Powell agent. You're just a consultant."

Derek chuckled. "I'm sure Griff didn't think twice about giving me the info. He knows we're working as a team on this case and we share everything." He winked at her. "Well, just about everything."

Maleah groaned.

"Where's your sense of humor, honey?"

"Do not call me honey!"

"Yes, ma'am, Ms. Perdue."

Maleah scowled at him. "Who did Griff add to the list?"

"His name is Tyler Owens, but he's actually not a suspect. His mother is Terri Owens, aka Candy Ruff. When Powell's tried to contact his mother to warn her about the murders and find out if she had received any letters, he explained that his mother had recently had a stroke and is recovering in a rehab center. He asked for the interview. He has three letters that were sent to his mother. He thinks receiving these letters contributed to her stroke."

"And we're going to waste our time interviewing him because?"

"Because he said he thinks he might know who the killer is."

Shelley Gilbert's call came into the sheriff's department at exactly 9:35 A.M. and two patrol cars were sent out immediately to Lorie Hammonds's home.

When Mike showed up at 10:05, he found the situation worse than he had imagined. He had expected to find reporters from the local newspaper and TV station and possibly a few nosy neighbors. But what he drove smack-dab into was pure bedlam. A horde of at least fifty people had congregated in Lorie's yard and the road in front of her house. When he got out of his truck, he counted six different TV cameras and a dozen photographers taking snapshots of the house, the crowd, and the uniformed officer guarding the front door. Mike assumed another patrolman was at the back door.

As he made his way through the mixed rabble of reporters and townspeople, Mike spotted more than a dozen faces he instantly recognized. He knew these people. They had voted for him. Two of them went to church with him.

"It's Sheriff Birkett," someone yelled and all heads turned to search for him in the crowd.

One cameraman zeroed in on him and the accompanying reporter called out a question. "Sheriff, is it true that you were once engaged to Ms. Hammonds?"

Someone else shouted, "Is she as hot in the sack in real life as she is in *Midnight Masquerade*?"

Mike clenched his jaw tightly. *Do not react. Do not respond. Don't let anyone goad you into saying or doing anything stupid.*

When he didn't reply to either question and continued walking toward Lorie's house, people gradually fell back enough to clear a path for him. A rumbling hush fell over the throng. He stepped up on the porch and spoke to the officer at the front door.

"I'm going in to see Ms. Hammonds," Mike told the deputy. "I'll be back out in a few minutes and make a statement. Until then, do your best to keep things under control. But under no circumstances is anyone to get any closer. If anyone tries to get on the porch, pull out your pistol to show them you mean business. That should be enough of a deterrent."

The deputy said, "Yes, sir."

Mike rang the doorbell and called, "It's Mike Birkett."

The door eased open. The crowd went wild, yelling questions and accusations that quickly blended together into an unintelligible roar.

Mike slipped inside quickly and closed the door behind him. Shelley faced him with a grim expression.

"Where's Lorie?"

"I'm here." She walked out of the shadowed corner of the dim hallway.

It broke his heart to see the hurt in her eyes. He couldn't comfort her, couldn't gently pull her into his arms and hold her. He didn't dare.

"This is all Ryan Bonner's doing," Mike said. "That little shithead might as well have shouted your name at Wainwright's press conference."

"He called," Shelley said. "Special Agent Wainwright. He got in touch right after the press conference to check on Lorie."

"Yeah, I spoke to him a few minutes ago and filled him in on the situation," Mike told them. "He's on his way to Dunmore right now."

"The phone has been ringing off the hook," Lorie said. "Shelley finally disconnected every line in the house."

"I'm sorry about this." Mike walked over to Lorie.

She stared up at him, her chin tilted defiantly, her expression one of steely determination. "I am not going to grovel and beg forgiveness for past sins. Not again. I've spent nine years paying penance. That's more than enough. From here on out, I don't give a damn what anyone in this town thinks of me." She looked him right in the eye. "And that includes you."

• • •

Sex Addicts Anonymous Arkansas Pioneer Saturday Group met every week at 10:00 A.M. at the Alano Club. Since the sessions were closed meetings, Maleah and Derek arrived at 568 West Sycamore shortly before 11:00. Armed with arrest photos of Casey Lloyd from four years ago when he had been picked up for possession of an illegal substance, Maleah and Derek waited outside the building. At five after, a mixed group of men and women straggled out, a few at a time, some talking and laughing, others scurrying away alone.

"There he is," Derek said.

"Casey Lloyd," Maleah called out to him.

A Pillsbury Doughboy–round man with puppy-dog brown eyes and fat, rosy cheeks threw up his hand and waved at Derek and Maleah.

"You missed the meeting," he said as he approached them. "The New Hope group meets on Wednesday nights or you can come back next Saturday. But I'd be happy to talk to you now, if you need immediate help."

"We're here to speak to you, Mr. Lloyd," Maleah told him. "We're not interested in your SAA group."

He glanced from one to the other, eyeing them speculatively. "What's this about?"

"If you would prefer to talk in private—" Derek said.

"I'm good here."

"Okay. That's fine with us," Maleah said. "I'm

Maleah Perdue and this is Derek Lawrence." She explained they worked for the Powell Agency and told him the bare facts about the recent murders. "By any chance you haven't received any threatening letters, have you?"

"No, I haven't, but I don't actually have an address either. I . . . uh . . . don't have a place of my own. I sleep most nights at one of the local church shelters, and during the week, I pick up whatever odd jobs I can find."

"When was the last time you left Fayetteville?" Derek asked.

"Christmas," he replied immediately. "My parents sent me a bus ticket and I went up to Bella Vista for the holidays with my family. And before you ask, yes, they've offered for me to come home and live with them, but . . . I've broken their hearts and disappointed them too often to risk it again. I take things one day at a time now, but I can't promise my parents or my sisters that I'll stay clean and sober and walk the straight and narrow from here on out."

Apparently Casey Lloyd, like Duane Hines, didn't have the financial means that would have enabled him to buy plane tickets and elaborate masquerade masks.

"Is there anyone you can think of from when *Midnight Masquerade* was filmed who would have a reason to want to see the actors in that movie dead?" Maleah asked.

"I have no idea. I really didn't get to know the actors all that well. When I coauthored that piece-of-trash script, I was high half the time."

"Were you sleeping with any of the actresses?"

"Laura Lou kept me on a pretty tight leash," Casey said. "The lady was my coauthor, my keeper, my lover, and my drug supplier. She'd have cut off my balls if I'd slept with another woman."

"Was Ms. Roberts a violent person?" Derek asked. "Would she be capable of cold-blooded murder?"

"That bitch?" Casey laughed. "She'd be capable, but she's a little long in the tooth to do the job herself. She'd hire a hit man if she wanted anybody killed. But I can't think of any reason she'd want to kill Dean or Hilary or Charlie. Travis Dillard is another matter. She'd love to see that old son of a bitch six feet under."

"There was bad blood between Mr. Dillard and Ms. Roberts?" Maleah asked.

"They had a business deal—she wrote the scripts for his movies for a little of nothing and she got a percentage of the take. Then Dillard and his lawyers screwed Laura Lou out of God knows how much, but she kept writing for him because nobody else would hire her until a few years ago."

"If Dillard was the victim, then Ms. Roberts might be our prime suspect," Derek said. "But he's very much alive, at least for now."

"What do you mean at least for now?"

"Travis Dillard has terminal cancer," Derek explained.

Casey grinned. "Maybe there is a little bit of justice in this old world after all."

By late afternoon, the crowd outside Lorie's house had dispersed, leaving behind cigarette butts, drink cans, and a variety of debris littering her yard and the road in front of her house. The flower beds on either side of her walkway had been trampled and the antique white wrought-iron settee in her backyard garden had been moved directly under a window, used by two peeping Tom reporters trying to see inside her house.

Mike had persuaded most of the townsfolk to leave, but it had taken a warning from Special Agent Wainwright to get rid of the press. At least temporarily.

"They'll be back," Wainwright had told her. "One at a time or in small groups. Your story is big-time news now that they know you're one of the Midnight Killer's potential victims."

"The Midnight Killer?"

"That's what the press is calling him, and it seems appropriate."

"Then y'all are sure it's a man?"

"Reasonably sure. Most serial killers are male."

*Most but not all,* Lorie thought. What if they were wrong? And what if, no matter what the FBI and the Powell Agency did, they couldn't keep the killer from getting to her?

"Lorie? Lorie . . ." Mike called her name several times before she snapped out of her thoughts and looked at him.

"Sorry, I was . . . It doesn't matter."

"Are you certain that you want to go to Jack and Cathy's homecoming party?" Mike asked. "It's only a small gathering, but—"

"I am not going to allow the media or the good citizens of Dunmore to make me a prisoner in my own home. My best friend is returning from her honeymoon this evening and nothing is going to keep me from being there to welcome her and her husband home."

"Then you'll go with me," Mike told her. "Ms. Gilbert, too, of course."

"That's not necessary," Lorie said. "If you show up with me, people will talk."

"Let them talk. If you're escorted by the sheriff, you'll be safer from the press and from anyone thinking about stalking you when you leave the house." He grinned. "Remember, I have the authority to arrest people, and for most folks that alone is a deterrent."

"Aren't you planning to take your girlfriend to the party?" Lorie asked.

Mike hesitated, and then cleared his throat. "Abby can pick up the kids and meet us there."

"What's she like?"

"Abby?"

"Yes, Abby." Not for the world would she tell Mike that his children had practically come out and told her that they didn't like Abby Sherman, the woman he had been dating on a fairly regular basis for several months.

"She's a really nice person. In many ways, she reminds me of Molly."

Molly, the woman who had taken her place in his heart and in his life. Molly, who had given him two beautiful children. Molly, who, in death, had been elevated to sainthood, at least in Mike's eyes. If Abby Sherman reminded him of his late wife, then she had to be damn near perfect.

"I look forward to meeting her," Lorie said.

Mike stared at her, a puzzled look in his dark blue eyes.

"If she makes you happy, I'm glad."

"What about you, Lorie, are you happy?" he asked, then quickly amended his question. "Were you happy before this mess with the threatening letters and—?"

"I was content," she told him. "It took me a long time to reach that point."

"I'd like to see you happy. I hate what happened today. I hate that people can be so cruel and unforgiving. In the past, I was one of those people. I wanted to hurt you the way you had hurt me."

"You did."

"I know."

"Mike?"

"Huh?"

"Don't ever settle for anything less than the real thing," she told him. "Don't convince yourself you should marry Abby Sherman or any other woman because she'd make a good wife and mother or because she reminds you of Molly. When you get married again be sure it's for the right reason."

"For love?" He grunted. "I've been in love twice in my life and I lost both of those women. I think the next time around, I'll gladly settle for something safer. Friendship, loyalty, fidelity, mutual respect."

The doorbell rang and a loud rapping on the front door followed immediately.

"Stay here," Mike told her.

Shelley came into the room from where she had been in the kitchen making a private phone call to Powell headquarters. While Mike headed for the front door, Shelley walked over and stood by Lorie.

Mike eased open the door. A uniformed deputy stood on the porch. Lorie sighed with relief. But her relief was short-lived.

"Sorry to bother you, Mike, but I knew you'd want to see this." He lifted his right hand and held up a single piece of paper. "Somebody has circulated these all over Dunmore. They're plastered to walls and telephone poles and even street signs."

Several choice profanities shot out of Mike's mouth in rapid succession.

"What is it?" Lorie asked, her pulse racing, her gut instinct telling her that whatever it was, it was bad news.

Mike turned and held up the paper so that she could see it. Oh, God, she'd been right. It was bad news. The single sheet was a printer copy of her *Playboy* centerfold. Lorie Hammonds, naked, smiling, posing seductively.

# Chapter 16

When he had phoned Abby and explained the situation, she had been far more understanding than he'd thought she would be.

"I'll be more than happy to pick up the children and bring them with me to Jack and Cathy's party," Abby had told him. "I think it's very brave of Ms. Hammonds to actually show up tonight. It's terrible the way people are talking about her, calling her all those awful names. Even though what they're saying about her is true."

He told himself that Abby's last comment hadn't been a catty remark about a woman she saw as a rival. If she were any other woman . . . But she wasn't. She was Abby. She didn't have a mean or hateful bone in her body; if anything she was too nice.

Mike knew he could have gotten one of his deputies to escort Lorie and Shelley to the party. Several of the deputies were Jack's buddies and would be there anyway. What had started out as a small get-together for a dozen or so people had wound up a big celebration with a guest list totaling more than forty.

Standing on Lorie's porch, showered, shaved, and wearing his best khaki pants and blue button-down, Mike hesitated before ringing the doorbell. Although both he and Lorie knew the real reason he was here to pick her up this evening, the whole thing seemed too much like a date to suit him. Memories from their teen years played in his mind like an old newsreel. Images of Lorie at sixteen when he had taken her to the junior/senior prom. Flashes of other dates over the years, a smiling Lorie eagerly welcoming him.

Steeling his nerves, he rang the doorbell.

Shelley Gilbert opened the door. "Come on in, Sheriff Birkett."

"Call me Mike." He walked into the house and glanced around, looking for Lorie.

"She'll be out in a minute, Mike," Shelley told him.

He nodded. "Had any more trouble from the reporters?"

"Not so far. I've seen several cars slow down as they passed the house, and somebody stuffed the mailbox with those *Playboy* centerfold flyers."

"Chief Ballard and I assigned crews from his office and mine to clean up those flyers as best they can. And if anyone is seen putting them out, they'll be arrested."

"That's good." She paused as if considering whether or not to say more. "But you and I both know that the damage has been done. Those flyers have accomplished their purpose."

"Yeah, you're right."

Lorie emerged from the hallway and glanced from Shelley to Mike. "Sorry to keep you waiting. I'm ready to go now."

Mike stared at Lorie. How was it possible that she was more beautiful now, at thirty-five, than she had been at eighteen? She honest to God took his breath away. She'd pinned her hair up, leaving dark rust-red curls framing one side of her gorgeous face. Her sleeveless beige dress hugged every voluptuous curve of her hourglass body and the heels she wore added three inches to her petite height.

Realizing that he hadn't been able to take his eyes off her since she entered the room, Mike hurriedly looked away and said, "We'd better get going if we want to arrive before the bride and groom."

"You two go on outside," Shelley said. "I'll set the alarm and lock up."

Mike escorted Lorie to his truck, opened the door, and gave her a hand up and into the cab. He waited for Shelley, and after she settled in, he rounded the hood and hopped up and into the driver's seat. Lorie sat in the middle, her shoulder brushing his right arm and her hip pressed against his.

*God, give me strength to control my reaction to Lorie's body touching mine. I sure as hell can't walk into the party with a hard-on.*

The three of them drove into town, a quick fifteen minute trip, in relative silence. Idle chitchat didn't seem appropriate. When they arrived at 121 West Fourth, cars lined both sides of the street. Mike pulled in behind a black Navigator, got out, and helped the ladies from the truck. They barely made it to the front door before Jack's Corvette pulled into the driveway.

"It's them," Lorie said.

The honeymooners emerged from the antique Vette, Jack's arm around Cathy's waist, both of them smiling.

"What's going on here?" Jack asked as he and his bride stepped up on the front porch.

"A welcome-home party that got a little out of hand," Mike replied as he reached out to shake his old friend's hand.

Lorie and Cathy hugged each other and then clasped their hands together, squeezing tightly, before letting go.

"You two look great," Lorie said.

"Apparently married life agrees with both of you," Mike added.

"Honeymoons agree with us." Jack grinned. "You should try it." He glanced from Mike to Lorie.

Ignoring the subtle reference to former lovers

reuniting, Mike opened the front door. "We'd better get you two inside before the party moves out here on the porch."

As Jack and Cathy entered the house, Cathy paused and looked at Shelley. "Hi, I'm Cathy Cantrell . . ." She laughed. "Correction. I'm Cathy Perdue. I don't believe we've met."

"I'm Shelley Gilbert."

"Shelley works with Maleah," Lorie said.

"Where is that sister of mine?" Jack asked.

"On assignment," Shelley told him.

Jack smiled and nodded, but Mike could tell that he suspected something was wrong. "You'll tell me later, right?" Jack whispered, for Mike's ears only.

"Sure thing," Mike said.

Jack clutched Cathy's hand and led her to the connecting double front parlors where most of their guests were congregated. The moment she saw Seth, she hurried toward him, her arms outstretched. Mike noticed the way Lorie watched as mother and son embraced—with a wistful look in her eyes. Did Lorie want a child? Did she regret—?

*Damn it! Don't think about what might have been.*

Mike caught a glimpse of Abby on the far side of the room, trapped in a conversation with Reverend Patsy Floyd, who was no doubt trying to persuade Abby to help with the Interfaith Youth Council that

258

Patsy had founded. The idea was for children and teens from various religions to meet once a month in a social setting that fostered understanding of and tolerance for one another's religious doctrines. He knew that Abby didn't totally approve of the fact that he allowed Hannah and M.J. to attend the monthly meetings.

"They're too young to be exposed to false doctrine," Abby had warned him. "You don't want them believing everything they're told."

"I'm not worried," Mike had said. "My children are being brought up in the same church I've attended all my life. I have confidence in their ability to choose the right path. But I want them to learn to be understanding and tolerant of people who are different from them. It's what Molly would have wanted. She had the biggest, kindest, most understanding heart of anyone I've ever known."

Abby had agreed with him, of course. She always did, easily changing her opinions to mimic his. Even though her physical appearance and generally sweet disposition reminded him of Molly, she didn't possess Molly's spunk. If Molly believed in something or someone, you couldn't change her mind easily. In that way, Molly had reminded him of Lorie.

Mike cast a quick glance around the room and noted that Lorie, with Shelley at her side, was talking to his mother. A tight knot formed in the pit

259

of his stomach. What could she and his mom possibly have to talk about? Nothing too serious, he figured, not from the way they were both smiling. He shouldn't stare too long. People would notice. People would talk. It was bound to happen now that the whole town knew the sheriff's department was involved in the Midnight Killer case. He figured people were already speculating as to just how involved he was in personally looking after Lorie.

*It's high time you paid attention to your date for the evening.*

He made his way across the room and slipped his arm around Abby's tiny waist. She was almost too thin. If not for her well-defined muscles, achieved through a strenuous exercise program, she would look unhealthy.

"Hello, sweetheart." She kissed his cheek.

He smiled. "Thanks for bringing the kids."

"As a matter of fact, I didn't bring them," she told him. "It seems your mother decided to come tonight and insisted on the children coming with her."

Mike knew for a fact that his mother had not planned on coming to the party. Only yesterday, she had told him that the arthritis in her hips was acting up and she was having to use her cane again.

"I'll see the doctor Monday and get one of those cortisone shots and I'll be just fine," she had assured him.

So what had happened to change his mother's mind?

"How are you, Mike?" Patsy Floyd asked. "I guess this Midnight Killer situation is keeping you pretty busy. We've heard all about it, of course, now that the FBI is involved. I'm terribly concerned about Lorie. Thank goodness she not only has a bodyguard, but she has you, too." Patsy looked from Mike to Abby. Her face flushed. "I mean in your capacity as the sheriff, of course."

Mike forced a smile. "Yes, ma'am."

"I'm very proud of Mike," Abby said. "He takes his duties as the county sheriff seriously. We can all sleep soundly in our beds at night knowing that he's in charge."

"Thanks for the vote of confidence, honey."

"If you two will excuse me, I want to say hello to Jack and Cathy," Patsy said. "Have you ever seen two happier people in your life? They're both simply glowing. There's nothing like being crazy in love, is there?"

Left alone with Abby, Mike managed to keep his strained smile intact. While she talked to him, he tried to listen and respond, but eventually, he allowed his gaze to casually drift around the room. When Abby said something about their plans for Sunday dinner tomorrow after church, he nodded agreement and kept smiling. Once again locating his mother's whereabouts in the gathering of Jack and Cathy's friends, he noticed how she held on to the handle of her walking stick and leaned slightly sideways, allowing the cane to help support her weight. She smiled broadly as she watched his son and daughter attach themselves to Lorie, one on either side of her. Lorie wrapped her arms around M.J.'s and Hannah's shoulders and began talking to them.

Just when had his children gotten so friendly with Lorie? Last year after he found out that she saw them every month at the Interfaith Youth Council meetings, he had warned her to stay away from them. But he hadn't told his kids to stay away from Lorie. After all, what reason could he have given them? The woman is evil? She wasn't. That she wasn't a proper role model for anyone, least of all his young children? That might have been true at one time, but for the past nine years, Lorie had lived an exemplary life.

Dunmore was a small town. His kids were bound to run into Lorie occasionally. And she had told him quite honestly that if and when she saw his children, she would not ignore them. And during the preparations for Jack and Cathy's wedding— he and Lorie both members of the wedding party —he had noticed how much his children liked Lorie. Especially Hannah.

But something else was going on and he felt certain that whatever it was, his mother had something to do with it.

Nell Birkett could be a devious woman when it

came to doing what she thought was best for her children and grandchildren. She had always liked Lorie, and as much as she disapproved of the choices Lorie had made in her late teens and early twenties, Nell had never bad-mouthed Lorie. Not to him or anyone else. When Molly was alive, his mother's allegiance had been to his wife. But after Molly's death, when he had started dating again, his mom had suggested he give Lorie a call. If anyone other than his mother had made that suggestion, he would have told them what they could do with it. But he had never spoken disrespectfully to his mother and never would.

"That's not ever going to happen." He had barely managed to keep his temper under control as he'd made his feelings perfectly clear. "And please, Mom, don't ever say her name to me again."

Was his mother using his own children as a means to reunite him with Lorie? He wouldn't put it past her, not if she had decided that Lorie was the right woman for him. But how could she believe that, especially now when the whole town had been reminded of Lorie's sordid past?

"I'm going over to talk to the kids," Mike told Abby.

She laced her arm through his. "I'll go with you."

There was no way to get out of taking Abby along with him. When they approached his mother and children, Lorie slowly dropped her arms from around M.J.'s and Hannah's shoulders.

"Well, there you are," his mother said. "We were just telling Lorie about Humphrey."

"Yeah, and Lorie said she had a pet rabbit, too, when she was a kid," M.J. told him.

"His name was Cottontail," Hannah added.

"Not very original, I admit." Lorie smiled warmly at both children, and then her gaze met Mike's. "Did your dad ever tell you about his pet raccoon?"

"No, he didn't," M.J. said, a cocky little grin on his face.

"Tell us, Daddy, tell us." Hannah tugged on his sleeve.

"Lord have mercy." His mother laughed. "His dad tried to tell Mike that he couldn't tame that wild thing, but he wouldn't listen."

"I'm surprised that you didn't catch a disease of some kind," Abby said. "Most animals are terribly nasty. I'm sure you learned that your father was right, didn't you, dear?" She snuggled against his side. "Wild animals are best left in the wild."

M.J. and Hannah frowned at Abby.

Before Mike could respond, his mother said, "Actually, it didn't take Mike long to have that raccoon eating out of his hand. He's always had a knack for gentling the wildest creatures."

When his mom gave Lorie a sidelong glance, Mike could have strangled her. Abby's perpetual smile wavered. Lorie looked downright embarrassed. And Mike didn't know what to say or do to ease the tension his mother's comment had created.

"Tell us about the raccoon, Daddy." Hannah tugged on Mike's arm again.

Lorie glanced around the room as if searching for someone, then said, "If y'all will excuse me, I want to find Cathy and bring her up to date on Treasures of the Past business." Before waiting for anyone to respond, she escaped. Shelley Gilbert, who had been standing nearby and being as inconspicuous as possible, followed Lorie.

Mike watched them until they disappeared into another room. Only then did he realize that not only were his children demanding details about his childhood pet raccoon, but Abby had been watching him watch Lorie. And his mother stood there smiling, looking as innocent as the day she was born.

Cathy actually found Lorie and not the other way around. In truth, Lorie had used Cathy as an excuse to make a hasty retreat. The last thing she wanted was to cause trouble between Mike and Abby Sherman. Apparently, Mike liked the woman a great deal; otherwise he wouldn't have been dating her and only her for several months now. Neither the fact that his mother obviously felt she was the wrong woman for him nor the fact that his children seemed to dislike her was any of Lorie's business. Mike's personal life was strictly off-limits to her. She had given up any rights she'd had to Mike seventeen years ago.

"There you are." Cathy discovered Lorie hiding out in the kitchen. "What are you doing in here all alone?"

"I'm not alone." Lorie nodded toward the open door that led to the adjacent mudroom. "Shelley's out there. She got a phone call, probably from the Powell Agency."

"Why didn't you call me and tell me what was happening?" Cathy asked. "Jack and I could have cut our honeymoon short and come home immediately."

"That's the reason I didn't want you to know." She looked Cathy in the eye. "How did you find out so quickly? You haven't been home fifteen minutes."

"Buddy Pounders just told Jack. As soon as Jack told me, I started searching for you so we could talk. I'm your best friend and yet I'm one of the last to know that your life is in danger."

"I'm sorry, but I refused to allow this insanity to intrude on your honeymoon. Besides, there was nothing you could have done. There's nothing you can do now."

Cathy grasped Lorie's hands. "I want you to move back in here and stay with us, you and Ms. Gilbert."

"No. I'm fine at home. Really. Shelley provides around-the-clock protection and Mike's seen to it

266

that for several hours around midnight every night, a deputy is stationed outside the house in a patrol car. There's no way I could be any safer. Besides, I do not want to run the risk of putting you and Jack and Seth in harm's way."

Cathy squeezed Lorie's hands. "They will catch him and put him away where he belongs. I'm sure of it."

Offering her friend the best confident smile she could muster, Lorie pulled free and said, "You're absolutely right. Not only is the Powell Agency involved, but the FBI has formed a task force. The killer doesn't stand a chance."

Cathy returned the smile, hers more fragile and uncertain. "I couldn't help but notice that Mike escorted you here this evening."

"It wasn't anything personal. After the press showed up at the house this morning and somebody distributed flyers of my *Playboy* centerfold all over town and half the county, Mike thought it was a good idea for him to bring me here tonight."

"He could have gotten Buddy or one of the other deputies to escort you."

"I suppose he could have, but—"

"If there's a silver lining inside this horrible cloud you're living under, it just might be Mike realizing how much he still cares about you."

A gasping laugh erupted spontaneously from Lorie's lips. "I'm not going there. I will not wish for the impossible or hope for something that can never be. I've wasted too much of my life waiting for Mike Birkett to forgive me."

"Never say never. In my wildest dreams, I wouldn't have thought that Jack and I would ever get a second chance. But we did. And it could happen for you and Mike, too."

"You didn't disgrace yourself publicly the way I did. You didn't pose naked for a national magazine. And you didn't costar in a porno movie that makes it possible for the whole world to watch you screwing a couple of guys."

"No, my sins were different," Cathy admitted. "But nonetheless unforgivable by some standards. I kept the truth about Seth's paternity from both him and from Jack for nearly sixteen years. My son grew up believing that Mark Cantrell was his father. And Jack never knew he had a son. And yet both Seth and Jack forgave me. Mike will—"

"Never forgive me."

Cathy's fragile smile melted away as she sighed quietly.

Shelley Gilbert cleared her throat. Lorie and Cathy glanced at her.

"Am I interrupting?" Shelley asked.

"No, of course not." When Lorie studied her bodyguard's expression, she felt a sudden uneasiness flutter through her. "Is something wrong?"

"Nothing to do with your case," Shelley assured her, then glanced away, but not before Lorie noted the sheen of moisture in her eyes.

Lorie and Cathy exchanged I-wonder-what-it-is? looks, and then Lorie said, "Is there anything we can do? I mean, you seem—"

"I'm okay." Shelley met their gazes directly and her facial muscles tightened in an obvious effort to retain control. "Nicole Powell called. One of the secretaries at the Powell Agency, a sweet kid—Kristi Arians—was killed tonight. The details are sketchy, but Nic said the Knoxville PD is treating her death as a homicide."

"Oh, Shelley, that's terrible," Lorie said.

"Ironic, huh? A Powell Agency employee murdered. I saw her only a couple of weeks ago. She was showing me her engagement ring."

"Is there anything—?" Lorie asked.

"No, thanks," Shelley replied instantly, not allowing Lorie to finish her sentence. "I'm okay. Really."

She wasn't and they all knew it, but Lorie didn't press the matter. And before either she or Cathy could think of anything to say, Jack entered the kitchen.

"Everybody's asking about you, honey," he said and then suddenly picked up on the strained atmosphere. "Is everything okay in here?"

"Everything's fine." Cathy slipped her arm through his. "I'm ready to go tell our guests all about our honeymoon."

"You don't want to tell them everything." Jack chuckled.

"None of the X-rated stuff, I promise."

As soon as Lorie and Shelley were alone in the kitchen, Lorie said, "We can leave whenever you're ready."

"I don't want you to cut your evening short because I got bad news about a fellow Powell employee."

"I don't mind," Lorie told her. "I wouldn't have come if Cathy wasn't my best friend."

"I'll let Sheriff Birkett know that we're ready to go," Shelley said.

"No, don't do that. Let him stay and enjoy the party. His mother and children and girlfriend are here. I'll tell Cathy and she can let him know later. You and I can just slip out the back door and go home."

Listening to the moans and groans, the cries and sighs of the men and women in the throes of sexual pleasure, he masturbated in a frenzy of excitement. When he sensed that he was on the verge of coming, he closed his eyes, blotting out the laptop screen, and imagined himself as one of the participants. As he climaxed, his ejaculation squirted onto the towel he had placed beneath him. His body trembled with release. He lay there on the hotel bed for several minutes as the after-shocks danced along his nerve endings. And then he got up, walked into the bathroom, and turned on the shower. Naked and beginning to feel

270

ashamed of what he'd done, he stood under the shower and washed himself thoroughly from head to toe.

This time, just as every time in the past, he had been unable to stop himself from being sexually stimulated when he watched *Midnight Masquerade*. He always jerked off, always had a mind-blowing orgasm, and always felt guilty as hell afterward. But no matter how hard he tried, he couldn't stop himself. He was addicted to this movie, its power over him stronger than booze or drugs.

He had lost track of how many old video copies he had destroyed. If only he could have bought every copy in the world. But now the movie had been rereleased—this past fall—on DVD. There was no way that he could escape from the sins of the past. Other people's sins as well as his own. Their wickedness had not only destroyed their own lives, but had brought such unthinkable misery into the lives of the people who loved them. They deserved to die. All of them. Once they were dead, each actor whose evil had tormented him and tempted him all these years, he would be free, wouldn't he? And she would be free, too, her sins atoned for.

After scrubbing himself until his flesh was cleansed, he dried off and dressed hurriedly. He had work to do, important work. That's why he was in Atlanta, why he'd been here for two days, plotting and planning in preparation for tonight's kill.

If she thought her bodyguard could protect her, she was wrong. Killing someone who wasn't on his list had not been a part of his original plan. But in order to follow through and eliminate all of the actors, he now knew he would be forced to kill their protectors. People who guarded the wicked against their rightful judgment were not innocents. They were tainted by association. He felt no qualms about doing whatever was necessary to rid the world of such evil.

He lifted the suitcase, set it on the bed, unzipped it, and flipped it open. There nestled inside was the mask that Ebony O had worn in the movie. She had been the only African American in the film, so she had stood out, her dark beauty a stark contrast to the paler flesh of her costars. Where Dewey Flowers, Lacey Butts, and Puff Raven had looked on film like the sluts they were in real life and Candy Ruff had somehow maintained a look of angelic blond innocence, Ebony O and Cherry Sweets had oozed a raw, earthy sensuality that somehow seemed natural and, oddly enough, even classy.

He knew these actors inside and out because he knew the film inside and out. Years ago he had memorized every line of dialogue and knew by heart every movement and every sound. He had studied their bios, investing time and money into digging deeply into their present-day lives. They had become not only his hobby, but his passion.

*And when they're all dead? What then?*

*I'll be free of my obsession.*

*Will you?* an inner voice taunted him.

# Chapter 17

Mike called her at 10:05 P.M. "We need to talk."

"Go ahead. Talk," she said.

"We need to talk face-to-face."

"Fine. Come by sometime tomorrow."

"It won't wait. We need to talk tonight."

"Has something happened?" she asked.

"Look, we're fixing to leave the party. I have to take Abby home first and then I'll come by."

He hung up before she was able to respond.

At 10:35 P.M., he drove up in the driveway and got out of his truck. Shelley unlocked the front door and let him in, then excused herself and went to the guest bedroom.

The width of the living room separated Mike from Lorie. He stood at the threshold in the foyer and she on the opposite side near the fireplace. They stared at each other, but neither of them spoke for several minutes.

"You left the party without telling me," he finally said.

"I gave Cathy a message for you. I didn't want to disturb you."

"I could have brought you and Shelley home. You didn't have to borrow a car from Cathy."

"Why are you making such a big deal about this?"

He huffed and shook his head. "You're right. I shouldn't have been worried about you. I shouldn't care. I shouldn't have left my girlfriend at her front door with just a kiss on the cheek. And I sure as hell shouldn't be here right now."

Lorie stared at Mike. He was furious. Furious with her? Or with himself?

"Whatever's wrong, whatever has you so pissed off, I'm sure it's my fault, isn't it? It's always my fault." She practically shouted the accusation.

He stomped across the room, his gaze focused on her, his dark blue eyes turning obsidian with anger. She stood her ground, her shoulders squared, meeting him face-to-face or as close as her five feet and one inch could bring her to his face level. If only she hadn't kicked off her three-inch heels when she and Shelley first arrived home.

"It's half your fault," he told her. He was breathing hard, his nostrils flared, his chest rising and falling rapidly. "Hell, it's not even half your fault. You can't help being beautiful and sexy. And it's not your fault the way my body reacts when I think about you."

Her eyes widened as she stared at him in disbelief.

"I thought I could do this—keep things strictly impersonal. I'm the sheriff. You're a citizen of my county whose life has been threatened. It's my duty to protect you."

Speechless, she simply stood there gaping at him.

"But I don't have to personally protect you," he told her. "I have deputies who can do that."

"Yes, you do," she finally managed to say.

"I've got a good life, a job I like, two great kids, a nice, respectable girlfriend."

"Yes, I know."

"Any man would be lucky to have a woman like Abby Sherman care about him."

"Yes, you're right. She's a fine woman."

Live wire tension pulsed between them. Throbbing. Intense. A millisecond from exploding.

"But God help us all, she's not you."

Mike grabbed her shoulders so quickly that she didn't have time to react before his big hands tightened almost painfully on her upper arms. She held her breath. Wanting. Needing. Uncertain what was going to happen. And afraid, afraid for both of them.

She recognized the anguish on his face and sensed the battle of wills going on inside him.

"It's all right," she told him. "If you want to kiss me, kiss me. I know that afterward, you'll walk out that door and nothing between us will have changed."

He closed his eyes and clenched his jaw. She suspected he was praying for the strength to overcome temptation. But God help her, God help both of them, because she didn't want to resist. She wanted him to kiss her, to touch her, to hold her in his arms. One last time.

He yanked her closer, cradled her face with his hands and lowered his head. Every nerve in her body rioted and every cell came vividly alive the moment his mouth touched hers. Tenderly, hesitantly, in direct contrast to the raging passion they both felt, he kissed her. Their mouths mated with gentle longing.

He lifted his head, kissed each cheek and then her forehead before he released his hold on her face and took a couple of steps back and away from her. Breathing heavily, their faces flushed, their bodies hot with arousal, they stood there and looked at each other for an endless moment. And then Mike turned and walked away. She didn't move from the spot until after he'd left her house. Only when she heard his truck pull out of her driveway did she draw a deep, aching breath.

He had parked on a back road that led into the woods behind Lorie's house and carefully crept up to one of the side windows. He often came here in the hopes of catching a glimpse of her naked, but that had happened only once. But once had been enough to show him that her body was still as perfect as the day she had posed for her *Playboy* centerfold.

What he hadn't expected tonight was to find Mike Birkett's truck parked in the drive. Mike shouldn't be here. He had no rights where Lorie was concerned. He didn't deserve a second chance with her, not after the way he'd treated her all these years.

If she'd been his girl, he would have forgiven her for everything she'd ever done wrong. He loved her. He appreciated her for the woman she was. No other man could take care of her the way he could.

*She's mine!*

He wanted to shout it from the rooftops, wanted everyone in Dunmore to know that Lorie belonged to him.

He would never let Mike have her. And he would never let the Midnight Killer claim her for his own.

Shontee had insisted on going to the club with Tony that evening, overruling all of his objections.

"The security here at the house is practically foolproof. You're safer here than anywhere else."

"What can happen?" she had whined. "You've got bouncers at the club, along with your own security team, and Tyrell follows me every step I take, except when I go to the bathroom. Please, Tony, please. I want to go out and have a little fun with you tonight."

"You know I can never say no to you, baby."

She had been going crazy cooped up at home, with no one to keep her company but Tyrell, the big, scowling brute who never said a word to her unless she asked him a question. No doubt Tony had warned him not to get friendly with Shontee. Tony was the jealous type. But Tyrell had taken his job as her vigilant but silent bodyguard to the extreme. He was like a gigantic stone statue hovering over her.

At least here at the Rough Diamond in Atlanta, Tony's first nightclub, she felt free, even with the tight security. Although he'd had to attend to business part of the evening, Tony had spent a lot of time with her. They had shared dinner in his upstairs office suite and then he'd taken her back down to the club and they had danced. He knew that she loved to dance.

They had been on the dance floor for quite a while when one of his flunkies came up to Tony and whispered something in his ear. He nodded to the guy, then let his hands drift down her back until they reached her hips. He caressed her butt as he leaned in and spoke softly into her ear.

"I love the way you feel, baby, and I hate to leave you, but we've got a situation that needs my attention." He motioned for Tyrell, who stood on the edge of the dance floor, a dark shadow keeping watch over her.

Tony escorted her off the dance floor where Tyrell met them. "Take her upstairs." He kissed her cheek. "I'll straighten out this problem and come get you soon. I promise."

Doing her best not to pout—after all, Tony had to take care of business—Shontee went quietly with Tyrell. They took the elevator to the top floor instead of using the stairs. Rough Diamond was housed in a three-story plus basement building that Tony had completely renovated from top to bottom. Although she'd never been in the basement, she knew most of the space was used for storage, a climate-controlled wine cellar, and the center of the club's state-of-the-art surveillance equipment. The club itself covered the entire main level, including two bars, a stage, a dance floor, and the kitchen in the back. The second floor contained small suites used by select clientele for intimate dinners and whatever other pleasures that required privacy. Tony's office and a deluxe apartment took up the entire third floor.

Cocooned inside the elevator, Shontee looked up at the six-six Tyrell. "Do you have any idea what situation Tony had to take care of?"

"No."

Tyrell punched the level three button and the elevator began its ascent.

"Do you think it'll take him very long?" she asked.

"Don't know."

Shontee tapped Tyrell in the center of his chest. He tensed. "Are you sure you're human? I'm beginning to think you're a robot."

He glared at her, but didn't respond.

Suddenly, the elevator stopped at level two. Tyrell stepped in front of Shontee as the doors opened. She had to lean her head to the side in order to see around his wide body. A man and woman, all wrapped up in each other, her kissing him and him pawing her, got on the elevator.

"This elevator is going up," Tyrell said in his deep, no-nonsense voice.

"We don't mind riding up and down, do we, doll baby," the guy said, laughter in his voice.

The redheaded woman's shrill giggles grated on Shontee's nerves. She was long, leggy and bosomy, and no doubt a high-price prostitute. Judging the man from his tailored dress slacks, expensive white shirt, neatly trimmed dark mustache, and the Rolex around his wrist, he was a wealthy businessman.

"I mind," Tyrell said. "Please, get off and wait for the elevator to come back down."

Disregarding Tyrell's request, the man reached around his "date" and hit the Close button. "Sorry, I can't do that."

Several things happened all at once, the events unfolding so quickly that Shontee had no time to react. Tyrell shoved back his jacket to expose his shoulder holster and reached for his pistol. The redhead shrieked at the sight of the gun. The businessman shoved the woman straight into Tyrell and by the time Tyrell pushed her out of the way, the man aimed his own weapon at Tyrell and then fired repeatedly. The redhead screamed. The man turned the gun on her and shot her between the eyes.

Shontee opened her mouth to scream, but nothing came out, not even a whimper. He stepped over the woman's body and around Tyrell's and grabbed Shontee's arm.

"Unless you want me to kill you right now, do not scream and don't fight me. Understand?"

She nodded.

The elevator, which had been climbing from the second to the third floor during the shooting, had stopped and the doors stood wide open.

He pulled her out of the elevator and down the hall toward Tony's apartment. She searched for any sign of cameras connected to the club's surveillance system, but saw none. Perhaps they were well hidden. If this guy was a robber or a rapist, she might come out of this alive. But if he was the person who had sent her the threatening letters, she would soon be dead.

Dead by midnight.

Oh, God, what time was it?

Wearing a pair of red silk pajamas and matching house slippers, Nicole Powell paced the living room floor while she waited impatiently for her husband to finish his telephone conversation with the Knoxville PD detective in charge of Kristi's case. Learning about the death of one of their secretaries who worked for the agency at the downtown Knoxville Powell Building had their household in an uproar. She had personally hired Kristi, a young, vibrant UTC graduate who needed full-time employment while she persued her master's degree in business administration. Everyone who knew the young woman liked her.

"I've made a pot of tea, if anyone would like a cup." Barbara Jean, wearing a green silk caftan that complemented her coloring, wheeled into the living room.

"Thanks. Maybe later," Nic said.

"Is Griff still on the phone?"

"Yes, he's talking to Detective Crawford and hopefully finding out exactly what happened to Kristi."

"Sanders is in the office sending out text messages and e-mails to all the Powell Agency employees." Barbara Jean rolled over to Nic, reached up, and grasped her hand. "Death is always difficult to accept, but it's especially hard when the person is so young."

"You're thinking about your sister, aren't you? Her death was senseless, as is any death at the hands of a cold-blooded killer."

Barbara Jean nodded, squeezed Nic's hand, and let go. "And yet we have no choice but to accept the senseless acts and do what we can to bring the perpetrators to justice. You accepted that as your role in life when you became an FBI agent. And instead of hiding away from the ugly side of life, I chose to work with the man I love, just as you did, to do everything possible to seek justice for those who cannot obtain it for themselves."

"Griff will become personally involved in this case," Nic said. "He thinks of all his employees as part of the Powell Agency family."

"Why don't I pour us some tea," Barbara Jean suggested. "I suspect that it's going to be a long night for all of us."

Just as Barbara Jean steered her wheelchair toward the open double doorway, Griffin and Sanders entered the living room together, the two men—a contrast in opposites with Griff big, tall, and blond where Sanders was medium height, stocky, and dark—deep in conversation. The moment Griff saw Nic, he stopped talking to Sanders and focused on her.

"Kristi was murdered at her apartment," Griff said. "Her throat was slit. Detective Crawford couldn't be persuaded to give me any other details about the murder."

"Do they have any suspects?" Nic asked.

"No."

Nicole knew her husband occasionally used unorthodox methods to obtain the information he wanted, those methods often bordering on the illegal. When she had worked for the Bureau, Griffin Powell and his vigilante agency had been the bane of her existence. Even now, she sometimes had a problem accepting his belief that "the end justifies the means."

"Barbara Jean has made tea," Nic said. "Why don't we all go to the kitchen and begin working on a plan for Powell's to obtain the information we need to find Kristi's killer."

The corners of Griff's wide mouth curved slightly as he gazed at her. "Sanders and I can handle the details, if you'd prefer not to know how and what—"

"I'm not an FBI agent now," she reminded him. "I'm your wife and the co-owner of the Powell Agency. I may not always approve of all your methods, but right or wrong, I want to know about whatever it is that you do to expedite matters."

Griff nodded. "Then let's go to the kitchen, drink our tea, and get down to business."

At 11:53 P.M., Theo Smith, who was monitoring the strategically placed cameras from the basement to the third level of the building, placed a call to Calvin James, the head of Rough Diamond's security team.

"I just picked up a man and woman in the hall on level three outside of Mr. Johnson's apartment," Theo said.

"Mr. Johnson just sent Ms. Thomas upstairs with Tyrell."

"I didn't see their faces, so the lady could be Ms. Thomas, but the man is not Tyrell. He's a much smaller man. And he's white."

"Can you still see them?" Calvin asked.

"No, sir. They've just moved out of camera range."

"If you see them again, let me know immediately."

"Yes, sir."

Calvin sent one of his guys to inform the boss about the intruders on level three while he took two other armed men and headed for the elevator, not knowing what they would find when they arrived in Mr. Johnson's private suite. Uncertainty pumped adrenaline through his body as he reached out and hit the Up button outside the elevator. He and his men waited while the elevator came down from the third floor. The doors swung open. Inside lay two bodies: a redhead in a clingy black silk dress, a single bullet hole in her forehead, and a large black man, his body riddled with bullets.

"Shit!" Calvin stared at the unknown woman and then at Tyrell Fuqua, Ms. Thomas's bodyguard.

"Please, don't kill me," Shontee pleaded with the man holding a gun on her. "Please, I'll do anything. I can pay you a lot of money. My fiancé is a very rich man. Just tell me what you want."

"I want you to die," he told her. "You and all the others."

"Others? You—you're the person who sent me the letters, aren't you?"

He smiled.

"Why?" she asked, wanting to keep him talking.

"At least tell me why you killed Dean and Hilary and Charlie."

"They had to be killed for the same reason you must die, Ebony O."

"I'm not Ebony O. Not any longer. I'm Shontee Thomas. I left that life years ago. I'm not that person now."

"You can't erase the past," he told her. "Not as long as you live. I watched you in *Midnight Masquerade* this evening. You're even more beautiful and sexy in person."

"You're a fan," Shontee said, forcing a smile, as she prayed that she could buy herself enough time for someone to realize Tyrell was dead and she was in big trouble.

"Yes, I suppose you could call me a fan."

His smile turned Shontee's blood to ice as they stared at each other. His weird expression hinted of madness. As she studied his face, she realized that he was wearing theatrical makeup, that his nose and chin were fake, probably plastic. That could mean his beard and mustache weren't real.

Why was he wearing a disguise? If he intended to kill her, there would be no witnesses. Ah, but what if there were hidden security cameras that she hadn't seen? Had he known about them or had he simply not taken any chances?

"Do I know you?" she asked. "Have we ever met before?"

His smile widened. Shontee's stomach knotted.

"You really want to know the answer to that question?"

"Yes." She held her breath.

"We've met before," he told her as he fired the pistol.

The bullet hit her in the shoulder. Crying out in pain, she clutched her wound. Blood trickled through her fingers.

Oh God, he had shot her!

*He's going to kill me.*

She lunged at him, her instinct for survival choosing fight instead of flight.

He shot her a second time, in the gut. The second shot slowed her as she doubled over in horrific pain.

"Why?" she asked, her voice so weak that she barely recognized it as her own. "Why . . . why . . . ?"

As she slumped to her knees, her life's blood draining from the two gunshot wounds, she prayed for help. Where was Tony? Where were the other people on his security force?

Standing directly over her, her attacker grabbed her hair and yanked, forcing her to stare up at him. While she looked into the eyes of her killer, he pressed his gun to her forehead. She grasped the cuff of his slacks with her bloody fingers.

"Don't," she pleaded.

"Dead by midnight," he told her and then pulled the trigger, sending the bullet straight into Shontee's brain.

# Chapter 18

Mike Birkett dropped his kids off at school and headed in to the office. Halfway between Dunmore Middle School, where M.J. was a sixth grader, and the sheriff's department, Mike's phone rang. Using the voice-activated command that responded to his calls, he answered immediately.

"Mike, it's Jack. Are you where you can turn on a TV?"

"No, I'm in my truck on my way into work," Mike said. "What's up?"

"Cathy and I have on the morning news. Special Agent Hicks Wainwright is being interviewed outside an Atlanta nightclub, some place called the Rough Diamond. Isn't he the FBI agent in charge of the Midnight Killer task force?"

"Yes, he is." The club's name sounded familiar. And then it hit him. "That club is owned by Shontee Thomas's fiancé. She was in *Midnight Masquerade* and has been getting the same kind of letters that Lorie's received."

"Yeah, from what Wainwright is saying, I figured as much."

"Did he get to her? Is she dead?"

"She's dead," Jack replied. "Wainwright is giving out basic facts, but no details. Ms. Thomas's death is being treated as a homicide.

And he's admitted that they have reason to believe she is the fourth victim in a series of murders."

"One a month," Mike said.

"What?"

"So far, since the first of the year, he's killed one person each month."

"Does this mean you think Lorie is safe for now, at least until May?"

"Yeah sure, if this guy doesn't alter his MO, but we have no guarantee of that."

"You should probably be the one to tell Lorie about Shontee Thomas," Jack said. "Or if you'd rather, I can do it. Cathy and I are heading out to her place in a few minutes."

Mike had intended waiting until Jack came in to work today to talk to him about taking over Lorie's case, but he figured, under the circumstances, now was the ideal time.

"Look, I had planned to discuss this with you later . . ." Mike paused. "As of today, I'm assigning you to Lorie's case. You'll be in charge. I . . . uh . . ." He considered lying to his old friend, to use any halfway reasonable excuse, but Jack knew him too well. The simple truth would work best. "I need to put some distance between Lorie and me. Things are getting too complicated."

"I see," Jack said. "Sure, I'll take over. No problem."

"Thanks. I appreciate your not trying to talk me out of my decision."

"I figure it wasn't an easy decision to make. Your gut is telling you to personally protect Lorie, but your head is warning you not to get too close to her or you'll wind up regretting it."

"Yeah, something like that." When Jack didn't comment, Mike said, "You'll keep me updated on a regular basis. Just because I won't be personally involved doesn't mean I don't care what happens to her."

"I get it," Jack told him. "The problem is that you do care, you care a lot more than you want to."

Lorie had turned on the small TV in the kitchen and muted the sound as soon as she'd poured her first cup of coffee thirty minutes ago. She liked catching the early morning weather report while she puttered around in the kitchen, drinking coffee and deciding what to eat for breakfast. Except for Sundays when she often cooked, she usually chose from among three menus: cereal and fruit, yogurt and fruit, or a muffin and juice. She liked routines because she found comfort and stability in daily habits that seldom varied. The craving for excitement and adventure had taken her into a world that had nearly destroyed her. Even though her life now was often boring and dull, at least it was safe and secure. Or it had been until recently.

She lifted the coffeepot from the warmer and poured her third cup into the decorative mug. "Want more coffee?" she asked Shelley.

Her bodyguard shook her head as she munched on cornflakes liberally sprinkled with banana slices and chopped walnuts.

Holding her mug in both hands, Lorie sat down at the kitchen table and glanced at the TV. Gasping when she saw Special Agent Wainwright apparently holding a press conference, she searched for the remote, found it in the middle of the table where she had tossed it earlier, and restored the sound.

The tickertape running across the bottom of the screen read: Fourth Midnight Killer victim murdered at fiancé's downtown Atlanta nightclub.

Shelley dropped her spoon into the almost empty bowl. Metal against ceramic clanged loudly in the quiet room.

"Was Shontee Thomas one of the actors in the porno movie *Midnight Masquerade*?" a TV reporter asked the special agent in charge.

Wainwright looked downright uncomfortable, as if trying to decide just how truthful he should be in answering the question. Apparently deciding that the info was easily accessible to anyone with an Internet connection, he replied, "Yes, Ms. Thomas did have a small part in the movie."

"Then isn't it obvious that she's the Midnight Killer's fourth victim?" another reporter asked while others clamored to be recognized.

"After we receive the medical examiner's report, I'll make an official announcement."

Wainwright was bombarded by a barrage of questions as he ended the brief interview and walked away from the microphone. "Do you believe all the actors from that particular movie are in danger?" "Do you have any suspects at this time?" "What can you tell us about the killer's MO?" "Is there anything, other than the fact the four victims were former porno actors, that links these murders?" "Is it true that Ms. Thomas had a personal bodyguard and that he was also killed?"

The camera swept over the slew of reporters outside the Rough Diamond nightclub and then panned out to show the crowd of curiosity seekers already congregated, even at this early hour.

Lorie set her coffee mug on the table and laid the remote down alongside the mug. "Shontee had a bodyguard."

Shelley's confident gaze collided with Lorie's nervous stare. "I know what you're thinking. Don't. Just because the killer got past Shontee Thomas's bodyguard does not mean that he'll get past me."

"I don't doubt your ability to protect me," Lorie said. "But you're only human, as was Shontee's highly trained bodyguard. They just said that the killer murdered her bodyguard, too."

"You not only have me, but you have the sheriff's department keeping a close watch and you have yourself, too. You own a gun and know how to use it. But if you'll feel safer with more protection, I'm sure we can arrange to add a second bodyguard to this detail."

"A second bodyguard?" For half a minute, Lorie actually considered the suggestion. "No. I feel like a charity case as it is. I can't ask the Powell Agency to provide two bodyguards when I can't afford one."

A lull in their conversation allowed them to hear the morning show anchorman's next statement. "And now to Joelle Piette, a reporter from our local affiliate in Atlanta. Joelle is speaking to Calvin James, the head of security at the nightclub where Shontee Thomas and her bodyguard, Tyrell Fuqua, were murdered last night."

The camera zoomed in on a young, attractive black woman with striking green eyes, her expression serious and concerned as she turned to the man at her side. The six-foot-plus black man with linebacker shoulders and neck stood at rigid attention, his dark suit jacket open to reveal a blood-stained white shirt.

"What can you tell us about the murders that took place inside the Rough Diamond last night?" Joelle asked.

"It came down around midnight," Calvin told her, his gaze riveted to hers and not the camera. "We've got surveillance throughout the building. An unknown man was seen with Ms. Thomas shortly before midnight, upstairs in the hallway leading to Mr. Johnson's private suite."

"Mr. Johnson is Anthony Trice Johnson, the owner of Rough Diamond and several other nightclubs throughout the South." Joelle looked into the camera as she spoke. "Shontee Thomas was his fiancée."

"That's right," Calvin said, as if Joelle's comments had been questions. "As soon as I was informed about the intruder, I took two of my men and headed for the elevator." He shook his head as if still not quite able to believe what he'd seen. "We found Tyrell and some redheaded woman in the elevator, both of them dead."

"And what did you do then?" Joelle asked.

"We took the stairs to the third floor."

"Is that where you found Ms. Thomas's body?"

Calvin nodded. "She was lying there, all shot up and bloody."

Four uniformed policemen appeared as if from out of nowhere and two flanked Calvin while one spoke to Joelle and the fourth motioned for the cameraman to end filming.

"You don't have the right to stop me from talking to the press," Calvin told the policemen. "Mr. Johnson wants people to know what happened to his fiancée. He wants to send a message to the killer."

Suddenly, the screen blurred and then went blank before the morning news anchor reappeared and hurriedly said, "We seem to have lost our live feed. But we will continue with this breaking story when we return from our regularly scheduled commercial break."

Standing in the back of the crowd assembled outside the Rough Diamond, he watched as the police escorted Calvin James away from the newswoman, Joelle Piette. No one—not the police, the FBI, the press, or Tony Johnson's security team—suspected that the person who had killed three people inside the nightclub only hours ago was now watching the media circus at close range.

When he had finished with Ebony O around midnight, he had gone back to his hotel. After he had put the fatal shot directly into her head, he had removed her clothes and then taken the mask from the briefcase he had brought with him. He had hidden the case on the third floor until he needed what was inside. Once he'd fitted the mask over her face, he had stuffed her clothes into the briefcase and made his way down the hall to a window that led to the fire escape. He had barely made it down the metal ladder to the alleyway behind the club before he'd heard someone shouting about the open window. He should have taken time to close the window, but he had known that every second counted. Clutching the briefcase, he had run up the alley for two city blocks and then entered his hotel through the back entrance.

After carefully removing the fake mustache, nose, chin, and hairpiece, he had taken off the theatrical makeup and showered. A few hours of restful sleep had been more than enough to revitalize him. On the way back to the Rough Diamond, he'd stopped at a fast-food place for coffee and a biscuit. Initially, he had intended to simply walk by, check out the scene, and circle back to his hotel. His flight home left at 11:55 A.M. But when he saw that a crowd had gathered, he joined them, acting like nothing more than an interested bystander.

Before he left Atlanta, he would mail the new batch of letters, one each to Puff Raven, Cherry Sweets, Sonny Shag Deguzman, Lacey Butts, and Candy Ruff. Four down, five to go.

When Jack and Cathy showed up at her back door a little before nine, Lorie knew that they had probably seen Special Agent Wainwright's interview on the morning news.

Shelley unlocked and opened the door for the couple. Cathy rushed to Lorie and hugged her. Neither said anything for a couple of minutes; they just gave and accepted comfort.

"We'll keep Treasures closed today," Cathy said as she glanced at her husband. "Jack's going to stay here with you and Ms. Gilbert for a while this morning."

"Look, there's no reason for me not to go to

work," Lorie assured her best friend. "If I stay at home, I'll go stir crazy. Besides, staying home today won't change anything. It won't change the fact that Shontee is dead and that I could be next on the killer's list."

"Show her the newspaper," Cathy told Jack.

Grimacing, Jack handed Lorie her morning newspaper. She eyed it as if it were a wriggling snake. "Is this my paper?"

"Nope, yours is still in the box. This is our copy of today's *Huntsville Times*," Jack said. "Page B-1, on the front page of the Region section."

Cathy stared at the newspaper as Lorie pulled out the Region section and discarded the rest, letting the pages fall haphazardly to the floor. The headline read: PORNO STAR ON KILLER'S HIT LIST. The cropped photo accompanying the article had been taken from an eleven-year-old publicity photo. In this particular shot, she'd been wearing a thong and a come-hither expression and nothing more. The picture had been altered to make it acceptable for the north Alabama readership.

"Oh, Lorie, I'm so sorry," Cathy said.

"Half the town gets the *Huntsville Times*." Lorie quickly scanned the article, then read one brief paragraph aloud. "Ms. Hammonds, co-owner of Treasures of the Past, a Dunmore antique shop, is the former fiancée of county sheriff Michael Birkett. The sheriff's department has taken a special interest in protecting Ms. Hammonds, at taxpayers' expense, even though a private female bodyguard has been provided to protect Ms. Hammonds twenty-four/seven."

"That damn little weasel." Lorie glared at the byline. Ryan Bonner. "Mike is going to be furious when he sees this."

"He's seen it," Cathy said. "Jack has spoken to him twice this morning. First to tell him about seeing Special Agent Wainwright's interview and then to tell him about the article in the *Times*."

"It's not fair that Mike will be judged guilty by association." Lorie crushed the newspaper in her hands.

"It's not as if most folks didn't already know that you and Mike were once engaged," Cathy told her.

"But that was old news, dead and buried in the past," Lorie said. "Ryan Bonner has made it current news. How is something like this going to affect Hannah and M.J.? Don't you think some of the other kids at school are going to ask them about it? And you've got to know that there will be at least one smart-mouthed kid who'll ask what they think about their dad having nearly married a *Playboy* centerfold."

"You let Mike worry about his kids," Cathy said. "You have enough to worry about as it is without—"

The phone rang. Four sets of eyes stared at the cordless telephone on the kitchen counter. Shelley picked up the phone and checked caller ID.

"It's a local number." She hit the On button. "Hammonds residence." She frowned. "Do not call again or I'll report you to the authorities." She laid the phone back on the counter and faced the others. "It's started again. I'll have to disconnect all the land lines so we don't have to deal with the phone ringing all day long. If the security system didn't require a landline phone, I'd leave them disconnected."

"Let them ring," Lorie said. "I won't be here. I'm getting ready and going to work."

"I don't recommend your doing that," Jack told her.

"Are you my keeper now?" she asked. "Did Mike turn me over to you?"

"He placed me in charge of your case."

"Fine. I knew he planned to . . ." Lorie paused to take a deep, calming breath and quickly rethought her decision to rush off to work. "How long do you think we'll have to keep Treasures closed?"

"I don't know," Jack said honestly. "A few days, maybe longer. It depends on whether or not there are more articles about you in the newspaper."

"And if there are?"

"Then the best course of action is to keep Treasures closed indefinitely."

Maleah and Derek had been brought back to Knoxville via the Powell jet at the crack of dawn that morning and had arrived at Griffin's Rest in time for breakfast. Although Griff and Nic were dealing with the murder of Powell secretary Kristi Arians, they had set up a meeting for all the top agents involved in the Midnight Killer case. The agency had been hired by the next of kin of two of the victims and they expected a call from Anthony Johnson or his representative before the end of the day. And they were representing, pro bono, Charlie Wong's family. The facts that Lorie Hammonds was Maleah's sister-in-law's best friend and Griff counted Jared Wilson among his close acquaintances changed the dynamics of the case for the agency. This case was personal.

The Powell Agency's main headquarters was housed in downtown Knoxville, in a renovated building Griff had purchased a number of years ago. The structure had been renamed the Powell Building in honor of its billionaire owner. A small group of administrative assistants, including the office manager, ran the day-to-day operations of the agency and reported directly to Griff and/or Nic. Fifty people, counting the in-the-field agents, were employed by Powell's. The computer experts worked in various capacities, but mainly doing research. The bookkeepers handled the finances, including taxes, accounts payable and receivable, and payroll. Griff kept former FBI profiler Derek Lawrence on retainer, as he did Camden Hendrix's law firm and a local psychologist.

Then there was Dr. Yvette Meng and her students. Maleah had no concrete proof, but she suspected that Griff was on the verge of utilizing Dr. Meng's special talents and those of her small conclave housed at Griffin's Rest to help with certain seemingly unsolvable cases. Personally, Maleah wasn't into all that woo-woo stuff, but she tried to keep an open mind. She knew one thing for sure—Dr. Meng was extraordinarily perceptive. Whether Griff's old friend and her pupils were actually psychic, she couldn't say. Maybe they were.

Griff worked from Griffin's Rest most of the time and had rarely visited the Knoxville headquarters in the past year. The real heart of the agency was located in a huge, state-of-the-art home office inside Griff and Nic's home. The space was divided into three areas, one of which was a meeting room equipped with two plasma televisions, DVD and CD players, and a wall lined with books and magazines. Plush leather chairs circled a large rectangular table.

Maleah and Nic had taken a few minutes, just the two of them, to catch up after breakfast. By the time they arrived at the office, Griff was seated at the head of the table and the other agents were milling around the room. Derek sat at the end of the table near Griff and the two were deep in conversation.

"Don't worry, they aren't discussing the Midnight Killer case," Nic told Maleah. "Griff wanted to speak to Derek about Kristi's murder.

We're waiting for a report concerning the details that the Knoxville PD are keeping top secret."

Maleah nodded. She never questioned Griff's methods of obtaining whatever information he wanted. Only on rare occasions did the agency come up against that rare human being—the man or woman who couldn't be bought for the right price. She wondered, if push came to shove, exactly what her price would be, because she knew only too well that *the price* wasn't always monetary.

Nic spoke to each agent present and then took her seat at the opposite end of the table from her husband. Maleah surveyed the group. Nic and Griff and Derek were already seated. Holt Keinan, who had been assigned to investigate Hilary Finch Chambless's murder in Memphis, sat down beside Derek. Ben Corbett and Michelle Allen spoke to Maleah as they headed for the table, coffee cups in hand.

After everyone was in place, casually seated around the table and still quietly chatting, Sanders entered and took a seat in the corner of the room, away from the others. Griff's right-hand man seldom participated in the meetings, but he often observed. Maleah didn't know why and had never asked.

Shaughnessy Hood, this month's head of security at Griffin's Rest, closed the door and then stood guard. His actions weren't actually necessary, but she understood the need for protocol. This was a private meeting where the agents would be discussing matters of grave importance and sharing confidential information.

Griffin Powell ended his conversation with Derek and turned in his chair to face the others. His gaze traveled around the table, silently acknowledging each Powell agent present. The room quieted. Everyone focused on Griff.

"Kristi Arians's autopsy will be performed tomorrow," Griff told them. "The funeral is tentatively scheduled for Thursday at noon. A by-invitation-only memorial service will follow that evening, here at Griffin's Rest."

"May I ask if Powell's will be doing an independent investigation?" Michelle Allen asked.

"Yes, we will," Griff replied. "Mitch Trahern will be heading that investigation." Griff waited for more questions and when no one else spoke, he continued. "Now, to the business at hand. The Midnight Killer case." He reached to his right and removed the top folder from a stack of thin binders piled in a neat bundle on the table. "Pass these around and once everyone has a copy, take a few minutes to look over the information."

"These folders contain reports from the six agents working in the field on this case," Nic explained. "Shelley Gilbert is not here because she is on bodyguard duty for a potential victim, Lorie Hammonds. But she filed her report this morning.

Derek has put together a rough preliminary profile of the killer, and Maleah has condensed the interviews they've had with possible suspects."

Derek explained, "Once I've gone over your reports, I will reassess the profile if there is any information that I believe changes my opinion."

"The report I submitted includes information about our interviews with four men we thought could possibly be involved in the murders," Maleah told them. "We have three other names on our list and hope to finish up with those interviews this week."

The agents passed around the binders of info and each took the allotted time to skim the reports.

"As you see, there is another report included, one put together by Powell's research team using certain information y'all submitted along with computer and legwork research," Griff said.

Maleah hurried through the report from Holt Keinan on the Hilary Chambless murder and Michelle and Ben's report on Dean Wilson's murder, but she took time to thoroughly go over Derek's profile. Even though they were partnered on this case, he hadn't discussed his profile with her and despite being curious, she had not asked him about it.

Midnight Killer's MO: Victims have all been former actors who starred in porno movies. Each victim had a part in the movie *Midnight*

*Masquerade*. Three of the four victims received two or more threatening letters that warned them they were going to die. (It is assumed that the first victim also received similar letters, but there is no proof that he did.) Each murder occurred sometime around midnight. Each victim was shot several times, with one final fatal shot to the head.

Midnight Killer Signature: This killer's "calling card"—he places a fancy mask (possibly the one from the porno movie in which the victim starred) on the victim postmortem.

The Midnight Killer shows traits of the organized serial killer, which means he is probably highly intelligent, socially and sexually competent, can be charming, is geographically and/or occupationally mobile, follows media coverage of his crimes, and was probably harshly disciplined or abused as a child.

Of the four distinct serial killer types, the Midnight Killer would fall under the Missionary-Oriented Motive type. He displays no psychosis to the outside world, but on the inside, he has an overwhelming need to rid the world of what he considers immoral or unworthy people.

To our knowledge, our unidentified suspect began killing in January and to date has killed four people. His need to kill has probably been fueled by certain fantasies that he's had and that have been escalating up for quite a while.

Maleah paused to consider the implications of what she had just read. She agreed completely with Derek's professional assessment of their UNSUB.

Hurriedly, she raced through the remainder of his report, which listed each of the four men they had recently interiewed.

Travis Dillard: Remains on our suspects list. Fits the organized killer profile to some degree. Has the intelligence to plot the murders and the financial ability to hire a professional killer.

Duane Hines: Removed from suspects list. Does not fit the profile. Does not have the intelligence to plot and carry out the crimes. Is virtually penniless.

Kyle Richey: Placed at the bottom of the suspects list. Partially fits the organized killer profile, has a criminal record, but is the type to commit a crime of passion and not premeditated murder.

Casey Lloyd: Remains on our suspects list. A reformed drug addict and alcoholic who displays pent-up anger. Most likely on the list of suspects to be a Missionary-Oriented Motive type.

"Keep these files, go over them, use them in any way that will help you in your investigation," Griff said, bringing everyone's attention away from the reading material and directly onto him. "We've learned a great deal already, but we're not even close to solving this case. Although there are four victims and more potential victims, this is one case, not several."

"I read where it's been determined that our UNSUB is probably taking a souvenir each time," Holt Keinan said.

"Yes," Nic replied. "The clothing the victim was wearing when he or she was killed disappeared. We believe the killer took the clothing, probably chose one article and discarded the rest. But no bloody clothing has been found either at the scene or in nearby garbage bins or Dumpsters."

"And he didn't use the same murder weapon for each killing," Ben Corbett commented.

"That's right," Griff said. "Ballistics reports confirm that each victim was shot with a different gun."

"And he's doing this for what reason?" Michelle Allen asked. "He can't think that by using different guns, the authorities won't link the four murders, not when he's gone out of his way to kill in the same manner, uses the mask as a calling card, and warns the victims in advance with identical letters."

"At this point, there's no way to know for sure why he's done this," Griff told the agents. "It could be as simple as him preferring not to pack a gun that goes through the airport's baggage security scanner. For a man with money, picking up a different gun in each city wouldn't be a major problem."

"We believe that our killer is using fake ID to purchase his plane ticket and to register at the hotels where he's staying. And more than likely, he's disguising himself in some way so that he can't be easily identified by anyone on the flights or in the hotels and restaurants. This makes it difficult to figure out if one of our suspects traveled on or near the dates of the murders. And for the same reason, we can't rule out any particular suspect."

"A check of airline passengers and hotel registrations the day of and the day before each murder might give us a single name," Holt suggested.

"We've thought of that, but so far, we've come up with nothing. No single name, which leads us to believe that he is possibly using several fake identities."

"Our guy is not only smart, but he's financially secure," Derek said. "And he's on a mission to rid the world of evil in the form of ten former porno stars."

# Chapter 19

Jeff Misner rammed into his wife, his upper thighs slapping against her still-firm ass as he took her from the rear. She huffed and panted and groaned, the sounds indicating sexual pleasure, but he never knew for sure if Jean was enjoying herself or not. He suspected that at least half the time, she faked her orgasms. During her career as Puff Raven, she had gotten plenty of practice. And to tell the truth, he didn't really care if she came or not.

"That's it, baby, give it to me hard and fast," Jean cried out as she moved in perfect rhythm to his thrusts.

He grabbed her hips tightly, probably bruising her darkly tanned skin, and hammered repeatedly until he climaxed. She screeched and shook and told him she loved him. He collapsed on top of her, shoving her facedown onto the bed. After his breathing returned to normal and the aftershocks of his delicious climax subsided, he rolled off her and then stood. She flipped over and looked up at him.

"I need to work on the new video for my Web site this afternoon," Jean told him. "You aren't going to need me, are you?"

"I'm fine for now." He winked at her. Jean was thirty-six, but she had taken good care of herself—boob and butt lifts, a tummy tuck, Botox, and a daily workout. "Have you got someone coming in to help with the video?"

"I'm flying solo on this one. Just me, a few toys, and my fingers." She laughed.

"I may drop by and watch."

"Sure thing. You know I love a live audience."

He held out his hand. She grabbed hold and he yanked her up and onto her feet. Her shoulder-length black hair—still natural and without a single silver strand—shimmered as she shook her head and stretched. Her body was toned, deeply tanned, and willowy slender. Since retiring from the regular porno film business, Jean had been making a healthy income via the Internet. The Puff Raven site was one of the most popular in the world. Once a month, she added a new video that customers could download and enjoy, for a very reasonable price.

Jeff figured that one of these days very soon the Internet sites would make regular porno movies completely obsolete.

After a quick kiss, he and Jean went their separate ways, she to her bathroom and he to his. He shaved, showered, and dressed casually in a cotton shirt and linen slacks. Just as he slipped into his leather sandals, his cell phone rang.

*Where did I put the damn thing? In my dressing room? On the nightstand?*

Then he remembered he had left it in his jacket pocket and hung the jacket across the back of the sofa in the sitting area of their bedroom. By the time he retrieved the phone, it had stopped ringing. Just as he started to check for a message, the phone rang again. He glanced at the caller ID.

Travis Dillard.

What the hell did that old son of a bitch want? After their last collaboration, he'd told Travis in no uncertain terms that they were kaput, finished, over and done. Travis needed to retire. He had lost touch with the new porno industry and still wanted to do things the old-fashioned way. Not Jeff. He was all about new and improved.

"Yeah, what's up?" Jeff asked when he answered on the fourth ring.

"Have you seen the news today?" Travis asked.

"Can't say that I have. I'm a busy man. Making deals, screwing my wife, enjoying my success."

"Think you've got it made, don't you? Well, Shontee thought she was living the good life, too, down in Atlanta with that rich boyfriend of hers, but her little pie-in-the-sky piece of heaven just bit the dust."

A sudden chill settled over Jeff. "What happened?"

"He got her," Travis said. "The Midnight Killer whacked Shontee last night."

"I thought she had a bodyguard."

"The killer filled him full of lead and then moved on to Shontee."

Jeff swallowed. Ever since the Powell Agency had contacted him and Jean, they had been careful not to leave the house without the private security that Jeff had hired. Around-the-clock protection didn't come cheap, but keeping Jean alive was worth any price.

"I thought you'd want to be forewarned," Travis said. "Tighten up your security and watch your back night and day. You never know when this guy is going to come for Jean."

"Is that a threat, old man?"

Travis laughed. "Don't talk nonsense. Why would I want to hurt Jean? She was one of my favorite fucks. I always loved the way she screamed when I made her come."

Jeff clenched his jaw. He would not rise to the bait. "I'll take care of Jean. And if I find out that you're behind these murders, that you've threatened my wife, I'll personally see to it that you rot in hell."

Jeff hung up, not giving Travis a chance for an acidic comeback.

After pocketing his phone, he left the bedroom and went downstairs. He had a sudden need to see Jean, to make sure she was all right. As he passed the living room, he nodded and threw up his hand when he saw one of their two security guards immersed in a game of solitaire. The second agent was posted outside and the two men rotated shifts indoors and out every four hours during the day. And every twelve hours, two fresh, alert agents took their places.

He entered the dark, soundproof room where Jean filmed her Internet videos. Reclining on a plush red velvet chaise longue, his naked wife touched herself intimately, one hand caressing her right breast, stroking the nipple, and the other hand between her spread thighs, rubbing her clitoris.

He watched her masturbate until she climaxed, her body jerking convulsively as she moaned softly and seductively.

"Did you enjoy that as much as I did?" she asked breathlessly.

Jeff chuckled. "Almost as much."

"I thought you said you wouldn't need me for a while."

"Travis Dillard called."

She rose from the chaise, slipped on a knee-length satin robe, and turned off the video camera set up on a tripod. "What did he want?"

"Shontee's dead."

Jean closed her eyes for a moment. "Oh my!"

Jeff rushed over to her and took her in his arms. Rubbing her back comfortingly, he told her, "Nothing is going to happen to you. I promise I'll keep you safe."

She laid her head on his shoulder and wrapped her arms around his waist. "I know you will."

As if he could hear her thoughts, his mind revised her words from "I know you will" to "I know you'll try."


As the lead investigator, Special Agent Wainwright called Mike and invited him to come to the field office in Birmingham and sit in on a general meeting of the Midnight Killer task force. Mike wasn't an official member of the force, so the invitation had been a courtesy. After Wainwright had come to Dunmore and interviewed Lorie, Mike had checked out the FBI agent and had found pretty much what he'd expected. Wainwright, at thirty-nine, was a seasoned investigator. He had the dedication, tenacity, and experience to direct every aspect of the investigation. Within days of being assigned the leadership role, Wainwright had established a computerized information management system to track tips and leads in the case. Under usual circumstances, Mike would have assigned one of his deputies as a liaison to work with the Bureau, but this was not just any case. Lorie's life had been threatened, and unless the killer was found and stopped, she would remain in danger.

A representative from each of the two states—Tennessee and Arizona—where the Midnight Killer had struck the first three times had been included on the task force, which at present numbered only five. A small group of experienced homicide detectives could be far more effective than a larger group of inexperienced lawmen. Wainwright had chosen one fellow federal agent and one Alabama state agent to complete the force.

Upon arrival at the field office, Mike was shown to Wainwright's office and introduced to the task force members by FBI Special Agent Luther Armstrong, who served as the force's co-investigator. Mike shook hands with the state reps, one a homicide detective from the Knoxville PD and the other a seasoned cop from Blythe, Arizona. When ABI Special Agent Karla Ross came over to him and held out her hand, Mike recognized her immediately.

"Good to see you again, Special Agent Ross," Mike said.

"Good to see you, Sheriff," she replied. "I don't think either of us thought we'd ever be working together on another serial killer task force."

"You're absolutely right," Mike said. "But just like the last time, I'm not an official member of the force. And you're the lead control officer on this one, right?"

Mike had become acquainted with Karla and her fellow ABI agent, Wayne Morgan, during the Fire and Brimstone murders that had ravaged Dunmore and several surrounding towns in northern Alabama for more than eighteen months. The lady was a hard-nosed, by-the-book type, a woman proving herself in a profession still dominated by men. She wore her hair cropped carefree short, didn't bother with makeup or nail polish, and walked with a swagger that said don't-mess-with-me.

Wainwright called the meeting to order and got down to business. The information he shared could be condensed down to one sentence: They did not have a suspect in the four murders. Basic facts were: The killer had used a different gun for each kill; he was probably using fake ID and different disguises; he killed each victim in the same manner, shooting each multiple times; he stripped the victim, placed an elaborate mask on him or her, and took the victim's clothes. Adding to that was the info that each victim had costarred in the same porno movie and each had received death threats prior to his or her murder.

"We got a break with this last murder," Wainwright told them as he motioned for Karla to turn off the overhead lights. "The surveillance cameras at the Rough Diamond Club in Atlanta caught our guy on tape."

"Are you saying we know what the Midnight Killer looks like?" Lieutenant Jon Yacup from Arizona asked.

"Yes and no," Wainwright replied. "We're ninety-nine percent sure the man is wearing a disguise, probably a fake nose and chin as well as theatrical makeup. But we can pretty much guess his weight and height from the video. And it's obvious that he's Caucasian."

Wainwright picked up the TV/video/DVD combo remote, hit a couple of buttons, and began playing the black-and-white surveillance tape. Mike watched closely as their killer appeared on screen, a medium-sized guy, with a prominent nose and a sharp chin. The dark-eyed, dark-haired man could be anywhere between twenty and fifty years old. The hair could have been dyed or was a wig, the mustache no doubt fake, and contacts could easily change very light eyes to very dark in a matter of seconds. And on black-and-white film, it was impossible to distinguish dark blue from dark brown.

After they watched the tape, Special Agent Armstrong said, "We admit that it's not a lot, but it's more than we had before, and piece by piece, we're gathering evidence. All we need are a few more lucky breaks and—"

"Let's hope no one else has to die before we get those lucky breaks," Sergeant Carter Fulton from the Knoxville PD said.

Everyone in the room agreed with Fulton.

A couple of hours later, Mike went out for lunch with Wainwright while Special Agent Ross drove Yacup and Fulton to the airport. After devouring barbequed ribs and finishing the meal with bourbon pecan pie, Wainwright wiped his hands on the disposable wet-wipe provided with his rack of ribs and then turned his attention to Mike.

"How's Ms. Hammonds doing?"

"She's okay, all things considered," Mike said.

"I spoke to Nicole Powell this morning. I guess you know she used to be a federal agent and still has friends at the Bureau." When Mike nodded, Wainwright continued. "Unofficially, we're utilizing the Powell Agency's investigation. Officially, we have no connection to the agency. Understand?"

"If you're saying that the Powell Agency is sharing their info with the task force, but y'all are not sharing with them, then yes, I understand."

"I'd never publicly admit this, but Powell's has a better record of catching the bad guys than we

317

do. And at least part of the reason for that is their ability to occasionally sidestep the law. We know Griffin Powell uses his wealth and power however he sees fit. But we can't prove he's ever done anything illegal."

"I'll take your word for that," Mike said. "I don't know Mr. Powell. I met him briefly a few weeks ago when he and his wife attended my deputy Jackson Perdue's wedding."

"I've met him only a couple of times myself. Nic—Mrs. Powell—is handling the communication between Powell's and our task force. And if it'll make you feel any better about Ms. Hammonds's safety, Mrs. Powell mentioned that Shelley Gilbert is one of their best bodyguards."

"I'm sure she is. But I figure that Tony Johnson believed the man he had guarding Shontee Thomas was one of his best."

"You're right. We're dealing with an intelligent, motivated killer who is enjoying outsmarting his victims, their protectors, and the law," Wainwright said. "With each murder, a new batch of letters have gone out. Ms. Hammonds and the others will probably receive another death threat via U.S. mail sometime in the next few days. As soon as she receives the letter, I want you to notify us. Her letter is our best chance of immediately getting our hands on a copy."

"I'll inform Deputy Perdue to contact you if and when Lorie receives another letter."

Wainwright cocked his brows as he stared at Mike. "Deputy Perdue will contact me?"

"I've put him in charge of Lorie Hammonds's case."

"Hmm . . ."

"Considering our past history, I thought it best to remove myself from any personal involvement in Lorie's case," Mike said, not sure who he was trying to convince that he had valid reasons for putting Jack in charge.

"You don't owe me any explanations," Wainwright told him.

"You're right. I don't. But I wanted to set the record straight so there won't be any misunderstandings later on."

"Okay. Sure. Just inform Deputy Perdue to notify me when Ms. Hammonds receives another letter."

Mike nodded. When Lorie received another letter warning her that she was on the Midnight Killer's death list, she'd need somebody to lean on, somebody to console her, somebody to protect her. But damn it, that somebody couldn't be Mike Birkett, county sheriff, M.J. and Hannah's dad, and Abby Sherman's boyfriend. Lorie had Shelley Gilbert and Jack Perdue to protect her. She had Cathy to console her. She also had other friends like Reverend Patsy Floyd that she could lean on. She didn't need him.

"I'd appreciate your keeping us routinely

updated," Mike said as he picked his bill up off the table and stood.

Wainwright stood, shook Mike's hand, and replied, "Your department will be kept in the loop. And if there is anything we can do for Ms. Hammonds, have your office contact us."

"Yeah, sure."

Why was it that Mike had a gut feeling that Special Agent Wainwright would like an excuse to see Lorie again?

*For obvious reasons, you dumb ass.*

What man wouldn't give his right arm for a chance with Lorie Hammonds?

Maleah and Derek arrived in Danville, Virginia, mid-afternoon for their appointment with Tyler Owens, whose mother, Terri, had once been known as Candy Ruff. Nestled in the foothills of the Blue Ridge Mountains, Danville, with a population of more than 50,000, was located in the Piedmont region of the state. And as Maleah drove along the area locally known as Millionaires' Row, she was reminded of the research they had done on Terri Owens, who was the descendant of one of the tobacco kings of long ago. How a Virginia debutante from one of the oldest and most respected families in the state had become a porno star puzzled Maleah.

"What's the address again?" Maleah asked.

When Derek recited the street and number, she

nodded. They were on the correct street of the Old West End Historic District.

"There it is." He pointed to the red brick Queen Anne Victorian home with the bed & breakfast sign on the front lawn. "Tyler Owens and his wife are the proprietors."

Maleah turned into the narrow drive at the Tyler House B&B and followed the paved lane to the back of the house where the parking area could accommodate a dozen vehicles.

"Mr. Owens booked rooms for us here tonight," Derek said. "Unless we gain any meaningful information about a suspect from Owens, we'll catch our flight to Louisville tomorrow to see Grant Leroy, known as Reverend Leroy these days since he's become a born-again Christian."

"Do you think Tyler Owens actually has some idea who the killer is?" Maleah opened the car door.

"Apparently, he thinks he does."

Derek got out and met her on the sidewalk and together they went to the office in the rear of the three-story house. An attractive young brunette wearing jeans and a Tyler House B&B T-shirt greeted them.

"Hello, I'm Amelia Rose Owens. Welcome to Tyler House."

"We're here to see Tyler Owens," Derek said.

"You must be Mr. Lawrence and Ms. Perdue. Tyler is expecting y'all. He's discussing the menu with our cook. Come with me into the front parlor and I'll let Tyler know y'all are here."

As they followed the woman they assumed was Tyler's wife out of the office and down the central hall, Maleah noted the similarities between this house and the one she had grown up in. Of course, Tyler House was much larger, had retained its original splendor, and was filled with priceless antiques.

"If there's anything y'all want to know about the house or about Danville, feel free to ask," the young woman said. "I've become a walking encyclopedia on the area since I married Tyler. His parents' families have lived in Virginia since the Revolutionary War. His mother's family, the Tylers, made their fortune in tobacco and his father's relatives were business associates of the entrepreneurs who founded Dan River, Inc."

"How long have you been married?" Maleah asked.

"Two years. We met in college and got married the summer after graduation."

A man's loud demanding voice echoed through the house, "Amelia Rose, where have you got off to, girl?"

Their hostess gasped, then shook her head and smiled. "That's Uncle Clement. He's Tyler's great-uncle. His maternal grandfather's brother. If y'all will excuse me. He'll keep hollering until I go see what he wants. He's a dear old thing, but a little addled. He's nearly ninety."

As soon as Amelia Rose went in search of Uncle Clement, Maleah and Derek exchanged closed-mouthed grins.

"I don't know if we've walked into a page of *Gone With the Wind* or a Victorian novel," Derek said.

"A combination of the two. What do you want to bet that the rooms are either called Rhett's Room, Scarlett's Room, and so on, or they're named after flowers? You know, the Lily Room, the Gardenia Room, and the Rose Room."

Just as Derek opened his mouth to speak, they heard a voice from the hallway. "Hello there. Sorry to keep y'all waiting."

When they turned to meet the speaker, Maleah barely managed not to gasp aloud. The young man—not a day over twenty-five—was strikingly handsome. The only thing about him that could be described as average was his height and body build. Large blue eyes, edged with thick brown lashes, were set in a chiseled, lightly tanned face that would make any Greek god envious. A tangle of golden blond curls framed those too-perfect features.

As he entered the room, he held out his hand to Maleah. "I'm Tyler Owens and you must be Ms. Perdue. It's a pleasure, ma'am."

My God, he was not only handsome beyond belief, but mannerly, too. Although she wasn't sure being called ma'am was a compliment.

"Maleah Perdue." She shook his hand.

He possessed a devastating smile.

When he turned to shake hands with Derek, Maleah couldn't help but notice the width of his shoulders encased in a soft, silk shirt and how tight his buttocks were in the faded, often-washed jeans.

"I certainly appreciate y'all coming here to Danville," Tyler said. "I could have flown to Knoxville next week, but this week, I simply couldn't get away. We're hosting a bridal tea Wednesday, a wedding rehearsal dinner on Friday, and the wedding on Saturday."

"Coming here wasn't a problem," Maleah assured him. "We're interviewing anyone connected to the *Midnight Masquerade* movie who might be able to help us find out who has been sending threatening letters and, to date, has murdered four people."

Tyler's eyes widened and his cheeks flushed. "We've taken precautions for Mother. The rehab center where she is recovering has been alerted to the threat on her life and no one is allowed to see her except immediate family and the staff, of course."

"How many letters has your mother received?" Derek asked.

"Three, that I know of," Tyler replied. "I have them if you'd like to see them." He glanced away, a melancholy expression on his gorgeous face. "I'm certain that those letters contributed to

Mother's stroke. She's not an elderly woman by any means. She's only forty-four."

"I'm very sorry about your mother," Maleah said.

He gave her another breathtaking smile. "Thank you, Ms. Perdue. That's kind of you to say."

When Derek cleared his throat, Maleah interpreted the action as a criticism. She could almost hear him accusing her of being dumbstruck by Tyler Owens's obvious physical beauty. Well, yeah. Duh. What red-blooded woman wouldn't be?

Tyler turned his attention to Derek, who got right to the point. "When you phoned us, you mentioned that you think you might know who the Midnight Killer is."

"Yes, that's correct."

"Well?" Derek asked.

"Of course, you want to know, don't you?" Tyler cast his sorrowful gaze toward the polished wooden floor, his actions bordering on the melodramatic. "I hate to accuse anyone." He lifted his gaze and moved from Derek to Maleah.

She wanted to scream, "For goodness sakes, just tell us already." But she waited patiently, allowing him to garner whatever satisfaction he could derive from prolonging the moment.

"I believe that it's possible my father is the Midnight Killer."

# Chapter 20

Lorie had almost forgotten the sound of her mother's voice. It had been nearly five months since they had spoken. Several times a year, usually on her birthday, at Thanksgiving, and at Christmas, her mother would call her and they would talk for five or ten minutes. Each conversation was precious to Lorie. She knew that her father had no idea that her mother kept in touch with her. Since her return to Dunmore nearly nine years ago, Lorie had visited her parents' home once. Immediately after she came back to Alabama, she had gone straight home, hoping and praying for her parents' love and support.

But within minutes of her arrival, her father had made it abundantly clear how he felt.

"I want you to leave," he had told her. "I don't ever want to see you or hear from you again. I don't have a daughter. As far as I'm concerned, my daughter is dead."

Glenn Hammonds had been a good provider, a faithful husband, and a spare-the-rod-and-spoil-the-child father. Known as a God-fearing Christian, he prided himself on being the head of his household. His family had been expected to accept that his word was law and never question his authority over them. No doubt her father had chosen her mother as his partner not only because

326

she was beautiful and he dearly loved her, but because she possessed a calm, sweet, easily manipulated nature. Sharon Hammonds had seldom disagreed with her husband and even when they had a difference of opinion, she always gave over to him in the end.

Although Lorie had accidentally run into them a few times and had seen them at a distance on a number of occasions, she was not a part of their lives, nor were they a part of hers. A couple of years ago when she had learned her father had suffered a heart attack, she had gone to the hospital. But her mother had stopped her outside of his room.

"I'm sorry, Lorie, but your father doesn't want to see you."

She had never forgotten the look of sadness and regret in her mother's eyes that day.

So was it any wonder that the sound of her mother's voice over the phone seemed almost unfamiliar to her?

"Lorie, are you there?" her mother asked.

"Yes, Mom, I'm here."

"We've heard about what's happening, about your being on that terrible Midnight Killer's list of people he intends to murder. You seem to be the main topic of conversation wherever we go lately."

"Yes, I suppose I am. I know how Daddy must hate that."

"He saw one of those flyers." Her mother lowered her voice to a whisper. "You know, one of the pictures you posed for a long time ago."

"I'm sorry that Daddy and you have to go through this again," Lorie said. "I'm sorry that you have to be ashamed that I'm your daughter."

"Oh, Lorie . . . I—I didn't call about that. I called because I'm worried about you."

Emotion lodged in Lorie's throat and for several seconds, she couldn't speak. "I'm okay. Thank you for calling . . . for caring."

"Of course I care. No matter what you've done, you're still my daughter and I love you."

"Do you, Mom?" Tears flooded Lorie's eyes, blinding her with a watery haze. "Do you . . . really?"

"It breaks my heart that you think otherwise, but I know you have good reason. Please, Lorie, don't hate me."

"Oh, Mom . . ." She held the phone away from her and took a deep breath. When she realized she couldn't stop crying, she held the phone to her chest.

By the time she managed to control her tears and lifted the receiver back to her ear, she heard only a dial tone.

"You think your father could be the Midnight Killer?" Maleah asked, slightly stunned by Tyler Owens's accusation.

Derek followed up immediately with another

question. "What makes you think that your father is the killer?"

"My father is unstable and has been for quite sometime." Tyler looked from Derek to Maleah and remained focused on her.

She suspected that Tyler sensed she was the more empathetic agent. "Is he mentally ill? Is he on medication?"

"I don't know. He has mental problems, but he's never been diagnosed by a doctor for anything other than anxiety. I have no idea if he's on medication or not. If he was, he'd hardly tell me. You see, we aren't close and haven't been for a number of years."

"Other than your father's mental instability, is there any other reason you think he could be the killer?" Derek asked.

"I'll have to give y'all some backstory," Tyler said. "It's the only way you can possibly understand."

"We're listening," Derek told him.

"Maybe we'd better sit down." Tyler issued the invitation with a sweep of his hand, indicating the plush velvet settee and chairs in the parlor. "Would y'all like some iced tea or lemonade? I can have Amelia Rose fix us—"

"Nothing, thanks," Derek replied.

After the three of them were seated, Derek and Maleah on the settee together, posing a united front, and Tyler in a chair across from them, Tyler began his story.

"My parents came from two of the oldest families in Danville. Their marriage was practically an arranged affair. Their parents were good friends and everyone pretty much expected the two of them to marry, which they did. Mother was only twenty-one when I was born eighteen months after they married and according to Dad, she soon felt trapped and wanted out of the marriage and out of Danville. When I was two years old, she just up and left one day. I didn't see her again until I was six. She came back to Danville to see me. That was the first time my father threatened to kill her.

"He was ashamed of the fact she had gotten involved in the pornography business and had posed in various magazines and had made several movies. They had an awful row and I heard everything. My mother left in tears and I didn't see her again for years."

"Your father's attitude was understandable, given the circumstances," Derek said.

"I suppose it was," Tyler agreed. "But you have to understand that I grew up listening to his tirades about my mother, how she was a slut who didn't deserve to live, how evil men had lured her into making indecent movies and all the actors in those movies should be taken out and shot."

"Those were his exact words—taken out and shot?" Maleah asked.

"Yes, ma'am. His exact words. I thought once he remarried—a fine lady named Brenda Lee—that things would get better. And for a while, they did. Then Mother moved back to Danville a few years ago and my father did everything he could to run her out of town. They've had some horrible fights, but the harder Dad tried to make her leave, the more she dug in her heels, determined to stay."

"What you've told us may prove that your father hates your mother and is ashamed of how she's lived her life, but not that he's a murderer," Derek said. "If he is a killer, then why did he wait all these years to start murdering porno actors and why only actors from that one particular movie? And why not start by killing your mother?"

"Dad had settled down the past couple of years, at least to a certain extent, even though he never accepted the fact that I had made a place in my life for Mother. But then when *Midnight Masquerade* was released on DVD this past fall, that set him off again. I think he zeroed in on that one movie and became obsessed with the people who were in it. And as for why he didn't kill Mother first—I don't know. Maybe he's saving her until last."

Silence fell over the parlor for several minutes and then Maleah asked, "You really do believe your father is the Midnight Killer, don't you?"

With a sheen of moisture dampening his big blue eyes, Tyler swallowed and said softly, "I don't want to believe such a horrible thing about my own father, but yes, I think there's a good chance that he's the killer."

· · ·

Feeling like a prisoner trapped in her own house, Lorie had decided she needed a project of some kind to keep her mind occupied. The idea of renting the empty store adjacent to Treasures of the Past and renovating the interior for use as a tearoom needed research and planning. When she'd mentioned this to Cathy, her best friend had agreed. So Lorie had spent most of the day speaking to a Realtor about the rental property and making various phone calls to suppliers and owners of teahouses in several different cities. And doing her best not to let her brief conversation with her mother this morning give her any false hopes about their relationship.

Shelley was engrossed in reading a new paperback and Lorie was going through magazines, such as *Tea Time*, and cutting out articles when the doorbell rang. Since they weren't expecting anyone, both she and Shelley froze for a couple of seconds. Then Shelley laid her book aside, got up, and headed for the front door.

Shelley peered through the viewfinder and laughed. "It's a couple of kids. They look like Mike Birkett's children." She opened the door.

Lorie jumped up and hurried to meet Hannah and M.J.

"We need to see Miss Lorie," M.J. told Shelley.

"Hey, you two, what are y'all doing here?" Lorie asked.

Hannah came rushing forward, threw her little arms around Lorie, and then hugged her. M.J. stood less than a foot away and looked up at Lorie with wide, misty eyes.

"What's wrong? Has something happened—?"

"Some kids at school were saying awful things about you," M.J. told her. "I punched Payton Carpenter in the mouth when he called you a bad word."

Oh dear Lord! Lorie had thought, short of her actually being murdered, things couldn't get much worse. But she'd been wrong.

Hannah lifted her head from where she had pressed it against Lorie's waist. "Jennifer Taylor said that you're a bad woman. Her mama said so. And—" Hannah puckered her mouth as she began crying.

"This is horrible." Lorie felt at a loss as how to handle the situation. What could she say to Hannah and M.J.? How could she explain?

"I told Jennifer that her mama was a liar." Hannah looked up at Lorie, her little tear-streaked face breaking Lorie's heart.

"I'm so sorry this happened." Lorie took Hannah's hand and held out her other hand to M.J. "It's very sweet of you both to defend me, but . . . I don't want either of you getting into fights with your classmates because of me. What is your father going to think about all of this?"

M.J. took Lorie's hand and as she led the children into the living room, M.J. said, "They said some bad things about Daddy, too."

"What?"

"Yeah, Colby Berryman said Daddy has the hots for you and he's letting his other head think for him." M.J. stood on tiptoe in order to reach her ear and then whispered, "I know what that means, but Hannah doesn't."

Crap! This was worse than awful. It was bad enough that Hannah and M.J. had to hear their classmates repeating the awful things their parents had said about her, but to have their father talked about in such a derogatory manner was shameful.

Lorie sat the children down on the sofa with her, one on either side. "I'm going to get Miss Shelley to call your father. He needs to know what's happened." *And I need him to help me explain to both of you why your classmates said the things they did about me and your dad.*

Up until that moment, Lorie had been so concerned about what had brought the children to her house this afternoon, both of them nearly in tears, that she hadn't thought about how they had gotten there.

"How did you two get here?" she asked.

M.J. and Hannah exchanged guilty looks before M.J. answered. "We sort of told a fib."

"What sort of fib did you tell and who did you tell it to?"

"Grams plays bridge on Monday afternoons, so

when Dad can't pick us up from school, we ride home with Mrs. Myers. She's got kids our age and . . . well, I told her that Grams wanted her to take us to Mrs. Shelby's house, because that's where they were playing bridge."

"My neighbor, Irene Shelby?"

"Yes, ma'am. I knew Mrs. Shelby lived down the road from you and that we could walk from her house to yours."

"Is your Grams playing bridge at Mrs. Shelby's house?"

"No, ma'am," M.J. admitted. "I told a fib. I guess I'll be in trouble for doing that, but we just had to see you."

Hannah cuddled up against Lorie. "We wanted you to know that no matter what anybody says, we don't believe you're a bad person. You're a nice person, Miss Lorie, and we like you. We like you a lot."

Lorie barely managed not to burst into tears. She put her arms around the children's shoulders and hugged them to her, then glanced across the room at Shelley, who shook her head and offered an understanding smile.

"Miss Shelley is going to call your daddy and let him know where y'all are. And I want you to tell us where your grandmother is so that she can call her, too. Nell is probably worried sick about you two."

"Yes, ma'am. We're sorry if we did something wrong."

"It'll be all right," Lorie assured him. "Your dad will understand."

Mike would understand, all right. And he would blame her. Well, better he take his anger out on her than on his kids.

He opened the briefcase that he had sent FedEx to himself from Atlanta and looked at Ebony O's bloody clothes. A slinky red dress that had accentuated her abundant curves. No bra, since she hadn't been wearing one. A pair of gold high heels. And a lacy red thong. He had not removed her ruby earrings and her gaudy three-carat diamond solitaire from her body. Jewelry was of no importance.

He fingered the red lace forming the V of the thong, lifted it carefully, and crushed it in his hand. Once a slut, always a slut. Shontee Thomas might have gotten out of the porno business, but she remained a worthless piece of trash until she took her last breath.

The others were no different.

Wicked. Immoral. Perverts. Tempting good men to think and do evil.

He brought the thong up to his face and buried his nose in the alluring scent of the whore's sweet pussy. A shiver of sexual excitement rippled through him. Even in death, a woman like that still held the power to entice a man.

He lifted his face and looked at the four window-

336

less walls surrounding him. Photographs of each person who had performed in *Midnight Masquerade* had been centered on individual cork boards. And attached to the boards beside each nude photo was a single article of clothing. Underwear. Dean's boxer shorts. Charlie's white briefs. Hilary's bra. And now Shontee's thong. He had acquired quite a collection in the past four months.

He took a small plastic box from his pocket, opened the box, and removed a couple of tacks. After he mounted the thong beneath Ebony O's picture, he stood back and smiled at his handiwork.

Four of the nine were now in God's hands and five were left, five who were yet to meet their rightful judgment. There was no doubt in his mind that all of them would be condemned to hell, a fitting end to lives not only lived in sin but lived in a way that catered to the most basic, animalistic nature in others. The only way to free himself once and for all from their evil influence was to kill them. He was justified in what he was doing. Killing them was like killing vermin, ridding the world of dangerous creatures who spread disease and destruction.

As he circled the interior of the storage rental, appreciating his collection, he paused in front of her photograph. Young. Beautiful. Sexy. And so very wicked.

"I'm saving you for last," he said aloud. "Always the best for last."

Mike's mother had phoned him, panicked and half out of her mind. His children were missing.

"When Kim hadn't dropped them at Gloria's by three-thirty, I called her and she said they had told her I was playing bridge at Irene Shelby's house. Now, why would they have told her such a thing? They knew where I'd be. Lord help us, Irene doesn't even play bridge."

"Did you call Mrs. Shelby and ask if the children were there?"

"Well, of course I did. She hasn't seen them."

While he had been reassuring his mother that M.J. and Hannah were okay and he would find them, his secretary had told him he had an urgent call on another line.

"It's something about your kids."

He had instantly put his mother on hold and taken the other call.

"Mike, this is Shelley Gilbert. Your children are here with Lorie. She said to tell you that they're all right, but you should get over here as soon as you can."

So here he was on Lorie's front porch, his mood alternating between relief and concern. Relief that his children were accounted for; and concern about why they had lied to Kim Myers and why they were at Lorie's house.

Before he rang the doorbell, Lorie opened the front door and stepped outside on the porch with him.

"Let's talk out here," she said.

"Where are M.J. and Hannah?"

"In the kitchen with Shelley. They're eating cookies and drinking milk. She'll keep them occupied while you and I talk."

"Okay. Talk."

"M.J. and Hannah told a fib—M.J.'s word—to get Kim Myers to drop them off at Mrs. Shelby's house so that they could walk here and see me. They both got in trouble at school today for defending me against some ugly things their classmates said about me."

Mike grumbled under his breath.

"I cannot begin to tell you how sorry I am that your children have been affected by what's happening to me now because of my past. I adore Hannah and M.J. and I'd never do anything to hurt them."

"I realize that." Mike frowned. "I guess I didn't know just how fond of you my kids are."

"It's my fault. I should have stayed away from them. If I had, they wouldn't even know who I am. But no, I couldn't leave well enough alone."

"Do they know about you—that you posed naked, that you made a movie—?"

"M.J. has one of the flyers, the photo of me in the nude. He told me that he hadn't shown it to Hannah." Lorie paused, took a deep breath and said, "Some kid told M.J. that you have the hots for me and that's why you're thinking with your other head."

"What!"

"Don't shout. The children might hear you."

"This is a damn screwed-up mess. I've stayed away from you ever since Molly died in order to protect my kids from shit like this."

"M.J. said he knew what thinking with your other head meant, but that Hannah didn't. Oh, Mike, he reminds me so much of you. He's such a wonderful little boy. He's been so protective of me. He told me that"—she swallowed—"if anybody else said anything bad about me, he'd sock them in the nose, too."

Mike groaned. "He hit somebody today?"

"I'm afraid so. Some boy named Payton something-or-other."

Mike made an odd noise, the sound a moan/laugh combination. "If Molly were here, she'd tell me that our son was acting way too much like me. But she'd say it with a smile. And she'd be right. I was always punching somebody in the mouth when I was a kid. I had a short fuse back then."

"Back then?"

"I manage to keep my temper under control most of the time. But I swear to God, when it comes to my kids . . ."

"We need to talk to them, you and I together. They deserve to know the truth or at least enough of the truth to understand why people are accusing you of having the hots for me. And I need to explain to them about the nude photo and—"

"I can't believe I'm saying this, but you're right. But we need to keep what we say as G-rated as possible. Kids these days know too much too soon as it is."

When Lorie opened the door and went inside, Mike followed directly behind her. They found M.J. and Hannah still in the kitchen, both sitting at the table finishing off their glasses of milk. As soon as Mike and Lorie entered the room, Shelley excused herself.

"Daddy!" Hannah set her glass on the table, shoved back her chair, got up, and ran to her father.

Mike swept her off her feet and set her on his hip. She gazed at him with a daughter's adoration in her dark blue eyes. "Are we in big trouble?"

"It isn't Hannah's fault." M.J. stood up and faced his father. "I'm the one who told Mrs. Myers the fib about Grams being at Mrs. Shelby's house."

"We'll discuss that later," Mike told him. "But right now, Miss Lorie and I need to talk to you two about the things y'all heard at school today."

"You mean about your having the hots for Miss Lorie?" Hannah smiled. "I know that means you like her for a girlfriend. And that's okay, Daddy. We like her, too. We like her a lot more than we do Miss Abby. We really don't like Miss Abby very much."

Mike wasn't surprised to hear that his children didn't especially like Abby. It wasn't as if their actions during the months he'd been dating Abby hadn't spoken for them.

"Miss Lorie used to be my girlfriend, a long time ago," Mike said. "Before I married your mama."

"Grams says that Mama would want you to get married again. You need a wife," Hannah told him. "And M.J. and I need a stepmama who would love us and maybe give us a baby brother or sister."

*Nell Birkett, you're a loud-mouthed busybody, that's what you are!* Mike would deal with his mother later.

"And we don't want Miss Abby. We don't like her and she sure doesn't love us," M.J. said. "We want Miss Lorie."

"Look, you two, stop playing matchmaker. Miss Lorie and I are not dating," Mike explained. "We're old friends. That's all."

"Oh, Daddy, you're telling a fib." Hannah smiled at him guilelessly. Mike set his daughter on her feet and cleared his throat.

"Miss Lorie and I are old friends and right now Miss Lorie's in trouble. Someone wants to hurt her, but we don't know who that person is. As the county sheriff, it's my duty to make sure Miss Lorie is safe. Do you understand?"

Both of his children stared at him and nodded simultaneously. M.J. said, "Yes, sir, we understand."

"A long time ago, when Miss Lorie was very young, she posed for some pictures that were printed in a magazine, and in those pictures, she isn't wearing any clothes." He waited, giving M.J.

and Hannah a chance to comment. When they didn't, he continued. "She also made one movie, a movie for grown-ups, and she wasn't wearing any clothes in that movie. Some people believe that what Miss Lorie did was wrong, and even though she's said she's sorry and that she wishes she'd never done it, there are people who won't forgive her."

"Those people aren't doing what God wants them to do," Hannah said. "We learned in Sunday school that God expects us to forgive other people when they do something wrong and then they have to forgive us when we do something wrong."

"You're absolutely right, sweetheart." Out of the mouths of babes. His nine-year-old daughter understood a great deal more about forgiveness than most adults. Certainly more than he did.

M.J. stared at Lorie. "Hannah and I forgive you, Miss Lorie." He glanced at Mike. "And so do you, don't you, Daddy?"

When Mike stood there, unable to utter a single word, Hannah tugged on his hand. "Tell her, Daddy, tell her. Tell her that you forgive her and that you really do have the hots for her."

Lorie laughed. Mike glared at her. And then he smiled.

He looked right at Lorie and said, "Forgiveness is a two-way street. If I forgive you, then you'll have to forgive me."

"It's a deal."

"Tell her the rest, Daddy," Hannah insisted.

"My daughter wants me to tell you that I have the hots for you."

Hannah giggled. "Now everything is going to be wonderful."

Mike and Lorie looked at each other. He knew that she realized everything was far from wonderful, but for now, for today, they could pretend it was. For Hannah and M.J.

# Chapter 21

Ransom Owens lived alone in the brick house built by his ancestors, an Italianate style with a low-pitched roof topped with a cupola. At present, he was divorced from his second wife, Brenda Lee. For all intents and purposes his only daily contact with the outside world was his housekeeper, Ramona. And it was she who opened the front door that Tuesday morning. The elderly woman, her short white hair permed into tight curls, wore a large floral apron over her polyester navy blue slacks and red T-shirt. Wearing no makeup or jewelry, and with her wrinkled face, thin lips, and hawk sharp nose, the tall, robust housekeeper could have easily passed for a man. Until she opened her mouth. The voice was Marilyn Monroe whispery, with a childlike tone.

"Please, come in. Mr. Ransom is expecting y'all." Ramona stepped back and swept her arm out in a welcoming gesture. "He's in the sunroom out back, having his morning tea break. The poor dear has probably been up since dawn working on his latest book."

Maleah sensed this old woman was genuinely fond of her employer.

"What sort of book is Mr. Owens writing?" Derek asked.

"Oh, the kind he always writes," Ramona replied. "A history book. He's had ten published, all of them about local Virginia history, from before the Revolutionary War to the present."

When they didn't comment, she added, "Mr. Ransom always was as smart as a whip. The boy had the soul of a poet. Neither of his wives appreciated him, that's for sure. But at least Miss Brenda Lee didn't shame him in front of the world the way Miss Terri did. Now that gal was a real piece of work. But you two probably know all about her, your being investigators."

"Then you were the family's housekeeper when Mr. Owens was married to his first wife?" Maleah asked.

"Sure was. I'm the one who had to look after Mr. Tyler when he was a baby. Miss Terri didn't take to motherhood. Finally Mr. Ransom hired a nanny for the little tyke."

"What sort of child was Tyler?" Derek inquired.

"Smart, just like his daddy, but every bit as beautiful as his mama. Too bad the good Lord wasted so much beauty on such a selfish, uncaring woman."

She led them down the hallway, talking nonstop all the way, and then paused and pointed to an arched open doorway. "Straight through there."

"Thank you," Derek said.

"Would either of you care for tea?" Ramona asked.

Maleah and Derek replied simultaneously, "No, thank you."

They found Ransom Owens sitting in an ornate white wicker chair, his eyes closed and a look of serenity on his long, narrow face. His brown hair, thinning on top, was neatly combed and he was cleanly shaved. He wore brown slacks, a beige shirt, and a tan sweater, the garments fitting loosely on his reed-thin body. When he heard them approach, he opened his tepid gray eyes, picked up the notepad in his lap, and laid it on the side table to his right. Maleah's first thought was that this man certainly didn't look like her idea of a killer. No, Ransom Owens looked like a well-to-do gentleman of leisure, a man most definitely born in the wrong century.

"Do come in and sit down." His deep baritone voice seemed at odds with his soft, scholarly appearance.

"We appreciate your agreeing to talk to us," Derek said as he slipped his hand beneath Maleah's elbow and guided her toward the wicker settee flanked by two massive, billowing ferns. Her initial reaction was immediate withdrawal, but she managed to stop herself from jerking away.

"I thought it best to clear up a few matters," Ransom said, watching them closely as they sat side by side on the settee. "I assume my son had nothing good to say about me. I did my best with him, but it was difficult raising a high-strung boy without a mother . . . a mother who shamed us both. We'd have been better off by far if Terri had died years ago."

Before either Maleah or Derek had a chance to respond, Ransom continued quickly. "And before you ask, no, I have no intention of murdering my ex-wife or any of the vulgar, uncouth people she associated with in the past. I know Tyler believes I may be this person the police are looking for, the Midnight Killer. I assure you, I am not. This is simply my son's way of tormenting me."

"Why would your son want to torment you?" Derek asked.

Ransom focused his weak, watery pale eyes on Derek. "A man does not like to admit such a shameful truth, but . . . My son hates me. Perhaps with just cause. I never understood him. I tried, but he was too much like Terri. He was willful and disobedient and never appreciated the way of life I offered him."

"We would like to take you at your word, Mr. Owens," Maleah said. "But we want you to know that the Powell Agency will be investigating further, so if you could tell us where you were and what you were doing on specific dates—the dates the four victims were killed—we could rule you out as a suspect."

"I am alone here in my home a great deal of the time," Ransom told them. "There are days when I see no one. Ramona comes in once or twice a week now, mostly to prepare and freeze meals for me to warm up later. She's too old to do much cleaning, although she runs the vacuum and stirs up a little dust with the feather duster. I have someone from a housekeeping agency come in every other week. Ramona pretends not to know."

Derek reached inside his jacket pocket and pulled out a list of dates. "We would greatly appreciate it if you'd take a look and see if you can account for your whereabouts on each date."

Ransom held out his hand and grasped the paper with long, bony fingers. He glanced at the dates, closed his eyes as if concentrating, and then handed the list back to Derek. "I'm not certain. I travel occasionally. I give lectures on Virginia history. I also do research. And I have friends who live out of state. I believe I was at home on all those dates. I know I was on the most recent date, when Shontee Thomas was killed in Atlanta."

"Can anyone corroborate your whereabouts?" Maleah asked.

"I'm afraid not. I live alone, eat alone, and sleep

348

alone. And I seldom answer the telephone. I don't like being disturbed when I'm working."

"Then you don't have an alibi?" Derek studied Ransom as if trying to decide whether the man was lying.

"No, I'm afraid I don't, but naturally, you'll dig around to see if you can find out if perhaps I was not here as I say I was. I understand. That's your job." Ransom glanced from Derek to Maleah. "Might I suggest that you check into my son's whereabouts on those dates. It's far more likely that he will turn out to be your killer."

Maleah and Derek exchanged a questioning glance. She knew he was thinking exactly what she was—that just as Tyler had accused his father, now Ransom was accusing his son. Talk about a dysfunctional family.

"Would you care to explain why you think your son is a murderer?" Derek asked.

"I thought I'd done that," Ransom said. "I sincerely hope my suspicions are unjustified. They probably are. I simply wanted to point out that between the two of us, Tyler is far more likely to be a killer than I am."

"Then you're not accusing your son of murder. You're simply saying that he's more likely to be a killer than you are. Is that right?" Maleah wanted Ransom Owens to clarify his comments.

"That's correct."

Maleah questioned Ransom for the next ten

minutes and received replies that revealed very little new information. If this man was a killer, she would be surprised. He seemed like a gentle soul, wounded and lonely. But it was possible that beneath that melancholy exterior, another man existed, a man capable of murder.

As she and Derek walked down the sidewalk toward their parked rental car, she paused and said, "So, what do you think?"

"I think Tyler Owens hates his father," Derek told her. "And I think there's more to Ransom Owens than meets the eye."

"Do you think either of them could be the Midnight Killer?"

"Sure. Either of them could be. But at this point, the way I see it is that each is pointing the finger elsewhere to take suspicion off himself."

"Great father-son relationship, huh? Makes me feel sorry for Tyler. Most fathers would do anything to protect their son, but Ransom Owens would be willing to sacrifice his son to save himself."

Doing her level best to keep her hand steady, Lorie gave Jack the letter she had received in today's mail. Another threat. The wording was identical to the other two messages she had received, and this envelope was postmarked Atlanta, Georgia. The son of a bitch had mailed the letter after he'd killed Shontee. Had the others

350

—Jean, Terri, Charlene, and Sonny—also received another letter? In her phone call last night, Maleah had told Lorie about interviewing Terri's son and their plans to interview her ex-husband.

"Tyler Owens thinks his father is the Midnight Killer," Maleah had said.

"What do you think?"

"Derek and I are both reserving judgment until we meet with Ransom Owens in the morning. After that, we're set to fly to Louisville in the afternoon and interview the Reverend Grant Leroy."

Lorie had laughed at the thought of Grant Leroy being a born-again Christian evangelist. The Grant she remembered had been a hard-drinking, womanizing, foul-mouthed SOB. On occasion, he had been charming, but only when he thought it would get him something he wanted.

"What about Sonny and Charlene?" Lorie had asked. "Has Powell's been able to track them down?"

"Sonny's in Europe somewhere, but that's all we know right now. As for Charlene Strickland, she seems to have dropped off the face of the earth. But eventually, we'll find them. The one good thing is that if we're having this much difficulty finding them, then so is the killer. If his letters aren't reaching them, he'd have no way to know since there's no return address."

Lorie watched as Jack scanned the letter and then carefully placed it in a plastic bag. Even though there was little chance the killer's fingerprints were on the envelope or letter, Jack followed the proper procedure.

"How many letters did Shontee receive before he killed her?" Lorie looked to Shelley for an answer. "And what about Hilary and Charlie?"

"The number of letters received before each was killed has varied," Shelley replied. "If each had received the exact number, then we could connect the dots and figure out who's next. We believe that's the reason the number of letters varies. He wants to warn the intended victims, frighten each of you, torment each of you, but not actually let you know for sure that you're next. It's all a part of the satisfaction he acquires from forewarning his victims."

Jack placed his hand on Lorie's shoulder. "I know it's rough staying cooped up here. The offer for you and Ms. Gilbert to stay with Cathy and me is an open invitation. You'd still be confined to quarters, but you'd be with friends. It might be good for you to be with Cathy, and if you were with us, she'd worry a little less about you."

"I'll consider it," Lorie said. "But for now, I'm staying put, here in my own home. And if that newspaper article hadn't come out and those flyers hadn't been circulated around town, I'd be going to work today."

"It's a good idea to keep a low profile a little while longer."

Lorie nodded. "By the way, did Mike tell you about Hannah and M.J. coming here to see me yesterday?"

"He mentioned it."

"Did he tell you that M.J. socked another kid because he said something ugly about me?"

"Yeah, Mike mentioned that, too."

"This crazy business with the Midnight Killer is affecting not only my life, but the lives of people I care about. You and Cathy and Seth. And Mike . . . and Mike's children. Maybe I should leave town, go somewhere—"

Jack grasped her by the shoulders. "You're not going anywhere. You're staying put right here where the people who care about you can look after you. If you left town, my wife would go with you."

When Jack offered her a comforting smile, she smiled back at him.

"Speaking of your wife—did she open Treasures today?"

Jack's smile faded. "No. We thought it best to keep the shop closed this week."

"That's certainly going to affect our bottom line."

Lorie's income came from her half of the profits from Treasures. Over the years, she had managed to buy a house and a car and open a savings account. But with the shop closed for a week—possibly longer—she would have no choice but to dip into her small savings, and it wouldn't take long to deplete every penny.

"Don't worry about money," Jack told her. "Cathy and I will—"

"No, you will not! I'm not taking money from y'all. I've got some savings. If necessary, I'll use it to tide me over."

Jack grimaced. "You're as stubborn as Cathy. I'll let you two hash it out." He gave Lorie's shoulder a tight squeeze. "I'm just a phone call away."

"I know. I appreciate everything you and Mike are doing."

As Lorie walked Jack to the door, Shelley's phone rang. They both paused and waited while she took the call. Her end of the conversation was limited to mostly listening and saying very little. The moment she hung up, she turned and looked directly at them.

"That was Maleah. She wanted us to know that Powell's found Charlene Strickland. She's dead."

Lorie gasped. "Dead? But how's that possible? He's been killing only one person each month."

"The Midnight Killer didn't murder her," Shelley said. "She died over a year ago from a drug overdose. She was working as a prostitute and had pretty much fallen off the radar. She wasn't using her real name, wasn't staying in contact with anyone she had known, not family or friends."

"I didn't know her all that well. She was an odd

sort of girl and even back when we made *Midnight Masquerade*, she was into the drug scene big-time."

"With Charlene Strickland already dead, that leaves only four actors from the movie left alive," Shelley said. "Jean Misner, Sonny Deguzman, Terri Owens, and—"

"And me," Lorie said. "The only thing we don't know is if he plans for me to be the May, June, July, or August victim of the month."

During the past six years, Reverend Grant Leroy, with the assistance of his wife and son, had built up a rather impressive congregation in Louisville, Kentucky. His followers had donated generously, allowing the reverend to build a huge church that seated a thousand people and a six-thousand-square-foot parsonage where he and his family lived. When Powell's had contacted the man who had directed numerous porno films in the past three decades, including *Midnight Masquerade*, his wife hadn't hesitated, even for a second, to set up an appointment.

"We have no secrets from our congregation," she'd told them. "They know all about Grant's past. They understand how the devil can tempt all of us to do evil things."

Renee Leroy had gone on to suggest the time and place for the meeting. "Grant teaches a young people's group on Tuesday evening. Have your agents come by the church office around eight o'clock and he'll meet with them then."

So, here they were at the Redeemer Church.

Maleah hadn't attended a church service in years. Her stepfather had insisted on the family attending services every time the church doors opened and had said a prayer of thanks before every meal. To outside observers, Nolan Reaves had appeared to be a good Christian. In truth, the man had been a sadistic monster who had made life a living hell for her mother, her brother, and her. Since leaving home for college at eighteen, Maleah hadn't been inside a church except for weddings, christenings, and funerals.

"Quite a place," Derek said. "An auditorium that seats a thousand. Can you imagine the cash they rake in from their parishioners?"

"Enough to allow Grant Leroy and his family to live the good life."

They entered through one set of five double front doors that led to the expansive vestibule. Dozens of young people, who appeared to range in age from thirteen to twenty, exited the sanctuary, many staying and milling around, everyone smiling and laughing. A tall, slender blonde wearing a fuchsia silk pantsuit and a string of black pearls approached Maleah and Derek.

"You must be the private detectives from the Powell Agency," she said as she held out her hand. "I'm Renee Leroy."

"Maleah Perdue."

She shook Maleah's hand first and offered her a warm, nice-to-meet-you smile; then she turned to Derek and her friendly smile suddenly came alive with feminine interest.

"I'm Derek Lawrence."

When he took the lady's hand, their gazes locked, and Maleah wanted to kick Derek and remind him that Renee Leroy, although at least twenty years her husband's junior, was most definitely a married woman. He should save all his charm for single women. Surely there were enough of those around to feed his monumental ego with their blubbering adoration.

"Come with me, please." Renee slipped her arm through Derek's. "Grant will meet us in the office."

When Renee led them down a long corridor, Maleah kept in step and gave Derek a scowling glance. He shrugged as if to ask, "Can I help it if women find me irresistible?"

Maleah hardened her frown. Derek smiled and winked at her.

Renee released Derek and punched the Up button on the elevator. When the doors opened instantly, Maleah and Derek entered the elevator behind her, and on the quick ride to the second floor, they didn't have time for conversation.

"This way," Renee said when they exited the elevator.

After seeing the size and grandeur of the Redeemer Church, Maleah wasn't the least surprised by the huge and expensively decorated office area housed on the second level. Renee led them through two outer offices and into her husband's private domain. Decorated in sleek black, white, chrome and glass, the 30' x 30' room all but screamed interior designer, which led to Maleah's question.

"Did you decorate the office, Mrs. Leroy?"

Renee beamed with pride. "Why yes, I did. How ever did you know that?" She giggled. "Silly me. You're an investigator. You probably did some background research on me as well as on Grant."

"As a matter of fact, we did." But Maleah did not recall any info about Renee Leroy ever having been an interior designer. She had been a waitress, a bartender, a restaurant hostess, and even a salesclerk in a paint and wallpaper store.

A robust man with impeccably styled salt-and-pepper hair and sparkling brown eyes came out from behind the enormous chrome and glass desk, walked across the room, and came right up to Maleah. Not handsome by any means, Grant Leroy did project an image of wealth and success with his neatly tailored pinstriped suit, his Italian leather loafers, and the gold and diamond jewelry that adorned his wrists and fingers.

"Ms. Perdue, I presume," he said as he grabbed her hand and gave it a sturdy shake before turning to Derek and doing the same. "And Mr. Lawrence. I understand you have a few questions for me about some of my old cronies from the days when I was trapped in that quagmire of sin and damnation, the adult movie business."

It was all Maleah could do not to laugh in the man's face. *Quagmire of sin and damnation? Give me a break.*

Derek jumped in with the first question. Apparently he was not on the verge of laughing. "You're aware, of course, that four former stars that you directed in *Midnight Masquerade* have been murdered, one each in the past four months."

Dramatically laying his hand over his chest, Grant heaved a deep sigh. "I was saddened to hear of their deaths, but not surprised. The evil that we do lives on, and if we don't repent of our sins and beg our merciful Lord to cleanse us, body and soul, then there is no hope for us."

Someone cleared their throat. Maleah looked over her shoulder and saw a young man in his twenties standing in the open doorway. He was Grant Leroy's image, only many years younger, with dark hair and eyes and a somber expression on his face.

"Come on in, son." Grant motioned with a come-here gesture. "This is my son, Heath. He's our youth minister and I'm proud to say my right-hand man helping me do the Lord's work."

Unsmiling, Heath moved his wary gaze slowly

from Maleah to Derek and then to his father. "I'm not sure you should be speaking to these people without a lawyer."

Grant dismissed his son's objections with a wave of his hand. "Nonsense. I'm not being accused of anything. And since I have nothing to hide, you shouldn't worry about these investigators asking me a few questions about my amoral past and the people I associated with back then."

"The Powell Agency has contacted all the actors, those who haven't been murdered already, to warn them that they're in danger," Maleah said. "And we're interviewing everyone associated with that movie, everyone from the producer to the cameramen."

"We believe the killer is in some way connected to that one particular movie," Derek said. "We are not accusing anyone. We're simply asking questions in order to eliminate as many possible suspects as we can."

"Then you consider my father a suspect?" Heath asked.

"Mr. Lawrence didn't say that," Grant told his son and then focused on Derek. "I am a changed man. I'm a devoted servant of God. I believe in and teach others to love the Lord and our fellow man. I am opposed to violence of any kind. I have only love in my heart for those poor, wretched souls who haven't found Jesus and are still plagued by their past wickedness."

"Have you kept in touch with anyone associated with *Midnight Masquerade*?" Maleah asked.

"I have had no communication with anyone in the past six years . . . well, except for Sonny Deguzman," Grant said. "Sonny came to see me and asked for my help. He wanted money, of course. At first I refused him, but then he convinced me that he truly wanted to change, to find salvation. He joined the church and even worked with us for several months. Unfortunately, he stole from us and I had no choice but to let him go."

"Grant could have had him arrested," Renee said. "But he didn't."

"How long ago was that?" Derek asked.

"A little over two years ago," Grant said. "And about eight months ago, I received a note from Sonny and a check for the amount he had stolen."

"Do you know where he was at that time?" Maleah asked.

"Somewhere in Europe." Grant looked at his wife. "Do you recall exactly where?"

"In Italy, I believe, some seacoast town," she replied. "He mentioned that he was fishing every day and enjoying the simple things in life."

"Messina!" Grant slapped his hands together. "That's it. That's where he was living eight months ago."

Maleah nodded. "That information should help us track him down and warn him. Is Sonny the only person from your days at Starlight

Productions that you've heard from in the past half dozen or so years?"

"Yes, he's the only one."

"Do you recall anything in particular that went on during the filming of *Midnight Masquerade* that resulted in threats being made?"

For the next twenty minutes, Maleah and Derek went through the series of questions they had asked the other possible suspects. And Grant's answers pretty much echoed what everyone else had said. Everyone had disliked Travis Dillard and hinted that if anyone from their past might be the Midnight Killer it was the owner of Starlight Productions, the man who had produced *Midnight Masquerade*. To a person, they had all agreed that Hilary Finch had been a first-class bitch and Charlie Wong had been a nice guy with a great sense of humor.

"Yes, of course I remember Lorie Hammonds. She was a good kid. She wasn't the usual type, if you know what I mean," Grant said. "Gorgeous and sexy, but classy, the type who came across as a lady. I've prayed for her and felt in my heart that she had probably found the Lord."

"One final question." Maleah knew that while she had done most of the talking for the two of them, Derek had been observing. After all, that was his area of expertise, using his off-the-charts IQ and noteworthy sixth sense to profile the people they interviewed.

"Certainly," Grant replied confidently.

"Can you account for your whereabouts at the time Dean Wilson, Hilary Finch Chambless, Charles Wong, and Shontee Thomas were murdered?"

Heath Leroy grumbled under his breath and then as he walked toward his father, he said aloud, "Damn it, Dad, I told you that you shouldn't have agreed to this interview without your lawyer present!"

Waking suddenly, Lorie shot straight up in bed. Her heart hammered maddeningly, the sound drumming in her ears. What had awakened her? She hadn't been dreaming, at least she didn't remember if she had. She sat quietly and listened, but heard nothing out of the ordinary, just the usual creaking and popping sounds that a house made. The foundation settling, the water pipes moaning, the wind sighing softly around the eaves.

A dog howled in the distance.

Once her breathing returned to normal, she reached over and turned on the bedside lamp, then tossed back the covers and got out of bed. She checked the clock. 3:15 A.M. Well past the witching hour. Or in her case, "the hour of death." Not bothering to slip into her house shoes and put on her lightweight robe, she left her bedroom and walked into the hall.

Why was she so jittery when there was no reason

to be? The Midnight Killer murdered once a month, and always around the hour of midnight. It had been only a few days since Shontee's murder. There was no reason to be so scared. The timing was wrong, both the month and the hour. She knew that the alarm system was armed and Shelley Gilbert was here. Shelley, a trained bodyguard who knew how to use the gun she carried.

She didn't want to wake Shelley, but she was now wide-awake and knew she wouldn't be able to go back to sleep. If she went down the hall and into the living room or kitchen, Shelley would hear her and get up to check on her. But what did it matter? It wasn't as if either of them had anything to do tomorrow, anywhere to be. They could take afternoon naps.

Thinking that perhaps a glass of chocolate milk and a few cookies might help her relax—sugar certainly might help to soothe her rattled nerves—Lorie headed for the kitchen. As she neared the kitchen, she noticed light creeping out from beneath the closed door. Was Shelley in the kitchen? Had she been unable to sleep and had gotten up and that's what had awakened Lorie?

She approached the door, then hesitated, her hand hovering in the air. "Shelley?" she called to her bodyguard.

No response. She called her name again. Silence.

A tremor of uncertainty began in Lorie's belly and spread out into her limbs. Reminding herself that it was highly possible that they had simply not turned off the kitchen light before they went to bed, Lorie grasped the doorknob. When she opened the door, her pulse raced at an alarming speed. But once she looked into the room and saw that it was empty and nothing was out of place, she breathed a sigh of relief.

She decided that maybe ice cream was called for now, to go with the cookies, instead of chocolate milk. As she reached to open the small pantry where the cookies were stored, she noticed that the back door was cracked open ever so slightly. How was that possible? Shelley always locked the outside doors, soundly securing them, before she armed the alarm system and went to bed. Had Shelley heard something outside and gone into the yard to check the grounds?

Shaking nervously from head to toe, Lorie forced herself to go straight to the back door and check the alarm keypad. The green light winked at her, warning her that the system was deactivated.

*Don't panic. Shelley's outside. There's nothing to worry about, nothing at all. But what do I do? Go outside to find Shelley? Close the door, lock it, and telephone Jack?*

Lorie stood behind the partially closed door and called Shelley's name several times, but did not get a response of any kind. She eased the door open wide and looked outside. Moonlight washed the backyard and nearby woods with a faded yellow-white hue. Pallid gray shadows hovered at the corners of the house and the trees spattered cadaverous silhouettes across the lawn, their tips splintering into thin, fingerlike shards.

Lorie shivered.

*Dear God, where are you, Shelley?*

Had the Midnight Killer come to Dunmore? Had he lured Shelley into a trap? Had he killed her?

*Don't assume the worst.*

Shelley was a trained professional. She wouldn't be easily duped.

*Something is wrong. Close the door and lock it!*

Lorie's heartbeat pounded in her head. Her pulse rate revved up as fear-induced adrenaline flooded her system.

When she reached for the door handle, she looked down and in her peripheral vision saw a dark puddle on the back porch. The light from inside the kitchen cast a dim glow over the red liquid.

Blood?

God in heaven, it was a pool of blood!

She stared at the dark stain, her gaze riveted to the spot.

It *was* blood. No doubt about it.

Was it Shelley's blood?

Off in the distance, a dog howled again. Lorie cried out, the unexpected sound startling her. Hesitating, uncertain what to do, she stood frozen to the spot, her unsteady hand hovering over the door handle.

Had he killed Shelley? Was he out there waiting to strike again?

But it was way past midnight. And he always killed at midnight, didn't he?

Something rustled through the brush in the nearby wooded area, the sound echoing in the predawn quiet. Lorie looked away from the bloodstain and searched the semidarkness for any sign of Shelley—or someone else, possibly the Midnight Killer.

*Whatever has happened, you can't help Shelley. Do what she would want you to do—protect yourself.*

Lorie slammed the door and locked it. And then she raced to the telephone. With trembling fingers, she dialed Jack and Cathy's number.

# Chapter 22

Deputy Buddy Pounders lived a quarter of a mile from Lorie, so Jack had gotten in touch with him immediately. When he arrived, Buddy instructed Lorie to stay inside with the doors locked until he canvassed the area around her house. She peered through the living room windows, watching, waiting, and holding her breath. She had turned on every outside light—porch lights, security lights, and even the miniature lights surrounding the patio. Five minutes later, Jack pulled his car up behind Buddy's. Cathy got out and rushed toward the front porch while Jack stopped to talk to Buddy. Lorie unlocked the door, and the minute Cathy came barreling into the house, Lorie grabbed on to her friend for dear life. Trembling uncontrollably from head to toe, she clung to Cathy.

"You're safe." Cathy hugged her fiercely. "I'm here and I'm not going to leave you."

"Shelley has disappeared and there's a pool of blood on the back porch. Putting the two together means that he's killed her, doesn't it? He's here in Dunmore and I'm his next victim."

Rubbing Lorie's back soothingly, Cathy said, "You don't know that for a fact. We don't know anything, not yet. Jack and Buddy will come in and tell us as soon as they finish checking the yard and—"

"How could he have gotten into the house? Why didn't the alarm go off? How did he outsmart a trained bodyguard?"

Cathy grasped Lorie's hands. "Listen to me. We do not know that Shelley is dead. Right now, she's only missing. And we do not know that the Midnight Killer is in Dunmore."

Lorie took a deep breath and then nodded. Cathy was right, of course. But if the Midnight Killer wasn't responsible for Shelley Gilbert's disappearance, then who was? And if she wasn't dead, why was there a pool of partially dried blood on the back porch?

"Let's go in the kitchen and I'll fix you some hot tea or cocoa." Cathy tugged on Lorie's hands.

Lorie fell into step beside Cathy. "Just go ahead and fix coffee since none of us will get any more sleep tonight. And it wouldn't hurt if you put a little whiskey in my cup."

"Do you have any whiskey?" Cathy asked as they entered the kitchen.

"In the cabinet over the microwave."

The following fifteen minutes passed slowly, each second unbearably long for Lorie as she sipped on the whiskey-laced coffee and prayed that Shelley Gilbert would be found alive. She and Cathy sat at the table, Cathy doing her best to make idle conversation in order to take Lorie's mind off the worst-case scenario. Suddenly, they heard the front door open and footsteps trod down the hall. It had to be Jack since he and Cathy were the only other people who had a key to her house.

"Where are y'all?" Jack called.

"We're in the kitchen," Cathy told him.

The door swung open and Jack came into the room with Mike Birkett directly behind him. Lorie's heart skipped a beat when her gaze met Mike's. She had never been so glad to see anybody. Despite the comfort Cathy offered and the protection Jack and Buddy provided, to her, Mike's presence meant safety and security.

"How's it going in here?" Jack glanced at Cathy.

369

"We're okay," Cathy replied. "Drinking coffee"—she eyed the whiskey bottle on the counter—"and doing our best not to jump to any erroneous conclusions."

"That's good," Jack said.

Mike came over to Lorie, dropped to his haunches, and looked into her eyes. "There's no sign of Shelley, but there is a blood trail from the back porch to the wooded area behind your house. I've put in a call for more men and a couple of dogs to search the woods."

"What about the blood on the porch?" Lorie asked. "Oh, Mike, there's so much blood out there."

Mike nodded. "Yeah, there is." He reached out and laid his hand over Lorie's. "Cathy is going to stay here with you and I'll have a couple of deputies watching the house. You're safe. Do you understand?"

"Yes, I'm safe. But what about Shelley?"

"I don't know," Mike admitted. "But as soon as I know something, you'll know it. I'm not going to keep anything from you."

"Thank you."

Lorie watched Mike as he rose to his feet and motioned to Jack. The two men went out the way they had come in, through the front entrance. Lorie figured they didn't want to risk disturbing anything on the back porch since it was probably the site of a homicide.

• • •

In that hazy, cotton-wrapped vagueness of being only partially awake, he lay there and gazed up at the ceiling. He knew that it would be necessary to alter his plans and speed up the process before the Powell Agency and the FBI closed in on him. Perhaps he had given himself too much credit for being able to outsmart them. When he had formulated his plan, he'd had no idea that the Powell Agency would become involved. Their resources were practically unlimited and their success rate was off the charts.

*The sooner I act again, the better. They won't be expecting another kill so soon. They believe they have until May before the Midnight Killer strikes again. They're wrong.*

Now completely awake and alert, he flipped on the bedside lamp and looked at the clock. 4:45 A.M. He rose from the bed and walked barefoot across the wooden floor, then eased open the door and made his way quietly down the hall. After entering his study, he locked the door behind him before going to his desk. He opened the bottom right drawer and removed a rectangular metal box secured with a combination lock. No one ever bothered his personal items, but the contents of the box would be lethal for him if anyone accidentally discovered them.

He rotated the lock, easily pausing at each secret number until the catch popped open, allowing him to carefully remove the lock and set it aside for the time being. After lifting the lid, he reached inside and removed a thin stack of letters secured with a rubber band. He fingered the envelopes, each one containing the identical message.

Charlene Strickland was to be his next victim, but when he had begun making inquiries about her this week, no one seemed to know where she was. He had been so sure that he had tracked her down to her most recent residence. As of eighteen months ago, she had lived in New York City, and that was where he'd sent the letters. Apparently, she had moved and left no forwarding address. He had to find her. As long as one *Midnight Masquerade* actor remained alive, he wouldn't be free. If all other search avenues failed, he would hire his own private detective to hunt down Charlene. Naturally, he would not reveal his true identity to the detective and he would pay him in cash.

He removed a photograph from the metal box. As his gaze moved slowly over the snapshot, tears gathered in his eyes. Things might have been so different for him, if only . . .

There was no point in looking back. The past could not be altered to suit a person's personal desires. A person had to accept his part in the grand scheme of things, in the divine plan that assigned a purpose to each human being. It had taken him a long time to understand what his true purpose was.

He had fought against his thoughts and feelings, believing them perverse, but now he understood that he must not only accept the ruthless side of his nature, but embrace it. Others would see him as a heartless killer, but he knew the truth. He had been given the ability to kill without remorse. That was a rare and special gift, one that should be accepted without question and used for the good of mankind.

He had eliminated four of the nine. Wicked. Immoral. Vile. Wanton. The devil's minions. They were creatures not content with reveling in their sins privately, but were evildoers who excited and tempted, who coerced and lured, flaunting their sins for the world to see.

Lacey Butts, also known as Charlene Strickland, was to have been his next kill. But all his efforts to find her had failed. However, he had no intention of allowing this minor setback to stop him from continuing with his important work. He would simply exchange one for another, swap their names on his list. Surely before he reached the final name, he would have located Charlene. He could alter minor items in his plan, but not the major things. All nine must die.

If at all possible, he wanted to save "her" until last. After all, she was the most important one. At least she was to him. All he had to do was close his eyes in order to see her as she had been in *Midnight Masquerade*. His body reacted the way it always did when he thought of her naked beauty being ravished by other men.

The voice inside his head, that incessant, condemning voice, tormented him. *Look at her. So beautiful on the outside and yet so very rotten inside. Black-hearted rotten. Watch her. See the way she moves, the way she talks, the way she smiles. She likes what those men do to her. And she enjoys what she does to them.*

Covering his ears with his hands, he tried to shut out the voice. But he couldn't.

*Stop fighting it. Listen to what he says. He knows the truth. She is evil. They're all evil. Once you've killed every one of them, the voice will stop. He won't ever say those things again. There will be no reason for him to make you listen.*

He closed his eyes and dropped his hands from his ears. The voice softened to a whisper.

*Look at her breasts. Full and round and lush. Her nipples are tight and berry pink and begging to be sucked. Watch the way she spreads her legs, unashamed to reveal the most secret part of her body to those men and to every man who watches her. Listen to the way she moans and sighs as they do all manner of unspeakable things to her.*

As the voice spoke to him, the movie played inside his mind as vividly as if he was watching the newly released DVD. He had seen *Midnight Masquerade* so many times that the images were seared into his brain.

• • •

By daybreak, a dozen deputies, along with two bloodhounds and their trainer, were scouring the woods behind Lorie's house. Mike had assigned two deputies to stay behind and guard Lorie and Cathy and keep the back porch cordoned off as a crime scene, while he and Jack joined the search party. He had spoken to Wade Ballard less than half an hour ago and the chief had offered Mike however many Dunmore police officers he needed.

"If we don't find Shelley Gilbert within an hour, I'll contact you again and you can send your people to help us widen the search."

While he'd been on the phone with the police chief, Jack had called Maleah to inform her that Shelley was missing and they felt certain foul play was involved.

"Maleah is going to contact Nicole Powell," Jack said. "I expect the agency will send in some people, even if we find Shelley alive and well."

"What are the odds of that happening?" It had been a rhetorical question. Mike knew that the odds were not in their favor. If that was Shelley Gilbert's blood on Lorie's back porch, then more than likely the Powell agent was dead.

"Do you think the Midnight Killer overpowered Shelley?" Jack asked as they entered the woods.

"Hell if I know," Mike replied. "If he did kill her, then why did he drag her off into the woods? Why didn't he just leave her on the back porch? And why didn't he kill Lorie when he had the chance, the way he did the others?"

They heard the bloodhounds' mournful wails off in the distance.

"They've picked up the scent," Jack said.

"I don't think the Midnight Killer is involved in Shelley Gilbert's disappearance. It doesn't fit his MO."

"Yeah, I agree, but who else would want her out of the way?"

Mike shook his head. "I've got no idea."

The deeper they treaded into Jernigan's Woods, stomping across knee-high grass in the open areas and through damp sludge and over mossy tree roots, the more distinctly they heard the dogs. Their barking continued nonstop as Mike and Jack caught up with the deputies who were following the hounds. As they approached the circle of uniformed officers surrounding the dogs that had stopped near the riverbank, Mike and Jack slowed their pace.

"They must have found something," Mike said to Jack, and then called out to Buddy Pounders, who had accompanied the hounds' trainer. "What is it? Have they found something?"

"Yes, sir. I'm afraid they have," Buddy said.

Mike and Jack exchanged this-can't-be-good glances and moved forward to join the others. Buddy and another deputy stepped aside to allow Mike and Jack an unobstructed view. Mike halted, closed his eyes for half a second, and mumbled an obscenity. Jack stared at the body, then leaned down and inspected it more closely.

Mike dropped to his haunches and surveyed the woman's butchered remains. Salty bile rose up his esophagus and lodged in his throat. Although Jack didn't seem fazed by the gruesome sight, Mike suspected that this type of bloody mutilation disturbed even a seasoned soldier such as Jack. It sure as hell disturbed Mike.

"Call Andy." Mike barked out orders, demanding the site be secured and sending all but a handful of deputies to regulate the flow of foot traffic into and out of the woods. It was only a matter of time before word of the grisly murder spread throughout the county. Reporters would eventually arrive, as would curious neighbors. Buddy Pounders and Ronnie Gipson would remain at the scene with Mike until Coroner Andy Gamble and his two-person crew arrived.

"Whoever did this didn't put a mark on her face," Mike said. "He wanted us to be able to identify her."

"Cut up the way she is, there's no way to tell for sure what actually killed her," Jack said, studying Shelley's body. "But my guess is that he slit her throat to finish the job."

Mike nodded. "Jack, I need you to go back to the house and talk to Lorie. Tell her that we found Shelley and she's dead, but leave out the details."

"Yeah, sure. And I'll contact Maleah. The Powell Agency needs to know. But God help us, they're going to descend on us like a swarm of killer bees."

"Tell Maleah to have Mr. or Mrs. Powell contact me directly. And I need for you to call Hicks Wainwright and let him know what's happened. My gut tells me that this has nothing to do with the Midnight Killer, but I'm no expert by any means." Mike took a deep breath. "As soon as you can, get back here."

"Want me to call Wade Ballard, too?"

"Yeah. Let him know that all hell's about to break loose."

Mike rubbed the back of his neck as he stood on Abby Sherman's doorstep. It had been a long, difficult day and it wasn't over yet. He hadn't stopped for breakfast or lunch, had drunk too much coffee, and had finally gobbled down a sandwich Jack had brought him around four that afternoon. As his mama would say, he felt like death warmed over.

He had left the crime scene secure. Dozens of officers, from his department and the state boys to the FBI, had gotten in on the act. He just hoped he was doing a halfway decent job of coordinating the various investigators. Andy Gamble, the county coroner, had turned Shelley Gilbert's butchered body over to the state, but not before he had examined the body at the site and taken it away in a body bag.

"We'll know more after the autopsy," Andy had told him. "But I'd say that the person who attacked her came up from behind and stabbed her in the back several times and possibly hit a kidney. The blood on the porch is from those initial stab wounds."

"He left a trail from the house into the woods," Mike had said. "Apparently he dragged her to the riverbank."

Andy had nodded. "And that's where he finished her off. He stabbed her repeatedly and then slit her throat. But even after she bled to death, he wasn't finished with her. He sliced up her arms and legs postmortem. I've never seen anything like it. He carved out little pieces the way you'd carve a pumpkin to make a Halloween jack-o'-lantern."

From hip to ankle on both legs and from shoulder to wrist on both arms, the killer had carved pieces of flesh from Shelley Gilbert's body. Thank God, she'd already been dead when her killer had etched the bloody, triangular designs.

Mike had finally left the crime scene once everything that could be done there had been done. Every precaution had been taken to protect both the back porch of Lorie's house and the area surrounding where the body had been found on the riverbank. The porch, back door, steps, and railings had been dusted for fingerprints. Soil samples had been taken from the yard, the path into the woods, and at the riverbank. The entire area had

379

been searched for any sign of the weapon. Shoeprints found near the river had been photographed, and after being sprayed with fixatives to stabilize the loose dirt, the prints had been filled with plaster. Mike hoped that the shoeprints didn't wind up belonging to one of his deputies.

He had left the press conference he'd held in front of the courthouse and had driven straight to Abby's. He hesitated before ringing the doorbell. He needed to be honest with her. He owed her that much.

*How can you be honest with Abby when you're not being honest with yourself? Admit the truth!*

But that was the problem—he wasn't sure he knew what the truth was.

He rang the doorbell. Abby opened the door instantly, as if she had been standing on the other side waiting for him to make his presence known.

She offered him a fragile smile. "Please, come in."

He stepped over the threshold. She caressed his arm.

"I can only imagine how difficult this day has been for you," she told him, concern in her voice and sympathy in her eyes.

Mike closed the door behind him.

"Have you had supper?" she asked. "I can fix you something. Scramble some eggs. Make a sandwich."

"Nothing, thanks."

"How about some iced tea or coffee or—?"

"Abby." He grasped her hands in his.

She stared at him, wide-eyed with uncertainty. "It's awful about that woman, the bodyguard. But Lorie Hammonds wasn't harmed. That's something to be thankful for."

"Abby, listen to me."

She looked directly at him. "All right."

"My mother is going to be staying at my place with Hannah and M.J. for a while, and I'm temporarily turning over some of my duties as sheriff to my chief deputy."

"Why?"

"When I leave here this evening, I'm going home to see my kids, and then I'm packing a bag and moving in with Lorie until she's no longer in any danger. I'll go into the office during the day, but in the evenings and at night, I'll be with Lorie."

Abby swallowed. "I see. But why, Mike, why does it have to be you? You can assign around-the-clock deputies or the Powell Agency can send a replacement. This isn't something you have to do personally."

He gave her hands a gentle tug, brought them up to his lips, and kissed her knuckles. "That's just the thing—it is something I have to do myself. I can't leave Lorie's safety in anyone else's hands."

"Why not?" Tears pooled in Abby's eyes.

Mike felt like the biggest jerk on earth. "I'm sorry. God, I'm so sorry. I never meant to lead you on and then pull the rug out from under you this way. I can't explain it, not really. But this is just something I have to do."

"You're still in love with her, aren't you?"

There it was, the one question he couldn't answer. "I honestly don't know."

"If it was just sex, I might be able to understand. But she has some kind of emotional hold over you. I can see it in your eyes when you look at her." Tears trickled down Abby's cheeks.

"It wouldn't have worked out between us," Mike said, without adding that not only did his kids not like her, but he wasn't in love with her.

"Do you honestly think it will work out with her?"

"This isn't about my expecting to build a future with Lorie. It's about keeping her alive, about my needing to personally protect her."

"And when this is all over, what then?"

"I guess I'll figure it out then."

Abby swiped the tears from her cheeks, tilted her chin staunchly, and looked right at him. "I'd like for you to leave now, please."

Mike nodded, and realizing there was nothing he could say or do to make this easier for Abby, he turned and walked away.

Lorie was thankful that Cathy and Jack were staying in her home with her, at least for tonight. She simply couldn't have forced herself to go beyond the front door. With her inside and the world outside, she felt relatively safe. Her best friend, who had stayed with her all day, gave her the comfort and reassurance she so desperately needed. And her best friend's husband, a sheriff's deputy who had once been an Army Ranger, provided her with personal protection. Also, there was a deputy stationed in the driveway who checked her front and back yards every hour on the hour.

She hadn't seen Mike since early this morning, but he had sent Jack to tell her that they had found Shelley Gilbert's body.

"Mike and I don't think that the Midnight Killer is the one who murdered Shelley," Jack had explained. "This isn't his MO, not even close. Even though he did kill Shontee Thomas's bodyguard, he shot the guy and then killed Shontee. Whoever killed Shelley used a knife." He had paused for a moment, and Lorie had suspected he was considering just how much to tell her. "He slit her throat."

For a second or two, Lorie had thought she'd throw up, but the nausea subsided and she'd managed to say, "And he didn't kill me and we both know he could have."

The day had been endless, each minute seeming like an hour. Investigators of every form and fashion had traipsed through her house, doing God only knew what to gather evidence. Deputies. Police officers. ABI agents. FBI agents. And when they had finished up inside, they had moved to the back porch, a taped-off crime scene being guarded by one of Mike's deputies. She and Cathy had lost count of how many pots of coffee they had made and how many cups they had filled. They had both been thankful to have something to do. And when Cathy had suggested making sandwiches and having them available for the slew of investigators, Lorie had immediately agreed.

She had watched from the kitchen window when Andy Gamble's team brought Shelley's body, cocooned inside a black body bag, out of the woods. Shelley, who only last night had been alive and well. Shelley, the person who had been responsible for keeping her safe. Shelley, whose bodyguard training and possession of a big gun had not protected her.

Jack and Cathy sat together on the sofa in Lorie's living room watching the ten o'clock newscast on Huntsville's CBS Channel 19. One of the countless reporters who had been kept at bay by the roadblocks set up and manned by Alabama state troopers had taped interviews with Lorie's neighbors. Supposedly, no one knew for sure what had happened, other than a woman's body had been found in the woods not far from Lorie's house.

"We heard it was that bodyguard who's been staying with Lorie Hammonds," Irene Shelby told the reporter.

Lorie, who had just taken a shower and put on

a pair of lightweight pink sweats and a lacy white T-shirt, came into the living room in time to hear Irene's comment.

Jack picked up the remote.

"No, don't turn it off," Lorie said. "Leave it on."

"Are you sure?" Cathy asked.

"I'm sure."

Jack laid down the remote.

The nighttime anchor appeared appropriately somber when he stared into the camera and said, "Sheriff Mike Birkett held a press conference late this afternoon." The taped interview appeared on the TV screen.

Lorie noticed how haggard Mike looked. His hair was windblown and disheveled and he sported a dark, heavy five o'clock shadow. He spoke calmly and with absolute authority, giving the basic facts and nothing more. The victim was Shelley Gilbert, who was employed by the Powell Private Security and Investigation Agency head-quartered in Knoxville, Tennessee. Ms. Gilbert was on assignment in the Dunmore area, working as a private bodyguard. The case was considered a homicide and both the ABI and the FBI were involved in the investigation.

Mike walked off, refusing to answer even one of the dozens of questions bombarding him from every direction.

"I hope he's home in bed and getting some rest," Lorie said. "He looked so tired."

The doorbell rang. Everyone froze. Before Jack got to his feet, a familiar voice called to them through the closed front door.

"It's me, Mike."

Lorie didn't move, could barely breathe. *What is he doing here?*

Jack walked across the room, unlocked the door, and opened it. "Everything's okay here. We were just watching the ten o'clock news before going to bed. You could have saved yourself a trip and just called, but I guess you needed to see for yourself that Lorie's all right."

"Yeah, something like that," Mike replied as he entered the living room, removed the navy vinyl carryall from his shoulder, and set it on the floor.

With the length of the room separating them, Lorie and Mike looked at each other. And then Mike turned to Jack. "You and Cathy can go on home. I'll stay with Lorie."

No one uttered a sound for a couple of minutes, and then Jack replied, "Sure thing, if that's what you want. I guess it makes sense for several of us to rotate shifts, but since I'm already here, you could have—"

"We're not rotating shifts," Mike told him. "I'm moving in. I'll be staying here with Lorie until she's no longer in danger. I'll go in to the office during the day, but I'll be here every night."

"What!" Lorie gasped. "You—you're moving in here with me?"

Mike looked her square in the eye. "That's right."

"But what about M.J. and Hannah?"

"My mother will be staying at the house with them."

"And Abby, what's she going to think about your moving in here with me?"

"Abby understands the situation," Mike said.

"Does she? I'm glad she understands, because I sure don't. How about explaining it to me?"

# Chapter 23

Lorie wasn't sure if she was relieved or not that Cathy and Jack had left so quickly. A part of her wished they had stayed, at least Cathy, for moral support. But on the other hand, she knew that this particular confrontation needed to be solely between Mike and her. His showing up at her door and announcing that he was moving in with her had come as a complete surprise.

No, surprise was too mild a word. Replace that with shock. Yes, that was how she felt. Totally shocked.

"My God, what were you thinking?" she demanded the moment they were alone. "People are already talking about us, so I can only imagine what is going to happen now."

When he stood there and stared at her, saying nothing, she marched over and stopped directly in front of him. "Why, Mike? Why are you doing this?"

"It's something I have to do," he told her, the words dragging out of him as if they caused him pain.

"And why is that?" She was not going to let him off with such a simplistic explanation. "It's not as if I didn't already have protection. Jack was here. And you have a deputy posted outside."

"Yeah, I know, but . . ." He hesitated, as if choosing his next words carefully. "I need to be the one protecting you."

She glared at him. "No, you don't. You need to be home with your children. You need to stay as far away from me as you can. Not only do you have a reputation to uphold, which you can't do living under the same roof with me, but you shouldn't put yourself between me and a killer. Hannah and M.J. have already lost one parent. I don't want to be the reason they lose another."

"Are you saying that you assume because Shelley Gilbert was murdered, someone will try to kill me?"

"Yes, of course, that's what I'm saying. You can't put your life on the line for me."

"But that's just it," he said. "If something happened to you and I knew that I hadn't done everything possible to keep you safe, I couldn't live with myself."

"Damn it, Mike, where is this sense of responsibility coming from? For nearly nine years, you were barely able to speak to me or even look at me, and when you did speak to me, you made it perfectly clear that you wanted absolutely, positively nothing to do with me."

"Yeah, I know. Thanks for reminding me of what a jerk I've been."

She was momentarily rendered speechless, her mind completely blank.

"I'm moving in and I'm staying until you're no longer in any danger. People can say whatever they want to say. I'm here as your personal bodyguard, not as your lover. If people want to believe otherwise . . ." He shrugged. "I have to do this. I wish I could give you a better explanation, but I can't."

"Hannah and M.J. will be—"

"For some inexplicable reason, my children seem to adore you. They're okay with my staying here. And my mother encouraged me to do this. She told me to do what I had to do."

Lorie huffed and threw up her hands in frustration, then glowered at him. "What about Abby Sherman? You can't tell me that she's honestly all right with her boyfriend living with another woman, even only as her bodyguard. She's well aware of the fact that the whole town knows all about our past history."

"Abby and I ended things this evening."

"What?"

Mike stayed focused on Lorie, his expression

grim. "It was never right between Abby and me. I tried to make it work. God knows she tried. She's a fine woman, but . . . I don't love her. And my kids don't even like her. And my mother . . . Hell, listen to me, would you? My personal life is none of your damn business and yet here I am explaining myself to you."

"You're right about that. Your personal life is none of my business. But your moving in with me is my business."

"I'm staying with you as your protector, to keep you safe. I'm certainly not standing here declaring my undying love for you or anything like that." He glanced down at the floor as he reached up and rubbed the back of his neck. "Our personal relationship hasn't changed. You're off-limits to me, the same as you've been ever since you came back to Dunmore."

"Screw you, Michael Birkett! I want you to leave. Get out of my house right now and don't come back."

He looked at her, his brow wrinkled, his gaze narrowed and anger brightening his blue-black eyes. "I'm not going anywhere. I'm here for the duration, to do whatever I have to do to keep you safe."

Barely able to refrain from hitting him, Lorie uttered a frustrated groan. "Damn you. You do not get to play the martyr, willing to lay your life on the line and die to protect me. Whatever your reasons for doing this, please don't. If you're doing this to make it up to me for treating me like the dirt beneath your feet all these years, then don't. I absolve you of any sins you think you've committed against me. Go home, Mike. Go back to your safe, uncomplicated, above-reproach life. Take care of your kids and keep looking until you find yourself another Molly."

She'd had it. All she could take. The very thought of having to endure Mike's presence in her home night after night was more than she could bear.

She walked past him until she reached the hallway, and then she ran into her bedroom and slammed the door. For half a second, she considered locking it, but if Mike wanted in, a locked door wouldn't stop him. And in all honesty, she didn't think Mike would invade her privacy. Hopefully, she had persuaded him to leave. But whatever he decided to do—go or stay—she didn't have to deal with him again tonight. There would be time enough for that in the morning.

After kicking off her shoes, she fell across the bed and onto her stomach. Turning slowly onto her side, she released the tears she had been holding in check all day. As she lay there crying, her body instinctively curled into a fetal ball.

After setting the security alarm, Mike picked up his vinyl bag, flung it over his shoulder, and walked down the hall. Jack had given him the security code right before he and Cathy left. Mike paused outside Lorie's closed door. He'd made such a mess of things. In his own redneck, He-Man, take-charge way, he'd barged in and told Lorie how it was going to be. What kind of fool did that make him? If he'd ever stopped and thought about the situation, he would have known how she would react. Lorie had always hated being told what to do. As a teenager, she had rebelled against her father's stern domination and had sworn she would never be any man's doormat, the way her mother was. If her parents had been different, if they had seen her through his eyes, as the beautiful, exciting, free spirit he had fallen in love with, maybe things would have turned out differently for her. But he couldn't lay all the blame on her parents. As much as he hated to admit it—and had fought against the truth all these years—if he had encouraged Lorie's dreams of becoming a movie star, if he had gone to LA with her and been there for her when things went wrong, she would never have made that damn porno movie.

If he had it to do over again, what would he do?

*Hindsight is twenty-twenty. No use crying over spilled milk. What's done is done.* A dozen different ridiculous sayings came to mind.

If he had gone to LA with Lorie eighteen years ago, they could have come back to Dunmore together, as man and wife, if her career had failed.

They would have built a life together here, the life he had always wanted for them.

But what if she'd made it big? What if she'd gotten just one lucky break and wound up becoming a star? Mike would have despised being thought of as Mr. Lorie Hammonds, the redneck hick husband that she'd brought with her from Alabama. He would have hated the glitz and glamour, the endless parties, the other social events, the premieres, and especially being hounded by the paparazzi.

So, he guessed that if he could do it over again, he'd make the same decision. He had done what he had to do. He had stayed in Dunmore. And Lorie had done what she had to do. She had gone to LA to seek fame and fortune.

Mike walked past Lorie's bedroom and glanced into the other rooms, searching and finding the room that Shelley Gilbert had used. The ABI folks had gone over that room with a fine-tooth comb. If Lorie had a second guest bedroom, he would prefer not sleeping in the room the murdered Powell agent had used.

He slipped his hand along the wall inside the open door of the pitch-black room at the end of the hall and flipped on the overhead light. He breathed a sigh of relief when he saw that it actually was a bedroom of sorts. A mahogany spindle double bed had been placed against the wall and covered with a white spread like the one his mother used on her own bed. He'd heard her call it a Martha Washington bedspread. Funny what a guy remembered.

A treadmill occupied the opposite wall in front of the wooden blind–covered double windows facing the backyard. A large desk, probably an antique, had been painted a dark green to match the old Windsor chair that had been painted the same color. A mahogany barrister bookcase stood beside the closet door, the case filled with a variety of hardcover books and paperback novels.

Mike dropped his vinyl bag down beside the bed, removed the four decorative pillows from the bed, and placed them in the armchair shoved into the corner. It had been a very long day. He was bone weary and all he wanted was a good night's sleep. He pulled back the covers—bedspread, light-weight quilt, and top sheet—and decided he really had no choice but to take a shower. The bed linens were light green, the hems of the top sheet and both pillowcases trimmed with lace. A guy couldn't lie down on stuff that fancy without cleaning up first.

After retrieving his pajama bottoms, a clean T-shirt, and a clean pair of briefs from his bag, he headed for the bathroom situated between the two guest rooms. He flipped on the light, closed the door, and turned on the shower. He'd searched through every drawer in his dresser at home before finding the one pair of pajamas he owned. He had stuffed the bottoms into his duffel bag, along with his shaving kit, underwear, and a change of clothes.

Dead on his feet, he nearly fell asleep beneath the warm spray of soothing water, but he managed to wash, step out of the shower, and dry off as quickly as possible. Once dressed in the PJ bottoms and white T-shirt, he gathered up his dirty laundry wrapped in his damp towel and walked out into the hallway. He'd had every intention of going straight to the guest room and falling into bed, but the same stupidity that had brought him here tonight urged him to check on Lorie.

He knocked softly on her door. No response. He called her name. She didn't reply. He grasped the doorknob and turned it. The door eased open.

She hadn't locked it.

He stood in the doorway and looked into her room, his gaze settling on her bed. She lay there, sprawled sideways, her body semi-curled, one arm draped over the second pillow. Plantation shutters covered both windows, their slats partially open. Only the light from the hall wall sconces and the minimum of moonlight from a crescent moon illuminated her still figure. He took several uncertain steps into the room and then paused.

What the hell was he doing?

He was checking on Lorie, making sure she was all right.

*She's fine. She's sound asleep. Now get your ass out of here pronto.*

Walking backward, he eased out of her bedroom

and left the door open. If she needed him during the night . . . Once out in the hall, he turned and moved quietly toward the guest room.

He dumped his dirty clothes in a loose pile beside his bag, then partially opened both window blinds to allow in a little moonlight. After turning off the overhead light, he crawled into bed and pulled the covers to his waist. He lifted up his arms, entwined his fingers, and slipped both hands under the back of his head. He lay there and stared up at the shadows dancing on the ceiling.

*Why, Mike? Why are you doing this?* Lorie's words played repeatedly in his mind.

He had told her the truth, or as much of the truth as he had been able to admit to himself. He was here because he had to be here. If he didn't do everything within his power to keep Lorie safe and the Midnight Killer murdered her, he wouldn't be able to live with himself. He had let Lorie down more than once, first when he hadn't been able to make himself leave Dunmore and go to LA with her. And the second time had been when she came home, her life in shambles, her pride destroyed and her reputation ruined. The first time, she had been equally at fault. She could have stayed with him. But the second time, when she returned to Dunmore nine years ago, he could have, at the very least, treated her with human kindness. His mother had pleaded with him to befriend Lorie. Even his wife had wanted him to offer Lorie a helping hand.

A man couldn't tell his mother and certainly not his wife that his bitter hatred for his former girl-friend was deeply rooted in one unbearable fact—deep down in the depths of his heart and soul, he still loved Lorie as much as he hated her. He didn't want to love her. God knew he tried not to love her, not to want her, not to need her on some basic, primal level. And over the years, he had been able to convince himself that all he felt for her was hatred and contempt. Odd, how a man could lie to himself so easily and could make himself believe what he wanted to believe.

So, what now? Now that he had finally admitted the truth to himself?

He could stop hating Lorie. Actually, he'd already done that.

And he could keep her safe. He could protect her from a deranged killer. He could do what he needed to do. This time, he wouldn't let her down.

Mike tossed and turned, flipping from one side to the other in an effort to relax and get comfort-able. He tried resting flat on his back, but that didn't work. He flopped down on his stomach and flung his arms, elbows bent, on either side of his head. Damn it, he needed rest, needed sleep. But sleep wouldn't come.

When this was all over, when the Midnight Killer had been stopped, when he knew for sure that Shelley Gilbert's murder wasn't in any way connected to Lorie, then he could resume his normal life. But in the meantime, he had to keep reminding himself that he and Lorie had no future together. It didn't matter that his mother liked her or that his kids adored her or even that he still loved her. And it really wasn't about forgiveness. He could forgive her and maybe she could forgive him. He might even get past the fact that every man in the county, including his friends, employees, and neighbors, had seen Lorie naked in *Playboy*. But how did he erase the memory of watching her having sex with two other guys?

*Face it, Mike, some things just weren't meant to be.*

She lay in his arms, her back to his chest, her naked butt pressed against his arousal. He nuzzled her neck and breathed in the sweet, floral scent of her hair, still damp from the shower they had taken together. He kissed her neck and her jaw and then moved up to circle her ear with his tongue. She moaned softly and cuddled closer as she grasped his hand and brought it to her mouth. She licked up and down each finger and laughed when he groaned deep in his throat.

"You're wicked," he told her as he turned her in his arms, bringing them face-to-face.

"And you love it." Smiling seductively, she winked at him.

"I love you," Mike said. "I love you so damn much."

"Not any more than I love you." Lorie reached up and twined her hands behind his neck. "Sometimes I love you so much it hurts."

He slipped his hand between her thighs and touched her intimately. "Tell me where it hurts, baby, and I'll make it stop hurting."

"Now who's being wicked?" She laughed as he lifted himself up and over her, bracing himself with a hand on either side of her head. "You know where and you know just what to do." She spread her legs in a blatant invitation.

Mike lifted her hips as he delved deeply and completely, taking her with a fierce hunger that equaled their mating in the shower less than an hour earlier. He could never get enough of Lorie. The more he made love to her, the more he wanted her.

She came first, crying out his name as her nails bit into his buttocks. That action sent him over the edge, headlong into an explosive orgasm.

He melted down on top of her and lay there until his heartbeat slowed and the aftershocks stopped rippling through his body. When he slid off her and onto his back, she eased away from him and got out of bed.

"Where are you going?" He held out his hand to grasp her and prevent her from leaving.

"I have to go," she said. "He's waiting for me."

"Who's waiting for you?" Mike sat up in bed.

"The Midnight Killer."

"No! You can't go. I won't let him have you."

She paused halfway to the door, and then turned and offered him a farewell smile. "I have to go. I have to pay for my sins. Once I'm gone, you can forget me. I can never hurt you or disappoint you ever again."

Mike jumped out of bed and tried to catch Lorie before she left the bedroom, but his feet were so heavy that he couldn't move.

"Lorie! I'll never forget you. Never. Please, don't go. Don't leave me again."

She disappeared down the hallway.

Mike's chest ached. His breathing became labored. He tried to move, to run after her, but it was as if his feet were glued to the floor.

If he couldn't stop her, couldn't save her, then she would die.

If she died, he would die.

Then he heard the gunshots. One. Two. Three. Four. And in between each shot, Lorie screamed, each an agonized plea for help.

He cried out her name repeatedly, his voice intermingling with her screams and the gunshots.

Suddenly silence.

He managed to lift his heavy feet and move toward the door. It seemed to take forever to reach the hallway. Halfway down the hall, he felt something wet beneath his feet. He looked down and saw a narrow red stream trickling along the hardwood.

And at the end of the hall—*God, please, no!*

Lorie's bloody nude body lay there, her beautiful brown eyes staring sightlessly through the slits in the decorative mask covering her face.

Mike woke instantly, but his head felt groggy and he ached deep inside, feeling the loss as if the dream had been real.

He sat up in bed and wiped the sweat from his face with his open palm. God in heaven, he had never had such a realistic nightmare. Yeah, sure, he'd had his share of wet dreams, a lot of them starring Lorie. But despite the orgasm that would require him to change into another pair of clean briefs, what he had experienced was far more than a sexual fantasy. It had been a horror show, a hellish vision that he couldn't seem to shake.

After pulling himself together, he got out of bed, searched his bag in the semidark and found another pair of briefs. He made his way to the bathroom, disrobed, washed off, and put on the clean briefs.

Before returning to his bed, he once again paused outside Lorie's room. Her bed was empty. *Where is she?*

Just as he barged into her room, halfway convinced that somehow the Midnight Killer had gotten to her, Lorie came walking out of the bathroom connected to her bedroom. When she saw him standing there wearing nothing but his briefs, she stopped cold and surveyed him from head to toe.

"Want something?" she asked.

"Just checking on you. When I saw that your bed was empty, I thought . . ." He huffed. "Hell, I don't know what I thought."

"I'm fine."

"Yeah, I can see you are."

"It's three-thirty." She pointed to the lighted bed-side clock. "I'm going back to bed. I suggest you do the same."

"Yeah, sure. I . . . uh . . . I . . ."

"What?" she asked.

He took a few tentative backward steps. "You know that you don't deserve what's happening to you, don't you?"

She eyed him quizzically. "Yes, I know."

He nodded.

"Is there anything else?"

He shook his head.

"Good night, Mike."

"Yeah, good night, Lorie."

He turned, walked away, and couldn't get back to the guest bedroom fast enough.

# Chapter 24

When Nicole Powell woke, she found herself alone in bed. She stretched her arm out over Griff's side and caressed the wrinkled sheet. The room lay in darkness, only the glow of dawn glimmering through the windows and balcony doors hinting of the time. Since Griff occasionally couldn't sleep and would get up at odd hours, she wasn't overly concerned. But she knew that Shelley Gilbert's murder weighed heavily on his mind, as it did hers. The death of a second Powell Agency employee so soon after Kristi Arians's brutal murder had the entire agency in an uproar. They had sent Mitch Trahern to Dunmore to represent the agency. As a former federal agent, his investigative skills were unequaled, so Griff trusted him to find out every detail, even confidential information.

She lifted her head enough to look at the bedside clock. 5:38 A.M. Groaning softly, she turned over and lay flat on her back. When Griff got in one of his pensive moods, she usually left him alone. He often sought her out in his own good time. And if he sometimes kept his thoughts to himself, she knew that he found comfort merely in her presence. She knew because he had told her so. Even now, after three years of marriage, she didn't always understand her husband.

Flipping over onto Griff's side of the bed, she grabbed his down pillow and hugged it to her body. She might not always understand him, but she always loved him, even when she was angry with him. He wasn't an easy man to live with and he would be the first to admit it. Demons from the past haunted him. Dark secrets lay buried in the depths of his soul, secrets that he had been unable to share with her. Secrets that bound him to Sanders and Yvette.

Nicole shoved the pillow aside and got out of bed. After putting on her robe and slipping into her satin house shoes, she went in search of her elusive husband. As she descended the stairs to the main level of their home, the early morning quiet surrounded her. The first place she looked was Griff's study, his private sanctuary from the world. But the door stood wide open and the room was empty. Had he left the house? Gone for a solitary walk around the lake? If so, he would return soon enough.

Knowing she wouldn't be able to go back to sleep, Nic headed for the kitchen. She could make coffee. She might even make scones or muffins and scramble some eggs and have breakfast waiting for Griff when he came in from his walk.

As she neared the kitchen, she noted light coming from beneath the closed door and heard the mumble of voices. Griff was in the kitchen. And he wasn't alone. Or perhaps he was on the phone talking to Mitch Trahern or one of the other agents.

She tiptoed up to the door and stopped. Listening quietly, she recognized the other male voice. Sanders.

"We must not assume anything," Sanders said. "Reading more into these deaths than there actually is would be foolish."

"And ignoring the possibility that Kristi Arians

and Shelley Gilbert were killed solely because they were both Powell Agency employees would be just as foolish," Griff replied. "If someone is targeting our employees—"

"If someone is—and that is a big if—then we have no way of knowing what his motive might be. It could have nothing to do with Malcolm York."

Nic gasped silently. What would make Griff think someone connected to Malcolm York had targeted Powell agents? York, the man who had kidnapped Griff when he was twenty-two and held him captive for several years, was dead.

"Sanders is right," a female voice said. "I thought we had agreed that the rumors being propagated in Europe about York being alive were entirely false. We know York is dead. We killed him. He has not come back from the dead."

An odd mixture of emotions swirled through Nic's mind. Griff was having a private meeting with Sanders and Yvette, and once again, he had not included her. He had shut her out and was continuing to keep secrets from her.

Her next thought was a totally unselfish one. How terrifying it must be for Yvette to even consider the possibility that her sadistic husband might still be alive.

"York is dead," Griff said. "On that, we all agree."

"And the deaths of the two Powell agents could be a coincidence," Yvette suggested.

"The murders were no mere coincidence," Griff told them.

"What do you know that we don't?" Sanders asked.

Nic swung open the door and entered the kitchen. "Yes, Griff, exactly what do you know that the rest of us don't know?"

Yvette and Sanders turned instantly and stared at Nic, each of them looking as if they wanted to explain their presence and yet waiting for Griff to respond.

Griff's body stiffened as if preparing for battle, bracing himself for the onslaught of enemy fire. He turned slowly to face her. "Good morning."

"Apparently not so good," Nic said.

"Sanders woke me half an hour ago with a report from Mitch Trahern," Griff said.

Nic slid her gaze over her husband, from his tousled blond hair, across his broad shoulders, and down to his size fourteen leather house slippers. He wore a silk robe over his silk pajama bottoms. When they had gone to bed last night, he had been naked.

"I must have been sleeping soundly," Nic said. "I didn't hear Sanders knock."

"I was already downstairs in my study."

"Then you were having trouble sleeping?" Not giving Griff a chance to respond, she glanced at Yvette. "How long have you been here?"

"Only a few minutes," Yvette told her. "Sanders

phoned and asked me to come to the house immediately."

"I see." She looked directly at Griff. "Another top secret meeting of the Amara Triad, huh?"

"Not top secret," Griff said. "I saw no reason to wake you since neither of us got much sleep last night. I thought you needed your rest. I intended to fill you in later."

"Fill me in now."

Griff nodded. "You know that the Knoxville PD did not reveal the details about Kristi Arians's murder, telling the press only that her throat had been slit and that was the cause of death. But we know that whoever killed her, mutilated her by cutting numerous triangular-shaped pieces out of her arms and legs."

"Go on." But Nic knew before he spoke exactly what he was going to tell them.

"Whoever killed Shelley Gilbert slit her throat and cut triangular pieces of flesh from her arms and legs," Griff said.

"Oh, my God." Nic felt sick to her stomach.

Smelling freshly brewed coffee, Lorie followed the scent straight to her kitchen. Bracing herself for whatever lay beyond the closed door—be that Mike still here or Jack having returned or another deputy on guard duty—she squared her shoulders and took a deep breath. Before leaving the bathroom, she had washed her face and brushed her hair, but she hadn't bothered with a robe since her lightweight sweats and T-shirt were presentable.

Mike stood at the stove busily scrambling eggs in a bright green nonstick skillet that she had bought at a discount store even though it didn't match anything in her red, white, and black kitchen. She had fallen in love with that stupid skillet the moment she saw it.

He glanced at her. "Morning."

"You're still here."

"Yep." He nodded to the table. "I heard you stirring about so I went ahead and set the table. I hope I used the right dishes."

She glanced at the white CorningWare plates she had bought at Wal-Mart for everyday use. "They're fine."

"There's coffee." He hitched his thumb in the direction of the coffeemaker.

After preparing herself a large mug of coffee, she pulled out a chair and sat down. Cupping the mug in both hands, she brought it to her lips and sampled the dark brew. Although it was a little stronger than she liked, she welcomed the caffeine fix.

Mike spooned half the scrambled eggs into her plate and the other half into his. Then he put the platter filled with buttered toast between the jars of strawberry and peach jelly.

"I couldn't find any bacon or sausage," he said as he picked up his mug and sat in the seat opposite her.

"I usually don't eat a big breakfast, just cereal and juice. I seldom buy bacon or sausage."

Mike nodded, then picked up his fork and dove into the fluffy scrambled eggs. After eating half the eggs and two half slices of toast, he washed it all down with the remainder of his coffee. He wiped his mouth, shoved back his chair, and got up.

"Want a refill while I'm getting mine?" he asked, holding up his mug.

"No, thanks. I'm good."

He glanced at her plate. "You aren't eating."

"I'm not used to someone making breakfast for me."

"Really?" He stared at her, a skeptical expression on his face. "I find it hard to believe that not one of the men you've dated cooked breakfast for you."

"Maybe that's because none of the men I've dated have spent the night and stayed over for breakfast."

"You don't expect me to believe that you've been celibate for the past nine years." Mike refilled his mug.

"I don't care what you believe. Maybe I have been celibate all these years. Maybe I haven't. It's possible that I've always spent the night at my date's house. Or maybe he came here and once we finished screwing each other senseless, I sent him away."

Mike sat back down at the table and looked right at her. "Do you get some perverse pleasure out of taunting me?"

Lorie laughed in his face. "Last night you told me that your personal life was none of my business. That works both ways, you know. Who I've had sex with during the past nine years or if I've had sex is none of your business."

"You're absolutely right," he told her.

She stared at him, surprised by his instant agreement. "That was too easy. What's going on?"

"I'm tired of every conversation we have turning into an argument. And since most of the time that's been my fault, I'm the one putting a stop to it."

"I'm amazed."

"You're amazed that I can be reasonable?" He grinned. "We're going to be together a lot from here on out. I don't want to spend most of that time fighting with you."

"You shouldn't be here, you know. You should let Jack look after me until I can hire a new bodyguard. I'm sure the Powell Agency can—"

"Damn it, Lorie, I don't want to argue about this. I'm here and I'm not going away. You're stuck with me."

"Until?"

"Until you're no longer in danger."

All right. If he could do this, then she could. If he could live in her house, see her day in and day out, sleep just down the hall from her and resist the undeniable attraction between them, so could she. But by God, she wasn't going to make it easy for him.

*Lorie, Lorie, Lorie, what are you thinking? Mike is doing what he believes is the right thing to do.* His reasoning might be a little skewed, but his heart was in the right place. Mike Birkett was a good man. Instead of making things difficult for him, she needed to help him. No matter what happened between them while they were together, when it was all over, she would have to let him go back to his normal life, a life that could never include her.

"I don't like that look in your eyes," Mike said. "You're plotting something."

"No, you're wrong," she told him and surprised both of them when she reached across the table and clasped his hand. "Thank you, Mike."

"For what?" He did not jerk his hand away as she halfway expected.

"For being you. For being the kind of man who would risk his life for an old friend."

He maneuvered their hands until hers was nestled inside his. They stared at each other for an endless moment, and then she pulled her hand away and got up to dump her cold coffee and pour herself a fresh cupful.

Oh dear God, this was going to be hard, damn hard. But she had to keep things on a platonic basis with Mike, for his sake as well as for hers.

Lila Newton had just come on duty at Green Willows Rehabilitation and Convalescence Center when Ransom Owens arrived at 8:05 A.M. His name was not on the list of acceptable visitors, a list that had been provided by his son, Tyler. As a general rule, Lila was a stickler for rules and regulations, but she also had a soft spot in her heart for Ransom. Actually, she'd had a secret crush on him when they were kids. Her father had been the Owens family's gardener and Ransom had always treated her kindly, always like the young gentleman he'd been. So, what did it hurt to allow him a few minutes alone with his former wife a couple of mornings each week? After all, it was obvious that the poor man still loved her. And he timed his arrival so that he could feed her breakfast, a chore that would have otherwise fallen to one of the aides. Of course, if his visits upset Ms. Owens, she'd have put a stop to them, but when Lila checked on her after each visit, her patient seemed quite serene.

"Morning, Lila," Ransom said as he approached the nurses' station.

"Morning, Mr. Ransom."

"How is she today?" he asked.

"I was just going to check on her," Lila said. "Would you care to walk with me? If they haven't brought Ms. Owens's breakfast, I'll see to it right away."

"Thank you, Lila. You've been a good friend to me and to Terri." He fell into step beside her as they made their way down the corridor.

One of the aides walked out of room 107, smiled

at Lila, glanced at Ransom, and hurried to the delivery cart parked in the hallway. Lila entered the room first and checked on her patient, who sat semi-upright in the bed, two pillows beneath her head. Theresa Lenore Tyler Owens, known to one and all as Terri, had once been a beautiful woman. Remnants of that youthful beauty remained, in the blue eyes, the golden hair, the slender curves of her shapely body. But her once peaches-and-cream complexion was mottled and splotchy, her arms and legs an unhealthy white. And her former full, pouting lips were now thin and drawn, the right side of her mouth drooping. She held her stiff right arm close to her stomach.

Terri had been a resident here at Green Willows for several months, her rehabilitation slow and emotionally frustrating. She suffered from aphasia, which affects the ability to talk, listen, read and write. The stroke had occurred on the left side of the brain, the side containing the speech and language center, and had created a severe weakness in the right side of her body. Unfortunately, Terri also suffered from a mild form of dysarthria, where the muscles used for talking were affected by the stroke, causing slowed, slurred and distorted speech.

"Good morning, Ms. Owens. You've got a visitor," Lila said as she spoke directly into Terri's face. "It's Mr. Ransom. He's going to feed you your breakfast."

Terri Owens's large blue eyes moved side to side and up and down as if searching for her ex-husband, but finally she gazed up and looked directly at him. He pulled a straight-back chair over to the edge of the bed and sat beside her.

"You'll have the usual twenty minutes," Lila told him before quietly leaving the room.

She stood in the doorway and watched while Mr. Ransom removed the plastic lid from his ex-wife's breakfast plate.

"You've got eggs and grits and a biscuit." Mr. Ransom picked up the single-serving size jelly. "And there's grape jelly."

Lila continued watching while he went about the task with the tenderness and patience of a mother feeding her infant. And all the while, he talked to Terri, telling her what a fine April morning it was and how the spring flowers were in full bloom. Lila shook her head sadly as she walked away and returned to the nurses' station.

*I wonder if Terri Owens has any idea just how lucky she is. Mr. Ransom is one in a million, that's what he is. After the way she up and left him and their little boy and brought such shame on his family and hers, you'd think he would hate her, that he wouldn't want to ever see her again.*

*But love is a strange and wondrous thing. And Sweet Jesus, it can certainly make fools of us all.*

"You don't have to do this, you know," Mike said.

"I want to," Lorie told him. "It's the least I can do for Shelley."

"You've already answered all our questions, mine and Wainwright's. You've signed an official statement. That should be enough. Let Griffin Powell read your statement and—"

The doorbell rang. Mike and Lorie looked at each other and then at the door.

"They're here," she said.

Mike crossed the room and opened the front door. Jack Perdue and Buddy Pounders had escorted their guests from their car to the porch. Mike had asked Jack to join them that afternoon, and Buddy was the deputy on guard duty.

Standing six-four, Griffin Powell towered over most guys, even men such as he and Jack, who both stood over six feet. The former UT quarterback filled out his fashionable suit with massive shoulders and thickly muscled arms. The man's size alone was intimidating. Add the fact that he was a billionaire into the mix and it was no wonder he had a reputation for always getting what he wanted, one way or the other.

Nicole Powell stood at her husband's side, a tall, attractive brunette, exuding an air of self-confidence. She held out her hand. "It's nice to see you again, Sheriff Birkett, despite the circumstances."

"Yes, ma'am." Mike held open the door. "Y'all

come on in. Lorie's waiting for us in the living room."

"We appreciate Ms. Hammonds agreeing to this meeting," Nic said.

"She and Ms. Gilbert hit it off right from the start," Mike said. "They were well on their way to becoming friends."

Nic Powell entered the living room first. She marched straight over to Lorie and spoke to her quietly. The two women shook hands.

"Won't you sit down, please," Lorie said.

When Lorie sat in her favorite easy chair, Mike took his place behind her, his hands loosely gripping the back of the chair.

Once everyone was seated, Griff Powell said, "Whenever you're ready, Ms. Hammonds, please tell us everything you remember about the day before Shelley was killed."

"The entire day?" Lorie asked.

"Yes, the entire day, from when the two of you got up until you went to bed that night."

"All right. I . . . uh . . . let's see. Shelley was already up when I awoke. We drank coffee, ate breakfast, talked, and—"

"What did you talk about?" Griff asked.

"I'm not sure. Nothing really. How I hated being a prisoner in my own home. How maybe we should both take up knitting." Lorie smiled. "Shelley was a nice person, you know. I liked her." Tears misted her eyes. "She told me that her parents were dead, but she had a sister who lived in Phoenix and a couple of little nephews. She was going out there for a visit when her assignment with me ended."

"Her sister is flying in to Knoxville tomorrow," Nic said. "She'll make all the arrangements, pack away Shelley's things and close up her apartment."

"Please continue with what you remember about the day before Shelley died." Griff steered her back to what he felt was important.

Mike reached down and gripped Lorie's shoulders and gave them a reassuring squeeze before releasing her. She tilted her head and gazed up at him, her fragile smile conveying her appreciation for his presence.

Lorie talked. The others listened. Occasionally either Griff or Nic would ask her a question and if she got off track, Griff would nudge her back onto the subject. An hour later, after she had shared every detail that she could recall with the Powells, Lorie rose from her chair.

"I'd like some iced tea. Would anyone else care for something to drink?"

"Iced tea would be nice," Nic replied. "May I help you?"

"That's not necessary, but thank you."

Without saying a word, Mike followed Lorie when she left the room. He exchanged an entertain-these-people glance with Jack and headed for the kitchen. The moment he opened the door, he stopped. Lorie stood with her back to him, her shoulders trembling as she muffled her sobs by placing her hands over her mouth. Acting purely on instinct, he went over and draped his arms around her. She leaned back, allowing him to partially support her as she cried. After taking a deep, calming breath, she turned, looked at him with teary eyes, and wrapped her arms around his waist.

He held her close, embracing her as she laid her head on his chest. "I'm here. I've got you, honey. Everything is going to be all right. I promise."

# Chapter 25

Casey used his friend Jason's cell phone to make the call. He had met Jason at one of their AA meetings and the two had hit it off immediately. It had been a long time since he'd actually had a friend—a real friend—so he did his best to never impose on Jason's kindness. From time to time, Jason gave him a few bucks, occasionally took him out for a decent meal, and had even offered to let Casey stay with him and his family. As much as he would have liked taking Jason up on the offer, he knew Jason's wife Heather had been relieved when he had declined. And who could blame her? Although the few times he'd seen Heather, she'd been nice to him, he realized she had genuine doubts about exposing her children to a guy such as he.

Sometimes he felt guilty for not telling Jason the

truth—that he was not penniless. He had chosen a low-key, under-the-radar homeless person's lifestyle. It suited his purposes, at least for the time being.

Finding an out-of-the-way park bench, Casey sat down, dialed the number, and waited. The warm afternoon sun warred with the cool April breeze. Summer was just around the corner, but a hint of winter lingered in the wind. Springtime birds chattered in nearby trees and squirrels scurried from branch to branch.

As always, the maid answered the telephone. "Laura Lou Roberts's residence."

"Please tell Ms. Roberts that it's Casey."

"Yes, Mr. Lloyd, I'll tell her."

Casey nervously tapped his index finger against the edge of the phone as he waited. A couple of minutes later, he heard that familiar throaty voice. A dozen years ago, he had found that husky tone sexy. One of his many deadly mistakes.

"Hello, sweet boy," Laura Lou said.

"How are you?" he asked.

"Doing okay for an old woman."

"You'll never be old. And you'll always be vibrant and sexy." He told her what he knew she wanted to hear. He had learned years ago how to please her in order to get what he wanted. "I miss you. Life isn't the same without you."

Her gravelly laughter grated on his nerves, the sound bringing back too many unpleasant memories from a time when he'd been little more than her lapdog.

*And what are you now? You're practically licking her butt, albeit via a long-distance phone call. Whispering sweet nothings in her ear, giving the old heifer a thrill.*

But it wasn't the same as in the past. This time, he was in control, even though she didn't know it. To get what he wanted, what he needed, he would have bedded the devil. And it wouldn't be the first time.

Her laughter quickly altered and changed to heavy coughing. When she managed to control the coughs, she told him, "One of these days, I'm going to come see you and collect on all your promises and IOUs."

He doubted seriously that the day would ever come when she would visit him. Her vanity would keep her away. She preferred for him to remember her as she had been in the past, not as she was now. He had heard through mutual "friends" in LA that Laura Lou had not gone under the knife for any recent nips and tucks, that she had lost so much weight she looked like a skeleton, and that her four-packs-a-day cigarette habit had resulted in emphysema that required her to haul around a portable oxygen tank wherever she went.

"I'd love to see you," he lied. "We had some good times, didn't we?"

She'd had good times. He'd been in hell. But it

had been a hell of his own making. Laura Lou had simply been the particular devil he had chosen to oversee his torment.

"Yeah, we had some good times," she said, a wistful quality softening her lifetime smoker's voice. "But your girlfriend wouldn't want me showing up, now would she?"

"I don't have a girlfriend at the moment," he assured her. That much, at least, was the truth. Until he got all his addictions under control, a committed relationship was out of the question.

"What's wrong with the girls in Arkansas?" Once again her laughter turned into uncontrollable coughing.

"Are you taking care of yourself? That cough sounds bad." He didn't give a damn how sick she was or if she lived or died. Correct that. He needed her to stay alive a while longer, long enough for him to accomplish his goals. He needed the old bat's money. Smiling to himself, he wondered how Laura Lou would react if she had any idea how he was using the cash she sent him.

"I've got bad sinus problems," she told him. "Apparently, they're chronic and I just have to live with them." She coughed a couple more times and then got straight to the point. "So, how much do you need this time?"

"What makes you think I'm calling to ask for more money?" They played this same game every time he called her. He understood two things about

Laura Lou. One: She needed the attention he paid her during these long-distance conversations. Two: She would send him the money he needed.

"Sweet boy, I know you."

"Inside and out," he agreed.

"So, how much this time?"

"A thousand should be enough."

"Want me to wire it to the same account there in Fayetteville?"

"Yes, please. Under the name of William Geisman."

"I hope you're using the money wisely," she said. "But if not . . . if you're doing anything illegal, be careful not to get caught."

"Good advice. But you always were the smart one, weren't you? Don't worry about me. I learned from the master how to get away with murder."

Lorie hung up the phone and turned to Mike.

"You already know what Maleah told me, don't you?"

He nodded. "Derek called Jack this morning and Jack relayed the information to me when he called a little while ago. He told me that Maleah planned to phone you and tell you herself."

"Sonny Deguzman's dead and the Midnight Killer didn't murder him."

"Yeah, it seems he was stabbed in a bar fight in Madrid about six months ago. He'd been living under an assumed name and that's the reason Powell's had so much trouble finding him."

"That narrows down the targets for our killer, doesn't it? The only actors from *Midnight Masquerade* left alive are Jean, Terri, and me."

"And all three of you have around-the-clock protection. Jean Misner's husband is keeping two bodyguards on duty at all times. Terri Owens is recuperating in a private facility, in a restricted section of the rehab center that screens all of her visitors. And you have me and backup from my deputies."

"Why haven't they caught him?" Lorie asked, simply voicing her thoughts and not expecting Mike to have an answer.

He put his arm around her shoulders.

She tensed.

He released her instantly.

She took a deep breath.

Whenever Mike touched her, she wanted to turn into his arms, hold him close and never let him go. And the odd thing was, she sensed that he felt the same way.

Dear God, what an impossible situation.

Lorie dove directly into the other subject she had discussed with Maleah. "Did Jack tell you that Shelley's sister plans to have her cremated, as she had requested in her will, and there won't be a funeral, only a private memorial service?"

"He did."

"If the state ME releases Shelley's body within a few days, the memorial service will probably be next week," Lorie said. "I'd very much like to go to Knoxville for the service."

"I think that can be arranged. I figured you'd want to go, so I've already mentioned to Jack that perhaps he and Cathy could go with us."

Despite their years apart, Mike still knew her so well that he could often second-guess her thoughts. "That would be good. I'm sure Maleah would appreciate their being there. Even though they didn't really know Shelley all that well, she and Maleah did work together and . . ." Tears lodged in Lorie's throat. She swallowed. "Damn it, I've got to stop tearing up all the time."

"Your bodyguard, a woman you liked and were becoming friends with, was brutally murdered two days ago," Mike said. "You wouldn't be human if you weren't upset over that fact. You have every right to cry whenever you feel like it."

"If I'm honest with myself, I have to admit that all this emotional turmoil isn't just about Shelley."

"I know." He looked at her with sympathy and understanding.

She tried to smile; the effort failed. "So many people have died. People I knew, people who were a part of my life years ago. Dean and Hilary and Charlie and Shontee, all murdered. And poor Charlene. And now to find out that Sonny died half a world away in some senseless bar fight." Her lips curved upward in an almost smile. "And knowing Sonny, the fight was probably over some woman."

Nodding, keeping his gaze connected with hers, Mike remained silent.

"You don't want to listen to me talking about the people I knew out in LA, especially the ones I got to know while making *Midnight Masquerade*. You probably think of them as the scum of the earth, but . . . they were real people, people who had hopes and dreams, people who did not deserve . . ." Lorie bit down on her bottom lip in an effort to control the tears threatening to overflow.

"Talk about whoever you want to talk about," he told her. "Do whatever helps, whatever makes you feel better."

"I'm not sure anything can make me feel better. It's as if I'm trapped in a never-ending nightmare."

"There will be an end to it, I promise you."

"Yes, I'm sure there will be, but will I still be alive to see it?"

"Don't say that. Don't even think it." He moved in on her, mere inches separating their bodies, and glared straight into her startled eyes.

"You're right. I have to think only positive thoughts."

She also had to put some distance between them. If she didn't, she couldn't be held responsible for what she might do. She wanted Mike so desperately, needed him so completely. She tromped across the living room and looked out the window. "Do y'all still believe that Shelley's death had nothing to do with the Midnight Killer's murder spree?"

Mike walked across the room and stood beside her. "Shelley's murder doesn't fit his MO. That's all we know. Powell's and the FBI are looking into old Powell cases that Shelley worked on hoping to find a link."

"What are the odds that a bodyguard on an assignment to protect a client from a serial killer would end up murdered by another killer?"

"Yeah, I know. It sounds implausible, doesn't it?"

Suddenly Lorie noticed an older model Buick turn off the road in front of her house and roll to a stop in her driveway. "Is that your mother's car?"

"Yeah, it is. I wonder what she's doing here."

Mike and Lorie watched while Nell Birkett emerged from the Park Avenue along with Hannah and M.J. The children ran ahead of their grandmother, straight toward the porch.

"Why the hell did she bring the kids here?" Mike grumbled under his breath as he headed for the front door.

By the time he unlocked and opened the door, he came face-to-face with his kids. Lana Ladner, the deputy on guard duty this evening, hadn't stopped his mother and children; instead, she had escorted them to the door.

Hannah hurled herself at her father. He swept her up into a bear hug and then set her on her feet. M.J. grinned broadly, evidently glad to see Mike.

"Hi, Miss Lorie," M.J. said.

Hannah went from her father to Lorie and grabbed Lorie's hand.

"What are y'all doing here?" Mike looked squarely at his mother.

"We're here for supper," Nell replied. "The children miss you and they asked if we could pay y'all a visit."

"You should have called first," Mike said.

"Never thought of that," she replied, a sly grin on her face.

"I'm afraid we were going to have sandwiches for supper," Lorie said. "But I can thaw out some chicken and—"

"Don't bother," Nell said. "I brought supper. Mike, go out to the car and bring in the picnic basket. It's on the backseat."

"I'll help you, Dad," M.J. said.

"Why don't you and Hannah both go help your father," Nell suggested.

Mike frowned at his mother, but did as she had asked. When Mike and the kids were out of earshot, Nell smiled at Lorie.

"How are you?" Nell asked.

"I'm okay."

"Is my son treating you well?"

"Mike's been very good to me."

Nell sighed. "Well, it's about time. That boy of mine is every bit as stubborn as his father was." Nell walked into the living room and sat on the sofa. "Tell me, is he thawing out any?"

"Pardon?" Lorie asked.

"Has Mike thawed out any where you're concerned? I know you said that he's treating you well, but is he . . . are you two . . ." Nell cleared her throat. "Has he at least kissed you?"

Lorie didn't know whether to laugh or cry, whether to tell Nell Birkett that it was none of her business or blurt out everything she was feeling.

"Mike and I are still attracted to each other," Lorie admitted. "But even if something does happen—and it hasn't—we both know that we have no future together."

"Hogwash."

Lorie stared questioningly at Nell.

"You made a stupid mistake when you were quite young and then Mike compounded the problem by acting like a complete jerk for the past nine years. But, honey, it's as plain as the nose on your face that if ever two people were in love, you and Mike are. As much now as you were when you were teenagers."

"That's not true. Mike may want me . . ." God in heaven, how could she talk to Mike's mother about the sexual attraction that was driving both of them crazy?

Before Nell could comment, Mike and the kids came in, Mike carrying a wicker picnic basket and M.J. toting a red and white cooler.

"Take that stuff out to the kitchen," Nell instructed them. "There's potato salad, deviled eggs, and tea in the cooler. Everything else is in the basket." As soon as her son and grandchildren did as they were told and headed for the kitchen, Nell put her arm around Lorie's shoulders and whispered, "Honey, if you want him, my son is yours for the taking."

Lorie didn't know how to reply to such a comment. She was beginning to believe that she actually could seduce Mike while he was acting as her protector. He'd probably put up a token protest before giving in to her. But as much as she longed to have sex with him again, she wanted more. A lot more. She wanted forever after.

Tyler Owens spoke to Lila Newton as he walked up to the nurses' station. He visited his mother several times a week, sometimes staying five minutes, sometimes half an hour. He usually arrived around 7:30 P.M. shortly before Lila's twelve-hour supervisor's shift ended. Occasionally, he brought flowers or a small gift of some kind for his mother, and he made a habit of bringing a dessert tray once a week and leaving it at the desk for the nurses and aides.

"How's Mother been today?" he asked.

"She's had a good day."

"I don't suppose she's said anything yet."

"No, sir. She tries really hard during physical therapy. She gets out sounds, of course, so it's only a matter of time before she's able to talk again. But she becomes terribly frustrated when she tries so hard and can't form the words."

"Has she had any visitors today?" he asked.

Lila hated lying and did so only in the sense that she deliberately omitted his father's name from the list she recited. "Reverend Harper came this morning. And of course you know your wife brought Mr. Clement by earlier this afternoon for their weekly visit. Seeing her uncle always seems to cheer Miss Terri right up."

"Yes, I believe Uncle Clement was like a second father to her when she was growing up and they were always quite fond of each other."

"Yes, sir."

Tyler nodded, then turned and walked down the corridor past the guard at the entrance to the row of deluxe private rooms.

Tyler Owens was a nice enough young man, cordial and mannerly, but never truly friendly. She always felt as if he believed he was better than she was, better than anyone who worked at the rehab center, even the doctors. He certainly wasn't the man his father was, not as good a man, not as smart a man. And in the looks department, he was pretty much his mother's son, all blond and beautiful.

Only Terri Owens wasn't so beautiful anymore.

Lila checked her wristwatch. She needed to begin her shift change rounds. If she started now, she would have more than enough time to check in on each patient in her care. And since at this time of day, patients often had visitors, it was a good way to be seen by the patients' friends and families and for her to take note of who seldom, if ever, had visitors. Those poor souls, so alone in the world, were the ones she felt the most sorry for.

Fifteen minutes later, as she paused outside the half-closed door of room 107, she heard Tyler Owens speaking softly to his mother.

"I have to go now, Mother. You get a good night's rest and I'll be back in a few days to see you. If you need anything, anything at all, just do your best to let someone here know and I'll see to it that you have it."

Terri moaned again and again, trying her best to speak.

Lila started to open the door fully and go into the room. But just as her hand touched the door to give it a gentle shove, she saw Tyler reach inside his shirt pocket and remove a newspaper clipping.

"Here it is, as promised," he told her as he placed the folded clipping into her left hand, the hand unaffected by her recent stroke.

Lila pushed open the door and entered the room. "I'm here to check on Miss Terri before I leave for the evening."

"Please, Lila, come on in," Tyler said. "I was just on my way out." He leaned over and kissed his mother's forehead.

Sitting perfectly still, no emotion showing on her slightly warped face, Terri gripped the newspaper clipping tightly in her good hand as her son walked past Lila and out of the room.

"Want me to put that away for you?" Lila asked as she paused at Terri's bedside and held out her hand.

Terri shook her head.

"Is it something you would like for me to read to you?"

Again, Terri shook her head.

"All right, then, is there anything you need before I say good night? Juice? Water? Help going to the bathroom? Another blanket?" She patted the cotton blanket lying across Terri's legs.

Terri nodded, unfolded her hand and shook the newspaper clipping as if it were a salt shaker. And all the while she kept mumbling, "Mu . . . mu . . . mu . . ."

"It's something about the newspaper clipping Mr. Tyler brought you?"

Terri nodded again and held up the clipping.

Lila took the clipping from her. The heading read: MIDNIGHT KILLER SLAYS 4TH VICTIM. Lila scanned the brief article. Shontee Thomas had been shot and killed in her fiancé's Atlanta night-club. The victim was a former porno star, the fourth one murdered since January. All four murders were believed to be the work of a serial killer dubbed the Midnight Killer by the press because the four victims had all starred in the movie titled *Midnight Masquerade*.

"Merciful heavens," Lila said. "Why on earth would Mr. Tyler bring this to you?"

Terri patted her chest with her left hand, the gesture speaking for her.

"You're trying to tell me that you knew these people, aren't you?"

Terri nodded and again tried to speak, but without success. She then reached over and slapped at the drawer in her bedside table.

"You want me to open the drawer?" Lila asked.

Terri nodded.

Lila opened the drawer and there beneath a silver mirror and brush and comb set lay several other newspaper clippings. Lila eased them out of the drawer and hurriedly skimmed each article. They were all about victims of the same serial killer.

When Lila looked at her again, Terri patted her chest.

"Oh, sweet Jesus. You're trying to tell me that you were in that movie?"

Terri nodded as tears misted her eyes.

Lila laid aside the clippings and grasped Terri's hand. "I don't understand why Mr. Tyler brought you these. He told the staff, of course, about the killer and that you were in the same movie as the victims. But we assumed you were to be kept in the dark so you wouldn't worry. We immediately tightened security to make sure you're kept as safe as possible. I don't know why Mr. Tyler . . ." Lila huffed. "There was no reason for you to know, no reason for you to worry."

Terri frowned and shook her head frantically.

"If you're concerned about that crazy man getting in here, don't be. You're well protected here, Miss Terri."

A lone tear escaped her left eye and trickled down her cheek. She tried again to speak, but when all that came out was a mumble of moans and groans, she pulled her hand out of Lila's, laid her head back against the pillows, and turned to face the opposite direction.

"Oh, you poor dear." Lila picked up the newspaper clippings and placed them back in the drawer. "I don't know why your son would bring those articles and show them to you, but I'm sure he had a good reason."

Lila walked out of the room, all the while grumbling to herself. "You'd think he'd want to keep his mother from learning that such terrible things had happened to people she knew. The last thing Miss Terri needs while she's recuperating is to find out that she could well be on that crazy man's hit list."

# Chapter 26

During the past couple of weeks, Lorie and Mike had fallen into a daily routine oddly resembling that of an old married couple. Minus the sex, of course. They took turns preparing their meals and shared in the household chores. They read the morning newspaper together and considered it a good day if neither Lorie nor the Midnight Killer was mentioned. Although a stray reporter showed up at least once a day, for the most part, the press didn't bother them, nor did nosy neighbors. Of course, Buddy Pounders had caught a couple of teenage boys spying on Lorie's house through binoculars and they admitted they were hoping to catch a glimpse of Lorie naked.

She had overheard Buddy tell Mike, "They had copies of that flyer of Lorie from *Playboy*. You can imagine what they've been doing."

She didn't want to imagine, but she knew. Boys and men alike often gazed at photos of naked women while they masturbated. Just when she thought there was a chance for Mike and her to put the past behind them, her past came back with a vengeance to put her in her place.

And just what was her place?

In hell, of course, with all the other wicked women.

Lorie's day-to-day life would be boring if not for Mike's presence. The sizzle sparking between them kept them both on edge, each acutely aware of the other. She lay in bed at night and thought about how close he was, just down the hall, only a short walk away. So close and yet so far away. And it was driving her crazy knowing that all she had to do was go to him, touch him, kiss him, offer herself to him.

Whether she showered or soaked in the tub, fantasies of a naked Mike joining her aroused her unbearably. When she closed her eyes, she could almost feel his big hands caressing her wet, naked body. She could feel his warm breath at her ear, his moist lips sucking at her breasts, his tongue stroking her intimately.

If their hands accidentally brushed or their bodies touched even for an instant, she felt a jolt of sexual electricity ignite between them. At odd moments, she sensed him staring at her. When she looked at him, their gazes would lock and each knew what the other was thinking.

Once a day, never at the same time, Mike escorted her outside for a short walk around her house. That morning, she had picked the last of the blooming tulips and daffodils from her flower garden and, once back inside, had trimmed the stems and placed the flowers in a crystal vase filled with water. The arrangement now graced the center of her kitchen table, where she and Mike were eating lunch.

Lorie wanted to return to work, but had agreed with Mike that it was best to wait for a while longer before resuming her normal schedule. Confinement at her home meant safety. It was easier to protect her in that type of controlled environment. At Treasures, she would be dealing with the public, and that public would include not only customers, but curious townsfolk, overeager reporters, and judgmental activists from the Women for Christian Morality organization. The WCM had done everything short of running her out of town on a rail when she'd come back to Dunmore nine years ago. Recently, she had received so many phone calls from reporters, both TV and newspaper, and publicity-seeking leaders of WCM that all her calls were now diverted to Powell's and monitored by the agency. It was a better solution than unplugging all of her phones during the day.

Mike alternated between working out of her home and going into his office during the day. Even though he was Lorie's bodyguard, he was still the sheriff, and with that title came certain responsibilities he couldn't delegate. But by suppertime each evening, he was always there with her and stayed all night. In his absence, the deputy on duty checked on her at regular intervals, and she never went outside.

Her life was in a state of nerve-racking limbo.

And she and Mike had run out of idle chitchat days ago. Now conversation between them was strained to say the least. They both struggled to find something to talk about, often resorting to the weather.

"Looks like it might rain," Mike said.

"Uh-huh. I think the weather forecast on the ten o'clock news last night predicted a fifty percent chance of thundershowers by this evening."

"We could use some rain."

"We sure could." Lorie picked up the half slice of her grilled cheese sandwich and took a big bite.

Mike scooped up a spoonful of hot tomato soup and brought it to his mouth.

Lorie took a sip of iced tea. "Your mom is bringing supper again tonight when she and the kids come over for a visit."

Mike nodded. "Uh-huh."

"You really should be at home with Hannah and M.J. instead of here babysitting me."

"There's no need to discuss that again," Mike told her.

Lorie voiced a concern that had been tormenting her. "What if I'm not his next victim? What if he's chosen someone else? Do you plan to stay with me indefinitely?"

"If that's what it takes. But I'm counting on Powell's and the FBI finding this guy before he strikes again."

"God, I hope so."

"It'll happen. I know it will."

She forced a smile and then concentrated on eating lunch.

Mike glanced at his wristwatch. "It's nearly one. We can take our apple pie in the living room while we watch *As the World Turns* and find out what Carly and Jack are up to today."

Lorie laughed. "You're the only man I know who'll admit he has ever watched a soap opera."

"Hey, I grew up with a mother who never missed an episode of *As the World Turns* and still doesn't. She records the show if she can't watch it when it airs."

"Yeah, I know. She's the one who got me hooked on the show when I was a teenager. Sometimes I catch it on my lunch break, and if not, I watch it on my DVR in the evenings." Lorie sighed.

"You miss work, don't you?"

"God, yes. I love being at Treasures. And I know my not being there is putting a burden on Cathy, and it's an added expense having to hire extra help."

"You know why you can't go into town yet, why being at Treasures is a really bad idea."

She blew out an exasperated breath. "I know, I know. Reporters and curiosity seekers would descend like a swarm of locusts if they knew I was there. Not to mention all those Bible-spouting, narrow-minded fanatics who think I'm the devil's spawn."

Mike looked at her and she knew he wanted to reach across the table and take her hand. But he didn't. He wanted to comfort her. But he didn't.

"It's okay," she told him. "Really. I can be a good girl and follow orders if that's what it takes to keep me alive."

"It won't be forever," he told her.

"I know, but right now it seems . . ." She paused, brought her hands together in a prayerlike gesture, and lifted them to her lips. After releasing a pent-up breath, she gazed down at the table, avoiding direct eye contact with Mike. "I never realized how much I wanted to live until recently. It changes your perspective on everything when death is staring you in the face. If I . . ." She emitted a grunting chuckle. "Scratch that thought. Not if I live through this, but when I live through this, I'm not going to waste any more of my life trying to make up for my many sins."

"All the time you've wasted is partly my fault. I couldn't stop punishing you. I could have been a friend to you. Mother and Molly tried to make me see reason. I should have listened to them and—"

"No, you shouldn't have. It wouldn't have worked, our trying to be friends. There was a time when I thought I wanted us to be friends, that friendship would be enough for me. But I was lying to myself." She looked right at him. "That's why our being cooped up together like this is bound to lead to trouble. Please, Mike, for both our sakes, leave and don't come back. Let me hire another Powell agent as my bodyguard."

Mike glanced away, finished off his sandwich, and then stacked his dirty dishes and carried them to the sink.

She shot up out of her chair. "Damn it, Mike, don't you dare ignore me."

He dumped the dishes into the sink, the silverware clanging against the stainless steel, and then he gripped the edge of the sink with white-knuckled strength.

She came up behind him, determined to make him answer her. "I can't stand this. Having you here is tearing me apart. I want you to go."

He spun around so quickly that he nearly knocked her down. As she wavered unsteadily, he reached out and grabbed her, his hands clutching either side of her head. Staring into his blue-black eyes, she held her breath as he lowered his head and took her mouth in a hungry, devouring kiss.

Heath Leroy despised the devil and all the sinners who worshipped him by committing evil. His father had once been the vilest of sinners and well on his way straight to hell, but praise be to God, Grant Leroy had found Jesus. The Son of God had spoken personally to his dad and called him to preach the Gospel. Heath counted himself blessed among men that his father had shared that special anointing with him, bringing him also into the glory of the Almighty. He had been a boy of seventeen when he had been reunited with his father, a man he'd seen very little of for most of his life. His parents had divorced when he was seven, and his only memories of his family together were of his mother and father screaming at each other.

Working side by side together, his dad and he had shared God's message with the people of Kentucky, his father's home state. They had started out small, going from town to town sharing the Good Word with anyone who would listen. Within a year, they had been able to rent a building in Louisville to house the Redeemer Church. His father's charismatic personality combined with the Lord's helping hand had quickly catapulted their small congregation into a group so large that they had been forced to rent a larger meeting place.

His father had sent him to college and two years ago, at twenty-one, he had become an accountant and now managed the Redeemer Church's finances. He was proud to say that their net worth was in the multimillions. With that kind of wealth, they were able to reach so many more people, people who needed to be saved.

Heath knew he had been saved by the grace of God and not through any action on his part. He himself was not without sin, but he fought the good fight every day of his life. A man could not give in to temptation, especially when that temptation was his own father's wife. Avoiding Renee wasn't possible. As long as he worked with his father, he couldn't escape her or the burning desire he felt whenever she came near.

He treated her with the greatest respect and he understood that her affection for him was that of a stepmother for a stepson. But how he wished she wouldn't hug him or give him sweet kisses on his cheeks or smile at him with such tenderness. Whenever he caught himself staring at her, longing no doubt obvious in his expression, he chastised himself for his evil thoughts and stayed for hours on his knees begging for God's help.

Just as his father had been able to overcome the evil inside him, the evil that coerced him into a life of depravity, Heath struggled to overcome the wickedness his father had passed down to him, an evil born and bred in the pornography business. If it were within his power to completely erase such evil from the world, he would. But for now, he had to settle for what he could do to save others from that most vile of all depravities.

Heath entered the Redeemer Church office complex, having come directly from a business lunch where he had interviewed Larry Williamson, a local contractor who had a spotless reputation as a God-fearing family man. The Redeemer Church had bought land down in LaRue County, five hundred acres on which they planned to build a youth camp. The church's largest contributors had pledged a quarter of a million dollars each for the construction costs. Heath was eager to see his father and discuss his recommendations for hiring Williamson Contractors.

He passed through the outer office, pausing only long enough to speak to the two secretaries as he made his way straight to his father's inner sanctum. His father's assistant, Maggie Stevenson—a plump grandmother of six and a good Christian woman —was nowhere to be seen, which undoubtedly meant that she was still on her lunch break.

In his eagerness to talk to his father, Heath didn't bother to knock before he opened the office door. What he saw stopped him cold before he took one step over the threshold. Completely naked, her breasts thrust forward and her thighs spread wide apart, Renee sat on the edge of his father's desk, which was positioned so that Heath had a sidelong view from his stance in the doorway. Grant Leroy, his tailor-made slacks hanging loosely on his hips, stood between his wife's legs and was pumping into her like a jackhammer boring into concrete.

Transfixed by the sight, Heath couldn't move. As he watched the intimate act between his father and stepmother, he became aroused, his penis hardening to the point of pain.

Dear God in heaven!

*Run, you fool, run.*

He managed to get his feet to cooperate long enough to turn around, but when he heard Renee's orgasmic cries, he couldn't stop himself from glancing over his shoulder. When he did, she looked right at him as she panted and sighed and gripped his father's hips, urging him on to achieve his climax.

Swallowing hard, Heath stared at Renee with what he knew was a stricken expression on his face. She had caught him watching them, but did she know that he longed to be there, between her legs, in his father's place?

Behind his father's heaving back, she shooed him away with the backward wave of her hand. She had given him a reprieve, silently telling him to go away before his father caught him.

Heath hurried past Maggie's desk and through the outer office, careful to keep his back to the secretaries so they wouldn't see his erection. Once safely inside his own office, he closed and locked the door. He immediately dropped to his knees and prayed.

Lorie had spent the rest of the day unable to think of anything other than the kiss she and Mike had shared after lunch. Just remembering the kiss sent her pulse rate into overdrive. It had begun passionately untamed. Hard. Hot. Deep. But it soon became a sensuously lingering expression of their need for each other.

Long after the kiss ended, they had stood together, Mike's forehead pressed against hers, their breaths mingling, as he held both of her hands down on either side of their bodies. Neither of them had said a word for several minutes. And then Mike had pulled back and walked out of the kitchen.

She hadn't followed him.

She had cleaned up in the kitchen and then, in the privacy of her bedroom, had called Cathy on her cell phone. After an hour-long heart-to-heart with her best friend, Lorie had ventured into the living room where she found Mike. He had glanced at her, acknowledged her presence, and then promptly ignored her. For the next few hours, they had avoided looking at each other or even talking. He had worked the crossword puzzle in today's newspaper while she had concentrated on sketching the layout for the tearoom she hoped that she and Cathy could open later this year.

If she were alive later this year.

When Mike's cell phone rang, Lorie gasped. She'd been lost in her own world of private thoughts and future plans.

Mike tossed the newspaper aside, got up, answered the phone, and paced the floor. Apparently the caller was doing all the talking because Mike didn't say a word after he identified himself.

Lorie checked her wristwatch. 4:40 P.M.

When she heard Mike say, "Thanks for calling. We'll see y'all tomorrow," Lorie shoved her sketch pad into her red leather briefcase and set the case on the floor.

"That was Derek Lawrence," Mike said as he returned the telephone to the holder on his belt. "He and Maleah are back in Knoxville. They got in sometime this morning."

"Did he have any news about—?"

"They've interviewed everyone they could find who was in any way connected to the making of *Midnight Masquerade*," Mike told her. "There's not a lot more they can do. They've ruled out a few people, but at this point, the possible suspects list includes half a dozen people involved with the movie."

"With the exception of the actors, most of whom are already dead."

Mike frowned. "Derek wanted us to know that Shelley's memorial service is set for tomorrow afternoon at two. I told him we'd be there."

"He didn't happen to mention if they have any idea who killed her and why?"

"I'm afraid not."

"They don't believe it was the Midnight Killer, but they haven't completely ruled him out, have they?"

"You know it's unlikely that it was the Midnight Killer. But no, they haven't ruled out the possibility."

"What time will we need to leave here in the morning to be in Knoxville for the service by two?" Lorie asked.

"I'm not sure. I'll check with Jack tonight and—"

"Don't forget that your mother and the children are coming over later for supper."

"I haven't forgotten. I'll get in touch with Jack after supper. I'm sure Maleah called him to let him know the time and place, just as Derek called me."

Lorie rose from her chair and walked toward Mike, who suddenly got a deer-in-the-headlights expression on his face as she approached.

"Didn't Mom say they'd be here around five?"

he asked. "That doesn't leave us much time. We should probably go ahead and set the table and—"

"Nell said five-thirty. We've got plenty of time."

"Oh, okay. I—uh, I'll go out and check with Buddy, see if he's got anything to report."

"Don't you think we need to talk about what happened between us, before Nell and the kids get here?"

"What's there to talk about?"

"We shared a pretty explosive kiss a few hours ago and we've both avoided—"

"It was just a kiss, that's all," Mike told her, but couldn't look her in the eye. "I won't let it happen again."

Lorie laughed. "You're kidding yourself if you think it won't happen again. And next time you may not be able to stop with just a kiss."

"Don't do this." He turned and headed for the front door.

She followed him. "The only way we can make sure it doesn't happen again is for you to leave."

He opened the door. "I'm not leaving and that's final."

"You stubborn mule!" she hollered at his back as he walked out onto the porch.

Without a backward glance, he stepped off the porch and onto the sidewalk. "That's the pot calling the kettle black," he said as he threw up his hand and waved at Buddy Pounders, who had just come around the corner of the house.

Lorie grumbled to herself, then yelled, not caring who heard her. "If you stay, whatever happens will be your fault, not mine!" She went back inside and slammed the door.

# Chapter 27

He had three days to make it happen. Three days to study Jean Goins Misner's daily routine, her comings and goings and the people allowed in and out of her home. Three days to find a way to get inside her house and kill her.

If he was gone longer than a few days, people would ask too many questions about his absence. As with the four other out-of-town trips he had made to inflict punishment and exact revenge, he had fabricated a reasonable excuse this time, a seemingly legitimate reason to be absent from his daily life. Of course, he was never where he was supposed to be. But he was always careful. He covered his tracks. He used fake ID and subtle disguises.

He was too smart to get caught.

Each execution had posed specific problems and, admittedly, he had created a scenario that complicated things, such as committing the murders as close to midnight as possible. But he preferred complicated to simple. He loved a challenge. And finding a way to get past the tight security surrounding Jean Goins, aka Puff Raven, would be a test of his superior intelligence.

As he gazed through the binoculars at Jean's Hollywood Hills home, he smiled to himself at the thought of killing her. Not only would she be taken by surprise, but so would the FBI task force and the Powell agents who had questioned him. No one expected the fifth murder to take place until May, the fifth month. And that element of surprise would work to his advantage.

He had arrived at eleven this morning, Pacific time. He had parked across from Jean and Jeff Misner's home for an hour and then moved his rental car down the street and parked it. With a digital camera hanging around his neck and a sightseeing brochure sticking out of his shirt pocket, he could easily pass himself off as a tourist, if anyone questioned him. After all, the homes of numerous old and present-day stars dotted the hills above the Sunset Strip, but only a handful had obtained their vast wealth in such a blatantly sinful way as the Misners had.

No doubt Jean had a full-time bodyguard. Perhaps she'd had one even before he had sent her the first death threat, but most certainly ever since. A bodyguard or even two or more could not stand between him and destiny. His destiny as the avenger, the righter of wrongs; his victim's destiny to be punished and rendered harmless. And having an obstacle such as a professionally trained bodyguard and overcoming that obstacle simply made success all the sweeter.

In typical tourist fashion, he meandered along leisurely, taking a snapshot every so often. He stopped and stared at the tall, decorative gates that protected the entrance to the Misners' estate. Jean's home was a five-bedroom, three-and-a-half-bath Mediterranean mansion set atop a sloping ridge. By going online and doing a minimum amount of research, he had discovered the community amenities included a heated pool and spa, a gym, a jogging path, and a grassy park for children and dogs. The Misners had come a long way from the time he had been a cameraman and she a supporting actor in *Midnight Masquerade*. Jeff was now an adult film director and Jean's porno Web site raked in a ton of money.

He couldn't remain there much longer without possibly bringing undue attention to himself. He would come back for a while tonight when he was less likely to be noticed. And then early in the morning, he would return in a different vehicle, a truck perhaps, and wear jeans and a tool belt and pretend to be a carpenter or a painter or even a plumber. He needed to know when the bodyguards changed shifts and who came and went from the house. A cook, maids, gardeners, hairstylists, masseuse, etc.

And if by tomorrow afternoon, he had not come up with a plan that would put him in direct contact with Jean near the midnight hour, he would resort to his backup plan. He would simply telephone her, tell her that he was in town and he would very much like to see her.

Maleah and Shelley Gilbert had been colleagues for several years and although they had never worked a case together, they had occasionally crossed paths at the Powell Agency headquarters and at various agency events.

Everyone who knew Shelley liked her.

She had been that kind of person.

The simple, dignified memorial service had lasted a little over an hour and a half. The ceremony had included two eulogies, one given by her sister, Stacy, and the other by Griffin Powell, several prayers led by the minister from the Baptist church Shelley had attended, and three hymns sung by the church choir. And all during the service, Maleah couldn't stop thinking about the fact that Shelley was the second Powell Agency employee who had been murdered in a very short period of time.

From the agency's inception, agent safety had been a top priority, and to Maleah's knowledge only two agents had been killed in the line of duty. All the agents were reasonably young, had passed strenuous medical and psychological exams, and had undergone extensive bodyguard training. Even the employees at the Knoxville office complex had received in-depth exams and had been given lessons in basic self-defense skills.

The funerals of two fellow agents in less than a month seemed surreal to Maleah and probably to all the other Powell employees. Griff had ordered the office closed for the afternoon, and to a person, the staff had attended the service, as had every agent who wasn't in the field and unable to return to Knoxville.

Although Maleah had become accustomed to Derek's presence and they had sat together at the funeral, she wished that her brother hadn't invited him to join them for an early dinner after they left the memorial service. Working with the man on a daily basis was bad enough without having to socialize with him. The fact that they appeared to be a third couple, along with the other two—Jack and Cathy and Mike and Lorie—aggravated Maleah. But it amused Derek. Damn him. He seemed to derive much too much pleasure from situations that made her uncomfortable.

Thankfully, they had all kept the dinnertime conversation light, almost as if by mental telepathy, they had agreed not to discuss the Midnight Killer or Shelley's and Kristi's murders.

"Y'all are welcome to stay over at my apartment tonight," Maleah told her brother as they left Chesapeake's Seafood House around 6:15 P.M. "I have two bedrooms and somebody can sleep on the sofa."

"Thanks, but we should head on home," Jack

453

said. "I took off work today and Cathy closed up Treasures so we could make this trip with Mike and Lorie. We all wanted to be here, to show our respect."

Maleah hugged Jack and then Cathy before turning to Lorie. "I'm sorry that we haven't solved this case and caught the Midnight Killer. But I promise you that we haven't given up."

"Powell's and the FBI are an unofficial team, and the combined manpower is formidable. It's only a matter of time before we get him." When Derek injected his comment into what Maleah considered a private conversation, she glared at him. And as usual, he acted as if he didn't even notice her non-verbal censure.

"I'm hoping that will happen very soon," Lorie said as she placed her hand on Derek's arm.

Lorie rubbed Derek's arm in what Maleah saw as nothing more than a friendly gesture, but apparently Mike Birkett saw it as more than that. His body visibly tensed and he gave Derek a get-your-hands-off-my-woman glare even though it was Lorie who had touched Derek. Then, as if sensing Mike's unspoken jealousy, Derek put his arm around Lorie's shoulder and leaned down to kiss her cheek.

Was the man crazy? Did he have a death wish? If looks could kill, Derek would be dead from the feral scowl on Mike's face.

"We should get going," Mike said, his tone gruff.

"As it is, it'll be close to eleven before we get home."

"Do you need a ride to your apartment?" Cathy asked Maleah. "I know you came to the service with the Powells."

"Don't worry about that," Derek replied for her. "I can take Maleah home."

Maleah forced a smile, not wanting to make a scene, today of all days.

After a round of quick good-byes that included promises to keep in touch and share information, Mike whisked Lorie away quickly. And since Jack and Cathy had ridden to Knoxville with the other couple, they followed them to Lorie's SUV.

Intending to get a taxi home, Maleah started to say good night—and good riddance—to Derek, but before she uttered a word, his cell phone rang. He answered, listened, and replied, "We'll meet y'all there in about fifteen minutes."

"I hope that 'we' doesn't include me," Maleah said. "I want to go home, take a long, relaxing soak in the bathtub, and sleep in my own bed tonight."

"I'll drop you by your apartment later, after we make a detour by the Powell Building," Derek said. "That was Griff. He wants us to join him and Nic and a few others for a Powell Agency powwow."

Maleah grumbled. "This couldn't wait until tomorrow?"

Reluctantly, Maleah slid into the passenger seat of Derek's sleek silver Corvette. When he got behind the wheel, she couldn't help noticing that his long legs and broad shoulders seemed over-sized for the small sports car. She found it oddly amusing that the blue-blooded Derek and her good-old-boy brother both had a passion for Corvettes. And it was downright annoying that Jack and Derek had become buddies last year when they'd worked together on the Fire and Brimstone Killer case.

On the short drive from the restaurant to the Powell Building, Derek didn't try to carry on a mundane conversation with Maleah. Thank good-ness. He parked his Vette in the underground garage and they showed their IDs to the guards on duty near the two elevators that rose from the base-ment level to the top floor of the restored 1928 structure. Griffin Powell's private office covered the entire eighteenth floor, the penthouse suite, which gave him a spectacular nighttime view of the city lights.

Apparently she and Derek were the last to arrive, because almost everyone else had taken seats around the conference table and had been served drinks by Sanders, who was acting as bartender this evening.

"Come on in." Griff motioned to them.

Nic smiled at Maleah when she chose the seat next to hers at the far end of the table. Derek declined Sanders's offer for a drink and chose a seat on the opposite side from Maleah.

Glancing around the table, she took note of the others assembled here this evening. Griff at the head of the oval table and Nic at his side. Sanders stood while Barbara Jean sat in her wheelchair by the bar. Holt Keinan leaned back in one of the thickly padded leather chairs and hoisted a beer bottle to his lips. Michelle Allen and Ben Corbett sat on either side of him.

Dr. Yvette Meng, along with one of her protégés, Meredith Sinclair, stood by the wide expanse of windows overlooking the city below. The two were deep in conversation.

Maleah leaned over and whispered to Nic, "What's Dr. Meng doing here?"

"Yvette and Meredith were allowed a few minutes alone with both Kristi and Shelley . . . before Kristi was embalmed and Shelley was cremated."

Maleah rolled her eyes skeptically and kept her voice low. "And did either of them sense something? Any information that will actually help us figure out who killed Shelley and Kristi and why?"

"As I understand it, empaths usually can't make a connection with the dead. Only mediums can do that," Nic said softly, keeping their conversation as private as possible. "And as you know, empathy is Yvette's talent."

"And Meredith Sinclair—what's her talent?"

"Yvette says that Meredith is multitalented."

Before Maleah could respond, Griffin Powell called the meeting to order. "We have two separate

457

issues to discuss this evening." He motioned to Barbara Jean, who lifted a portable folder onto her lap, opened it, removed a stack of files, and returned the folder to the floor. "Barbara Jean will hand out updated information on the Midnight Killer case and all the info we have at present on the murders of Kristi Arians and Shelley Gilbert."

While Barbara Jean distributed the stapled documents, Griffin continued. "Take a look at Derek Lawrence's most recent profiles and you'll see that he has somewhat narrowed the list of possible known suspects. His educated guess, as he himself calls it"—Griff glanced at Derek—"is that one of the following could be the Midnight Killer."

Griff gave everyone a couple of minutes to locate Derek's report before he said, "As you'll note, Powell's research data on the comings and goings of these suspects, along with all personal records that we could access, narrows down the list to Grant Leroy and his son Heath, to both Tyler and Ransom Owens, and to Casey Lloyd."

"That's still five suspects," Michelle Allen said. "And those are only the known suspects."

"Which is all we have to work with at the present," Griff told her. "We concentrate on what we've got. As of this coming Monday, the last Monday in April, agents will be assigned to each of these suspects to keep track of where they go and what they do. And as added protection, we will offer to assign a Powell agent to each of the three remaining potential victims: Terri Owens, Jean Misner, and Lorie Hammonds."

"What sort of problems can we expect to run into with Special Agent Wainwright and his task force?" Ben Corbett asked.

Griff looked at his wife. Nic said, "Unofficially, Hicks Wainwright will cooperate by giving us a wide berth as long as we don't publicly step over the bounds. He's aware of the fact that Powell's has the resources to allocate manpower to this investigation that the Bureau doesn't, such as keeping the five suspects under surveillance. At present, Powell's is working on numerous cases, but two take top priority—unmasking and stopping the Midnight Killer and"—she glanced around the table, pausing briefly on each employee—"and finding the person who killed Kristi and Shelley."

"Are we assuming that they were killed by the same person?" Holt Keinan asked. "Do we have evidence to back up that assumption or—?"

"That info is in the report." Griff tapped his copy of the documents. "The two murders were almost identical in nature. The killer's MO for their murders was the same. It's highly unlikely that two different killers would use the same method to murder two Powell agents less than a month apart."

"What's the consensus concerning the possibility that Shelley's and Kristi's murders are somehow connected to the Midnight Killer murders?" Maleah asked the question that had been troubling her ever since Shelley's murder, a question that she and Derek had discussed.

"We have no evidence that there is any connection," Griff replied, then looked at Derek. "What's your educated guess on that one?"

"I'll tell you what I told Maleah when she and I discussed the possibility—it's improbable that the Midnight Killer murders and the murders of the two Powell employees are connected. The MOs are completely different. And just as important, the Midnight Killer would have no reason to kill Kristi Arians, who was in no way connected to that investigation."

"Does that mean someone is targeting Powell employees for a reason totally unrelated to any ongoing investigations?" Michelle asked.

"Possibly," Griff said. "We've already beefed up security here at the Powell Building and at Griffin's Rest. And every agent will be contacted and warned to be extra vigilant concerning their own safety. Shelley Gilbert's death tells us that whoever killed her was a highly trained individual. No amateur could have overpowered her."

"Then you think we're dealing with an assassin?" Ben asked.

"I think it's possible," Griff agreed.

Silence fell over the room, each person no doubt considering his or her own fate as a Powell employee. Maleah sensed that there was a lot more to Griff's suspicions than he was revealing. Only her friendship with Nic gave her an insight into Griffin Powell's personal life, one that the other employees did not have. If someone was targeting Powell employees, there had to be a reason, and her gut instincts told her that that reason was Griffin Powell himself.

"Any idea why somebody would target your employees?" Holt asked.

"Nothing concrete," Griff said.

"We're moving forward with the Midnight Killer investigation." Nic stepped in with a comment that purposely changed the discussion. "We want each of you to study the updated information and make any additions you feel are necessary. We'll meet back here in the morning at ten. Thank y'all for coming tonight."

Nic had effectively ended the meeting and dismissed the agents. Taking their cue from Nic's abruptness, Holt, Ben, and Michelle made a hasty retreat and headed for the elevator. As Derek and Maleah followed, Griff called to them.

"You two, wait up."

They stopped, turned, and faced Griff.

"Derek, we need your area of expertise," Griff said, then looked at Maleah. "Nic has requested that, as her close friend, you be included in this very private conversation. Anything said from this point on is to be kept in the strictest confidence and mentioned to no one outside this room. Do you understand?"

"Yes, I understand."

Maleah understood that Griff didn't want her here and had probably objected when Nic had asked that she be included. But he was hardly in a position to deny his wife the loyalty and support of one friend when he had included Sanders and Yvette Meng. And although Barbara Jean and Nic were dear friends, Barbara Jean's first allegiance was to Sanders, and Sanders's allegiance was always to Griff.

She shouldn't be thinking in terms of having to choose sides or considering the possibility that Nic and Griff might be at odds over whatever top-secret information Griff was going to reveal. But when she glanced at Nic and sensed some odd vibes coming from her friend, she realized her instincts were probably right on the money. Yvette Meng's presence here tonight, along with her unnervingly spooky fellow psychic, Meredith Sinclair, bothered Nic a lot more than she wanted her husband to know.

As soon as Derek and Maleah sat back down at the conference table, Sanders closed the double doors and Yvette and Meredith took seats at the far end of the table. Sanders removed one of the chairs and Barbara Jean eased her wheelchair up to the table. Sanders took the seat next to her.

Standing in front of the small assembly composed of their most trusted confidants, Griff remained quiet and still for a couple of minutes, as if considering what to say and how much information to share.

"Yvette and Meredith, as all of you know, possess certain talents that can often be used to help Powell's. Not in all cases, of course. Only in a specific few. They were allowed to see Kristi and Shelley, after their autopsies. Yvette was unable to ascertain any information that might help us. But Meredith did pick up on something."

Maleah was somewhat of a skeptic. A partial skeptic. She didn't actually believe in the supernatural, but she didn't completely disbelieve either. Was it possible that some people possessed a greater degree of psychic instinct than most? Yeah, sure. But that was as far as she was willing to suspend disbelief.

Griff looked at Meredith. The shy, withdrawn young woman with the wild, curly red hair and an abundance of freckles kept her head bowed and didn't make eye contact with Griff or anyone else.

"Can you tell us what you sensed when you were with Kristi and then with Shelley?" Griff asked.

Meredith swallowed. "They did not know their killer and he did not know them."

A cold trickle crept up Maleah's spine. This was just a little too weird to suit her. Were they supposed to believe that Meredith Sinclair was able to speak to the dead?

"And?" Yvette Meng prompted her protégé to continue.

"He felt nothing when he killed them. No regret. No passion," Meredith said. "To him, it was simply a job well done."

"Thank you," Griff said and then focused on Derek. "I want you to work with Meredith to form a profile of our killer. There's a good possibility that he is a hired assassin, which will make discovering his identity difficult. But if I have a profile of this man, it will assist me when I begin searching for him."

Maleah had remained quiet as long as she possibly could. "Why would someone hire an assassin to kill Powell Agency employees?"

Griff's hard glare bored into Maleah and for a split second she regretted being so bold.

"That is *the* question, isn't it," Griff said. "And I intend to find the answer before anyone else associated with Powell's is murdered."

An uneasy silence permeated the room. The soft, rapid drum of her heartbeat hummed in Maleah's ears.

# Chapter 28

Lorie had just stepped out of the shower and wrapped a towel around her wet hair when an explosive streak of lightning lit up the sky, so bright that it was visible through the white lace

Roman shade covering the bathroom window. When they had been half an hour outside Dunmore on their trip home from Knoxville tonight, distant thunder and lightning had forewarned of an approaching springtime storm. After dropping Cathy and Jack by their house, she and Mike had hurried home, hoping to outrun the impending rain. They had almost made it, but as they emerged from her SUV, the bottom fell out, drenching them both to the skin. Once inside, she had gone straight to the bathroom while Mike locked up and secured the alarm system.

Suddenly a riotous boom of thunder followed another blaze of lightning. Lorie shuddered. The lights flickered several times as she reached for a second towel. And then the electricity went out and everything turned pitch black. Lorie gasped and jerked her hand away from the decorative metal towel rack.

She kept a flashlight and a box of matches in her nightstand and there were scented candles on top of her dresser. Taking it slow and easy, she felt her way to the door, cautiously moved into her bedroom, and managed to make it to her bed without running into anything. Another vivid slash of lightning illuminated the room for a couple of seconds, long enough for her to grab the handle and open the nightstand drawer. She rummaged through the drawer's contents until her fingers encountered the flashlight.

"Lorie," Mike called from the hallway outside her closed bedroom door. "Are you all right?"

"I'm fine," she told him.

"A transformer probably blew," he said. "I've already put in a call to the emergency line at the utility company."

Without warning, Lorie's bedroom door opened and there stood Mike, fresh from his shower, wearing only his pajama bottoms and holding a flashlight, which he pointed directly at her. Both of them stood unmoving, each of them transfixed by the knowledge that Lorie was stark naked. Mike ran the flashlight over her from her wide eyes and gaping mouth to her bare feet. As if finally realizing what he was doing, he cast the flashlight's glow away from Lorie and waved it around the room as if searching for something.

"I—I had just gotten out of the shower when the power went out," she told him.

"Where's your robe?" he asked, his voice rough and husky.

"Uh, in the bathroom, on the door hook. I wasn't thinking about anything except getting my flashlight."

"Find your robe and put it on, for God's sake."

Loud, repetitive knocking at the front door gained their attention before the sound of a man's voice identified the person as Tommy Dryer, the deputy on guard duty tonight.

"Stay in your room." Mike barked out the

order. "And put on your robe or your gown or something."

Trembling inside and out, Lorie sucked in a deep breath. She could still feel Mike's gaze as it raked over her, the intensity of his stare so powerful that it was as if he had actually been touching her. She had wanted him to look at her, to find her desirable, but she knew that tempting him could be dangerous for both of them.

As she used the flashlight to find her way back into the bathroom, she heard the sound of voices coming from down the hall. Apparently Mike and Tommy were discussing the sudden blackout. Springtime storms such as this were common in Dunmore and occasionally losing power for an hour or two was the norm.

When she located her silk robe hanging on the back of the bathroom door, she set the flashlight on the vanity so that the beam shot straight up at the ceiling. She slipped into the ankle-length yellow robe and tied the belt into a loose bow at her waist. Just as she reached up to remove the towel from her hair, a soft rap on the partially closed bedroom door gained her attention.

"Are you decent?" Mike called to her.

Leaving the towel draped around her head, she picked up the flashlight and walked out of the bathroom. "I'm wearing a robe now, so yes, I suppose I'm decent."

When she shined the light toward the door, it hit

Mike mid-chest. He had a gorgeous chest. Broad, muscled, covered with a heavy dusting of curly black hair. Quickly, she lifted the light to his face.

He blinked and held up his hand to shield his eyes. "Damn it, Lorie, are you trying to blind me?"

She jerked the beam away from his face. "Sorry. I guess I should light some candles."

"It's late," he said without moving from the doorway. "I don't think you need to light candles when all we'll be doing is sleeping."

"It'll be a while before I can sleep. It's nearly midnight, you know, and the power is out and it's storming and . . ." Leaving her sentence unfinished, she went over to the nightstand, removed a box of matches from the drawer, and then lit the three fat round candles sitting atop her dresser in decorative crystal holders. "There, that's better."

A delicate muted glow illuminated her bedroom, the soft golden shimmer casting wavering gray shadows over the floor and ceiling.

"I'm going to grab a quilt and a pillow off my bed," Mike said. "With the power out, you're jittery, and I think we'd both sleep better if I'm close by. I'll bunk down outside your door in the hall."

"There's no need to do that," she told him. "You won't get any sleep on the hard floor."

"I won't get any sleep worrying about you if I'm down the hall."

"Then sleep on the chaise longue over there." She pointed with a flick of her fingers. "There's already a pillow and afghan on the chaise that you can use."

Talk about tempting fate! It had been difficult enough for them to keep their hands off each other with him sleeping down the hall. But on the other hand, the thought of Mike nearby was extremely comforting, all things considered.

"The alarm system's backup batteries are good for about eight hours, I think," Mike told her as he came into the room. "I figure the power will be back on long before that. The guys at the utility company are used to these frequent spring storms. And even if the phone line goes out, we both have our cell phones and Tommy's got the radio, of course."

"Then we're as safe as we can be," she said.

Lorie knew that if she stayed right where she was, Mike would have to walk past her to get to the chaise. So, she waited for him to come to her. As he approached, he slowed his gait and finally stopped right beside her.

While they stared at each other, sheets of heavy rain pouring down and the wind whipping through the trees outside, the mantel clock in the living room struck the midnight hour. Lorie gasped.

"It's okay, honey," Mike said. "Remember, you're safe."

"I know." She wrapped her arms across her chest in a hugging gesture. "But for how long? We both know that he's going to come for me."

469

"And when he does, he'll have to come through me to get to you."

"Oh, Mike, that's what frightens me. I can't bear the thought of you risking your life to protect me." Of its own accord, her hand lifted, reached out and rested, palm down, in the center of his chest.

Mike stiffened. His chest rose and fell heavily with each breath he took. Their gazes locked, neither of them able to look away.

Why had she done something so monumentally stupid? She knew better than to touch him. Correcting her error in judgment, she jerked her hand away, but Mike grabbed her wrist midair and brought her hand back to his chest.

"I want you to touch me," he told her, his voice a rasping whisper.

She shivered, sexual longing spreading quickly through her body. "Are you sure?"

"I'm sure." He maneuvered his hand holding hers to his chest and rubbed her open palm from one tight nipple to the other. He groaned as her fingers slid across his body. He guided her hand over his belly and down the arrow of dark hair that disappeared into his pajama bottoms.

She had dreamed of this moment for such a long time that it didn't seem quite real. And it wasn't real, not in the way she longed for it to be. Mike wanted her, but only for now, not forever. He wanted sex, not love and marriage. But she wanted him any way she could get him, even if tonight was all he could give her.

When he released her hand where it was poised above his navel, she slid her open palm down the fly of his pajama bottoms until her hand covered the bulge of his erection. With gentle seduction, she cupped his penis through the cotton material and tightened her fingers around him.

Moaning deep in his throat, Mike closed his eyes, and she knew how much he was enjoying her intimate caress. Ever so slowly, she lifted her hand to the waistband of his pajama bottoms, inserted her hand inside against his bare skin, and circled his sex with her fingers.

"Damn, honey. Damn," Mike growled.

She pumped him very slowly, using her thumb to stroke the bulbous head of his penis. He was big and hard and ready.

"I'll give you until daylight to stop doing that," he told her, and she smiled as she remembered how that phrase had been a joke between them in their teens when they had first become lovers.

"You're not twenty anymore," she reminded him in the same jovial manner. "Are you sure you can keep it up until daylight now that you're no longer in your prime?"

"I think I can manage . . . given the right incentive." He chuckled.

She smiled. "I'll see what I can do to keep you aroused."

"Honey, all you have to do is breathe to keep me aroused."

While she caressed him, he gently grasped the back of her neck with his right hand, tilted her head upward, and brought his mouth down on hers. She opened herself to him, sharing the kiss, giving and taking in equal measure. His left hand glided down her back, over the silky robe, and cradled her butt.

He bunched a handful of silky material in his hand at the base of her spine. "Take this damn thing off."

"Put your robe on. Take your robe off," she teased as she moved her caressing hand up and out of his pajama bottoms. "Make up your mind, will you."

He tore at the loosely tied belt around her waist and when it fell away, he yanked the robe apart and stared at her. She could barely breathe. He covered her breasts with his open palms and gently squeezed. Her heart stopped for a half a second. Cupping her breasts in his hands, he stroked each nipple with his thumbs.

Lorie's knees buckled.

He lowered his head and took one nipple into his mouth while his fingers toyed with the other. Her body tightened and released as a tingling sensation spread from between her legs and zipped along every nerve ending. Moaning with pleasure, she leaned into him while he slid one hand between her thighs and delved two fingers inside her.

"Next time I'll make it slow and sweet," he vowed.

"Next time," she echoed his sentiments.

He shoved the robe off her shoulders and onto the floor, and then marched her backward until they reached the bed. While she watched him, her gaze moving over him with great pleasure, he shucked off his pajama bottoms and tossed them aside. Lorie sucked in her breath. All she could say was that Mike's body had improved with age. Hard and pulsating, eager for action, his sex jutted out from a nest of thick black curls. Without a word exchanged, he pushed her onto the bed, spread her dangling legs, and stepped between them. She scooted back a few inches until her hips rested near the edge of the mattress. And then she reached up as she lifted her legs and wrapped them around him. He came down over her and grasped her hips. Hoisting her higher to bring their bodies into a perfect alignment, he thrust into her and pushed himself to the hilt.

Oh God, how she loved the feel of him inside her. This was Mike, she reminded herself. Her Mike. Her first love. Her only love. It had never been the same with anyone else.

He took her with a frenzy that brought them both quickly to the pinnacle. First she and then he climaxed, their orgasms so close together the aftershocks rippled through them simultaneously. Mike fell on top of her, his big body pressing her to the bed, pinning her beneath him. She loved his heavy weight covering her, his broad shoulders blotting out the world.

And then it ended as quickly as it had begun. Mike lifted himself up and off her. Standing over her, he held out his hand. When she put her hand in his, he pulled her to her feet so that they stood facing each other. He smiled. She smiled. And then he led her into her bathroom and turned on the shower.

Thirty minutes later, freshly showered and her hair towel dried, Lorie lay in Mike's arms in the center of her bed and listened to the soft, sweet hum of his breathing as he slept. It had been a long, long time since she had been this happy. It wouldn't last, of course, but while it did, she intended to savor every moment.

# Chapter 29

He stood in the woods, darkness surrounding him, as the rain poured down, soaking him completely. He kept one hand over the binocular lenses, partially protecting them from the rain. The power had gone out over an hour ago, leaving all the houses in the neighborhood dark. But he had seen flickers of light through Lorie's windows. Flashlights no doubt. And perhaps candles.

At present, she was under tight security with Sheriff Birkett living under her roof, there every night, and a deputy on guard duty 24/7. But divine providence would eventually smile down on him at the right moment, leaving Lorie vulnerable. And then she would be his.

He had loved her so deeply and completely and she was betraying him with another man. With Mike Birkett, the son of a bitch who had treated her so badly. Some women were just that way. The worse a man treated them the better they liked it. If only he had realized sooner that Lorie wanted to be punished.

He released his hold on the binoculars. They dangled from a strong, leather strap hanging from his neck.

He envisioned what the moment would be like when he claimed Lorie as his own, how she would look, what she would say, what he would do. The thought of her naked body aroused him unbearably. He would punish her and then screw her and then punish her again.

He would give her what she needed.

He would make her forget all about Mike Birkett.

He would become her hero. Her lover. Her protector.

He and no one else, not even the Midnight Killer, would decide Lorie's fate.

Easing his hand out of his raincoat pocket, he reached under the coat and unzipped his jeans. He had to end the aching need. If he didn't, he would do something foolish. Freeing his penis from his briefs and jeans, he thought about how Lorie looked in *Midnight Masquerade*. As he jerked off, images of her giving one of the actors in the movie a blow job flashed through his mind and helped him achieve a fast and furious orgasm.

Something aroused Nic from a light sleep. Had it been a sound? A light? Or simply instinct? With her eyes still half shut, she turned over in bed and wasn't surprised to find Griff's side empty. Scanning the room, semidark in the dawn light, she saw her husband's silhouette poised on the balcony, his huge hands gripping the railing as he gazed out over the lake at the back of their house. How many times during their three-year marriage had she awakened to find Griff out of bed, often on the balcony or downstairs in his study? She knew that he seldom slept more than four or five hours at a time and that occasionally he would wake from a nightmare drenched in sweat.

Nic slipped out of bed, still naked from their lovemaking late last night, and walked across the room. Before she reached the open French doors, a cool breeze hit her skin. Griff lifted himself to an erect position and turned around to face her. She stood in the doorway and looked at her husband, daybreak painting the sky over the lake in vivid shades of pink and gold directly behind him.

He held out his hand to her.

She went to him.

He pulled her into his arms and held her against him.

"You're cold," he said as he ran his hands over her shoulders and down her arms. "Let's go back inside."

"How long have you been awake?" she asked as he slipped his arm around her waist and led her back into the bedroom, leaving the doors open behind them.

"Not long."

"We should talk."

"Talking is overrated."

"Communication between a husband and wife isn't," she told him.

Griff led her to the bed, removed his robe, and lowered his head to kiss her. Nic lifted her hand between them and covered his lips with her fingertips.

He stopped and looked her in the eye. "You're going to make me talk, aren't you?" His lips curved in a hint of a smile.

"Put your robe back on and I'll put on mine so our being naked won't be a distraction." She reached down, picked up his robe, and handed it to him.

While he put on the robe, she found hers lying on the floor and quickly retrieved it. After slipping into it, she motioned to Griff and he followed her into the sitting area of their bedroom. When they were seated together on the sofa, Nic reached out and took his hands in hers.

"Talk."

"Someone is targeting my people," Griff said. "It's my responsibility to find out who and stop them before anyone else is killed."

Nic squeezed his hands reassuringly. "I think you're right. My gut instincts are telling me the same thing. The only difference is that you're convinced the killer is someone from your past on Amara and I'm keeping an open mind. It could well be someone from your more recent past, even someone from our past together, someone who has nothing to do with Amara or Malcolm York."

He pulled his hands out of hers and knotted them into fists. After working his hands open and closed a couple of times, he rubbed his palms up and down his robe-clad thighs.

"Sanders and I have begun going over records that date back to the inception of the Powell Agency, searching for anyone who might have a grudge against me personally or the agency in general. So far, we've found nothing that aroused our suspicion, but I've assigned half a dozen employees to go over the files and another half a dozen to work exclusively on this case."

"You've already done all of that without discussing it with me." Nic knew that by now she should be used to Griff making decisions and acting on them and then telling her after the fact.

He couldn't seem to get it through his thick skull that they were a team, as husband and wife and as business partners.

Griff frowned. "Do you object to what I've done?"

"No, I think you're handling this in the best way possible, but it would have been nice if we had made these decisions together, if I'd known beforehand."

"You know now." He shot up off the sofa. "Damn it, Nic, I wasn't hiding anything from you. I'm not keeping any secrets about this. I thought . . ." He paced back and forth in front of the fireplace.

Nic sighed heavily. "It's all right." She patted the sofa. "Come sit back down."

He eyed the sofa. "If what Meredith sensed is correct, then the killer is an assassin. He's been hired to do the killing. That probably means there is someone rich and powerful behind the murders, someone who is striking out at me through my people."

"Meredith could be wrong."

Griff sat beside Nic, but didn't touch her. "I don't think so. Yvette says that her abilities are the most powerful she's ever seen."

Yvette. It always came back to her, didn't it? Yvette thinks. Yvette believes. Yvette wants. Yvette needs.

"Don't look at me that way," Griff told her.

"What way is that?"

"I thought we had finally worked through your suspicions about Yvette. You told me that you were going to try to be friends with her."

"I am trying. I know she's important to you."

Griff grasped Nic's shoulders. "She is important to me and so is Sanders, but no one is more important to me than you are."

God, how she wanted to believe him. Damn it, she did believe him. He loved her with the same passion and devotion that she felt for him. She would bet her life on it. "I know," she managed to reply in a choked whisper.

He caressed her cheek.

After clearing her throat, she asked, "So, while we have agents examining the records looking for someone from the agency's past who might have hired an assassin, what are we going to do to find out if whoever hired the killer is someone connected to your past on Amara?"

"By retracing the steps Yvette, Sanders, and I took from the day we escaped from Amara until I returned to the U.S."

"And will this involve your going back to Europe and Asia and searching for pieces of your past with Yvette and Sanders?"

"At this point, I see no need to do more than send agents overseas to do some in-depth digging, highly trained agents, men I trust implicitly. I plan to put Luke Sentell in charge, and if Yvette agrees, if and when he unearths something, I'll ask Meredith to help him."

"It seems you've given this a great deal of thought," Nic said. "But there is one possibility that you haven't considered."

"What possibility is that?"

"That whoever killed Kristi and Shelley may be someone from my past. After all, I worked on some high-profile cases when I was with the Bureau."

Alone in his hotel room in LA, he watched with morbid fascination as the two men cornered the woman and dragged her down to the floor. She fought them halfheartedly, her arms flaying, her head turning from side to side as one of the men lay down beside her and pulled her over and on top of him. The camera got a close-up of their genitals as the man rammed his penis into the woman and then quickly withdrew. The other man stood over her, a thin black whip in his hand. As the woman rode the man beneath her, the man behind her cracked the whip and brought it down over her bare buttocks. Again and again.

By the time she and her partner reached simultaneous orgasms—probably faked—her butt bore a series of red stripes. The skin had not been broken, only reddened and possibly bruised.

Moments afterward, the man standing over her tossed the whip aside and jerked the woman up and onto her knees. He reached down and yanked off her fancy mask, revealing Candy Ruff's beautiful face. Terri Owens's face.

At this moment in the movie, the revelation of Candy's identity always excited him. Oddly enough, far more than any of the blatantly sexual acts.

As he pleasured himself, his hand moving rapidly up and down the length of his penis, tears trickled down his cheeks. He hated them, every last one of them. If not for their wicked acts captured on film for the world to see, he wouldn't be doing this. It was their fault that he found it difficult to achieve an orgasm unless he was either watching *Midnight Masquerade* or thinking about it, reliving the scenes in his mind.

The man on screen threaded his fingers through Candy Ruff's long, blond hair and forced her face against his erection. Without being prompted, she opened her mouth and began licking him from tip to root.

Candy Ruff took her fellow actor's cock into her mouth.

Watching her on film while she sucked her on-screen partner's dick, he wept. His body shook with a combination of pleasure and shame when he climaxed. As the tremors continued rippling through his body, he turned onto his side and glanced at the bedside clock through a haze of tears.

2:30 A.M. Pacific time.

• • •

She felt his warm breath against her cheek when he nuzzled her ear. Coming awake languidly, her nipples peaking and awareness tightening inside her, Lorie sighed as she turned and reached for Mike.

*If this is a dream, dear God, I don't ever want to wake up.*

Her body ached with pleasure and longed for more. More of Mike. His mouth on hers, his lips tasting every inch of her, his tongue flicking across her nipples and between her thighs. His big hands smoothing over her from head to toe, his fingertips seeking and finding every erogenous zone. Mike on her, over her, behind her . . . inside her. Their first time had been fast and fierce, the second time slower, more sensual, more explorative. They had slept briefly, awakened, made love, slept and awakened again.

Mike ran his hand down her back and cupped her butt, pulling her toward him and pressing her into his morning arousal. He kissed her, a light brush of his lips across hers. Sighing dreamily, she caressed his cheek, her fingers encountering dark, scratchy beard stubble.

"I need to shave," he said.

"Later. First things first." She rubbed herself against him.

He laughed. "That's what I like, a woman who has her priorities straight."

"Do you have to go into your office today?" She

483

kissed his shoulder, bit it softly, and then licked the bite.

Mike groaned. "I'm afraid so. But I don't have to be there until ten." He threw one big, hairy leg across her and hoisted himself up and over her. "That gives us plenty of time for more important matters."

She brought her arms up and around his neck as she stared into his eyes. "I wish . . ." She had been about to say that she wished this could last forever.

As if reading her mind, he said, "It is what it is. Not the past, not the future, just here and now. Is that enough for you?"

"Yes." She lied to him, told him what she thought he wanted to hear.

"I do love you, Lorie. I always have and probably always will."

She saw the truth in his eyes, but she also saw the sadness and regret.

"I know. I feel the same way."

He lifted her hips and lowered his mouth to hers, kissing her as he pushed slowly and deeply inside her. They lay together, their bodies joined, their breaths mingling, as they kissed with tender passion.

If only she could capture this perfect moment and keep it for the rest of her life. But the moment passed, as all moments do. The gentle kisses turned passionate. The blissful stillness of lying together in the preliminary stage of lovemaking exploded into fulfillment-seeking action. They exchanged dominant positions twice. She shoved him over and got on top, riding him hard and fast as he urged her on and then after she reached her first climax, he toppled her onto her back again and brought her to a second climax before he came.

# Chapter 30

"There's a problem with Mrs. Owens," Ashley White said as she came rushing toward the nurses' station. "Monique is with her and trying to calm her down, but she's real agitated. I've never seen her like this."

"Do you have any idea what upset Miss Terri?" Lila Newton asked the nurse's aide. Mr. Ransom hadn't shown up this morning, so she knew his morning visit had not caused the problem.

"No, ma'am, I don't have the foggiest."

"Is there someone in her room?"

"No, ma'am. I didn't see a soul. Of course, one of the other patients from a nearby room could have wandered in and out before we heard Mrs. Owens throwing things and hollering like crazy."

"Let me see if I can't calm her down without resorting to medication." Lila came out from behind the waist-high counter and hurried down the corridor past the security guard, Ashley on her heels. Halfway down the hall, she heard an awful

485

caterwauling coming from Terri's room, and Monique, one of the day-shift aides, talking to her sternly yet pleadingly.

This was worse than she'd thought, so Lila turned around and went back up the hall. She logged out a vial from the locked medicine cabinet and picked up a hypodermic in case she needed to sedate Terri. She would use the medication only as a last resort.

The door to room 107 stood partially ajar, enough so that Lila immediately got a glimpse of the items that had been thrown onto the floor. A plastic water pitcher and matching cup, Terri's breakfast tray, with food splattered in every direction, and the extra blanket that was usually folded and tucked neatly at the foot of the bed.

Lila entered the room, careful not to step on the specks of scrambled eggs and the small puddles of coffee. Monique looked at Lila and shook her head.

"I don't know what set her off," Monique said. "It's not like Mrs. Owens to act up this way."

"Did you say anything that might have upset her?"

"No, ma'am. I swear I didn't. I didn't say nothing to her except I guess she'd miss her son's visits while he was out of town."

"That shouldn't have upset her," Lila said. "Mr. Tyler's gone out of town before and it hasn't seemed to bother her."

"No, ma'am."

"Miss Terri," Lila called as she approached the bed where Terri sat straight up, her good arm flaying wildly as she mumbled incoherently. "What's got you so all-fired upset this morning?"

Terri's gaze met Lila's and for a couple of seconds she quieted. "Mu . . . mu . . . su . . . su . . . buh, buh . . ." Frustrated by her inability to communicate verbally, Terri pointed to the adjustable wheeled table from which she had tossed her breakfast tray.

Lila gazed down to the spot where Terri's purple-tipped finger pointed. Grape jelly had been smeared on the top of the over-bed table. Apparently, Terri had used the index finger of her left hand to try to print out a word using the grape jelly as paint.

Terri concentrated on Lila's face as Lila tried to read the word, but all the letters weren't legible. She managed to make out what appeared to be a "T" and an "L" and maybe either an "S" or a very crooked "R."

"T-L-S?" Lila asked.

Terri shook her head.

"T-L-R?"

Terri nodded.

T-L-R. T-L-R. Lila looked at the smeared lettering again. Tyler? "Were you trying to spell out Tyler?"

Terri nodded and motioned wildly with her left hand.

"You want to see Mr. Tyler?" Lila asked.

Terri nodded. "Mmm . . . mmm . . ."

"But don't you remember, Mr. Tyler went out of town for a few days."

Tears pooled in Terri's eyes.

Lila leaned over and whispered, "Do you want me to call Mr. Ransom?"

An odd expression crossed over Terri's face before she shook her head.

Knowing that Lila was right-handed and the stroke had paralyzed her right side, Lila asked, "All right then, do you think you could use your left hand if I got you a pen and some paper?"

Terri pursed her lips and tried again to speak. Puffs of air emerged through her lips, creating the sound of the letter "F" that she repeated several times as she glanced at the bedside table.

Lila glanced at the table, completely bare after Terri's tirade, except for the telephone. Since she was unable to verbally communicate, Terri received very few telephone calls. "Did you receive a phone call that upset you? Did Mr. Tyler call you?"

Terri stared wide-eyed at Lila as she reached out and grabbed Lila's arm.

Lila pulled Terri's hand from her arm and patted her gently. "Did Mr. Tyler's wife or your uncle Clement call you and tell you something that upset you?"

Terri shook her head.

"Did Mr. Ransom call?"

Terri shook her head and then, slapped her chest repeatedly. "Mu . . . tok . . . Ty."

"Oh, you need to talk to Mr. Tyler. Is that it?"

Frowning and shaking her head, Terri squeezed Lila's hand, a look of desperation in her blue eyes.

"You relax and I'll see what I can do to get in touch with Mr. Tyler and Mr. Ransom—"

Terri went wild again, flaying and hollering and fighting Lila's attempts to calm her. Feeling as if she had no choice, Lila prepared the hypodermic and with Monique's assistance, administered the mild sedative. Within a few minutes, the medication took effect, enough so that Terri settled down, but she kept mumbling incoherently as she finally drifted off into a light drug-induced sleep.

"Please, stay with her for a while," Lila instructed Monique. "And have someone check on her every thirty minutes the rest of the morning."

Once back at the nurses' station, Lila telephoned Mr. Ransom's home. Ramona Cosgrove answered, "Owens residence."

"This is Lila Newton, the RN in charge of Mrs. Terri Owens here at Green Willows Rehabilitation and Convalescence Center. May I please speak to Mr. Ransom?"

"I'm afraid you can't talk to him," Ramona said. "He's not here."

"When do you expect him? This is rather important."

"Couldn't say. He went out of town."

"Oh, I see." Lila debated whether she should ask for a way to reach Mr. Ransom, but since technically the situation with Terri was not an emergency, she said, "If you hear from Mr. Ransom, would you please ask him to contact me, Lila Newton."

"I don't expect he'll be in touch. He's off somewhere upstate doing research for his new book. When he goes off that way, I never know when he'll be back. Sometimes it's a week or more, and other times, he's gone only a few days."

After speaking to Ramona, Lila gave some thought to phoning Mr. Tyler's wife, but decided against it. She and the staff would simply deal with Terri the best they could for the time being. After all, that's what they were paid for, wasn't it, to take care of their patients' needs, both physical and emotional? Who knew what was going on in Terri Owens's mind? It could be little to nothing, and certainly not cause enough to have either her son or ex-husband rush back to Danville.

For over a week, Lorie had been trying to talk Mike into allowing her to go to Treasures, to work in the storeroom, do inventory, price merchandise, or prepare brochures for their new summer sales items. She needed to do something—anything— that would get her out of the house and help keep her mind off the Midnight Killer and Shelley's murder. This morning, she had finally persuaded him to drop her by Treasures on his way in to work.

"Please, I promise to stay out of sight in the back of the store. I can do inventory and place new orders and have lunch with Cathy and we can discuss plans for the tea shop and—"

"Stop!" Mike had held up a restraining hand. "I'd rather you stayed here, but I know you're going crazy being cooped up this way."

She had given him her best begging-puppy-dog look. "Please, please, please. No one other than you and Cathy will even know I'm there. And you can post a deputy to watch the shop if that will make you feel better."

"Okay, against my better judgment, I'll take you to Treasures. And I'll have Buddy keep an eye on the shop. He's got guard duty today."

She had thrown her arms around Mike and kissed him. That kiss of gratitude had quickly led to other things, and those other things had required removing a few clothes.

An hour later, Mike had escorted her into Treasures through the back entrance and given her strict instructions on what she could and could not do. He had also told Cathy that he expected her to see to it that Lorie followed orders and had made Cathy practically sign a blood oath that she would look after Lorie.

Everything had gone smoothly until midafternoon, when UPS made a delivery. As usual, Kerry Vaughn, the UPS guy, brought the stack of boxes in on a dolly and wheeled it straight to the storeroom.

When Lorie heard the door open, she looked up from where she sat on the floor going through the merchandise on the bottom shelves in the storeroom. She had been marking the sale prices on the winter, Valentine, and hadn't-sold-in-six-months items. Kerry's unexpected appearance startled her. She had promised Mike that no one other than Cathy would see her while she was at Treasures.

"Afternoon, Lorie," Kerry said as he pushed the dolly into the room. "Sure is good to see you back at work."

"Uh . . . hi, Kerry. It's good to be back, but I'm keeping a low profile for the time being." She glanced at the open door. "So don't mention to anyone that I'm here, okay?"

"Sure thing. I understand." Kerry shoved the door partly closed and then he unloaded the boxes and stacked them in the corner. "It's a shame the way some people around here have been acting. I just want you to know that I think the world of you and so do my mom and my wife. We're hoping the FBI catches that crazy Midnight Killer real soon."

Looking up at Kerry, she smiled. "I appreciate that. Right now, I need all the friends I can get."

When Lorie started to get up, Kerry held out his hand to assist her. Once on her feet, she signed for the delivery and they chatted for a couple of minutes before Kerry grabbed hold of the empty dolly and turned to leave.

Suddenly, they heard a woman's voice calling from outside in the shop. "Is that you back there, Lorie?"

With her heartbeat rapidly accelerating, Lorie glanced past Kerry and saw Cathy trying to block Tracie McLees's charge toward the storeroom. Tracie was one of their best customers, a real sweetheart of a person, but Lordy, Lordy, did that woman love to gossip.

"My goodness, why didn't you tell us that Lorie was back?" Mrs. Webber followed Tracie. Mrs. Webber, another valued customer and Nell Birkett's first cousin once removed, had befriended Lorie the moment she returned to Dunmore nine years ago.

"Please, ladies." Cathy blocked the storeroom entrance. "Lorie's doing inventory. She's not back at work full-time and we'd appreciate y'all keeping her presence here hush-hush."

"You can trust us not to say a word," Paul Babcock said from where he stood in the middle of the shop. As usual, he was going through the display of antique postcards. "We don't want anybody causing trouble for you, Lorie."

Kerry shrugged. "Sorry. I guess I was talking too loud or something. I didn't mean to give you away like that."

"It's all right. It couldn't be helped, I guess."

After Kerry left, Cathy came into the storeroom. "Should I call Mike?"

"Heavens, no. He'll blow this all out of proportion and come rushing over here for no good reason."

"I'm sorry I didn't stop Kerry, but Mrs. Webber had me so distracted that I didn't realize—"

"It's not your fault. No harm done. Thank goodness the customers here in the store are people who genuinely like me and won't rush out of here to tell the whole town that I'm at Treasures."

"I hope you're right. And it should be okay, if Tracie can keep her mouth shut. You know how she is."

An hour later, a small group representing the WCM—Women for Christian Morality, a radical, fundamentalist organization—showed up outside Treasures. Within ten minutes after those five ladies began marching up and down the sidewalk in front of the shop, reporters from two Huntsville TV stations and from the local newspaper appeared on the scene.

So much for trusting people who liked her. Lorie would lay odds that Tracie had accidentally let it slip about Lorie being at Treasures. Depending on who she told or who overheard her, the news probably traveled at the speed of light.

"I recognize three of those good Christian women out there protesting," Cathy said. "One is a

494

former customer, Sheila Smith, one is Rita Martin, a friend of my mother's, and the other is our old sixth-grade teacher, Doreen Culp."

Lorie sneered. "I always hated Miss Culp and she didn't like me. She's the type who never should have been allowed to teach children. If she'd been around during the Spanish Inquisition, she'd have loved getting the chance to torture people."

By the time Mike showed up, spitting mad and barking orders to his deputies to disperse the crowd, the streets were lined with curiosity seekers, some having left the downtown stores where they worked in order to join the horde and see what all the fuss was about.

Cathy, who had closed Treasures to keep the would-be intruders at bay, unlocked the door to let Mike in and then quickly locked up again. Lorie could hear him clearly from her hideaway in the back of the shop.

"I was afraid something like this would happen." Mike tromped into the shop. "Where's Lorie?"

"In the storeroom," Cathy said. "Buddy's standing guard at the back door. Unfortunately, a small crowd has gathered out there, too. I swear I don't understand this herd mentality that has turned normal people into raving lunatics. How five uptight, narrow-minded rabble-rousers like Miss Culp could stir up such a stink in such a short period of time is beyond me."

"I put in a call for help to Patsy Elliott. I'm hoping that in her capacity as a minister, she can talk sense into the WCM ladies," Mike said as he marched toward the storeroom. "I brought three deputies with me, including Jack, and five more are on their way to help with crowd control. I want this situation ended peacefully."

Cathy followed Mike. "Do not blame Lorie for any of this. If it's anybody's fault, it's mine. I was busy with Mrs. Webber and couldn't get away from her in time to stop Kerry Vaughn before he took a delivery back to the storeroom."

"It's not your fault," Mike told her. "It's my fault for letting Lorie talk me into bringing her here this morning. I knew better, but . . ." He walked into the storeroom and glared at Lorie. "When I get you safely back to your house, you'll be lucky if even I let you take a walk in the backyard."

Lorie bristled. She knew he was upset with the situation and worried sick about her, but damn it, she would not let him take his frustration out on her. "With that attitude, you'll be lucky if I let you step foot in my house again."

Mike huffed, blowing off steam, and then grabbed Lorie's shoulders. He stopped just short of shaking her. "I'm sorry, honey. God, I'm so sorry." He pulled her into his arms and the rest of the world faded away completely.

She relaxed her tense body and wrapped her arms around his waist. "I'm sorry, too. I shouldn't have nagged you day after day about letting me come into town to Treasures."

Cathy cleared her throat. Lorie and Mike pulled apart and looked at her.

"I don't mean to break up this tender moment, but I think I hear my husband calling out and banging on the back door."

"You two stay here," Mike ordered. "I'll see what's up with Jack."

Lorie and Cathy stood in the storeroom doorway while Mike went to the back entrance, exchanged a few words with Jack, and then opened the door. Jack escorted Reverend Patsy Elliott into Treasures.

"Patsy and I have talked to the mob out front and half the folks have gone on their merry way," Jack said. "There's maybe a dozen people out front, along with three of the ladies from the WCM, who are still ranting and raving. Of course, the TV reporters are still here, cameras ready, and Ryan Bonner just arrived. He must have broken every speed limit between Huntsville and Dunmore to get here so quickly. One of the reporters is out back, along with maybe five or six people, including two of the WCM ladies."

"Thanks." Mike glanced from Jack to Patsy. "I want to take Lorie home as soon as possible. It's just a matter of deciding on the best route— through the back door or front door. Either way, we're going to have to maneuver her safely away from the reporters and the WCM."

"Front door," Lorie said. "I want to go out the front way, flip Miss Culp a bird as I pass by, and watch her faint dead away."

"I'm glad you find this so all-fired amusing." Mike's brow wrinkled in a censoring frown. "You've got this town riled up. People are taking sides, pro-Lorie and anti-Lorie. My mother and my kids have to defend me to their friends and acquaintances because I'm personally protecting you. Keeping a deputy around the clock at your house is costing the county money it doesn't have. And this little scene today is only adding fuel to the burn-Lorie-Hammonds-at-the-stake frenzy the WCM has stirred up."

Lorie felt as if Mike had slapped her.

"I did not ask you to personally protect me. And I never asked for around-the-clock protection from the sheriff's department." Lorie barely managed to keep her voice calm. What she really wanted to do was scream at Mike. "Don't do me any favors, Sheriff Birkett!" She turned to Jack. "I'd appreciate it if you'd take me home. And if no one else has anything to say, I'm getting my purse and going through the front door and out onto the sidewalk to meet the press and those uptight old bags. They're just jealous because I look so damn good in those *Playboy* photos and they know that nobody would ever want to see any of them naked."

"I'll take you home." Mike grabbed her arm.

She jerked away, planted her hands on her hips and yelled, "Don't touch me, damn you, Mike Birkett!"

"Lorie." Patsy said her name softly. "As the county sheriff, Mike is under a great deal of pressure trying to protect you and at the same time pacify his constituents. He's just terribly frustrated. I don't think he meant what he said as a condemnation. He's not blaming you. He was simply stating the facts."

Lorie crossed her arms over her chest and refused to look at anyone in the room.

"How about a compromise?" Jack said. "Let Mike and me take you out of here through the front door and straight to my patrol car and then I'll drive you home. And you won't shoot Miss Culp a bird."

"That sounds like a reasonable plan," Patsy said.

"If you'd like, I'll go home with you," Cathy offered.

When Lorie was angry and hurt the way she was now, she tended not to think straight. Cathy had been her best friend since they were kids and Patsy had become a dear friend during the past few years. She needed to listen to them because they wanted what was best for her.

"No, you stay here and close up shop," Lorie told Cathy. "Once I'm gone, the WCM will leave and the reporters will no doubt follow me home." She turned to Jack. "You can take me out of here through the front door. And I promise to behave myself."

"I'll need Mike's help," Jack told her.

She nodded and then glanced at Mike. "I'd appreciate it if you could post a deputy outside my house until I can hire another Powell agent. I'm sure Maleah can get someone down here in the morning."

"There's no need to call Maleah and hire another agent," Mike said. "I'm not going anywhere."

Before Lorie could reply, Jack intervened. "For now, let's just get you to my car and then home. You and Mike can work out everything else later."

"He's right," Cathy told Lorie. "Please, do what Jack says."

"Okay." Lorie stiffened her spine, determined to hold her head high as she faced the reporters and the WCM witches.

Jack and Mike flanked Lorie as she picked up her purse and marched out of the storeroom, through the shop and to the front door. When Mike opened the door, three deputies moved in to stop the reporters from storming toward Lorie. Mike walked out onto the sidewalk and the minute she emerged from Treasures, he grasped her arm tightly. Their gazes met briefly, his stern look telling her he wasn't letting her go, not now or later. Jack came up on her other side, the two men providing a physical barrier between her and everyone else.

"Leave Dunmore today, Jezebel!" Rita Martin bellowed at the top of her lungs. "We don't want your kind in our town. Not nine years ago and not now."

"Ignore her," Mike whispered as he picked up the pace, hurrying Lorie down the sidewalk toward Jack's patrol car.

"You're a shame and a disgrace to your parents," Doreen Culp yelled. "You broke their hearts with your wickedness."

"We're almost there," Mike told her. "Don't slow down. Don't acknowledge them."

*Oh, Mike, Mike, don't leave me. I can't do this without you.*

"Whore! Slut! Harlot!" Sheila Smith hurried after them, repeating the slurs over and over again.

Jack opened the passenger door. Mike practically shoved Lorie into the car.

"Is she worth risking your career, Sheriff Birkett?" one of the TV reporters asked.

Mike froze to the spot, his hand on the door handle.

"She must be," Ryan Bonner said. "Tell us, Sheriff, is her body still as perfect as it was in those *Playboy* photos? Are the blow jobs she gives you as good as the one she gave that guy in *Midnight Masquerade*?"

Mike snapped around and lunged at the *Huntsville Times* reporter. Jack grabbed Mike in time to stop him just short of attacking Ryan Bonner.

"Don't do it," Jack said.

Mike took a deep breath and then turned around to Lorie. "I'll see you later." He slammed the door and walked away, not looking back at her or the reporters.

# Chapter 31

Puff Raven had been and still was an extremely sexy woman, with long legs, slim hips, and enormous breasts. Her huge brown eyes beckoned a man to come closer. Her full red lips promised untold delights. It didn't matter that she wasn't classically beautiful. Who cared if she didn't possess a face that could launch a thousand ships? A guy wasn't likely to worship at her feet or write love songs in her honor. The typical man would never ask a woman such as she to marry him and be the mother of his children. Only somebody as depraved and wicked as she was would want her on a permanent basis, somebody like Jeff Misner. The woman was good for only one thing—sex. And she had capitalized on her singular talent, making herself rich in the process.

But no matter how wildly vulgar and degrading her online videos were, they could never compare to *Midnight Masquerade*. That movie was a legend in the business, and that legend had followed its actors to their graves.

He sat alone in his hotel room, alternating

between watching *Midnight Masquerade* on his portable DVD player and checking the time.

All the preparations had been made. The gun and the mask were in his small suitcase, as were several disguises he could choose from for his return trip home. But tonight, he wouldn't wear a disguise. It wouldn't be necessary.

Deciding that the only way to get to Jean Goins, aka Puff Raven, was to walk through the front door as an invited guest, he had telephoned her.

"Well, what a pleasant surprise," Jean had said when he called.

"I'm out here in LA on business and just wanted to check on you to make sure you're all right."

"Of course, you know all about what's been happening, about the Midnight Killer. I've thought about everyone else and wondered how they're holding up. About like I am, I guess."

"It's horrible," he'd said. "I hope you're well protected. Better to be safe than sorry."

"I am. I am. Jeff has made sure there are a couple of bodyguards here at the house with us all the time. And I'm not going out at all these days. Lucky for me, I can work at home."

Her seductive chuckle had sent a shiver of excitement as well as loathing through him. "I hate to ask, but I'm wondering if I could impose on you. There's been a mix-up in my hotel reservation. They don't have me checking in until tomorrow—"

"Say no more. You'll come straight over here and stay with Jeff and me for your entire visit."

"That's very generous of you, but I won't impose on you for more than one night. I promise."

"Don't be silly. We'd love to see you again after all these years. My goodness, how long has it been?"

Gaining entrance to the Misners' private domain had been the easy part. They would open their doors and welcome him in, feed him dinner and serve him drinks. The difficult part would be disposing of their two bodyguards and then Jeff before turning his attention to Puff. Quick action would be called for. That's the reason he had purchased the Glock 17, a semiautomatic with an extended ten-round magazine. He could fire repeatedly, in rapid succession, taking out the two guards and Jeff before they knew what had hit them.

Jack had stayed with Lorie until Cathy arrived a little after six, and she was grateful that, for the most part, he had left her alone. He hadn't tried to start up a conversation or offer her comfort or advice. While she had reclined on the chaise, alone in her room, the shades pulled and a meditation CD playing, Jack had protected her from the reporters who had followed them from Treasures. And he had telephoned his sister Maleah to ask that Powell's have another bodyguard ready to send if Lorie didn't change her mind about Mike. Which she wouldn't and had tried to tell Jack, but like most men, he listened only when he wanted to. By the time Cathy arrived with grilled chicken sandwiches, fries, Cokes, and single-serving apple pies from Burger King, the reporters had left. All except Ryan Bonner.

"Can't you make him go away?" Cathy asked as she spread out their meal on the kitchen table.

"He's not on Lorie's property," Jack told her. "He's parked across the road in the Summervilles' driveway. Apparently, they have no objection to him being there."

"Maybe you should call and ask them."

"And maybe you should calm down and pretend he's not there," Jack said.

"Is that your subtle way of telling me that ignoring him is the best course of action?"

"Something like that. At least for now."

"All right then." Cathy smiled at Lorie and urged her to sit. "Let's eat before everything gets cold. There's nothing worse than cold fries."

"Maybe cold coffee." Lorie returned Cathy's smile.

The last thing Lorie wanted was food. But if she didn't at least go through the motions, Cathy would probably force-feed her. It was an effort to swallow each bite, but to appease Cathy, Lorie slowly ate a third of her sandwich and a few fries.

"Is that all you're going to eat?" Cathy asked.

"For now. I promise I'll eat the pie later." She set the unopened dessert box in the center of the table.

Just as she gathered up the remainder of her food and headed for the garbage can, the doorbell rang. Apparently still a lot more rattled than she realized, Lorie gasped, her hands jerked, and the remnants of her partially eaten meal fell to the floor.

"You two stay here," Jack told them as he rose from the table. "I'll see who it is."

When Lorie bent down to clean up the mess she had made, Cathy got up and rushed over to her. "Let me do that." She grabbed Lorie's shaky hands. "You need to pull yourself together."

By the time Cathy cleaned up the floor and dumped everything, including her leftovers and Jack's, into the garbage, Lorie had managed to calm her rattled nerves. But relief was short-lived. Jack returned to the kitchen with a guest.

"What are you doing here?" Lorie glared at Mike, who stood in the kitchen doorway, a few feet behind Jack.

Mike glanced at Cathy. "Would you two mind giving Lorie and me a few minutes alone?"

"Don't you dare go anywhere," Lorie told her friends as she glowered at Mike. "I want you to leave."

"Just talk to him, will you?" Jack said as he and Cathy made a hasty exit.

Lorie stood her ground in the middle of the

room, her arms crossed over her chest and her chin tilted defiantly.

"I apologize," Mike said. "Everything I said was the truth, but I said it all wrong. It didn't come out the way I meant it."

"And how did you mean it?"

"I was angry with myself for letting you talk me into taking you to Treasures today. If you'd just stayed at home, none of this would have happened." Before she could protest, he held up his hand in a wait-a-minute gesture. "It's my fault. Not yours."

"No, it's my fault for nagging you about it day after day."

"Look, honey, I've kept a lot bottled up inside me. I should have told you that my mother and the kids are still being harassed by a few stupid people about my moving in here with you. And I should have explained that I've been getting some pretty nasty phone calls from a handful of people letting me know how displeased they are by my conduct."

"Your conduct?"

"Oh, the objections about my conduct range from my setting a bad example by living in sin with a woman of ill repute to I should be forced to resign for spending taxpayer dollars to protect a woman like you."

Poor Mike. No wonder he had exploded the way he had.

"I guess I owe you an apology, too," she said. "I think the stress is getting to me more than I realized. I thought everything had settled down somewhat, that the sharks were no longer circling and it was reasonably safe to go back into the water. But apparently the ladies from the Women for Christian Morality were just waiting for a chance to attack."

"I think Patsy Elliott set them straight today," Mike said. "In her own diplomatic way she told them that their actions were neither moral nor Christian and that by deliberately being cruel to another human being they were going against Christ's teachings. 'Love one another.' 'Judge not that ye be not judged.' She quoted Scripture to them, chapter and verse."

"Patsy is one in a million," Lorie said. "God bless Patsy Elliott. If only all ministers could be like her."

"She's a good person." Mike centered his gaze on Lorie's face. "Am I forgiven?"

"There's nothing to forgive," she told him. "It's been a terrible afternoon, and the sooner we put it behind us the better."

"I agree." Mike nodded toward the closed kitchen door. "I'll tell Jack and Cathy that they can go on home."

"No, don't. I mean, wait just a minute."

"Is there something else?"

"You can't stay," she said.

"What do you mean I can't stay? I thought—"

"I wish you could stay. I want you to stay. But

not at the cost of your reputation and your job. And not when Nell and the children are being put in such an awful position. It's not fair to ask you to pay such a high price—"

Mike grabbed her by the shoulders and shook her. "I'm not walking away from you. Not while you're in danger. I won't do it. I can't."

"No matter what the personal cost to you and your family?"

He loosened his hold on her shoulders, eased his hands down her arms, and took her hands in his. "I can't promise you a future and I'm sorry about that. But I can offer you my protection. I need to do this, Lorie. Please, don't send me away. Not yet."

Biting down on her bottom lip in an effort not to cry, she closed her eyes and prayed for guidance. How could she possibly refuse his request knowing what it meant to him? If he could keep her safe, no matter what the personal cost, then when all was said and done, he could walk away with a clear conscience. He would then be able to forgive himself for the way he had treated her in the past and move on with his life.

"You can stay," she told him. "But I'm not sure about—"

"I'll sleep in the guest bedroom tonight."

"All right."

The Misners' cook had prepared dinner before she left and the housekeeper would clean up when she came on duty in the morning, so only the Misners and their bodyguards were there to welcome him. He was glad that he wouldn't be forced to kill the cook; after all, she was just an innocent bystander. The bodyguards were, unfortunately, collateral damage. The 8:00 A.M. to 8:00 P.M. guards had been relieved by the night shift before he arrived. Lucky day shift. Unlucky night shift.

Feeling safe and secure in their mansion on the hill, behind locked gates and with two trained professionals guarding them around the clock, Jean and Jeff had been the perfect host and hostess. The three of them had sat around after a delicious meal and discussed the past while they downed several drinks and he nursed the one scotch and soda Jeff had prepared for him.

As the midnight hour approached, Jeff yawned several times and mentioned going to bed. Thinking quick on his feet, he managed to revive the conversation and keep it going without arousing suspicion. Then at fifteen till, he rose to his feet just as both bodyguards came into the living room after making their rounds inside and outside of the house. Jeff had explained that at 11:30 each night, the guards double-checked to make sure the house was secure.

"Before we all turn in for the evening, I have something in my suitcase that I brought for you, Jean. A little gift. Let me go get it and give it to you."

"That's so sweet," Jean said. "You didn't have to do that."

"Oh, but I did." He moved toward the hallway that led to the guest bedroom. "Just give me a couple of minutes. In the meantime, prepare yourself for a surprise."

Jean laughed. "I do love surprises."

She wasn't going to love this one, but at least he could give her one final, truly impressive surprise before she died. A little parting gift to the woman who had given so much to so many. The woman who had played a part in ruining his life. Of course, she hadn't single-handedly destroyed him. She'd had a lot of help. Dean and Hilary and Charlie and Shontee. Charlene and Sonny and Lorie. And Terri.

*Look at them cavorting around naked as the day they were born.* The voice inside his head boomed loudly in his memory. *Wicked, evil, depraved, sex-craved men and women. See the way he touches her, without love or respect. All he wants is to use her for his own perverted pleasure. How can she let him do those things to her?*

*Watch and learn. And never forget.*

He entered the bedroom with its gleaming hardwood floors and huge windows that overlooked the patio and pool. When he had first arrived, one of the bodyguards had showed him to the room Jean had assigned him so that he could freshen up for dinner. He removed his small

511

suitcase from the closet where he had stored it earlier this evening, set it on the bed, and flipped it open. First, he removed the beautiful mask that Puff Raven had worn in *Midnight Masquerade* and carefully peeled away the protective tissue paper surrounding it. Then he put on a pair of thin plastic gloves he had brought with him and removed the Glock 17 from the quilted pouch attached to the back side of the case. He had purchased the weapon this morning from a rather unsavory character, but then what other kind sold illegal guns? Over the past few months, he had learned that buying a gun that couldn't be traced back to him was a relatively simple matter. All it required was enough cash in hand and knowing how to go about locating a seller.

He checked the semiautomatic. He would come back for the mask later, once he had killed Jean and removed her clothes.

With the Glock inside his sports coat jacket, he slipped out of the bedroom and back up the hall. A minute before reentering the living room, he pulled the gun from his pocket.

He would have to go into the room shooting. The two bodyguards would still be with Jean and Jeff.

"They are both always with Jean at midnight," Jeff had told him.

With the element of surprise on his side, he opened fire the minute he saw the first bodyguard, striking the guy three times in rapid succession, the third bullet entering his heart. He then turned to the second bodyguard, who had pulled his pistol from his shoulder holster, but before the guard got off the first shot, he took him out with a lucky hit right between the eyes. Adrenaline surged through his body as Jean screamed and Jeff cursed.

They stared at him in utter disbelief.

He aimed the Glock at Jeff.

"It was you?" Jean asked, her eyes wide with shock. "You—you're the Midnight Killer?"

"Don't do this," Jeff pleaded. "I'll give you whatever you want. I'll write out a check for every cent we have and—"

"This isn't about money," he said. "This is about what your wife and the others did to me."

"What did I ever do to you?" Jean held out her hands in her typical dramatic fashion.

He caught Jeff trying to sneak toward the desk in the far corner. Without issuing a warning, he aimed and fired, hitting Jeff in the belly.

Jean screamed again. "Oh, God, Jeff, Jeff . . ."

He turned the gun on her when she started to go to her husband. He fired instantly, deliberately striking her in the shoulder. She cried out in pain.

On his knees and doubled over as blood gushed from his abdomen, Jeff sobbed loudly and continued pleading for his life and Jean's.

"Shut the fuck up!" He'd heard all he wanted to hear.

He shot Jeff four more times until he fell over on his face and didn't say another word.

And then he turned back to Jean, who had inched her way slowly back against the wall. "Please, please . . ."

The modern chrome-finished wall clock chimed the midnight hour. Before the clock had struck six times, the next bullet hit Jean in the thigh, and by the ninth ring, the third bullet entered her chest. She slid down the wall and onto the floor, moaning and groaning, and taking her time to die.

Enough of this!

He walked across the room, stood over her, pressed the muzzle against her temple and said, "Dead by midnight." Then he fired the fatal shot.

Puff Raven was dead.

After glancing around at his handiwork, he slid the Glock back into his coat pocket and knelt down beside Jean. He took his time undressing her and discarding her bloody silk caftan. Beneath the single garment, she was naked except for an indecent orange lace thong. With the utmost care, he slid the string out from between her butt cheeks and pulled the scrap of cloth down her legs. He crushed the thong in his hand, brought it to his nose, and sniffed the musky scent of Puff Raven's pussy before stuffing the thong into his pocket.

Only one final touch was needed to complete the scene. He walked leisurely down the hall to the guest bedroom, picked up the beautiful mask, and returned to the living room. Once he had placed the mask over her face, he stood back and admired his handiwork.

Perfect.

Taking all the time he needed to do a thorough job, he went through the house, systematically wiping down or washing every item he had touched tonight. No need to take chances by leaving behind evidence that could be traced back to him. Not that he was a suspect, but it was best to err on the side of caution.

Once he had completed his clean-up chores, he went back to the bedroom, removed the plastic gloves, and tossed them and the tissue paper that had covered the mask into the suitcase, along with Jean's caftan. He picked up the suitcase and carried it with him when he left the Misners' fabulous Hollywood Hills mansion. Once outside, he tossed the suitcase into the backseat of his rental car and then slid behind the wheel. The locked gates opened automatically for vehicles exiting the premises, so he drove straight out onto the street and off into the night.

# Chapter 32

At 8:15 on the last Friday morning in April, Lila Newton received a phone call from Mr. Owens shortly after coming on duty at Green Willows. Yesterday, she had had debated whether or not to contact Terri Owens's daughter-in-law and explain the situation. They had been forced to keep Terri sedated all day. Each time she resurfaced from the effects of the medication, she quickly went from slightly agitated to almost hysterical. And since Terri couldn't speak coherently and her attempts to write looked like little more than hen scratches, the staff had no way of knowing what she was trying to tell them. Finally, Lila had telephoned Amelia Rose around 9:30 last night.

"I'll call Tyler and tell him what's happening and that his mother wants to see him. He's due home tomorrow evening anyway."

"I've never seen Miss Terri this way," Lila had said. "For the most part, she's usually cooperative, even docile. But ever since she found out that Mr. Tyler went out of town, she's been acting up."

When Lila took the phone call, she assumed it was Mr. Tyler calling to check on his mother, so when she heard Mr. Ransom's voice, it momentarily startled her.

"Lila? Lila, are you there?" Mr. Ransom asked.

"Yes, sir. Sorry. I . . . uh . . . I was told that a Mr. Owens was on the line and I expected it to be Mr. Tyler."

"Is there some reason you were expecting Tyler to call?"

Lila hated to tell Mr. Ransom over the phone, with him off on a research trip somewhere, about his ex-wife's condition. But he would want to know, and if Mr. Tyler couldn't get to the bottom of the problem when he came home this evening, maybe Mr. Ransom could.

"I had to call Amelia Rose last night. We had a time with Miss Terri all day yesterday, from the time she woke up. I've never seen her that way. The doctor examined her and didn't find any physical changes, so we assume it's something entirely emotional. She seems desperate to see Mr. Tyler."

"And you have no idea why she wants to see Tyler? She's been unable to communicate in any way?"

Lila sighed. "Well, she did smear grape jelly on the top of her over-bed table and tried to write Mr. Tyler's name with her finger. I believe she wants to tell him something that she thinks is important."

"And you have no idea what that might be?"

"No, sir, I don't."

"It's possible that she's dreamed up something in her mind or she's blown a minor problem out of proportion. After all, she hasn't been herself since the stroke. Naturally, the best course of action is to keep her sedated for the time being. Has Tyler been in to see her?"

"Mr. Tyler is out of town."

"Is he?"

"He's due home this evening."

"Lila, would you please do me a favor?"

"Yes, certainly, Mr. Ransom."

"Keep a close eye on Terri when Tyler visits her

and let me know what transpires between them. I wouldn't ask, but since Tyler refuses to even speak to me, I—I . . ."

"Don't you worry. I'll be real discreet, but you can count on me to watch over Miss Terri."

"Thank you. And I'll do my best to return to Danville in time for my morning visit with Terri tomorrow."

After her conversation with Mr. Ransom, Lila made her morning rounds, all the while thinking how sad it was that Mr. Ransom and Mr. Tyler were estranged the way they were. Despite their father/son differences, they both loved Terri, and were both devoted to her. Why, she didn't know. The woman certainly didn't deserve their love or devotion.

Jack arrived at Lorie's house a little after ten that Friday morning. When Mike opened the door, he could tell by the look on his deputy's face that he was bringing bad news.

"Where's Lorie?" Jack asked.

"In the shower," Mike said. "She slept late this morning. I don't think she got much sleep last night."

"I just got off the phone with Hicks Wainwright."

"And?"

"He's struck again. Last night. Out in LA."

"The Midnight Killer?"

"Yeah. When their housekeeper arrived at six

this morning, she found a bloody massacre at Jean and Jeff Misner's home in Hollywood Hills."

"Jean Goins Misner."

Jack nodded. "Also known as Puff Raven."

"I thought she had two around-the-clock body-guards."

"He killed both guards, probably first, and then the Misners. Shot all four of them repeatedly. He followed his usual routine. He stripped Jean Misner and put a mask on her face after he killed her."

A loud gasp from behind them alerted Mike to the fact that Lorie had overheard Jack's last statement.

She stood a few feet away, dressed in faded jeans and a white pullover and with her damp hair pulled back in a loose ponytail. "Jean's been killed? But it's still April. He wasn't supposed to strike again until May."

"Derek warned us that he might begin escalating the kills," Jack reminded her. "Killing again before May indicates that he's altering his MO, at least to some extent."

"There are only two of us left," Lorie said. "Terri and me."

"But he probably doesn't know that. It's unlikely that he's found out Charlene Strickland and Sonny Deguzman are already dead." Mike reached out, put his arm around her, and pulled her to his side. What could he say or do to make this easier for her? He wanted to comfort her, but how? He felt helpless.

"Wainwright has contacted the rehab center where Terri Owens is recuperating," Jack said. "He's been in touch with her daughter-in-law. Everything possible will be done to protect her. And we're going to keep you safe."

She jerked away from Mike. "You have to leave. You can't stay here. He'll kill you if you stay."

"That's nonsense," Mike told her. "If he comes after you—"

"When, not if," Lorie said. "When he comes after me, he'll kill anyone who gets in his way." She shook her head. "I am not going to let you risk your life for me."

"Honey . . ." Mike held out his hands, wanting to pull her into his arms, but when he saw the stricken look on her face, he didn't touch her. "Listen to me."

She kept shaking her head. "Jean had two body-guards and he killed both of them. How did that happen? How could he have gotten past all that security?"

"I don't know," Mike admitted.

"Wainwright got a call from the LAPD," Jack said. "He called me from the airport. He's on his way to LA by now. Our conversation was brief because he was in a hurry. I got in touch with Maleah on my way over here. She'll share the info with the Powells and Derek. Maybe he can come up with an explanation of how a woman who was supposedly surrounded by the best security money can buy is now dead."

While preparing for dinner out with her husband, Renee Leroy turned on the small TV in her dressing room in order to catch the evening news. Tonight they were dining with the Bellamys, an older couple completely devoted to the Redeemer Church and two of their biggest contributors. Celia and Earl were sweet people, but so boring. All he talked about were his horses and his golf game. And Celia seemed to be interested in only one thing—her six grandchildren. Renee knew the Bellamy grandchildren's names and ages and had looked at countless photo albums filled with their pictures.

Renee slipped into her calf-length navy silk sleeveless dress. As she removed the matching jacket from the pink padded hanger, the TV announcer's last comment caught her attention.

"We go now to Los Angeles where the FBI and the LAPD will be issuing a joint statement concerning the murder of adult film star Jean Goins Misner, aka Puff Raven, wife of producer Jeff Misner."

The navy jacket dropped from Renee's hand. She stared at the small screen as two men stood in front of a crowd of reporters. The camera scanned from one man to the other. Their identities appeared in print at the bottom of the screen. One was the LAPD chief of police and the other was FBI Special Agent Hicks Wainwright.

The police chief made a brief statement, giving only the basic information that the bodies of Jean Goins Misner, her husband, and two bodyguards were found by the Misners' housekeeper at approximately 6:00 A.M. that morning.

Using the house intercom, Renee called Grant, who had gone down to his study a few minutes ago. "Grant, are you there?"

"Yes, darling, what is it? You sound upset."

"Turn on the TV," Renee told him. "They're making an announcement about Jean and Jeff Misner. They've been murdered."

"Dear God in heaven. He's killed another one."

"Watch it," Renee said. "We'll talk later."

Renee sat at her vanity table, her gaze fixed on the TV, and listened while Special Agent Wainwright told the world that the FBI suspected the Midnight Killer was responsible for the murders, that Jean Goins was the fifth actor who had starred in the porno movie *Midnight Masquerade* to be killed.

Renee wondered if Grant should call Heath to let him know. He had voiced his concerns about his father's welfare the moment the news first came out about the Midnight Killer. After all, Grant had been the director, and even though so far only actors had been killed, who was to say when that maniac would move on to others with any type of connection to the movie?

If he thought it necessary, Grant would contact Heath. She certainly had no intention of calling him. Although she and her stepson had never had a cross word, they had, until recently, given each other a wide birth. Both knew they were important to Grant and his ministry and accepted their unique places in his life and in his Christian organization.

But if there was one thing Renee knew a lot about, it was men. And her instincts warned her about Heath. She knew he was infatuated with her, and despite being flattered and admittedly having flirted a bit with the boy, she had become concerned about his unhealthy interest in her. Ever since he had walked in on her and Grant making love, he'd been acting weird. Well, weirder than usual. Heath always had been a bit of an oddball. His preoccupation with his father's past—what he referred to as Dad's days of debauchery and depravity—seemed unnatural to her. Yes, Grant had publicly condemned his former lifestyle, but he didn't dwell on it in his sermons or in his private life. He had put his past behind him, mentioning it only when he used it as an example of how anyone could, through the Lord Jesus Christ and His ultimate sacrifice to save all mankind, find salvation and forgiveness.

But Heath often seemed obsessed with the porno business and its effect on decent people. On more than one occasion, she had heard him raving to his father about how he wished he had the power to remove all such wickedness from the world. When she had spoken to Grant about Heath's fixation on how evil porno movies were, he had dismissed it as nothing more than his son's zealous dedication to Christ and the Redeemer Church. So she had tried to convince herself that her husband knew his son far better than she did. And when the thought had crossed her mind that perhaps Heath was the Midnight Killer, she had immediately dismissed the idea as ludicrous.

Her doubts about her stepson's mental stability were one thing, but to suspect him of cold-blooded murder was something else entirely.

Just because he had been out of town the past few days and a new murder had taken place didn't mean he was the killer.

But was it simply a coincidence that Heath had also been out of town when Shontee Thomas had been murdered?

Yes, it was a coincidence. It had to be. She refused to think otherwise.

*I am not going to do anything with my suspicions except forget them. I will not dig into Heath's travel records since the first of the year. I will not!*

Tyler Owens arrived at the Green Willows Rehabilitation and Convalescence Center shortly before seven that evening. He had not stopped by

524

the nurses' station on his way to his mother's room, but Lila had caught a glimpse of him as he hurriedly passed by. By the time she caught up with him, he had already gone into Terri's room and closed the door. As a general rule, she would never intrude on a family member's visit, but she had promised Mr. Ransom that she would keep close tabs on Miss Terri. Glancing right, left, and behind her, Lila grasped the handle and cracked open the door a couple of inches, just enough so that she could see into the room and could hear what Mr. Tyler was saying.

He leaned down and kissed his mother's cheek. Still mildly sedated, Terri opened her heavy eyelids and glanced up at her son. She stared at him for the longest time, but made no attempt to speak.

"I hear you've been giving the nurses a difficult time," Tyler said. "I wish we knew what was wrong, why you've been so upset."

A peculiar shiver shimmied up Lila's spine when she saw Tyler smile as he took his mother's frail right hand and squeezed it tightly. Terri moaned as if she were in pain. "You mustn't be difficult, dear. When you allow yourself to become so agitated, they have no choice but to sedate you." He held her hand tightly. "And no more of this smearing jelly on your table and trying to write in the jelly. Promise?"

Terri nodded.

"That's my good girl." Tyler released her hand and laid it back at her side.

"Amelia Rose called me while I was out of town to tell me that Ms. Newton had contacted her and told her you were acting up and wanted to see me." He pulled up a chair and sat by her bed. "I'm here, Mother. But unfortunately you can't tell me why you wanted to see me, can you?"

"Mur . . . mur . . . da."

Tyler tensed. "What was that?"

"Mur . . . da."

"Well, listen to you. You did manage to say a word, didn't you."

Terri patted her chest and then pointed to him.

"Yes, I'm afraid there's been another murder. The Midnight Killer has struck again. He killed Jean Goins this time. You and Jean were great friends at one time, if I remember correctly. She was certainly nice to me whenever Uncle Clement took me to visit you. Dad still doesn't know anything about those secret trips, does he?"

Tears welled up in Terri's eyes as she stared at her son.

"You mustn't worry," Tyler said, his voice soft and soothing. "You're safe. No one can get near you except those I personally allow to visit."

"Ra . . . ra . . . so," Terri mumbled.

"Ra-so. Ra-so. Are you trying to say Ransom?"

Terri nodded.

"Is that what this is all about? You're afraid Dad will try to get in here to see you?"

Terri patted her chest again.

"I'm sorry, but I don't understand."

She lifted her right hand, pulled back three fingers, and using her thumb and index finger, formed the shape of a gun. She pointed directly at her head. "U . . . Ra-so . . . hup."

Tyler stared at his mother, a stunned expression on his beautiful face. "You can't be saying what I think you're saying." He laughed nervously. "You want me to protect you from my father. That's it, isn't it?"

Lila barely managed not to gasp aloud. She stepped back away from the door and closed it quietly. Why did Mr. Tyler think his mother was afraid of Mr. Ransom? Lila had never seen any indication that his visits upset her or that she was in the least bit afraid of him.

What to do, what to do! Should she call Mr. Ransom and tell him what she had overheard? The man had a right to defend himself, didn't he? Besides, if Terri was beginning to form words that could be understood, it would be only a matter of time before she told Mr. Tyler that Mr. Ransom had been visiting her on a regular basis. And then, the shit sure enough would hit the fan.

Lila hurried up the hall, went into the nurses' lounge, and when she saw that it was empty, she removed her cell phone from her pocket and dialed the phone number Mr. Ransom had given her when he'd called her that morning.

# Chapter 33

Carrying a newspaper under his arm and with the straps of a midsize backpack hanging over one shoulder, Casey Lloyd got off the bus at the Greyhound terminal on Wedington Drive in Fayetteville Saturday morning. Unfortunately, he'd already missed his SAA meeting, but it couldn't be helped.

After each trip, he felt like celebrating because he knew he was coming closer and closer to achieving his ultimate goal. But what did a guy who had sworn off liquor, drugs, and addictive sex do in order to celebrate? He had a little money left in his wallet, enough to buy himself a steak for lunch, and then afterward, maybe he'd go see a movie. But first, he needed to run by his friend Jason's house and leave his backpack. He kept his personal items stored at Jason's for safekeeping. He trusted his friend not to break open the locked case containing these items and pilfer the contents.

When he passed a garbage can, he stopped and tossed away the newspaper. While away from Fayetteville, he had kept up with the news, so he knew the whole nation was abuzz about the Midnight Killer's latest murder.

Casey remembered Jean Goins with affection, mostly because Jean had despised Laura Lou with a passion and had often called her a hack who couldn't write her way out of a paper bag.

Poor Jean. Destined to die along with her *Midnight Masquerade* costars. There were only four of them still alive: Sonny Deguzman, Charlene Strickland, Terri Owens, and Lorie Hammonds. He hoped the final four were living it up these days, enjoying life to the fullest. It was only a matter of time before the Midnight Killer executed each of them.

And who knew, maybe when the great executioner, the righter of wrongs, finished with the actors, he might get rid of the producer and the head writer. Casey knew one thing for sure—the world would be a better place without Travis Dillard and Laura Lou Roberts.

Derek Lawrence kicked back on the sofa and placed his feet on the overstuffed leather ottoman in Griffin Powell's study. Sanders served iced tea and then quietly left the room. Derek sipped on the sweet raspberry-flavored tea as he gazed casually about the room, concentrating on the people and not the décor. Griff and Nic were seated in the large armchairs flanking the fireplace and Maleah sat on the opposite end of the sofa. He'd been staying with the Powells for the past few days, and Maleah had driven in from Knoxville that morning. The gruesome murders of Jean and Jeff Misner and their two bodyguards had been front-page news the past two days. And as Powell's gathered more and more information, Derek had been working on a new updated profile of the Midnight Killer.

"I think it's obvious that whoever the killer is, Jean and Jeff Misner not only knew him, but trusted him," Derek said.

"I think we all agree with you on that." Griff downed a hefty sip of tea.

"The LAPD says there was no forced entry." Derek flipped open his notepad. "Both bodyguards were shot to death in the living room, as were the Misners, so the killer didn't enter the house and immediately start shooting. The cook had prepared a meal for the Misners and a guest. Drink glasses were found in the living room, indicating that the Misners had entertained their dinner guest after the meal. So far, all the fingerprints found belonged to the Misners and their bodyguards. Apparently, our killer was very careful not to leave behind any evidence."

"I assume the cook left before the guest arrived?" Maleah asked. "Otherwise, he would have killed her, too, since she'd have been able to identify him."

"That's right," Griff said. "And when questioned about if either of the Misners had mentioned their guest's name, she said she didn't recall his name being mentioned. She thought Jean Misner had referred to him by a pet name, but for the life of her she couldn't remember what it was."

Nic entered the conversation. "She did remember that Jean Misner said their guest was staying overnight and that they hadn't seen him in years."

"It was a rather simple plan and practically fool-proof," Derek theorized. "An old acquaintance from out of town phoned the Misners and finagled an invitation to stay with them, at least for one night. They never suspected that he intended to kill them. Why would they have trusted him so implicitly, knowing the person who murdered Jean's costars might well be someone connected to *Midnight Masquerade*?"

"What if he wasn't directly connected to the making of the movie?" Maleah suggested.

"Y'all ruled out any crazed fans, specifically those obsessed with *Midnight Masquerade*," Griff said. "So who does that leave? The most likely suspects are those who were involved in the making of that particular movie."

"You both could be right." A couple of ideas had occurred to Derek yesterday after he'd thoroughly gone over all the information Powell's had accumulated. He had worked on two profiles for a hypothetical killer. "Let's say that the killer is not directly connected to the movie but is someone all the actors knew."

"Like who for instance?" Nic asked.

"A boyfriend, a husband, a father, a son." Derek paused to allow the others time to absorb his theory. "This person's life was in some way adversely affected by their girlfriend, wife, daughter, mother, or father being involved in the porno business, and for some reason they focused all their rage on the actors in *Midnight Masquerade*. Something happened shortly before the first of this year that triggered all his pent-up rage and sent him off on a killing spree."

"The movie was rereleased on Blu-ray DVD," Maleah said. "Could something like that have been the trigger?"

"Yes, it could have," Derek replied.

Silence fell over the room.

Finally, Griff said, "As scenarios go, it's not a bad one."

Derek grinned. "If you like that one, I have another almost as good."

"I'll just bet you do." Maleah rolled her eyes. "Let's hear it."

"The killer either is or was in the business. He just wasn't an actor. He was the writer or director or producer or even one of the cameramen. He associates a turning point in his life with that particular movie, and something occurred six months ago that freed the demons inside him, demons he had been able to control up until then. Possibly the rerelease of the movie triggered his murder spree."

"We've ruled out Travis Dillard, unless he hired someone to do the killing for him," Maleah said. "He's too old and sick to be our guy. Kyle Richey hasn't left Mexico since we interviewed him, so that rules out one of the cameramen. And Jeff Misner was the other one. Who does that leave? Grant Leroy and Casey Lloyd."

"From the files I've read on those two, I'd pick Casey Lloyd over Grant Leroy," Griff said. "Leroy's life is better now than it's ever been. If anything, his past in the porno business has helped him more than it's hurt him. He uses himself as an example of how even the wickedest sinner can be redeemed. But Casey Lloyd, on the other hand, has hit rock bottom. He could blame the porno business and the actors from *Midnight Masquerade* in particular for his failures."

"If I had to choose between those two, I agree that it would be Casey," Derek said. "So, let's say he's one of our major suspects."

"But we also have your other scenario," Maleah reminded him.

"So we do." Derek grinned. "Want to name those suspects and rule out any of them?"

He could see that she had taken his request as a challenge. So like Maleah. She was a prickly pear, her sharp needles always on the defensive.

"I'd pretty much rule out boyfriends right off the bat. At the time the movie was made, most of the actors were dating one another or at the very least sleeping with one another. I don't recall that we found any evidence that anyone was in a long-term relationship with someone outside the business."

Maleah thought for a moment. "Do we happen to know how many fathers are still alive?"

"Actually, I did my research," Derek said. "Of all the actors and Starlight Productions personnel who worked on the movie, only three have a father living now—Lorie Hammonds, whose father hasn't left the state of Alabama in three years; Casey Lloyd, whose father was injured in a car wreck a few years back and is confined to a wheelchair; and Charlene Strickland, whose dad retired from the army and has been living in Hawaii for the past eight years."

"Okay, we've ruled out boyfriends and fathers," Maleah said. "That leaves husbands and sons. In the husband category, I'd put Ransom Owens at the top of the list. That guy is strange. And sons . . . hmmm . . . Heath Leroy and Tyler Owens, although I hate to think of anyone as gorgeous as Tyler Owens being a murderer."

Derek snorted. "Pretty boys can be deadly. Despite your finding him oh so attractive, he's still a suspect. That gives us four—Casey Lloyd, Ransom Owens, Tyler Owens, and Heath Leroy."

"Then those are the four we should keep close tabs on starting immediately," Nic said.

"Have we been able to get any info on their comings and goings the past few months, and do we know their whereabouts right now?" Maleah looked from Derek to Griff.

"Nailing down specifics is difficult when you're

playing catch-up," Nic said. "Hicks Wainwright has shared bits and pieces of information with us, but he may well know things we don't. On the other hand, we've shared everything we know with him. Phone records, airline records, and credit card records are not impossible for us to get, but it takes time. And although the FBI could access all of that for each of our suspects, they can't do it without some type of evidence against the suspects, which they don't have. And neither do we."

"What are the odds that all four men just happened to be out of town and unaccounted for when the Misners were murdered? Reports have been coming in the past few days with updates on their conspicuous absences from home." Derek tapped his notebook. "Casey Lloyd disappeared several days ago and just showed back up in Fayetteville today. We have no idea where he's been."

"We believed he was penniless, but it seems we were wrong. Some deep digging resulted in our discovering, only yesterday, that Laura Lou Roberts has been wiring money to an account in Fayetteville to a Mr. William Geisman," Nic said. "From the description the bank tellers gave our agent, we're pretty sure Mr. Geisman is Casey Lloyd."

"Both Ransom Owens and his son Tyler left home shortly before the Misners were murdered. According to his wife, Tyler Owens is off somewhere on a fishing trip. And the elder Mr. Owens's housekeeper said he had gone off, in her words, on another one of his digging-up-bones research trips."

"What about Heath Leroy?" Maleah asked.

"According to his secretary, Heath has been in LaRue County, Kentucky, inspecting some acreage that the Redeemer Church recently purchased," Nic said.

"Damn," Maleah cursed under her breath. "It's taken us too long to narrow down the suspects. We should have had tails on these four men long before now. If we had, maybe at the very least Jean Misner and Shontee Thomas would still be alive."

"Powell's has been on this case less than six weeks," Griff reminded her. "We started out with nothing except three unsolved murders that we—the Powell Agency—figured out were connected. If not for us, the FBI probably wouldn't have gotten involved as soon as they did. We're not miracle workers. We're just investigators."

"Sorry. I'm frustrated and worried sick about Lorie Hammonds. Until the Misners were murdered, we thought we would have a month between kills, but now . . ." She glared at Derek. "Don't say it. I know you told us that it was a possibility that the killer would deviate from his MO, which could mean killing more than one person per month."

"We're all frustrated," Griff said. "But from here on out, our four suspects will be under constant surveillance." He turned to Nic. "Call Wainwright and let him know what we're going to do. We don't want our agents getting in the Bureau's way during their investigation. It won't help if we're working at cross-purposes."

He didn't want to kill her. But he had known all along that it was inevitable. If she were the only one left alive, it was possible that those stupid FBI agents would wonder why she hadn't been killed and actually would put two and two together. His original plan had been to save her until last. Killing her would be difficult for him because he loved her. She didn't deserve his love; she never had. If only . . .

The past couldn't be altered no matter how much a person wished it could be. Her unforgivable actions had colored every aspect of his life. He had never been able to recover from her desertion. Had she ever loved him? If she had, how could she have left him?

He had spent most of the day considering his options. He didn't dare risk waiting another day. If he didn't act immediately, it was only a matter of time before his identity would be revealed.

At this time of night, the Green Willows Rehabilitation and Convalescence Center was eerily quiet, with only an occasional cry from a restless patient or laughter coming from the nurses' lounge. The front door was locked precisely at eleven every night and not reopened until six the next morning. The night-shift nurses didn't make rounds except when they first arrived at eight and then again at six the following day. For the most part, they spent their time in the lounge, checking on their charges only if a patient buzzed for assistance. The night watchman was responsible for the overall security of the building, but only the restricted area of the center had its own private guard, who worked eight-hour shifts.

Timing was crucial to his success. He knew he had no more than ten minutes to get in, kill her, and get out. It had to be done during the time one guard left his post at ten o'clock and the other settled into his comfy seat at the entrance of the center's deluxe suites. Officially, there was supposed to be a guard on duty at all times, but he knew for a fact that at shift change, the incoming guard usually took his time storing items in his locker, using the bathroom, chatting with the nurses, and getting himself a cup of coffee or a Coke from the machine in the lounge.

Terri's death had to appear totally unrelated to the murders of the other *Midnight Masquerade* actors. He couldn't risk being found out, especially not before he had killed the remaining three. If only one was left alive, it would have all been for naught. In order to free himself from his never-ending torment, they all had to die.

He had parked his car several blocks away,

walked to the center, and then checked out the visitors' lounge directly inside the entrance to make sure the night watchman was nowhere to be seen. Once inside, he moved quickly down the corridor toward the west wing, luckily not encountering a single solitary soul.

So far, so good.

Pausing at the point where the hallways crisscrossed, he peered around the corner and scanned the nurses' station. A heavyset, dark-haired aide came up the hall toward the station, apparently having just left a patient's room. She bypassed the station and went straight into the lounge.

He took in a deep breath, waited a couple of minutes, and watched as the guard rose from his comfy seat, stretched, and headed for the lounge where the employees' lockers were located. Once the coast was clear, he ventured around the corner and rushed past the guard's empty chair. The sound of voices and laughter from the lounge followed him down the hall as he hurried to room 107.

He opened the door and gazed into the dark room. Coming from the well-lit hall, he had to wait a couple of minutes for his vision to adjust to the darkness. She lay on the bed, her body turned away from the doorway, the covers pulled up to her neck. A combination of excitement and dread shot a dose of adrenaline through his veins.

*I can do this. I will do this. She doesn't deserve to live any more than the others.*

His attention focused on Terri's still form as he closed the door behind him and moved toward her. Feeling around in the bedside chair, he found the extra pillow that the aides placed behind her back during the day. Smothering her would take only a few minutes. She wouldn't suffer, not as the others had. In a way he was glad. But somehow it didn't seem fair that she, the one who was the most responsible for all of his pain and misery, would be allowed such a gentle death.

Suddenly, his peripheral vision caught a flash of movement on the other side of the bed. Holding the pillow over Terri's head, he stopped dead still when he saw a dark silhouette standing in the corner, only a few feet away.

Even in the darkness, he recognized the man.

"Hello, son," Ransom Owens said.

# Chapter 34

"What are you doing here?" Tyler Owens stared in total disbelief at his father.

"I could ask you the same question," Ransom replied as he reached out and pulled the lever that turned on the light over Terri's bed.

Tyler gripped the pillow tightly. "I came to check on Mother."

Ransom glanced at the pillow. "What were you going to do with that?"

Tyler swallowed hard. "I thought she might need another pillow."

"Over her face perhaps?"

"Don't be ridiculous." Perspiration peppered Tyler's forehead and upper lip.

Ransom hadn't wanted to believe that his son was capable of murder, let alone that he had come here tonight to kill his own mother. But somehow the possibility didn't surprise him. He had spent years denying his concerns about Tyler, who had been a sullen, moody little boy whom he had suspected of killing numerous birds and several neighborhood pets.

Thank God, he had taken his ex-wife seriously tonight when she had managed to say those few damning words—*Tu kull. Me. I nuw.*

He had translated. "Tyler is going to kill you? You know. You know what?"

Terri had pointed to the number twelve on her bedside clock. "Kull. Kull awl."

Cold fear had permeated Ransom's body at that moment, hours ago, after Lila Newton had lied to the guard and convinced him that Ransom's name had been added to the visitors' list. Lila had been the one who had called him to warn him that she believed Terri had asked her son to protect her from his father. Ransom had instantly realized something was wrong, that either Lila had misunderstood or that Terri's mind was playing tricks on her. He had never done anything that would make

Terri believe he might harm her. God, he loved her. Always had. Always would. Yes, there had been a time, years ago when she had broken his heart, a time when he had wished her dead. But he hadn't meant it.

But how many times had he watched that damn movie—*Midnight Masquerade*—and drank himself into a stupor, often with Tyler at his side. Tyler, who had been just a little boy. God in heaven, what had he done to his son by forcing him to watch that movie with him, over and over and over again? He could barely remember the things he'd said, horrible things, about Terri and the other actors.

Late this afternoon when Ransom had finally been able to understand that his ex-wife was trying to tell him that their son was the Midnight Killer, he had wanted to deny his own gut instincts. And he had, at least at first. But then Lila had shown him the newspaper articles about each murder that Tyler had brought Terri and stored in her bedside table.

"How do you know for sure that Tyler killed all these people?" Ransom had asked Terri.

"Tul mu."

"He told you?"

Terri had nodded.

"When? Last night or before then?" Realizing that was two questions, he had rephrased. "Before last night." She'd nodded. "And last night, did he threaten you?" She had nodded again.

542

"Why would he tell you?"

Tears had pooled in Terri's eyes and he had known she couldn't answer, that whatever reason their son had confided in her, no one would know unless Tyler chose to tell them.

"I know what you've done," Ransom said to his son. "Your mother told me."

Tyler's flushed face dripped with perspiration. "Her words are just a jumbled mess. How could she have possibly told you anything?"

"We understood enough to figure out what she was trying to say."

"We?"

"Lila Newton and I."

Tyler dropped the pillow on the floor, then reached out, grabbed the form lying in the bed, and shook it. "Mother! Mother, tell them it's not true. Tell them that they misunderstood."

The figure in the bed turned slowly and a pair of dark brown eyes stared up at Tyler.

The door flew open and armed FBI agents quickly surrounded Tyler as the agent who had been lying in Terri's bed rose to her feet.

"Mother!" Tyler screamed.

"Your mother isn't here," Ransom said. "She was moved into a different wing of the center a few hours ago, shortly after I got in touch with Special Agent Wainwright."

Right before his eyes, Ransom watched his son—his only child—emotionally disintegrate. He blamed himself. He and Terri had done this to the boy. When he had looked into his ex-wife's eyes as she had tried so desperately to tell him that Tyler was the Midnight Killer, he had seen not only terror, but regret. He realized that she accepted her share of the blame for the damage they had done to their son.

Tyler dropped to his knees, covered his face—that beautiful face so like his mother's—and wept uncontrollably.

The FBI agents circling Tyler waited and watched. When Ransom moved toward his son, every instinct within him urging him to comfort and protect, the agent in charge grasped Ransom's shoulder and shook his head. He looked the agent squarely in the eye and nodded.

Two agents holstered their weapons, reached down and grabbed hold of Tyler under either side of his arms. As quickly as he had burst into violent tears, he stopped crying, came to his feet wildly, and struggled against the agents' tight hold.

"I had to do it," he screamed. "It was the only way I could be free."

Emotion welled up inside Ransom and it was all he could do not to weep.

Shoving Tyler facedown onto the bed, the agents used force to subdue him. He kicked and flailed and screamed.

"Please, don't hurt him." Ransom barely managed to get the words past the lump in his throat.

Turning his head sideways, Tyler laughed hysterically. "You don't want them to hurt me. Such fatherly concern. Too little too late, you son of a bitch."

Ransom sighed heavily as the agents handcuffed his son and yanked him off the bed and onto his feet.

Tyler glared at Ransom, pure hatred in his blue eyes. "Aren't you happy that they're all dead? You hated them, every last one of them, but you hated her the most, didn't you? Candy Ruff. How many times did I hear you say you wished she were dead? If you hadn't tried to play the hero tonight, she'd be dead. Dead before midnight."

Tyler's sinister smile unnerved Ransom. Had he created this monster, this sick, angry, dangerous monster?

As the agents dragged Tyler out of the room and down the hall, he kept talking. "He used to sit there in front of the TV screen playing that movie over and over again. Watch it, he'd say. See what evil truly is. That's your mother up there screwing those men. She enjoys it, damn her. Hell, she loves it. That's what he'd say."

Long after the agents escorted Tyler out of Green Willows, Ransom stood alone in room 107, his son's accusatory voice echoing inside his head. Choking on his unshed tears, he gasped for air and finally gave in to his emotions. He wept quietly, his shoulders shaking and his hands trembling.

"Mr. Ransom?"

He cleared his throat, wiped his face with his fingertips, and turned to face Lila Newton.

"Is there anything I can do for you?" she asked.

"Would you take me to Terri?"

"Yes, sir, of course I will."

Lila led him from the west wing to the east wing of the center. As they approached room 118, he noticed that a nurse's aide sat in a chair outside the closed door. Lila spoke to her as she opened the door and then went with Ransom into the semidark room, the only illumination coming from the night-light in the bathroom. He slowly walked over to the edge of the bed and only then did he see that Terri was wide awake and staring at him.

"Tu. Tu?" she asked, her voice quavering.

Ransom took her small, slender right hand in his and held it tenderly. "The FBI took him away. They didn't hurt him. Tomorrow, I'll hire him a lawyer. I'll call my old fraternity brother, Robert Barlow. He'll take Tyler's case. I'm sure of it."

Terri squeezed his hand.

"Robert can use an insanity plea," Ransom told her. "Tyler's sick. He's very, very sick."

Terri squeezed his hand again and slowly closed her eyes. Ransom reached down and wiped the tears from her cheeks.

Mike's cell phone rang at 1:15 A.M. Although he kept the volume on low at night, the distinct ring woke him immediately. He flopped over in bed, flung his arm out toward the nightstand, and grappled across his wallet, keys, and holstered S&W semiautomatic before finding his phone. He grabbed it, pressed the Unlock button, and stared bleary-eyed at the caller's name and number.

Hicks Wainwright.

Mike shot straight up in bed and tossed back the covers. He took the call as he rose to his feet. "Mike Birkett here. What's going on?"

"Mike, it's Hicks Wainwright. We got him."

"What!"

"The Midnight Killer. We arrested him tonight, just a few hours ago. And we have a full confession."

"How? Who? My God!"

"Tyler Owens, Terri Owens's son," Hicks said. "For some reason, he confessed to his mother, and despite not being able to speak coherently since her stroke, she managed to make her ex-husband understand what she was trying to say. We set a trap, waited for Owens to try to kill his mother, which he did, and took him into custody. He's been singing like a bird ever since."

"I can't believe it's over," Mike said. "You're sure. A hundred percent sure."

"As sure as we can be at this point," Wainwright told him. "But my gut tells me that there's not much doubt he's our guy."

"Thanks for letting me know so quickly."

"I thought Ms. Hammonds should be one of the first to know. She and Terri Owens are the only two survivors. All the other actors from *Midnight Masquerade* are dead."

"I'm sure she'll have some questions."

"Maybe I'll be able to answer them in a few days."

As soon as Mike said good-bye and placed his phone on the nightstand, he grabbed his jeans off the nearby chair where he'd hung them earlier, put them on, and ran up the hall to Lorie's room. Per his instructions, she had left her door open.

He knocked on the door frame. "Lorie? Honey, wake up."

She lifted her head and stared at him; then she sat up, sending the covers sliding to her hips. "Mike? What's wrong?"

"Nothing's wrong," he told her as he entered the room and went straight to her. "They got him. Hicks Wainwright just called. They arrested the Midnight Killer a few hours ago." He sat down beside her.

"Say that again." She looked at Mike, happy tears in her eyes.

"It was Terri Owens's son, Tyler," Mike said. "The FBI set a trap for him, and when he tried to kill Terri, they arrested him. He's confessed to everything."

"Oh, thank you, God." Lorie threw herself into Mike's arms and hugged him fiercely. "I've got a million questions, but none of them seem to matter right now. Oh, Mike, Mike . . . Is it really over?"

"Yeah, honey, it's over. It's really over."

He wished he could go right up to Lorie's house and look in the windows the way he used to do before Mike Birkett had moved in with her. It was too risky now. He had to watch from afar. But the day would come when she'd be alone, all alone, and then he could make his move. He was tired of waiting, but as long as she was guarded so securely, he couldn't risk getting caught.

For more than two years, he had hoped she would notice him the way a woman notices a man she's interested in; but that hadn't happened. He had been patient, waiting for her to see him as more than a mere acquaintance. But the only man Lorie could see was Mike Birkett.

If only she could see him in a different light, he would help her seek and find forgiveness for her many sins. But he had come to realize recently that she was beyond forgiveness now. She would never repent, never find redemption, and never plead with him to help her cleanse her soul of its wickedness. Not now that she had Mike back in her life—and in her bed.

*I loved you so, Lorie.*

*I would have done anything for you.*

But she had betrayed him with a man unworthy

549

of her. A man who could never love her the way he did.

He understood now that there was only one way he could save Lorie from herself. And he loved her enough to do what had to be done.

# Chapter 35

The Powell Agency wrapped up their investigation into the Midnight Killer case two weeks after Tyler Owens was arrested and signed a confession. Ransom Owens had hired Robert Barlow, a high-powered attorney from Richmond, but Tyler had refused any help from his father and gone instead with a court-appointed attorney. The news media was having a field day with the story.

Griff had called a final meeting of all the main agents involved in the case, giving each instructions to report to their respective clients for one last time in order to help them find some measure of closure. Griff had gone to see Jared Wilson to tell him about Tyler Owens's arrest before the news leaked to the press. Michelle Allen and Ben Corbett would return to Knoxville for a follow-up visit with Jared. Holt had already left to catch a flight to Memphis to finalize the case with Tagg Chambless, Hilary Finch's husband. Other agents had been assigned to speak with the families of all the victims, whether or not they had been Powell Agency clients.

Nic had told Maleah that Griff had arranged for Charles Wong's wife to receive a sizable check that would give her and her daughters modest financial security for a number of years. Mrs. Wong would be told that the money came from a life insurance policy her husband had purchased a year before his death.

"If Casey Lloyd hadn't been so secretive about what he was doing, we could have completely eliminated him as a suspect," Maleah said.

"I suppose collaborating with a world-renowned author on a tell-all exposé about his years in the porno business wasn't something he wanted to broadcast," Derek said. "Besides, I think Casey enjoyed the cloak-and-dagger secrecy of visiting the reclusive author in Arizona without anyone being aware of what he was doing."

"Information after the fact doesn't help us, does it?" Griff told them. "If we or the Bureau had found out sooner that when he was a Boy Scout, Tyler Owens had earned a merit badge for rifle shooting, it would have given us reason to suspect him since whoever killed the victims was quite adept at using a firearm."

"I suppose none of that matters now," Nic said. "The killer was apprehended. And our Midnight Killer case is closed."

"And Lorie Hammonds is alive and well," Maleah added. "Cathy tells me that life is gradually returning to normal for Lorie and she went back to work at their antique shop this week."

"Hmm . . . I just might make a detour through Dunmore on my way to my beach house on St. George Island." Derek winked at Maleah.

Griff chuckled. Nic rolled her eyes and smiled.

"And what makes you think Lorie would want to see you when she's got Mike Birkett around?" Maleah asked him.

"Are they engaged?" Derek grinned at Maleah.

"No, but—"

"Maybe Mike needs a little healthy competition."

"Maybe you need to mind your own business."

"Maybe I'd like to make Lorie Hammonds my business."

Maleah huffed loudly. "She doesn't want you. No woman in her right mind would want you."

"And no sane man would put up with you."

Five minutes later, Maleah and Derek realized that sometime during their childish argument, Nic and Griff had left the room.

Mike had moved back home a couple of days after Tyler Owens's arrest, but as a precaution, a deputy had remained posted outside her house every night from ten until two for the rest of the week. Although she still got curious stares and an occasional off-color comment from a few men, for the most part, the community as a whole pretty much treated her the way it always had. Some people were friendly, some ignored her, and a few were downright hostile. The Women for Christian Morality hadn't picketed the shop since she returned to work at Treasures, thanks in great part to Patsy Elliott's intervention.

Customers came and went on a regular basis, along with the occasional curiosity seeker. After she had granted Ryan Bonner an exclusive interview—against Mike's wishes—and three articles about her past and present and her connection to the Midnight Killer appeared in the *Huntsville Times*, the media interest in Cherry Sweets and Lorie Hammonds had begun to wane.

She was, slowly but surely, getting her life back on track. Except for her relationship with Mike. It could never go back to the way it had been before, not now that they had become lovers again. And yet neither of them was sure they had a future together. She was still a woman with a notorious past, at least notorious in the eyes of small-town America. If they could move away from Dunmore, escape the narrow-minded bigotry that judged her as unfit wife and mother material, and live in a big city like New York or Chicago or Atlanta, they might have a chance of making it as a couple. But Mike's life was here. His children's lives were rooted in this community, and his mother's family had lived in Dunmore for generations.

She and Mike had agreed that they needed time apart, time to recover from recent events, time to put their lives back in order and make rational decisions about their future.

He and the kids had cooked dinner for her one night and she had cooked for them another night. She and Mike had gone out on one date that had ended with a good-night kiss at her front door. And she was no longer forbidden to spend time with Hannah and M.J.

"No matter what happens between us, I want you and my children to get to know one another a lot better," Mike had told her.

She wanted that, too.

Actually, what she really wanted was the chance to be a good stepmother to Mike's kids, something that might never happen.

"I'm off now," Cathy said as she retrieved her purse from under the checkout counter. "My appointment is at four o'clock." She grabbed Lorie's hands. "I'm so nervous. I've taken four home pregnancy tests and all four were positive, but I want to hear Dr. Evans tell me that I am definitely pregnant."

Lorie and Cathy laughed like schoolgirls.

"Jack is so excited," Cathy said. "He missed out on the whole experience when I was pregnant with Seth, so in a way, this is his first time. You should hear him. He's convinced it's a girl. He's already coming up with names."

"I'm so happy for you." Lorie hugged Cathy. "You deserve the wonderful life you have with Jack."

"You deserve a life with the man you love, too," Cathy told her. "I swear, I want to shake Mike Birkett until his teeth rattle."

The bell over the entrance tinkled loudly as the front door opened and Nell Birkett followed her grandchildren into the shop. "Hello, girls," Nell called to them as she came inside and closed her wet umbrella while M.J. and Hannah ran over to Lorie.

"I brought them a little early," Nell said. "It's raining cats and dogs out there and I always drive slower when it's raining. Another thing, I'm going to stop by the farmer's market on my way back from the dentist if it's slacked up some and I feel like it. Thank goodness Dr. Springer could fit me in. This tooth is killing me." Nell rubbed her swollen jaw. "It's probably an abscess. Sure feels like it. And I sure do appreciate your looking after the kids."

"No problem. I love spending time with Hannah and M.J."

"Gotta run." Nell waved good-bye as she headed out the door, reopening her umbrella on her way out.

"Me, too," Cathy said. "I'll call you the minute I leave Dr. Evans's office."

"Don't forget your umbrella." Lorie picked up the bright red umbrella from the counter and handed it to Cathy.

Left alone with the children and a few browsing

ustomers, Lorie suggested that M.J. and Hannah go with her to the kitchenette in the back. "I have milk and cookies. Or Cokes and chips."

"Milk and cookies," Hannah said.

"Coke and chips." M.J. grinned.

After settling the children at the table, each with the snack of their choice, Lorie told them, "When you finish eating, clean up after yourselves and then start on your homework. I'll be outside in the shop if you need me for anything."

"Yes, ma'am," they said in unison.

On her way out, Lorie overheard Hannah say, "Miss Lorie would make a great mom, wouldn't she?"

*Oh, Hannah, more than anything, I'd love to be your mom.*

"If Dad marries her, she'd be our stepmom," M.J. corrected his sister. "But she wouldn't be one of those mean stepmothers. She'd be like a real mom because she likes both of us so much."

*I love you both. More than you'll ever know. I love you because you're great kids. I love you because you're Mike's children. I love you because you were almost mine.*

Customers came and went and Lorie rang up several nice sales. Mrs. Webber hurried in for a quick look through the blank invitation cards that were on sale, bought two dozen for her sister's birthday party, and hurried off. Paul Babcock showed up and took his usual stance at the antique postcard table. Mike called to check on the kids and told her that he'd drop by and pick them up before she closed at 6:00 P.M. One by one, her customers hurried off to their cars, eventually leaving only Paul and a lady Lorie didn't recognize in the store.

The heavy springtime thunderstorm that had rolled into Dunmore, bringing a torrential downpour along with booming thunder and dangerous cloud-to-ground lightning, grew progressively worse. Concerned about Hannah and M.J., Lorie carried two flashlights with her when she went to check on them. She gave one to each of them and cautioned them to stay away from the single window in the room.

"Keep these with you, just in case the power goes out," she told them. "With a storm this bad, there's a good chance the electricity will go out at any moment. During these spring storms, we average losing power at least once a month."

"I don't like the thunder and lightning when it's like this," Hannah admitted.

Lorie hugged the child, kissed her forehead, and said, "You're safe in here. I promise. And as soon as I shoo the last of my customers out the door, I'll close up early and come back in here with y'all until your dad shows up."

That promise seemed to pacify Hannah. Lorie could tell that although he was putting up a brave front, M.J. was a little unnerved by the incessant under and repeated flashes of lightning. "Take care of your sister," she told him.

"Yes, ma'am. I will."

When she went back out front, she found the shop completely empty. Good. She was glad she wouldn't have to rush any customers out the door and into the rain. Peering through the full glass door, she realized she could barely see the sidewalk in front of Treasures, let alone the buildings across the street. Just as she started to flip over the sign to read Closed, a clap of thunder rattled the shop windows, making her gasp and jump. Suddenly the front door swung open, startling her. Buddy Pounders tromped into Treasures, tossed back the hood on his raincoat, and smiled at Lorie.

"It's coming a damn monsoon," he said.

"I was just closing up," Lorie told him. "Is there something you need?"

He glanced around the shop. "Are you here all alone? No customers left?"

"No customers," she told him.

"Well, I came by to ask you something," Buddy said.

"You did?" She couldn't imagine what Buddy needed to ask her. Something about Mike maybe?

"I . . . uh . . . are you and Mike a couple?" he asked. "I mean, are you two dating each other and nobody else?"

She started to tell Mike's deputy that it was none

of his business, but instead she said, "Mike and I are trying to figure things out."

"Well, while you're trying to figure things out, would you consider dating somebody else?" Buddy's lopsided boyish grin probably appealed to most women.

"Are you asking for yourself or for someone else?"

"For myself," he admitted. "I've admired you for a long time, Miss Lorie. You're one fine-looking woman and I'd be proud if you'd go out with me sometime."

Lorie managed not to laugh in Buddy's face. He was a sweet guy with youthful good looks to go with his adorable smile. But he was years too young for her, probably not a day over twenty-five. And she was and always would be in love with Mike Birkett.

She placed her hand on Buddy's arm covered by his damp raincoat. "I'm flattered. Very flattered. But right now, I'm not seeing anyone except Mike."

Buddy's face turned beet red. "I sure hope he's got sense enough to marry you. But if he doesn't, well, somebody should tell him that there are plenty of guys who'd be interested, me included."

Smiling warmly, she said, "Thank you, Buddy."

He cleared his throat. "Well, I guess I'd better be going. You lock up after I leave."

"I will." And she did.

With the door locked and the CLOSED sign prominently displayed, Lorie headed for the kitchenette. The lights flickered. Oh, dear. She didn't make it across the shop before the lights flickered again. Another deafening roar of thunder, followed by a blinding lightning flash, stopped Lorie in her tracks. The lights went out, sending the entire shop into darkness. Only the fading daylight coming through the glass door and the display windows across the front of the shop enabled her to see anything at all.

The children were alone in the back, Hannah probably frightened and M.J. trying to be brave. Since she was halfway across the shop, she decided not to go back and search for a flashlight under the checkout counter. Feeling her way more than seeing, Lorie took small, careful steps, doing her best not to run into anything. Once she reached the back wall, another streak of lightning illuminated the open door leading to the rooms behind the shop. She stepped over the threshold, placed her hand on the wall, and took her time going down the hallway between the storeroom and the kitchenette.

Feeling a whoosh of air coming from somewhere nearby, she stopped and listened. Just as she started to call out to the children, someone grabbed her from behind and placed a sweaty hand over her mouth.

• • •

*You're mine now. I'll never let you go.*

He had been patient. He had waited for such a long time. Too long. Didn't she understand that she belonged to him, that they were destined to be together forever. And there was only one way he could make sure Mike Birkett would never have her, that she would truly be his and only his for all eternity.

He supposed he had known all along how this would end despite how much he wished it could end differently.

*We will make love, sweet Lorie, and then . . .*

They would be found lying together, naked lovers whose souls could never be separated.

Lorie tried to scream.

He yanked her backward so that her butt hit his groin and she felt his erection pressing against her. She struggled to free herself but he held tight.

"I don't want to hurt you," he whispered, his breath hot against her ear. "Not yet."

Who was he? His voice was so soft she could barely hear him, but it sounded familiar.

"I've been watching you for a long time," he told her. "I used to stand outside at night and look at your silhouette through your window shades. I wanted you so much. But you never looked at me once. You couldn't see anybody except Mike Birkett."

Was it Buddy Pounders? No, no, it couldn't be Buddy. The voice was too soft, a tenor instead of a baritone. And this man wasn't tall enough to be Buddy. He wasn't much taller than she was. Buddy was six feet tall.

"You are mine, not Mike Birkett's and not the Midnight Killer's. You belong only to me. We are going to be together forever now."

Whoever he was, he intended to kill her, that much was clear. But she'd be damned if she'd let that happen. She had no intention of giving up and going to her death like a lamb to the slaughter.

His lips touched her neck. She shivered.

"You like that, don't you? You want me as much as I want you. God, Lorie, I want to fuck you. I want to fuck you so bad."

He stuck his hand between her legs and kissed her neck. She took advantage of the moment when he was distracted by his own sick desire. She bowed her head and then reared back and bashed him in the nose. He hollered in pain and momentarily loosened his hold on her long enough for her to pull away from him.

"Lorie, is that you?" M.J. called out in the darkness.

Oh God, the children! How could she have forgotten, even for a moment, that Mike's children were in the kitchenette.

"I thought you were here alone," he said. "Who is that?"

Inching her way along the wall, trying to get farther away from her attacker and stop M.J. before he came out into the hall, Lorie called, "Go back. Do you hear me? Close the door and lock it. Do it now."

A child's frightened scream reverberated off the walls. No, no, no!

"M.J., answer me."

"Help me, Miss Lorie," Hannah cried. "Somebody's got me."

"So help me God, if you hurt that child, I'll kill you, you sick son of a bitch," Lorie yelled at the top of her lungs.

"This is Mike Birkett's little girl, isn't it?" The man chuckled. "She's a pretty thing, sweet and tender and—"

"Don't you hurt my sister!" M.J. shouted as he moved his flashlight's beam in a semicircle.

That was when Lorie saw Paul Babcock standing inside the kitchenette, Hannah hoisted up in front of him, his forearm pressing firmly across her throat. M.J. stood outside in the hall, only a few feet from Lorie.

"Let her go," Lorie said. "Please, Paul, we can lock the children up in the storeroom and then you and I can have our time together, all alone, just the two of us."

Hannah whimpered. M.J. shined the light directly on his sister. Paul's arm tightened across her neck. It would take very little for him to choke her without meaning to or even break her fragile little neck.

"Tell me what you want me to do and I'll do it," Lorie said. "Anything. You name it and it's yours."

She inched closer and closer to M.J. and when she was within touching distance, she held out her hand, wriggled her fingers, and mouthed the words "stay here." Knowing what she wanted, M.J. gave her the flashlight. Holding the light in front of her and keeping it aimed directly at Paul, who was using Hannah's head to shield his eyes from the flashlight's glare, Lorie took small, tentative steps forward until she entered the kitchenette. And then she turned off the flashlight.

"Why did you do that?" Paul asked. "Where are you? I want to see you. Turn the flashlight back on. If you don't, I swear I'll break her neck."

Lorie reached out and ran her hand across the counter and into the sink where she had left a paring knife after peeling an apple for her midafternoon snack.

"Don't play games with me, Lorie," Paul said. "I'll do it. I swear, I'll kill her."

Lorie grabbed the knife, slid it into her pants pocket, and then hurriedly turned on the flashlight and held it under her chin.

"I'm here. See?"

"Where's the boy?"

"M.J., tell Paul where you are," Lorie called to Mike's son.

"I'm in the hall."

"You stay there, boy, or I'll kill your sister."

"Let her go," Lorie pleaded. "We'll lock her and M.J. in the storeroom and then you and I—"

"You don't tell me what to do." He lowered Hannah to her feet, put his hands around her throat, and squeezed.

Dropping the flashlight, Lorie screamed and lunged at him, every protective, maternal instinct within her coming into play. She yanked the knife out of her pocket and stabbed his arm. He yelped and instinctively released his hold around Hannah's neck.

"Run, Hannah, run," Lorie yelled as she jumped on Paul Babcock before he knew what had hit him.

He grabbed her just above her waist, his grip so tight that she felt as if he were cracking her ribs. Barely able to breathe, pain radiating through her body, she managed to lift her hand and plunge the paring knife into Paul's neck. As he eased his tenacious hold on her, she jerked the knife out, fully intending to stab him again. Blood gushed from the puncture wound like water from a geyser and Lorie knew she had hit his jugular. He dropped to the floor, one big hand gripping his neck. Blood spurted through his fingers. He took her down with him as he fell to the floor and she lay there pinned beneath his stocky frame. He moaned and gurgled and then became unconscious within a couple of minutes. Lorie shoved him off her and crawled a few feet away. She sat there on the floor, her hands and face and clothing wet with Paul Babcock's blood.

"M.J.," she called out to Mike's son.

No reply.

Lorie struggled to her feet, her knees weak, and her legs shaky. Where were the children? She searched and found the flashlight, turned it on, and staggered out into the hall. Dancing the light up and down and around, she found the hall completely empty. The back door stood wide open. Breathing raggedly, she walked to the door and looked out into the alley.

"M.J.? Hannah?"

The worst of the storm seemed to have passed, leaving behind a slow, steady rain falling from a gray sky. She stepped outside and let the clean, cool rain wash away some of Paul's blood.

"Hannah? M.J. Where are you?" The alley was dark and shadowy, lit only by the dim dusty daylight that was quickly fading.

"Miss Lorie," a little voice called from inside the nearby Dumpster.

"Hannah?" She rushed to the Dumpster and saw Hannah hiding there between two large black garbage sacks. Lorie reached down and lifted Hannah up and out. She flung her arms around Lorie's neck.

"Where's M.J.?" Lorie asked.

"He put me in the Dumpster and told me to hide," Hannah explained. "He went for help."

Hannah clung to Lorie for dear life as Lorie's knees gave way and she eased them down to the ground there in the alley. Hannah sat in Lorie's lap, her little head pressed against Lorie's breast. Lorie wrapped her arms protectively around Mike's baby girl.

Ten minutes later, that's where Mike found them, his daughter and the woman he loved. Both of them drenched to the skin, Hannah clinging to Lorie and Lorie's wet clothes stained red with blood.

# Chapter 36

When Lorie walked out of the sheriff's office the morning after stabbing and killing Paul Babcock, M.J. and Hannah on either side of her, she was met with an unpleasant surprise. A huge crowd of townsfolk had gathered, along with TV and newspaper reporters, including Ryan Bonner.

"What's going on?" Hannah tugged on Lorie's hand.

Scowling as he took in the scene before him, Mike came up behind Lorie and called to his mother, who stood just inside the doorway. "You kids go with Grams." He glanced over his shoulder at Jack. "Take them out the back way and drive them home."

"But I want to stay with Miss Lorie," Hannah whined.

"Miss Lorie needs us," M.J. told his father. "We want to tell all these people how she saved our lives. They need to know that she's a hero."

"I'll tell them," Mike promised. "I'm going to make an official statement as the sheriff and then another one as your father. Now, you two do as I told you and go with Grams. I'll see y'all at home in a little while."

Hannah reached up and pulled Lorie down to give her a kiss before going to her grandmother. M.J. stood straight and tall in front of Lorie, then quickly hugged her before following his sister.

"Are you up for this?" Mike asked her.

"There's not much more anyone can do to me," she told him. "If the good people of Dunmore want to tar and feather me, then I say let 'em bring it on. I'll face every last one of them. Hell, I'll face the devil if I have to."

"I think you did that last night," Mike said as he escorted her to the top of the steps.

A roar of shouts rose up from the crowd. Mike cleared his throat and said in a loud, clear voice, "Late yesterday afternoon, Paul Babcock, a life-long resident of Dunmore, assaulted Lorie Hammonds and took her and my children hostage inside Treasures of the Past. In order to save my daughter's life, Ms. Hammonds fought Mr. Babcock, and during the fight, she stabbed him in the neck."

The reporters bombarded Mike with questions,

which he did not answer. Instead he said, "This morning, Ms. Hammonds and my children gave sworn statements concerning the events that led up to Paul Babcock's death. Ms. Hammonds killed Mr. Babcock in self-defense and in order to save my children." Mike turned to his chief deputy. "Chief Deputy McCorkle will take over now and try to answer any other questions you have."

"I have a question," a female reporter called out as she waved one hand in the air to gain Mike's attention. "I'm Alice Kendall, the editor of the WCM's weekly newsletter."

Mike took Lorie's arm and started to walk away.

"What sort of example do you think you're setting as the sheriff of this county by having an affair with a woman like Lorie Hammonds? Do you think your constituents will reelect a man involved with a woman of such inferior moral character?"

Silence fell over the crowd.

Mike turned and looked the woman in the eye. "Lorie Hammonds is a kind, caring, loving woman who made some mistakes years ago. Mistakes she's atoned for many times over." Mike slid his arm around Lorie's waist and held her against his side. She knew he could feel her trembling. "I'd like to think that my constituents are good people who believe in the Bible—'judge not that ye be not judged.' But if they choose not to reelect me because of my wife's past, then I'll just have to find me another job, won't I?"

"Your wife?" Lorie gasped.

Mike looked at her and smiled. "This wasn't quite how I'd planned to ask you to marry me, but—"

"You're going to marry her?" Alice Kendall asked. "Won't it bother you knowing that any man with the price of a DVD can see your future wife not only completely nude, but having sexual intercourse with other men?"

Lorie stiffened. God, if only a hole would open up and swallow her.

"The way I see it, the men who watch that movie will envy me," Mike said loud and clear for everyone to hear. "They'll know how lucky I am to have such a beautiful sexy woman giving herself to me and only me for the rest of our lives."

Lorie looked at Mike with teary eyes.

"I love you, Lorie. Will you marry me?" Mike dropped to one knee.

The crowd went wild with applause and shouts of congratulations. "Way to go, Mike." "You're sure as hell one lucky SOB." "We'll dance at your wedding."

"You're out of your mind," Lorie told him. "You know that, don't you? You're crazy and brave and wonderful and—and yes, I'll marry you."

Mike grabbed her and kissed her, there in front of God Almighty and half the town of Dunmore, Alabama.

• • •

Griffin Powell took the call at 3:17 that afternoon. He listened carefully, made a few necessary comments, and ended the brief conversation. If there had been any doubt in his mind before now, the news he had just received erased those doubts. As he mentally processed the information, he left his study and went in search of his wife. He found Nic on the patio, stretched out on a chaise longue with a book lying in her lap as she gazed out over the lake behind their house. When she heard him approach, she glanced up and smiled at him.

And then her smile disappeared. Apparently she had sensed that something was wrong.

"What is it?" she asked as she got up and laid aside the book.

"I just got off the phone with Holt Keinan," Griff said. "His brother was murdered sometime last night."

"Oh, my God!"

"His throat was slit," Griff told her.

"No, no, please don't tell me that—"

"His body was mutilated postmortem. The killer carved triangular pieces of flesh from his arms and legs just as the person who killed Kristi and Shelley did to them." Griff clenched his jaw, and then looking squarely at Nic, said, "Apparently, he's not just targeting Powell agents. Now he's killed a member of an agent's family."

571

# Epilogue

Lorie had tried to convince Mike that they should have a small, private wedding, just family and closest friends.

"As much as I want to give you whatever your heart desires, I'm afraid we are outnumbered when it comes to decisions about the wedding," Mike had told her. "My mother says that since this is your first marriage, you deserve a big, fancy wedding. And Hannah is already talking about being a junior bridesmaid and M.J. told me that if your father won't walk you down the aisle, then he wants that honor."

So in the end, with Cathy joining forces with Nell and the kids to insist on the wedding being a major event, Lorie and Mike had agreed, if somewhat reluctantly. A June wedding, with a guest list in the hundreds. A church wedding nonetheless, at Dunmore First Methodist, with Reverend Patsy Elliott officiating.

But Lorie had drawn the line at wearing white.

"I'm not that much of a hypocrite," she'd told Cathy.

"Mike was your first lover and now he'll be your husband. Wear white if you want to. You have as much right as three-fourths of the brides today."

"I don't want white. I want yellow. A pale, shimmering yellow. It's what I've always wanted."

Today, Lorie Hammonds had walked down the aisle on her father's arm, the two now on speaking terms even if their relationship remained somewhat strained. For the first time in her married life, Sharon Hammonds had stood up to her domineering husband and told him what's what.

"You are going to walk our daughter down the aisle on her wedding day. And if you refuse, then you'll be sleeping on the couch the rest of your life!"

Lorie had indeed felt like a fairytale princess in her strapless, butter cream yellow wedding dress, the bodice heavily decorated with pearls and rhinestones and intricate beading that culminated in a cluster at her waist. The only jewelry she wore were small diamond stud earrings and the half-carat yellow diamond that Mike had given her the first time they had been engaged, all those years ago. She had sent it back to him from Los Angeles seventeen years ago and Nell had kept it for him all this time.

The entire wedding had seemed like a dream to Lorie, every aspect of the event as perfect as perfect could be. From the warm and sunny June weather to the approval of a town that had once scorned her, Mike and she had exchanged their vows surrounded by family, friends, and well-wishers.

Jack and Cathy, as matron of honor and best

man, had insisted on hosting the reception at the Dunmore Country Club.

With his hand over hers, she and Mike sliced into their seven-tier wedding cake as the photographer snapped shot after shot of the happy couple. But breaking with tradition of the bride and groom sharing the first bites of their cake, they had brought Hannah and M.J. with them and offered the children the first pieces.

They were a family now, she and Mike and his children. *Their children.* She would never try to take Molly's place. What she wanted was to carve out her own place in their hearts and in their lives.

As the foursome posed for more photographs, happiness beyond her wildest dreams swelled up inside Lorie.

*Thank you, dear God, for blessing me with a second chance at happiness.*

She closed her eyes and made a solemn vow to Molly Birkett. *I promise that I will take care of your family for you, Molly. I'll love Mike forever and be faithful to him until my dying day. And I will always love M.J. and Hannah as if they were truly my own.*

**Center Point Publishing**
600 Brooks Road ● PO Box 1
Thorndike ME 04986-0001 USA


**(207) 568-3717**


**US & Canada:**
**1 800 929-9108**
www.centerpointlargeprint.com